Swimming to th
By Kristin Bill
Copyright 2012

All rights reserved. No part of this publication may be reproduced, stored in a retrieval system, or transmitted in any form or by any means, electronic, mechanical, recording or otherwise, without the prior written permission of the author. This is a work of fiction. The characters, incidents and dialogues in this book are of the author's imagination and are not to be construed as real. Any resemblance to actual events or persons, living or dead, is completely coincidental. Createspace Edition.

## Summary

She was tired of life…
He was tired of death…
Can one miracle restore them both?

Kelsey Mitchell's dreams of happily ever after were washed away when her emotionally abusive husband succumbed to the pride of his religious illusions and abandoned his family. Years later, raising two kids alone in the beachside community of Santa Cruz, Kelsey's faith is again tested when her daughter's life is in jeopardy. Now, she must make a choice to drown under the weight of her past or resurface triumphantly in the faith and hope she left behind.

Alex Bechtel traded his successful CPA business for his first love: Pastoring a small church in a quaint seaside village. But when he discovers the church is long on rules and short on compassion, he must question his decisions and his own definition of faith.

Can two people with troubled pasts find hope and love in one another? Or is Swimming to the Surface worth the effort?

## Chapter 1

Once upon a time, Kelsey Mitchell harbored hope. Perhaps, dream was a better word. She dreamed that a handsome prince (or at least a well-paid doctor) would whisk her away from life's drudgery into a romantic, happily-ever-after with 2.5 children tucked safely inside a European station wagon. But, reality had a way of stepping on hopes, snuffing out dreams and landing her squarely behind the wheel of a beat-up minivan on its third transmission.

Kelsey squinted in the bathroom mirror, touched the lines at the side of her eyes and realized how off-course her life had become, how off-course *she* had become. Inside her circa 1964 bathroom, when bulbous, plastic crystal faucets were all the rage and linoleum was a lifelong product, she didn't seem to belong. She rubbed her hand along the faucet handle and thought only of its beauty. The beauty of her freedom was far more fabulous, far more priceless than genuine crystal or her former life wrapped in a gilded cage. An alarm clock droned on from the other side of the apartment.

"Nathan!" she wailed. "It's time to get up" Her son moaned his annoyance. "Nathan!" she squealed again, though she wasn't without compassion for him. She'd never been a big fan of mornings either, and it was just harder to pad along the dirty carpet or get into the dingy shower. Gone were the granite countertops and travertine floors they were used to, and somehow, the environment made it more difficult to face the day.

It started early in Silicon Valley, this concept that life was not your own and running the treadmill of life was a necessary evil. First, you're taught to rise at an ungodly hour to get to a place you don't even want to be: school. Then, shortly after you realized school was the fun part of life, you're thrust into the workforce, where not only is punctuality expected, but you must appear respectable at the same time. While pajama bottoms paired with a T-shirt may have been cute in college, later in life it is cause for a mental health check-up.

The alarm clock pierced her eardrums. "Nathan, get up!"

Kelsey looked at her hair, dangling like wet noodles upon her shoulders. It had to be blown out, a daily redundancy that annoyed her. It all seemed so hoity-toity and ridiculous. If everyone came to work straight out of bed, there'd be no cause for everyone wasting his or her time. Perhaps they'd find the workplace more productive, as they did when they went to casual Fridays. But that was probably the depression talking. She'd never much cared for change, and now everything in her life was different—turned upside and tossed like wilted lettuce leaves

She sighed. People expected performance in the workforce, as well as coiffed hair and a friendly attitude before coffee. It was all too much. And it was all based on other people's notions. After all, she didn't want to be the woman who didn't wash her hair, anymore than she wanted to be the kid who ate paste.

"Nathan!" she wailed one final time. "Get out of bed now!" Thirteen years old and yet every morning he faced the world like a college student after a binger. More groans emanated from his room. "We leave in fifteen minutes!"

This morning, the responsibilities seemed to rise like a wave and cover her until she couldn't breathe from the pressure. She left the hairbrush dangling in her knotted hair, picked up a snapshot of her with the kids at Disneyland that was tucked into the mirror and sighed again.

Then, she pictured her mortgage statement for her apartment; an apartment that only a selling real estate agent and loan broker would call a *spacious condominium*. She finished the stroke of her brush. "There's got to be more than this," she announced to her reflection. "I've got to be more than a stereotypical single mother," she paused as she remembered to count her blessings. "I have this condo," she said as if she were selling toothpaste on television, but her spirits dropped with her inability to buy what she was selling. "Yeah, life sucks."

"Nice sentiment for a Monday, Mom." Kelsey turned. Her daughter Meagan was nine…going on thirty-five. Meagan was the very picture of organization and enthusiasm; a testament to the fact that more than genetics played a role in Creation.

"Do you even know what sentiment is?" Kelsey cupped her daughter's chin. "Why are you so warm?"

"It's hot in here, your shower steamed up the whole place. We've got to get these fans fixed. They just make noise." Meagan bent lanky elbows and placed her cutlet fists to her middle. "I'm in the fourth grade, you know. I know what sentiment means. Like, it's a disturbing sentiment that my mother uses the word, sucks."

"Is it?" Kelsey grinned, looking up at the bathroom fan that was supposed to draw all the steam from her bathroom. They didn't make them like that anymore. It sounded like a tank and worked with industrial strength…but only in the bathroom. Somehow, the fan shot out the steam through other ducts in the house, making the apartment swelter like a sauna when someone showered as if it was a group activity. She shuddered at the thought of the bacteria dwelling in the carpet since whatever decade it had been laid down. She wouldn't let the kids sit on it, in fact. "Would you rather I didn't shower?" she asked Meagan. "Because I'd be happy to comply."

Meagan rolled her eyes. "Whatever, Mom. If you want to dress and smell like a hobo, go for it."

"We need a vacation. Do you ever think about that?" Kelsey stood on the toilet and looked outside at the weather. The slender, horizontal window afforded the only ocean view from the apartment. She hated to admit how much time she'd actually spent dreaming while standing on the john since they'd moved there. She looked down at her daughter. "If you could go anywhere, where would you go?" She hoped the enthusiasm in her voice would search and rescue the dreamer lurking within her serious daughter.

"You're going to dry your hair, aren't you?" Meagan gave her an Elvis-upturned lip. "You can't go to work like that."

"What are you, Martha Stewart?"

"Mom, lots of people short of Martha Stewart dry their hair in the morning. It doesn't make you a perfectionist to get ready for work."

"I think it does, actually. Is your brother up?"

"It's Monday." Kelsey was struck by how her daughter crossed her arms, just like her own mother had done to express annoyance. Meagan yanked a brush through her tangled hair. There were some genetic connections one just didn't want to make, especially on a Monday morning. "Meagan, tell me you didn't iron your outfit."

She nodded. "Last night. I like that little crease in my pants. If you lay everything out, and just add coordinating socks, there's nothing to do in the morning. I highly recommend the system for both you and Nathan."

Kelsey thought that their iron hadn't made it with them in the move. She should have guessed Meagan had confiscated it with glee. "I'm sure you do. Now where would you want to go on a vacation?"

Meagan shrugged her small shoulders. "I don't know. Somewhere that I didn't have to stand on a toilet to have a view, I guess. So what if I made you and Nathan a schedule. You know, wrote it all out like they do in preschool."

Some people were born without a sense of fun and Kelsey counted people who used irons unnecessarily, among them. "We'll talk about it later, Meagan, thanks. Can you go turn on Nathan's sunlamp and put his alarm clock next to his ear? I can't be late this morning. My boss is about on her last nerve with me."

Nathan was not simply a teenager; he was not a morning person, not even as a baby. He'd been too lazy as an infant to wake up Kelsey in the middle of the night. Of course, she'd heard all the horror stories about 3 a.m. feedings, and then her son failed to rouse. At first, she worried something was wrong, but after a week she came to appreciate his ability to sleep through the night. When Nathan slept, it was like waking the dead, except the dead would have slightly more enthusiasm. Nathan greeted the day like an unwelcome friend come to borrow money.

A coworker had recommended the sunlamp, which imitates morning sunlight and awakens the

Melatonin naturally. Kelsey wasn't sure her son possessed Melatonin. Perhaps he had some rare childhood disease where he'd been born without it. Or maybe he possessed an excess of it. Whatever had occurred, Kelsey thought her family an extremely odd threesome.

She watched Meagan smooth her cotton pants like an old lady in summer linen. "I need you to sign my Friday folder." She thrust forward a perfectly kept paper folder. "Pictures are tomorrow, so you need to fill out the form and send a check—"

Kelsey winced. The only thing worse than a relentless series of have-tos was a child who remembered them for you. In order. She was like a speaking BlackBerry. "Meagan, go turn on Nathan's sun lamp."

Meagan rolled her eyes again and Kelsey thought childishly, *right back atcha*. "Your eyes are going to get stuck like that! And your crease is crooked in the back!"

Meagan rushed back into the bathroom, and Kelsey laughed as she jumped down off the toilet. "Only kidding."

"Mom, that's not funny." Her four-foot perfectionist left the bathroom and Kelsey giggled again.

With the touch of fall in the damp air and the morning fog off the coast, Kelsey knew she'd freeze if her hair weren't dried, so she unwound the cord from her hair dryer, believing herself industrious for a Monday. Of course, it was hard to be appreciated when Meagan had razor-sharp creases with a matching part in her hair.

"It's definitely time for a vacation when I want to sing my own praises for something as mediocre as drying my hair."

"And stop talking to yourself, it's weird!" Meagan yelled from the hallway. "I can only handle one crazy parent!"

Before Kelsey plugged in the dryer, she heard an odd clunk that sounded like the time she'd knocked over her mother's grandfather clock. With all the natural clunks part of their apartment's paper-thin walls, something told her this one was different. She looked at the floor while she processed the sound. She waited, but there were no telltale signs that the old woman next door might be cleaning out her closet again.

"Meagan?" she called. "Is that you?"

No answer.

"Meagan, answer me!" When her little girl didn't, Kelsey's sixth sense kicked in and she dropped the hair dryer and ran into the bedroom. Meagan lay slumped on the floor alongside the unmade bed. Kelsey lifted her off the floor. "Meagan!" she screamed. Meagan was dead weight, still and heavy. Seeing her daughter so limp and unlike the natural dictator she'd raised, dread spread through her. Meagan's eyelids were closed, but her eyelashes fluttered, and Kelsey could see her dark pupils rolled back into the drawn lids.

"Meagan!" Kelsey felt slightly disconnected, as though her body acted on its own volition. She couldn't bear to be in the moment. "Sweetheart, wake up! I'm sorry I made fun of your crease. Mommy just wishes I could be more like you, that's all. Wake up, sweetie!" She searched for the inner light of her daughter's personality, confused by the foreign invasion of something altogether different within the delicate, familiar body. "Come on Meagan. Mommy won't have time to dry her hair," she threatened, hoping her daughter's eyes would pop open in fear of humiliation. But they didn't, and her heart dropped like lead in her chest. "Meagan, please," she whispered, before looking to the ceiling, "God, please!"

    Meagan roused with a few moans. Her limp frame lifted slightly, and she vomited all over her mother. Kelsey brought her daughter close to her breast. She wiped Meagan's face with her jacket collar and realized how great it felt to be needed by Meagan, so self-reliant and adult by nature. "Meagan, look at me!" Kelsey lifted her daughter's chin, but Meagan's lids fell heavy again. "Meagan, wake up! Please Meagan, don't do this! Wake up, sweetheart!"

    Kelsey played back their conversation in the bathroom when everything had been so normal. She rubbed her forehead and tried to rationalize the experience. She looked around the room for something that might offer a clue to a sudden illness, but she saw only her bed made, Meagan's doing, no doubt, complete with throw pillows at attention and Meagan's *iCarly* backpack on the floor, the girl's green eyes staring mystically at them.

Her mother instinct terrified her, but her body acted for her. She mentally noted Meagan's eyes were glassy and that she burned with a fever. Kelsey murmured soft words and said a prayer while her body lifted Meagan to the bathroom and ran the bath water to clean them off with a damp, warm washcloth. She hadn't even finished sponging them off when she realized Meagan needed a hospital.

"Nathan!" she screamed in that voice that he knew was serious, the one where she'd yelled, *earthquake, get under something!* "Nathan, get in here!"

Nathan appeared instantly at the bedroom door, rubbing an eye with the back of his hand. "What's the matter?"

She forced her voice to remain steady. "Nathan, we have to go to the hospital. Get your clothes on and get in the car. Don't make me wait for you! This is not the time."

"Mom, what's the matter with Meagan?"

"She doesn't feel well," Kelsey answered in perfect monotone. "She has a fever. Do as I tell you, Nathan." The fear in his eyes was palpable, but she kept her wits about her. "Nathan, it will be fine, just get in the car and we'll go. Meagan needs a doctor. She'll get to the doctor and everything will be fine."

Unrealistic tasks and mundane actions like drying her hair suddenly felt like a perfect dream. She would give anything to be rustling the children into the minivan for school right now, trying to shove a granola bar down Nathan. She shouldn't have complained. She should *never* complain.

Once in the car, Kelsey wondered how they all managed to get there. Meagan's feeble frame was conscious now and she took the time to manage her mother's life. "Mom, you left the light on in the kitchen. PG&E…" she trailed off and Kelsey grinned, never happier for an environmental sermon.

"We'll go green, baby. As soon as we get back. Keep talking, honey. Stay awake. Tell me how to get to the hospital." Kelsey locked Meagan into her seatbelt and her heart skipped a beat as she remembered her baby daughter fighting the car seat by stiffly thrusting her hips and screaming bloody murder, as though Kelsey had been a kidnapper rather than her flesh-and-blood mother. Once, she'd been chastised by an avid Dr. Laura fan, who told her how the baby's mother shouldn't leave her with such an inexperienced nanny like herself.

"She won't get into the car-seat willingly because she feels abandoned by her mother," the stranger offered. "You tell that woman to quit her job and come home where she belongs."

Kelsey smiled at the memory. Meagan was nothing if not a fighter, and she took solace in that fact as she drove. Nathan might have been unwilling to fight, too lazy to bother with a struggle, but Meagan…Meagan hadn't planned for this day off school, and she knew her daughter would be plotting how to make up the day before it was over.

Nathan usually rode shotgun, a position he announced the moment he awoke. The truth was, Meagan didn't care one way or the other, but she liked to save it for the power struggle once in a while.

She could have beat Nathan to the car any day by at least thirty minutes without even trying. Nathan's eyes were wide as he watched his sister. "Will she be all right, Mom?" His voice quavered.

"She'll be fine, Nathan." But in her mind, she raced through the childhood illnesses that could come on so quickly. Since she came up with nothing good, she forced the thoughts away. "She'll be fine," she said again. She saw Nathan's fear-filled eyes in the rear-view mirror and reached into her mommy brain for something light to say. "I'll give you some money when we get to the hospital and you can find the cafeteria and get breakfast. I'll bet they have donuts! The waxy kind without nutrition!"

Nathan never ate breakfast. Since he was a baby, she'd tried to force it down him in the shape of scrambled eggs, smiley-faced pancakes and plain toast, but it sat there untouched. *Another testament to my failure as a mother*, she thought. Once, when Nathan was going through his bathroom humor stage, she'd even tried baking 'Banana Butt Bread' – which had the nuts taken out and was formed into the shape of his rear end to get him to eat.

"That's disgusting!" was all he said, leaving the lumpy loaf to rot on the counter until the summer ants came and she had to throw it away.

Meagan moaned, and she realized she should have simply called 911. *Meagan would have thought to call 911.*

"I want Teletubbies. The fish one," Meagan said.

"What did you say?"

"Potatoes love science."

"Nathan, get the cell phone out of my purse and dial 911."

"What do I say?"

"Just dial it, I'll do the talking." She pressed her foot to the floor, and raced through a yellow/red light. Looking in the rear view mirror, she saw she'd gotten away with it, and she dashed to the next light, which was red. She honked her horn in short succession and gingerly drove through the intersection against the light.

Nathan handed her the phone. "911, what's your emergency?"

"I'm bringing my daughter to the emergency room to Santa Cruz General. I need someone to meet us at the door. She's very sick. It was very sudden. I want her taken to Lucille Salter to Stanford's Children's Hospital. Can you get an ambulance to meet me?"

"You want EMTs to meet you at one hospital to take you to another?" the woman asked incredulously before returning to her bland, uncaring voice. "What are her symptoms?"

"Just call them, please! I'll handle them when they get there. She needs Stanford Children's Hospital. This is something serious. It came on so suddenly!" She tried to transfer a portion of her trauma onto the operator, but the woman would have none of it.

"How old is the child?"

"She's nine. She's nine and she's talking nonsense, she spiked a fever and she's been vomiting."

"Ma'am, can she move her neck?"

Kelsey pulled to the side of the road. "I don't know, she seemed limp to me, not stiff," she said, warding off the very thought of meningitis. "Yes, limp."

"Ask her to try to touch her chin to her chest."

"What about the ambulance?"

"There's one in route, ma'am. How far are you from the hospital?"

"About three minutes. Maybe four with traffic." Kelsey estimated as she pulled back into traffic.

"Ask her to touch her chin to her chest."

"Meagan?" Kelsey put her hand under her chin. "Meagan, can you hear me?"

"Mom, the state of California can hear you. Turn right, Mom. The school traffic will get in your way."

Kelsey did as she was told. "Meagan, I need you to try to touch your chin to your chest. Can you do that for me?"

"No," she said without trying. "Hurts."

She was grateful Meagan made some sense. "She was fine fifteen minutes ago. This just happened. Could she have swallowed something?" Yet she knew her daughter wouldn't so much as swallow a piece of bread if it contained hydrogenated oil, much less something inappropriate for human consumption.

"How far are you from the hospital now, ma'am?"

"About two minutes. Will they be there? The EMTs? I want her taken to Lucille Salter at Stanford. It's serious."

"That will be up to the attending doctor. Ma'am, is your daughter alert?"

"Yes, my daughter is alert. I want her taken to Stanford, no attending doctors!"

Kelsey gritted her teeth. She might have been president of the human doormat league, but when it came to her children, she had the ferocity of a starving great white. Generally, she inherited all the work no one else wanted to do because she couldn't speak up for herself. She'd simply rather do it than garner a useless confrontation, but she'd learned that fighting for her children was the only option. No one else would do it, and the last thing she wanted was for him or her to think they, too, deserved nothing from life. She found this one element of parenthood crucial and unavoidable. Something about the operator's snide tone gave her strength, and she clicked the phone shut. It started ringing shortly after, but she ignored the buzzing pulse.

"Mom, can I do something?" Nathan asked.

"Just pray, Nathan. You're good at that. Pray that this will all be over soon and we'll have our little Martha Stewart back." Kelsey held back tears. "Meagan, Mommy can't live without you. You know that!"

"Maybe I could ask for a Rachael Ray instead?" Nathan snickered.

The side streets, which she thought would be faster than Highway 1, were jammed with mommies in minivans taking their kids to school, as Meagan predicted, so she used the shoulder and let them berate her with their horns, while she committed the cardinal sin of cutting into the drop-off lane. They arrived at the hospital, and Kelsey honked the horn continuously until someone came out to meet them. She stared at Meagan, slumped in the passenger seat and she prayed like she never had before.

## Chapter 2

Kelsey pressed her horn while people dressed as doctors, or at the very least hospital staff, looked at her as if she had the wrong address. She stepped out of the car, raced around to the passenger side and opened the door to let them see Meagan for themselves.

Her legs weakened at the sight of her daughter, bent over like a wilted tulip. "Help me!" she screamed at one of the men, who pretended she was invisible. "I need help, it's my daughter. She's lethargic, talking nonsense, and she vomited. I want her taken to Stanford." The men just continued to stare past her, as though she'd said nothing, as if Meagan wasn't lying there helpless.

When she spotted a man walking out in his white coat, the word "Doctor" embroidered on his chest pocket, she abandoned the perfect for the present. He walked to the side of the building, and

Kelsey followed. He reached inside his pocket, when she grabbed him by his lapels. "Listen to me! I need help. Didn't you take some kind of vow of something?" Her shout may have frightened him. In fact, she probably scared herself, so out of character was her reaction. But no one seemed to feel her stress, and she desperately needed someone to get it.

The doctor calmly removed her hands from his shoulders, which forced her to realize they were there in the first place. "She's speaking strangely, you say?"

"Words that make sense, just not together."

"Is she slurring her words?"

Kelsey nodded.

He peeked around the corner at Meagan in the front seat. The little girl smiled, and Kelsey marveled at her daughter's polite response. "She should have been born in the Victorian age. I can practically hear her calling for her smelling salts."

The doctor ran the few steps to the curb, seized a pen-sized flashlight from his breast pocket and shined it into Meagan's eyes. He knelt alongside Meagan and shined the penlight into her eyes again. He clicked it on and off, and did the same for her other eye. Then, he motioned with his forefinger to two underlings in white coats; the ones who had previously ignored her. The doctor grasped the back of Meagan's neck and tried to press it to her chest. Kelsey followed suit and stretched her own muscles to set an example. Meagan only moaned at the movement, and Kelsey's insides turned, an uneasy sickness that felt as much hers as Meagan's.

"I'm not going to get my smoke," the doctor said, as if Kelsey should care. "It's the only reason I came out here, but it's not safe out here. Ambulances, people, you name it."

"My daughter is *sick*," she explained. What exactly did he expect her to say? Did he want her to be upset that her daughter's illness had interrupted his nicotine urge? She couldn't think of anything else to say, and yet he kept staring at her as if waiting for the appropriate response.

Kelsey drew a deep breath. She despised doctors as it was. Her mother used to parade her into specialist after specialist, asking countless questions of them. Such inane things as, "Why can't she play the piano like all her other friends?"

"She's six," the doctor might say, so Mother would find another doctor to get to the root of the 'problem'. Consequently, she didn't think much of the profession, though her mother always told her she was destined to marry one. She had married one of course, but rather than the medical sort, in some sort of strange rebellion, she'd found the biggest, nerd PhD in all of Harvard. As if to say, *here he is, Mother. Your doctor. Am I free now?* All these years later, she often wondered if she hadn't done it just to make her mother right in the wrong sort of way.

Dr. Nicotine only resurrected her lifelong animosity.

"Life's a female dog," she told him. "You can kill yourself with cigarettes after you help my daughter." The seconds ticked by, and her rage grew with the doctor's slow pace.

"Ain't it a dog? That's why I started smoking in the first place."

"Is Meagan going to be all right?" she asked him, though her first inclination to get to Stanford echoed in her brain. She thought living in this backwoods' town, where the air regularly smelled of marijuana, had never been the proper place to raise children. Now she was paying the price for not taking action. Or rather, her daughter was paying the price. "I want her taken to Lucille Salter. They probably see this sort of thing every day." She paused before adding, "But it isn't serious, right? Just a little bug? Is there something going around?" She ventured another glance at her daughter and ignored all the sirens in her head.

"Stanford is too far," the doctor said. "You want her on IV antibiotics as soon as possible. Trust me, they would do the same thing I would. If there's possible meningitis, it's always better to be safe than sorry. We'll take a spinal tap, but we have to know what type of bacteria is there for the right antibiotics to be used, and this needs to be done as soon as possible. They may save her life."

*Save her life*. Kelsey wouldn't even go down that road. She couldn't bear it. "She doesn't have meningitis," she said assuredly. "She was fine. Not even an hour ago, Meagan was fine."

He offered no protection from her fears, no soothing words to quiet her mind. "And order a CT Scan, STAT," he said to the orderly before addressing Kelsey again. "The faster the tests, the better for confirmation." His hardened look softened momentarily. "If you still want her sent to Stanford, she can go as soon as the tests are run, but you take her there, you're adding...I'd say at least three hours with traffic over to the hill and triage before she gets seen. Not to mention all the teaching doctors who will want to take their crack at diagnosing her. If it's meningitis, especially bacterial"—he looked down at his cheap watch. It brought her some kind of peace that he entertained a cheap timepiece—"you don't have that kind of time."

She left his warnings to hang, unable to hear any more dire predictions. "Will the spinal tap hurt her? Meagan isn't fond of pain."

Meagan's eyes grew wide at her question, but she quickly lay back in the seat. Nathan sat behind her with his hand on his sister's shoulder, his eyes clasped shut. She should have felt peace that her son prayed, but she wanted to kick something. Why did she have to face crisis after crisis alone? She wasn't cut out for that sort of thing.

"I haven't met the patient who is fond of pain. Maybe you can introduce me sometime," the doctor said with a slight smile. He motioned for the orderlies to get Meagan on a gurney. "It will hurt more for you to watch, Mrs.—I'm sorry, I didn't catch your name."

"Kelsey," she answered.

"Kelsey, I'd suggest you stay and fill out all the necessary paperwork. Is Meagan up-to-date on her vaccines?"

"Yes, all of them." His eyebrows lowered. "Really, she is." Living in Santa Cruz, vaccines were pretty much of the devil, but the schools required them, and after Todd left, Kelsey didn't have the gumption to fight the system even if she'd wanted to. Her kids kept up with the growing list of California disease requirements, even though Meagan would print out a list of Internet warnings about why she shouldn't have this shot or that. What plagued Kelsey now was the notion that maybe Meagan had been correct, and all of those shots had harmed her immune system. What if taking the easy route killed her daughter? What then?

*More guilt. More shame.*

"Get her inside," the doctor ordered and she watched them wheel Meagan away.

The notion of them taking Meagan from her sight caused all Kelsey's fears to flame and she stared at Nathan, then ran after the gurney. She grabbed her daughter's hand and studied the pudgy fingers, marveling at their beauty. Meagan could give her all the advice in the world, she was still the tiny baby who snuggled into the crook of her arm. Her precious girl. "I love you, baby. Mommy will be right here." She let go as the doctor brushed past her.

"I'll be back," Dr. Nicotine said gruffly. "I want to oversee the test." He pat his chest where the cigarettes were, clearly he lamented that their call went unheeded. His expression softened once again as he turned and walked toward Kelsey. "I trained at Stanford Medical School if it makes you feel any better. The doctors there probably went to some flyover state college."

Perhaps she had touched a nerve, but hoped his cocky swagger testified to his expertise as a doctor.

"Mommy loves you Meagan. Don't worry about a thing," she called after the gurney.

"She is so embarrassing," Meagan murmured.

The doctor never promised them any hope or prognosis, and it offered her no comfort that he didn't have time for a cigarette. Typical man, she thought, but in her heart, she prayed he was not a typical man. He needed to be a spectacular man who would bring her precious girl back to her, Friday folders, straight creases and all.

Nathan didn't look at his mother, and his eyes were wet. His arms were crossed in front of him. "Why does this crap happen to us, Mom? Did you ever ask yourself why it always has to be us? Isn't there anyone else God could pick on for a time?"

"I don't know, Nathan. I only know we have to make the best of what we've been dealt." She should have offered better, more spiritual advice, but she was dry.

Even if her family did seem like some great cosmic joke to the Almighty. What choice did they have but to put one foot in front of the other and keep on walking? Nothing was sacred, Kelsey thought. Not her marriage, not her kids, nothing, not even after a lifetime of faith. Her devotion to all had meant nothing in the grand scheme of life. It was impossible not to view God in the vein of her mother and father, her husband – people who promised to love her but abandoned her all the same.

Adding God to the mix only seemed natural. She didn't please Him either. And she was tired of trying.

Nathan clenched his arms tighter. "Is this all there is? One crappy day after another? My friends get iPhones and I get this." He shook his head. "You gotta call school and tell them we're out today or we'll be doing detention on top of missing homework. Then, when Meagan wakes up she'll have a cow, and I don't want to listen to her anal-retentive freak-out session." He walked ahead of her, his anger clearly covering for his fears. Her children were far too experienced with Freudian vocabulary.

It was moments like these that she wanted to throw in the towel because she didn't have answers for Nathan. If she had a path out of the muck, she would have taken it a long time ago. It didn't seem to matter that she wasn't destined for leadership, everyone still looked towards her to navigate them out of the crooked maze. There was no one but her, and like Moses, she couldn't have felt less qualified.

"I'm sorry, Nathan. I don't know why this stuff happens. We just need for Meagan to be all right."

He put his head on her shoulder, a move he rarely ventured now that he entered his teen years. "Me too, Mom. I don't mean to complain. I don't want you to feel worse."

"I want you to be angry, Nathan. It's better than ignoring the feelings."

"Ya think?" He shrugged. "I think it's easier to ignore them."

"The counselor would say we're not ignoring them, we're suppressing them, and they'll come out somewhere else."

"The counselor likes to hear himself talk."

"Now we're poor and stuck with our own problems." She smiled, and her son lifted his head and put it back on her shoulder.

Meagan maintained what control she could through Martha Stewart idiosyncrasies and organizing her often-chaotic mother, but Nathan had always been a bigger concern. He'd stopped reacting at all. *"We're getting a Nintendo Wii for Christmas,"* incurred the same response as, *"there's no money this season for a soccer uniform."* Nathan went through life waiting for the next blow and absorbing the pain without the slightest twitch. But today, Kelsey saw his humanity return in his sister's pain. She saw it and took solace in the fact that he had not flat-lined emotionally. Yet.

But darn if that kid didn't deserve some goodness of his own.

"We're going to get out of this, Nathan. We are. This is our year," she said without conviction.

"You've been saying that for three years, Mom."

"But this year…this year I feel it, buddy. This is our year. We're going to walk out of this desert."

Kelsey had grown too angry to pray, livid in fact. Despite that, desperation gave way and a prayer formed easily in her mind, just like it used to a long time ago. The anger certainly hadn't helped. What did she have to lose at this point?

*Heal my Meagan, Lord. Isn't it bad enough that she's got me and Todd for parents? Nathan can't take another blow; he's such a sensitive soul. Take me if you need someone. . .or maybe their father would be better since I have to raise them, but it's up to You. I'll go either way. I won't ask for anything else, just spare my children. This isn't their fault. It's been a long time since I asked for anything, God, so if You've got one left in there for me, make it this one.*

## Chapter 3

Visitations were, by far, the worst part of Alex Bechtel's job, and the kicker? They took up the majority of his time. Each morning, after he jogged Obadiah (an oversized, over-enthused mutt) along the beach path, he dressed in his Sunday best, positioned his tie, and climbed into an enormous, old Lincoln—tithed to the church by an elderly member who no longer drove. He'd spend the first several blocks worrying if the mountain of kibble would be enough for Obadiah, whether or not the squeaky toys would entertain him until lunchtime, and then he'd think to himself how pathetic it was that he had nothing more to worry about than his dog. That, and the sofa being eaten.

Alex would maneuver the mammoth vehicle to the hospital or sometimes the homes of those elderly church members, who'd been on his regular visitation list or stricken with illness in the night. It wasn't the visitations he minded, it was the disappointment on people's faces when they saw him rather than Pastor Underwood.

The pastor thought it beneath him to check on his flock personally, so Alex was the go-to man. If Alex considered himself the arms of the church body reaching out, Pastor Underwood was the untouchable place, off-limits and unseen to the general population – except of course on Sunday when he preached with fire and brimstone until his face flamed red and sweat poured from his temples. It was like any other job, the boss got the perks and the underling, Alex, got what was left.

One hand on the steering wheel, he reached behind him to find what was digging into his back. Sure enough, one of Obadiah's toys. Smiling, he returned his attention to the road.

It wasn't all bad. He'd wanted to come to California, perhaps not Santa Cruz, the Wiccan Mecca of the west coast, but he'd come to feel at home among the cacophony of misfits who made up the community. It was several communities in actuality. First, it was a tourist town, famous for its Coney Island-type pier and surfing; a college town, known for its laid-back UC campus; a New Age center attracting a variety of hemp-wearing hippies of all ages; an environmentalist sanctuary providing a place of beauty and security for wildlife, and finally, an outland suburb of Silicon Valley over the Santa Cruz mountains. In other words, no one really fit in, and because of that, Alex felt at home. Santa Cruz was like an independent country filled with the remnants of some other country and pressed together into a laid-back life with upscale shops, fast food joints, and the newer, modern strip malls like Everywhere, USA.

Mrs. Willits had been "ill" since he'd come west, and though he always enjoyed her company, he knew that's all she was looking for – a little companionship, for which she'd write a tithe check each week. Alex felt like a kept man when she handed him the check with her careful, all-capital, squared print.

Every week, as he'd walk up Mrs. Willlits' path with its chipped brick-colored paint over cement, he'd think the church should do more to help keep the elderly woman comfortable. Even the windows were so dingy from the ocean's salt air, one could barely see through them. He wondered if the neighbors thought her money might be better spent on a handyman than the church tithe she saw to. The dilapidated houses like hers were mostly gone now, replaced by mini-mansions and renovated homes worthy of their beachfront address. No doubt, the developers were circling like vultures waiting to swoop in on her property.

It sent a pang of guilt every time he saw the old desperate house. But every afternoon, back at the office, when he might have arranged a work party from the congregation, Mrs. Willits evaporated from Alex's mind and all was forgotten until the following week when he entered through the shabby doorframe. Wood, paint and the salty air of the Pacific didn't mix, not without constant upkeep.

This morning, the door opened wide before he'd had a chance to knock.

"Good morning, Alex." Mrs. Willits' raspy voice greeted him as she stood behind the tired screen door, part of its netting flapping in the breeze. Slight and brittle in stature, he thought of Mrs. Willits as unflappable. Storms came and went, but she weathered them all with the practicality of an eagle scout.

"Good morning, Mrs. Willits. How's the hip today?"

She might have faded into the background, if not for her strong personality, with her graying skin and thinned straight frizz of hair, she reminded him of that famous Albert Einstein picture. In a way, she was like that picture, hiding her wisdom behind a persona that might fool the less astute. A person only made that mistake with her once. She afforded respect.

Alex reached for the screen door, and she held it closed. He pulled again, and she brought it toward her. "The hip is sore. I'll bet it rains tomorrow. You know you're getting old when your bones become the local weather vane."

"I'd think it be convenient," he said. "Like your own personal Doppler system, tracking the storms."

"A what? Oh Alex, some days, my boy, you talk another language altogether. You needn't remind me I'm a dinosaur. I'm well aware of that fact."

"Well, let's hope it doesn't rain. Obadiah gets covered in mud every time it does. It takes me an hour and two loads of laundry to get him back to rights. I don't have the time for rain and I don't know how many more big loads the old washer will take."

She laughed dutifully, but made no move to open the screen door. "It's the rain in life that makes things grow."

He shifted uncomfortably on the front porch and pulled at the door one more time. "Is something the matter?" he asked. "If I didn't know any better, I would say you were telling me to take a hike."

Her smile flattened. "I hear Dan Tognotti isn't doing so well this morning. You should probably be on your way to the hospital, now that you've confirmed that I've lived through another night."

"That is not why I come."

"I'll have the tithe check tomorrow. Come by then."

"That's not why I come either."

"So you are coming to court me, is that it? My papa would have never let me marry a preacher man. Didn't have much use for them. He thought they were lazy, and I suppose during the war they may have looked that way."

The word *lazy* resonated with Alex. "I've been thinking about how I should come do some work around here. What do you think about my arranging a work party to get this place into shape?" He ran his hand over the screen. "It would take less than an hour to fix this door, and the outside could really use a coat of paint."

"Pshaw." She waved her bony hand his way. "Paint it when I'm dead. The last thing I need is a bunch of do-gooders outside my window all day." Her expression warmed. "I don't mean to be ungrateful, Alex. You're a good man, but if I wanted the place painted, I'd hire someone. When I kick the bucket, someone is going to come in here and raze this house, so why put any money into it now? We learned not to be wasteful in my day. Get to the hospital, they'll be needing you."

Alex stalled. He hated to hear her talk about death. "I wish you wouldn't say things like that. It makes it sound like no one will care when you're gone, and you know that isn't true. Not to mention you've got too many years left. You know, they say the mean ones last like vinegar."

She laughed. "Go on, git!"

For a woman who rarely left her house, she managed to know everything about everyone within the congregation, and beyond. One day he'd work up the courage to ask her how she became the central source of information for the entire town without so much as a computer or a Facebook account to get her data.

Alex shifted foot to foot till Mrs. Willits waved him away again. "Go. You're dawdling."

He nodded. "Yeah, I know. I'm going." Like a repentant teenager searching for a lost baseball, he had a purpose. Mrs. Willits seemed determined to thwart it. "Did you give the kids back their balls when they went over the fence? I'll bet you didn't."

She ambled out to the rickety porch as if to shoo him away. At the sight of her wrinkled, crumbly hands, he felt guilt. Mrs. Willits possessed the same skills his mother perfected.

"This isn't like you, Alex. I did give the boys back their baseballs incidentally, though only twice. After that, they had to go buy new ones. Some days I just thought they wanted to see the old lady throw a pitch."

He smiled. He knew it. He pulled a leaf off the bush, and she only pursed her lips. "I guess I'll be going."

"I guess you will." Mrs. Willits turned, hobbled to her porch and shut the door gently. They both knew what he had to do and understood instinctively that no one likes to head toward death. Once on the sidewalk, he looked back at the overgrowth in front of her house. He'd definitely plan the work party that afternoon, whether or not she objected.

Looking across the street to the unencumbered view of the Pacific, he inhaled deeply. He'd never get tired of seeing the ocean every morning. It changed colors depending on the weather, but mostly stayed a sapphire blue with sparkling caps under the sun. When he first arrived he thought it was God winking at him. It amazed him how with familiarity something so spectacular could become just a plain background.

He sighed as he made his way back to the gigantic boat of a car as though the tantalizing view was only there to taunt him between illnesses and prognoses.

The sight of the car added to his down mood of the morning. He hadn't had many dates since moving to California, and when he looked at the car he knew the reason. Or one of them anyway. He didn't care how pious a man was, he didn't want to show up for a date in a car big enough to sleep six inside. This car could house an immigrant family after a day of picking strawberries down the road in Watsonville, and the last thing any woman's father wanted to see was a vehicle drive up with an enormous backseat.

"You are going to get in that car?" Mrs. Willits had returned to the porch.

"Eventually."

"You're as bad as a toddler this morning, Alex. I have a good mind to call Pastor Underwood."

"You'd tattle on me?" He grinned.

"Alex, you'll be sorry if you're not there." A car sped by and he didn't bother answering her. He just got into the boat, turned the key, and the engine roared to life.

He and his friends would have loved the old Lincoln in high school when they might have stuffed the entire class of 1998 in the trunk. But now? Now it only served as date control, because he wasn't about to suffer the humiliation of not being able to afford his own vehicle. All the degrees he'd collected and *Doctor* Alex Bechtel barely afforded gas for his floating tank. He'd bought himself a very expensive, and so far, useless title.

His cell phone rang, and thankful for the interruption, he answered on the first ring. "Alex Bechtel."

"You're still not moving." Mrs. Willits' voice berated him. "Dan needs you, Alex."

A wash of guilt flushed through him. He wasn't a heartless man, but he wasn't Mother Theresa either, and the job had started to strip him of purpose. He sat in the car, staring at the ocean and hoping for some other urgent need to pop into his head. "I'm going," he finally said, and he heard her click the phone down.

His nature was given to teaching, and he'd hoped to pastor a large congregation, studying God's Word for exactly the right message each week, but that dream seemed so distant now – if Alex were asked what he hoped for, he probably wouldn't remember.

The Lincoln coughed as he pressed on the gas pedal, and the car ambled down W. Cliff Drive. He tried to ignore how the Pacific twinkled this morning. As a preaching man, his vocation was to comfort those in need, but the loss of humanity had its effect on him and it showed in his stooped posture. The job was getting harder because it was becoming easier to watch people flirt with death's door. He'd grown accustomed to the sound of life's last breath exhaled. It was a sound that haunted him at night.

"I'm thirty-one and I know more eighty-year olds than twenty year-olds. There's something seriously wrong with that." He didn't know who he was talking to – God gave him the job, and considering all of Alex's other offers (zero), it wasn't like God's will wasn't made clear.

If his friends from back home could have seen him today, they would have claimed he'd sold out and looked like any other pastor they'd mocked in seminary. Sold-out, burned-out, and growing more detached by the minute.

They'd teased him when he'd left that he'd probably come home with a buxom blonde in a convertible, and the idea seemed less ridiculous the longer he stayed. The women all seemed to be shaded the same orangey-brown, and blondes never did much for him. They bore far too close a resemblance to Samson's Delilah for his tastes. Though he knew through careful study and geographic cultures, that Delilah was no doubt as brunette as he. *She's blonde by nature*, he reasoned. A long-standing prejudice, and he had no idea where it had come from, although Jamie Linder from fourth grade may have had some influence on it. She told everyone at school he wore Sesame Street underwear. The worst part was that it was true. He stayed the same size from Kindergarten to fourth grade, or relatively close, so his mother saw no reason to buy different underwear. His grandmother had purchased all these packs of perfectly good Big Bird briefs in bulk, and their supply never dwindled. He used to pray to grow. And he finally did, but not before the damage was done. And he'd developed an unnatural rage against large avian creatures.

He pulled up to the hospital and dropped his head onto the steering wheel. He'd never run from his calling and he knew it, it was just that morning, wanting to put off his calling to a later date. He pulled his jacket on, buttoned it and lifted the black leather notebook from the seat.

Dr. Mackinaw stood outside the hospital doors, drawing deep breaths and watching his own stomach expand. He had his hands flat and pressed together, like that old painting of Jesus where the Savior was a blonde. He nodded at Alex, and a look passed between the two men.

"Today?" Alex asked.

"Soon," Dr. Mackinaw answered. "No one can ever be sure, but soon."

"Does it ever get easier?"

The doctor nodded. "It does. Not sure if that's a good thing or not." He shrugged and focused on his abdomen expanding and contracting again. "I thought we had this one, Alex."

"Me too, Doc."

Alex existed in Santa Cruz, watching other people's lives play out, while he sent the dying onto their next destination. The families looked to him desperately, as though he were a doctor of prayer fitted with special powers. He gazed back with uncertainty, making him feel like the powerless rube he'd become.

"I'd better get in there." The two men parted, and Alex mumbled prayers to himself, asking for strength and a light heart. *God is in control. God's will is not for us to know. Someday, we'll get answers.*

It all sounded trite when life seemed so unfair. Not everyone was afraid of dying, naturally, but cases like today's got to him, where no matter how bright the send-off, the sad truth lingered. There would be fatherless children. A wife left to navigate the world on her own.

Alex walked into Dan's room and felt like an intruder. He clutched his notebook tighter and felt for the small Bible in his jacket pocket. "Good morning, Tognottis!"

"Alex, we were wondering when you'd get here. Come on and sit down." Dan motioned to the empty chair by the window. "Did you have coffee yet? Crystal can run down to the cafeteria. She might like the break."

Crystal, a small blonde, appeared too tired to run anywhere. She bore dark bluish circles under her eyes, and if Alex hadn't known any better, he would have thought it was she stricken with the disease. She made light conversation to keep the mood breezy, but he could see it was all an act.

"Angela scored her very first goal, Pastor Bechtel."

A little blonde nodded her head, and Alex cupped her chin in his hand. "You little Beckham, you."

"I scored two!" Danny announced with his face upturned for his reward.

Alex mussed the little boy's hair. "And you, a regular Wayne Rooney. The San Jose Earthquakes will be scouting this family."

Naturally, the children were too young to have any idea what he was talking about, but he figured they understood the tone because they both looked proud as punch.

Alex swallowed hard. He said all the right things, but reality overwhelmed him like never before. A young father, surrounded by his four small children made conversation focusing on soccer scores and new ballet moves. Only four months ago, Dan started a fight with a brain tumor and the tumor had scored significantly higher.

Crystal jittered about the room, trying to keep the unruly children from losing focus on their father. "Kids, tell Pastor Bechtel about the new Bible song you learned."

For months now, Crystal had acted like Snow White on steroids. She sang happy songs and encouraged the kids to sing along and regularly broke into courtship tales about mommy and daddy. This morning was no different. He worried what might happen when she allowed the hard truth to penetrate her system.

"No," Angela said. "Tell us about Daddy meeting us on our birthdays! Daddy likes those stories. Don't you Daddy?"

"I do," Dan affirmed.

"Well…" Crystal clapped her hands together. "Angela took her sweet time in coming." All eyes focused on their mommy as she no doubt embellished and romanticized their entrances into the world. Each child fidgeted with anticipation while they waited for their sibling's story to be told. "I thought she might never come, and your daddy"—she looked straight into Angela's eyes—

"your daddy said, 'Well, she's like any woman. She tells you she'll be five minutes and then realizes she is having a bad hair day and must go back and fix it. When she gets it right, she'll join us.'"

Crystal told the story with just the right inflection, as if they were all at Disneyland hearing a great fable. "And when you came, Angela, your daddy said, 'you see, she waited to be absolutely perfect, and wasn't she worth the wait?'"

Crystal and Dan both had tears in their eyes, and yet, there were three children left. By the end of it, Alex was exhausted. He couldn't imagine how Crystal held it together. Dan's pale gray pallor signaled that his fight was nearly over, but his proud smile never waned. He looked at each of his children as though he couldn't believe he'd had a part in something so right.

Alex felt totally useless in contrast. "Why don't I take the kids to get a snack so you two can have some time together?"

Dan shook his head. "Not now, Alex. I don't want to part with them just now." Dan struggled for his next breath, and the children cowered at the sound.

Alex wished he could kick something.

*"Daddy went to heaven,"* Crystal would say softly with a smile, but Alex couldn't help but feel the kids' future betrayal, as they discovered this sweet place called heaven meant that daddy wasn't ever coming home. In the near future, they'd forget his face, then his voice, and then him altogether, except for the stories Crystal patch worked together. Alex thought

without this man's wife and her happy tales, this father would cease to exist, and the idea filled him with an Ecclesiastical sorrow.

"Doesn't his color look good today, Pastor Bechtel?" Crystal asked.

Alex roused from his thoughts. He gazed at the merry wife, whose zeal appeared to the average bystander like a quad jolt of espresso shots, while her four children shackled themselves to her ankles like Ebenezer's ghosts, their gut instinct keeping them away from their father.

"Yes, Crystal. He looks good today." Alex patted Dan's shin under the blanket. "But he can speak for himself. Dan, you're looking good today. How ya feeling?"

Alex didn't mention that often in the last twenty-four hours of life, people would awaken with clarity and joviality to create positive memories of the end. Perhaps, it was God's gift to the family for enduring the tragedy. Heaven would connect them all again one day. What kind of pastor would he be if he didn't believe in that joyful reunion? But one couldn't be human and not mourn the present.

"She keeps saying I have good coloring. What color am I today, Crystal?" Dan grinned.

"You're a fresh pink," his wife said. "Like a newborn's bottom."

The two of them laughed, and Alex seemed to feel their connection, as if he were an intruder between their loving gaze. It made a man want to watch another man receive that kind of love.

"Doesn't my wife tell the best stories, Alex? I can see the Kingdom. It's close and full of color, more than we've ever seen on our spectrum." His eyes thinned. "You be sure and tell my kids how their daddy whooped you in basketball, all right? How I sent you home hurting and whining. And don't let Crystal marry any doofus who doesn't know how to play basketball. If a man isn't fast on his feet, there isn't any way he can keep up with her."

"Dan!" Crystal chastised. "In case you haven't noticed, I'm going to be a bit busy. Call me crazy, but I imagine my four ducklings following on my heels aren't exactly going to open up a big dating pool for me."

"Mom, are we getting a pool when Daddy goes to heaven?" Angela asked.

"No, sweetie. Daddy's making a joke."

"That's not funny, Daddy. We want a pool."

He gazed straight into his wife's eyes. "Crystal, you could have fourteen kids and any man would be lucky to have you as his wife. I certainly never deserved you, and nothing made me happier."

He watched as Crystal squeezed her husband's hand and the children jumped onto the bed, momentarily forgetting their fears. "Daddy, can we wrestle?" one of them cried.

He noticed the moment happening between the family, and he backed out of the hospital room to leave them to their revelry.

He'd become like that cat in the nursing home who could smell death, and soon, no one would want Alex around, any more than the since-murdered feline. There was something inherently creepy about a pastor who only handled death and illness. He'd become more of a mortician than a preacher, which if he thought about it, infuriated him. Morticians made a lot better money.

He eyed the muted walls of the hospital, all too familiar now, and walked with a resolute gait, anxious to get back to the office and his first love, teaching. This job was tearing at his soul.

Alex stumbled, and he looked down to see a young teen propped up against the wall. This strange image took a moment to register. His eyes fell on the oversized, puppy-like feet in untied skate shoes with the extra fat laces tucked into themselves, and his eyes came to rest on a familiar face under a mop of wild, sandy-blonde curls. The boy's body was inclined against the wall in a slovenly right angle, and his lanky arms were crossed.

"I'm sorry, son. I wasn't paying attention. Are you all right? I didn't hurt you, did I?"

The adolescent smirked and pulled his legs toward his chest, wrapping his arms around them and resting his forehead on his knees. He'd seen tears in the boy's eyes before he crumpled into a ball, and the dichotomy between the "cool" image and the boy's mood caught Alex by surprise. Visitations had already taken him an hour longer than he'd planned, and he had a Sunday school lesson to prepare back at the office, so the boy's tears represented an inconvenience that Alex hoped to ignore. After a full minute without an answer, Alex stepped over the boy, and he walked about three yards before his callous actions startled him. He turned around, and in a half-hearted way, asked, "You need to talk, son?"

The boy shook his head back and forth. "You don't even know who I am, do you?"

Alex searched his memory, but out of context and with the morning he'd had, there was little chance of him offering the youth a satisfactory answer, so he opted for honesty. "I'm sorry. I don't remember, but it's been a full day already. You know me?"

The corner of the boy's lip curled upward. "No, I don't know you. And I'm glad! You should be ashamed to call yourself a church over there at St. Rude Evacuation."

"Pardon?" The boy had obvious taken the time to come up with an angry alternative to Santa Cruz Evangelical, so whatever the kid felt, it was personal.

"The Bible says when a man is in sin, he should take one witness, then two, then the elders and cast him out if he still won't repent. You think I don't know that? You think my family doesn't know what the Bible says?"

"You have an advantage on me, I'm afraid. Did my church harm you in some way?"

Alex heard footsteps, and then registered another pair of feet tucked neatly into black heels. He focused on the feet first, his mind so lost in his thoughts, and he followed the black hosiery up the shapely legs until his eyes rested upon a face he did recognize. She had cut her long, beautiful hair that he'd once dreamed of running his hands through, only to wish he were Catholic to make a public confession of his lustful thought. Just to be done with them.

The room suddenly felt very warm. He yanked at his tie and looked for the nearest exit as though there were a fire behind him. He didn't know her name, but her classic beauty and pensive eyes inspired him to dream of a wife who looked like this, and cared for him like Crystal now did Dan. Even now, he found his thoughts drifting to what kind of man it would take to have a woman like her focus with eyes only for him. Silky hair and creamy skin with soft angles molded straight from heaven forced Alex's eyes back to the boy on the floor.

"You have barf in your hair, Mom," the boy said.

The woman fingered her hair, and then struggled with her purse until she pulled out a packet wipe and opened it. She ran it through her hair. "Did I get it?"

"Just a little right here." Alex took the wipe from her and made a final brush through her hair. The action felt far more intimate than he'd have liked, but everything about her unnerved him.

"Thank you, Alex," she said. "Nathan, we have to go. Your sister's tests should be done by now. I've signed our lives away so we can go see her"

"Nathan Mitchell from youth club," Alex said.

He remembered Pastor Underwood counseled the brunette beauty and her husband. From what Alex could recall, her husband expressed a desire to see his wife learn proper submission, and that led to a month of sermons on godly submission in a wife. Perhaps it was that unbroken spark in her that enraptured a man's attention, like the adulteress whose words drip honey. Maybe she would only be tamed by the one man meant for her. He coughed away the thought. Which was her husband, naturally.

"I tripped over your son," he said. "I think we may have offended him at youth group, but I haven't yet discovered the slight." He looked straight at the boy. "Whatever it is, we could work it out, Nathan. You seem to know your Scriptures well." Alex sneaked a glance in Mrs. Mitchell's direction, but he found himself so taken up with her infinite beauty that he couldn't permit such harmful thoughts about her. They felt nothing short of treason.

"I'm not interested in attending a country club church," Nathan said, as if he were fifty years' old.

Alex noted, by Nathan's cool tone, that the boy wasn't fooled for a minute by his sudden recognition. Nathan looked knowingly at his mother just to let the pastor know how transparent the scene was, and a rush of shame burned in him.

"Nathan! Mind your manners. I'm sorry, Pastor…Bechtel is it?"

He nodded. "Call me Alex."

"It's been a hard day for us. If you'll excuse us." She began to walk away, then suddenly turned back to him. "If you wouldn't mind putting my daughter Meagan on your prayer list."

"Certainly," Alex's voice squeaked, as though he were in seventh grade again. "I don't remember your name."

"It doesn't surprise me in the least, Alex. I remember you quite well. You attended one of our last counseling sessions with Pastor Underwood. Did you learn anything? Like how a proper wife should act, perhaps?"

"I don't remember," he lied. Why on earth would he lie? It slipped out of him as easily as Peter denying his Lord. "I hope everything worked out all right."

"We're legally separated, and he left us two years ago. Does that answer your question?" She peeled her sweater from her arms and helped her son from the floor. Without another word, she turned on her heel. The thought of death was far from Alex's mind as he watched her hips sway back and forth down the hallway.

Alex rubbed his palm over his mouth and reached for the small New Testament in his breast pocket. He chastised himself that lust for another man's wife is exactly why he wasn't fit for a full pastor position. Who wanted to hire a pastor without any responsibility but an oversized dog? But as he shut his eyes against the thoughts, he saw the silhouette of her again, sucked in a deep breath, and rested his palm against the wall.

"It's all this death. I'm losing my mind," he whispered. And then he heard a small voice, like a child's. It called to him, and he stopped trying to discern where it came from.

"Help me," the weak voice pleaded.

He looked around, but there was only him in the hallway. An eerie feeling crept over him, but he wasn't scared, only intrigued.

"Help me," the angelic voice sang, and he followed the feeling, a sort of force that pulled him along. He felt as if a shaft of light hovered over him and led him to where the voice became audible, but never louder, simply with more clarity of where he was being led.

"Right here," the voice sang. "Here I am, help me Pastor Bechtel."

## Chapter 4

"Mom, why were you so nice to him? Don't you remember what they did to us?"

Kelsey brushed her son's face. "They didn't change anything. They simply made it feel worse. People do that, Nathan. I've come to realize it's mostly ignorance, they don't mean to dole out extra. Focus on Meagan, sweetheart. Revenge of any kind is a waste of energy."

She walked up to the reception desk behind the great, glass partition that kept you, the sick, separated from the warden of health. The warden was a dead-ringer for what she imagined an evil, patient killing nurse to look like. The kind who could no longer work with patients, but as a nurse was too valuable to be let go. From behind a bulletproof shield, she peered over colorfully painted glasses with harsh, kohl-lined eyes and bright red lipstick, which highlighted her age.

"Help you?" her gravelly voice asked.

"My daughter was brought in this morning. She's with Dr. Levin for testing."

"Insurance card and identification please." She held her hand up to the circular hole. Kelsey placed her driver's license and insurance card in the aged hand.

She used ten-key to punch in the numbers before letting her gaze rise and fall over Kelsey, as if she were buying alcohol for an underage friend. "Is something the matter?" she ventured.

The woman ignored her, picked up the phone and made a phone call. She slammed her plastic barrier shut and after what felt like an eternity, sliced open the window.

"The insurance company says this card isn't active. We can't admit"—the pointy-faced woman looked down at the paperwork—"Meagan, is it?" She tried to hand back the insurance card through the hole, which Kelsey couldn't help thinking would easily handle the barrel of a gun. Kelsey refused to take the card.

"You've already admitted her. That's why I'm here."

"Will it be a cash pay then?" She shoved the card at Kelsey again, gesturing in animated form.

"A cash pay? Of course not. I'm a single mother. Check the card again. There must be something wrong with your system. I have a court order stating this must be paid." She reached into her purse to pull out the orders, which she took with her everywhere. The waiting room was full, and though she'd been rejected publicly, Kelsey looked around and thought no one in the room probably understood a word of English. She took solace in that.

"Mom, let's just go." Nathan tugged at her arm. "Meagan's probably fine by now."

"Go where, Nathan? Your sister is sick. We can't leave."

"Everyone's looking at us," he whispered.

She turned around, and all eyes averted. "Nathan, I'm sorry. If this embarrasses you, why don't you go to the cafeteria and wait? I'll come get you before I go in to see Meagan. They have to admit her, honey, it's California law." At her knowledge, the woman behind the glass bristled. "Honey, you'll feel better after you eat." She brushed the hair off his forehead and he turned around to the small crowd of coughing, staring folks. Didn't anyone have a general doctor any longer?

"Stop looking at us!" Nathan snapped. "Mom, dad didn't pay the bill and you know he didn't. What did a court order ever mean to him?"

"Nathan," she whispered. "Everything will be fine. I have to think of Meagan right now, so if this bothers you, you need to go to the cafeteria. I don't think any of them understand, anyway."

"They're all getting seen. Everything's not fine, Mom. I'm tired of being told we aren't good enough. We have another piece of plastic that's useless. Stop telling me that as if I don't get it. I get it. We're poor now."

"We have a roof over our heads and we're here, aren't we?" She rubbed her forehead. She didn't have the strength to argue, not with Nathan anyway. She hadn't even had her coffee yet, and therefore, her brain had yet to kick in for the day. "I want to get back in to see Meagan, so let me handle this. All right, sweetheart?"

"One day, Mom. I'm going to belong to the most exclusive country club and I'm only letting good people in. I'm not going to judge people by their wallets!"

Kelsey tried to focus. She leaned in, hoping to find a heart in the woman behind the glass. She kept her voice low for Nathan's sake. "My ex-husband has a court order to keep this insurance active. Do you need to see it? It's a guarantee of his financial responsibility."

"All I know is what the insurance company tells me. Court order or no, the guy has to pay the bill. That's something you gotta take up in court, but you see what it says?" She swiveled the computer screen toward her where it blinked, "INACTIVE. LAST PAYMENT APRIL 2012."

"So you're telling me all these people have active insurance cards?" Kelsey swept her hand around the room. "Two of them don't even have shoes. My daughter is very sick and it's hardly her fault her dad is a deadbeat. What am I supposed to do? Legally, you have to treat her, so what are my options?"

"There's a payphone in the lobby if you'd like to call your ex-husband, but I should warn you, I just spoke with the woman in charge of your group number. I always call and check to verify if payment has recently been made," the woman said, as though Kelsey should nominate her for employee of the month. "And she said the insurance had been unpaid for over four months."

"Four months! Shouldn't I have gotten a letter or something saying our coverage was up?"

"Sometimes they'll grant you service if it's only one payment missed, but this… Numerous requests for payments were sent out." She pushed the microphone aside and came close to the dotted opening in the window. "When coverage is denied, we turn over every stone. Insurance is notorious for ducking payment. Your daughter will get treatment, but payment is going to be up to you."

"My daughter needs a spinal tap and she's been taken in already. I'm a single mother with absolutely no help, how would I afford that kind of bill?"

"We'll bill you, Mrs. Mitchell. Standard procedure. We wouldn't ever deny services to a person in need." After a pitiful smile, the woman went on, "You can take it up with your insurance company later if it's appropriate or at least show the courts your ex will be responsible for the money. You're sure you don't want to call your ex?" She eyed the payphone.

Kelsey shook her head. "He's not in the country, but thank you for your help." She packed up her wallet and what was left of her shredded dignity and walked a few steps to the triage nurse with Nathan behind her. What was another outlandish bill anyway? It was all just crazy numbers on statements that she couldn't afford to pay. One more red bill to add to the mix. Money was the least of her troubles; her daughter was having a spinal tap. "Can I see my daughter now?"

The triage nurse exchanged a look with the admitting nurse. "Dr. Levin said he'd be out to update you after the procedure. Have a seat. I'm sorry about the insurance. We're seeing more and more of that, what with the economy being so bad and all. In my day, men provided for their children."

She nodded, grateful for a little solidarity, but she wanted to see Meagan and Nathan didn't need to hear any more ugly details. "The procedure should be over by now. Would you mind checking?"

All pretense of the gentle nurse disappeared. "If it were over, Dr. Levin would be here. They probably had to wait for anesthesiology. Have a seat." The triage nurse stared at Nathan in a way that made Kelsey uncomfortable, as though her son was a hoodlum of some sort. He may have been in desperate need of a haircut, but his sweet toddler face was all Kelsey saw. She draped an arm around him.

"My daughter's only nine. I'd like to be with her if possible. She'll be afraid, she's never been in a hospital before. Aren't mothers normally there?" Granted, by now, Meagan was no doubt interrogating the doctors and ordering up breakfast in bed, but the triage nurse didn't know that.

"She's being cared for. As I said, Dr. Levin will be out to update you. Have a seat."

Kelsey took a seat and thumbed the plastic insurance card, no more useful than the plastic versions of the American Express card that came in the mail. *Your name here.* Well, the cards that used to come in the mail when she'd been married and her husband paid the bills.

"We have no insurance," Nathan said, with a roll of his eyes. "We're like, total losers. What's next? The soup kitchen we used to work at."

"Don't give God any ideas. I'm sure it's just a misunderstanding and besides, we're not defined by money, remember?"

"Sure," he said without conviction.

"We'll get it cleared up and my insurance at work will kick in soon." She swallowed the thick lump in her throat. There were no words to describe her powerlessness.

"*If* you can keep this job." He walked away and stood in front of a snack machine, studying the contents. Kelsey walked after him and rested her hand on his shoulder.

"Listen Nathan, I know it's been tough, but employers expect a lot out of people these days. I can't work those kind of hours and be there for you two." One person can't do it all, she thought to herself, but at least I'm here trying. She knew better than to expect kudos from a teenager.

"We have nothing, Mom. Does he even care?"

"As much as he's able to. He does. But he's sick, Nathan." She never imagined herself vocalizing such words about the father of her children -- words that echoed of neglect. Never in her wildest nightmares did she imagine a solitary life with her in charge of the day-to-day decisions. She'd never been allowed to venture out on her own, never imagined the trouble her own decisions could lead her into – because she'd simply never been allowed to imagine. Dreams and happily-ever-after were all she saw in her future because that's all she'd been told were possible. Her parents had seemed so sure of it, that Kelsey couldn't have imagined a world outside what they envisioned for her. She wasn't that intelligent.

"College?" She'd heard her mother say with a laugh, though only a junior in high school, Kelsey knew what she meant, and she stood outside the dining room, listening intently to the discussion of her future. "Whatever will she need college for?"

"We have to provide her with an education, Dee."

"Are you thinking of a community college?"

"She can't very well get an educated man in my shop now, can she? You've given her everything, Marion. How do you think she'll survive without money and fine clothes? You've taught her nothing but your silly parlor tricks to snare a man. It's the least you can do to get her a decent one."

The conversation grew more heated, "It's just like you to blame me for her simple ways. I never heard you complain when she played piano for your employee Christmas parties. Or when she painted you a picture for your office wall. No…then, it was all well and good that she excelled in the arts. I specifically remember you touting her sweetness and how she'd never be in need of a real education with a charm like hers. She's not a puppy, but you were perfectly happy when she sat at your feet and fawned over you."

"Stop your back-mouthing, woman, and get that girl into a college. I'll be at the London office for a week." Kelsey's dad slammed the door, and her parents' conversation ended the same way most of their conversations ended. With Kelsey's future sealed.

Contrary to all statistical probability, she entered Harvard and majored in math. She imagined a healthy alumni gift had something to do with her entry. Only one year later, she'd achieved her parents' goal and met a graduate student named Todd Mitchell, whose thesis, which she personally typed, was based on the future of quasi-particle physics. She'd hit the mother lode and her greatest goal in life had been achieved. She had officially been transferred out of her parents' responsibility and under Todd's rule. It never occurred to her, she'd had choices all along or that an alternative might be worse.

"Mom, when I grow up, I'm going to buy you anything you want. You won't have to beg or plead or give me a reason either. I'm going to give you what you deserve."

She fought the sting of tears. "I have everything I want, Nathan. As long as Meagan is all right, and we're together, nothing else matters."

They were free of the endless litany of regulations that came with being a part of the Mitchell clan: heat water on the stove versus the microwave (dangerous radiation); all can labels must face outwards in the same direction (that's simply the right way); deal only with credit cards and ATM cards, paying them off each month (there should be a record of every purchase, and you wouldn't have to touch dirty, filthy money); there could be no Christmas lights because they might not be turned off at night and cause a fire, dishes needed to be lined up smallest to biggest from left to right. It seemed every day that Todd added a new rule to their lives and they tried to keep up, rather than endure his wrath. It all seemed so ridiculous now.

Walking on eggshells and tiptoeing so as to go unnoticed came naturally to Kelsey, but when she witnessed her children doing it, something in her snapped. Todd's extreme version of Christianity got stranger and stranger, his finish line farther away, unattainable. Like a rainbow, the closer she came, the more distant he became.

"I didn't make the rules," he'd say. "Take it up with God. Man is meant to rule over his household, and you forget, I'm the one who will be judged on my performance as a leader."

If she had been as simple-minded as her parents deemed her, she would have had a much easier time in life as Todd's wife. She wouldn't have struggled against daily unrighteousness, but realized sooner that dysfunction breeds dysfunction. And a loveless marriage, contempt. *That was probably unfair.*

It wasn't loveless. She had, after all, loved Todd in the beginning, been awestruck that such an intellectual man could fall for a ninny like her. She'd felt…well, she'd felt grateful.

Todd's science brain was filled with calculations and algorithms that rendered his emotions useless; cobwebs among the synapses. They say the eyes are the first thing to go – what a strange and heartless place the world was when it's the soul.

A wave of desperation hit at the memory. "Can we please see Meagan now?"

The triage nurse gave her a standard look of disdain. Kelsey simply knew when disdain came naturally to a person. For this nurse, it was a secondary benefit alongside her paycheck. Kelsey pulled at the door, which was locked from the other side. The nurse smirked.

"I'm her mother," Kelsey said again. "She's nine years' old."

"Are you going to call Dad or am I?" Nathan tugged at his jeans. "This has to get straightened out."

Too many sounds buzzed in Kelsey's head. She snapped at Nathan. "I will call your father when we get home. Nathan, I will handle this. It's the middle of the night there anyway."

"It's 9 p.m. there," he stated. Nathan definitely inherited his father's mind for science and numbers. She reached for words to answer him, when she saw movement in the triage office.

"Ma'am, I'm not going to ask you again. Sit down! I will call security if necessary."

"Call them. What right do you have to keep me from my daughter?"

Dr. Levin walked into the triage nurse's station and the nurse was so startled, she spilled a small amount of coffee onto her white uniform. A kinder, perhaps more educated woman than Kelsey, would not take pleasure in this, but she was not that person. Not today anyway. Dr. Levin tapped his chest pocket, ensuring his cigarettes were at hand. His face gave nothing away, but when he opened the door, a loud buzzer alerted everyone to his arrival. She grinned widely as she and Nathan were swallowed up into the hallowed hallway.

"Dr. Levin, I'm so grateful." Her eyes focused on his embroidered name over the cigarettes.

"Meagan's asking for you. She may be back to sleep by the time you get back there. She's drifting in and out of consciousness, but we've got her started on the IV antibiotics. We believe they're the right ones, but we'll have to keep an eye on her to know for certain."

She squeezed Nathan's hand, more so for her own strength than because he needed leading. She paused and tried to brace herself. "What did the spinal tap show?"

"The lumbar puncture went straight to the lab." The doctor shut the door behind them and garnered a severe expression. "We don't have results yet, I'm afraid. I'm going with my gut." He dropped his head and scratched the back of it. "I'm afraid Meagan does have what appears to be bacterial meningitis. Of course we can't be certain, but we treat it as though we are. Her glucose levels were low, her white blood cell count was high, and her opening pressure was higher than 200." He looked down. "None of that is good I'm afraid, but we're doing all we can for her. Has she been sluggish lately?"

If she had, Kelsey wouldn't have noticed. Meagan's low gear was like most people's overdrive. Once again, she clutched Dr. Levin's hand with both of her own. "Tell me in English. What does this mean for Meagan? Are you telling me that my daughter is really in trouble here?" she sputtered. She tried to use her daughter's name as often as possible, so he'd know this wasn't just any child. "My children are all I have, Dr. Levin. We're not talking life or death here." She let out an uncomfortable laugh. "Right?"

"It means you did the right thing bringing her in so quickly. We've got her started on corticosteroids," he corrected himself. "Intravenous steroids to combat swelling, and we're also giving her fluids and antibiotics through the IV. I'm not going to lie to you, Mrs. Mitchell. This is very serious, but I am encouraged at the way Meagan has revived after the steroids. Her energy is low, but I believe the swelling was cause for her confusion, and we hope to keep that down with the steroids. We're going to keep her here for observation, naturally, and we're going to be following up until we know for certain she's in the clear. It's touch and go. I highly recommend you don't try to do anything like transfer her at the moment."

"I don't understand. There's no chance—" she couldn't finish the sentence. There wasn't any chance; she wasn't even going to go there.

He rubbed her upper arm, which caused her to flinch. Human contact had become a foreign concept unless her children fought one of her hugs, or Nathan waited for his sister to become sick to allow her to take his hand.

"Bacterial meningitis is a disease we don't fully understand and I can't, with any certainty, predict its course from what I've seen today. It reacts differently in everyone. I do believe we've caught this early and that the swelling was hopefully caught before any damage was done to her brain or spinal cord." He pat his chest again. He was like a caged animal that wanted an escape. "She's in the second room on your left. I'll be back after my smoke." The way he couldn't look at Kelsey, with his kind, blue eyes told her more than she wanted to know. The fact that he used so many words to say so little frightened her to no end.

"Dr. Levin," she said after him.

"Yes, Mrs. Mitchell?"

She fought back a tear. "Thank you. Thank you for coming in and attending to Meagan. I owe you a carton of cigarettes."

"Save your money and my life."

Her head swam; she wobbled before slamming her head into the wall. Dr. Levin and Nathan caught her and held her steady. She swallowed her anguish and stood tall, forcing back her shoulders. "Second door on the left you say?" She cleared her throat.

He nodded.

She and Nathan made their way down the hallway and paused outside Meagan's door. As she entered, she startled at the sight of a man in the room. Nathan took her hand and they stared at one another. She quietly stepped into the hallway and checked the number on the room. "Didn't he say this door?"

They both peeked into the room again, and noticed Meagan's clodhopper Mary Janes on the side table. She then saw that the man, wearing an ill-fitting suit, was none other than Pastor Alex Bechtel from earlier in the hallway. Her hackles went up, but his presence rendered her silent for some reason. Though inside she roiled, her body stayed planted in the doorway as if paralyzed by his presence.

He mumbled what she believed were words of prayer, and his hands were outspread over Meagan, who was asleep on the bed, oblivious to his presence. She looked beautiful and peaceful, like the times Kelsey watched her asleep.

Alex's hands hovered over her daughter in a strange way that felt New-Agey to her. Naturally, with all of Todd's crazy churches, she'd seen pastors lay hands on the sick, but this was different. The two of them seemed locked in some kind of hypnotic trance, and it wasn't until Nathan knocked over a bedpan with a deafening clang that Alex jolted and turned around.

Her anger suddenly flared like an accelerant to the flame. "What do you think you're doing?" she shouted as she rushed to Meagan's side and grasped her daughter's hand, which was warm to the touch. She brought it to her face and exhaled, relishing in the familiar curves of the bony knuckles and short, rounded nails, now impaled by a needle and tube taped to her wrist. "Meagan," she cried, as she knelt at her bedside. "Meagan, Mommy is right here." Like a great storm brewed within her chest, she directed her rage at the preacher, who seemed to embody all that his religious world had cost her. "Get out of here right now before I call the police!"

"I had a word," Alex stammered. "I wouldn't have come in, but—"

Kelsey clenched her teeth and growled through her tightened jaw. "Get out! Get away from my daughter and don't ever come near my family again, do you understand me?"

"Please Kelsey. I had a word. Let me just explain." He looked innocent enough, but didn't they all? Right before they stole all your money and told you your entrance to heaven would be assured.

"A word?" She laughed maniacally. "Would that be the same word that told my husband to go off his medication? The same word that sent him to Laos to witness to prostitutes? Oh and please, leave your family behind so that God can prove His faithfulness. Is that your word from the Lord?" She struggled for breath and felt empty after spewing so much of her anger. "You guys are unbelievable! Is there nothing you won't stoop to? Speaking of love while all you do is use repression and submission to keep women where they belong, in your harems."

From the corner of her eye, she could feel Nathan's expression curdle before he sprinted from their presence. The sudden silence and chill in the room brought instant clarity.

"Now look what you've done!" She'd just told her son the truth. Not in careful, calculated, monotone sentences like she'd practiced, but with gale force strength while he stood emotionally naked and unprotected.

Alex let his hands drop to his sides. "I don't understand."

"Of course you don't. You preachers never understand the whole story, but that doesn't keep you from opening your big mouth, does it? Wielding Scripture like a sword, does it?"

An instant flash of light illuminated the room and she looked around for a camera. Another flash sparked, and Kelsey sheltered her eyes with the back of her forearm. She pressed the call button frantically while Alex closed his eyes and the powerful surge came again. She felt it more this time than she saw it, as if a lightning bolt hit beside her. "Did you see that?" she asked Alex. She ran to the window and looked out to see perfectly sunny skies. "Did you feel that?"

He nodded wordlessly.

"What was that?" She gazed around at all the machinery, and red lights abounded. Meagan's heart monitor had stopped, and the rest of the machines beeped incessantly. Alex had his eyes shut again. "Do something!" she screamed at him.

"I am doing something. I'm praying!"

"I asked you a question. What was that?"

"I don't know!" he yelled back. The most passion she'd ever seen in his insipid self. She grabbed him by the shoulders. "Stop doing that," she demanded, shaking him. "Get out!"

"Mom, calm down, I asked Pastor Bechtel here." Meagan sat upright in her bed, fully conscious. She began ripping off the monitors. Her daughter looked up longingly at Alex and grinned like a flirtatious Hannah Montana. "I knew I could trust you. You have a warm spirit."

"Meagan." Kelsey brushed the hair off her daughter's forehead. "You've been asleep, sweetheart. You couldn't have asked anyone here."

She shook her head. "I saw him in the hallway and I asked him to come in and help me. It was the weirdest thing, Mom. I patted him on the shoulder. Remember?" She looked to the pastor.

Alex nodded.

"Stop encouraging her! Meagan, you've had a traumatic morning and you have a lot of drugs in your system, sweetheart. They make us think strange things." Her stomach surged with panic. Meagan was still hallucinating and after what she'd experienced with Todd, Kelsey couldn't stand the thought of her daughter dwelling in another world, a world where truth made no difference to one's belief system. She looked to Alex, hoping for his clarification, but his face was mystified and confused. If she was looking to him for clarity, perhaps it was she who was hallucinating.

"I'll be back, Meagan," Alex said, in a low tone, like an action movie hero.

"You won't be. Meagan, you've been lying here in bed." Kelsey pushed her daughter's hair behind her ears.

"Mom, I heard the doctor talking. He said it didn't look good, the infection was everywhere, and I could feel it, my body felt strangled by a giant kelp bed. Then, I was suddenly released and it felt like I was flying, hovering over the doctor and the room. He said he couldn't believe I'd lasted this long with no overt symptoms. The bacterial levels were through the roof, and he didn't know how he was going to tell you because he said there wasn't much hope. He said you were the hysterical type, and boy, I thought he had to be talking about my mom. That's how I knew it was me they were talking about. I thought, 'how many sick girls could there be with hysterical mothers in the hospital at this very moment?'"

"You were dreaming, sweetheart." Kelsey said the words commandingly, like Todd might have done.

She shook her head violently. "He made it sound like the inside of me needed a good bath. So I said to myself, my mom can't even dry her own hair without me. There is no way I'm going anywhere. Then, I decided to pray the way you taught us when we were young, in Jesus' Name." She looked at Alex to explain. "I don't usually pray anymore, just so you know. I sort of take a more studious look at the whole religious thing. I stopped praying a long time ago. Anyway, I saw Pastor Bechtel below me and he just felt like the answer—"

"Below you?" Kelsey's heart sped.

"It kind of felt like I was on the ceiling looking down. I can't explain that part. Anyway, I said, 'Help me, Pastor Bechtel,' and showed him where to go. When he came in here, I told him that I needed prayer, but not any old prayer, I needed the kind that got results." She smiled broadly and tapped the bed with both palms, quite happy with herself. "And I'd say, I got them. It was just like I got zapped awake."

Kelsey looked at Alex and he merely shrugged. Dropping her head into her hands, she didn't know what to think. She wanted to tell her daughter that the drugs had muddled her thoughts, but if Meagan came back to her, what did she care if her daughter thought the Tooth Fairy had done the work? Truthfully, she didn't care as long as Meagan was out of danger, and she certainly looked out of danger. She grabbed Meagan and forced her into a bear hug, the kind she'd stopped appreciating years ago.

"So Mom," Meagan said into her hair. "Did you call work yet and let them know you weren't coming in?"

"I didn't get the chance—"

"You see, Pastor? Was I right or was I right? She needs me. You smell like barf, Mom." Meagan tossed her hair back. "She'd never make it without me. I had no choice but to come back. I'll bet you didn't call our schools either."

She hadn't. She'd had no time to process anything, but with one crisis averted, she had to see to Nathan. "I need to find your brother."

## Chapter 5

Alex stared intensely at Kelsey and searched for an answer in her dark eyes. Something extraordinary had happened, as if the morning passed seamlessly before his eyes, but there was no recognition in her expression.

Kelsey remained in the doorway between her daughter's room and the hallway where he stood. She struggled with the purse strap on her arm, as if looking for direction, torn between her son and daughter's needs. She seemed oblivious to the gift she'd been given while he longed to dissect what just happened to them.

"Kelsey," he said gently. "Before you go after Nathan…" Her eyes glazed over, and she may as well have been a million miles away. "Kelsey," he repeated, waving his palm in front of her face.

"I don't want to discuss it," she finally said.

"Are you afraid if you talk about it, the miracle might unravel?"

She nodded slightly.

He shook his head. "God doesn't work that way."

Any reaction from Kelsey seemed locked up and shut tightly, put away for the night, though it was only ten-thirty in the morning. She looked away, down the hall, her gaze once again vacant. He wondered if she was always like that. Void of emotion? Unable to see the goodness in front of her?

Initially, she'd made all the right gestures, hugged her daughter, smiled warmly, but there was something about her now that wasn't present in the moment. It was as though she longed to escape the confines of the hospital and the inexplicable light they'd just experienced.

His stomach sank as he realized he'd just done the same in Dan's room. One thing he'd learned as a Christian; the minute you started to raise yourself onto another level, God was more than happy to show you the way back down to reality.

"Did you want me to go and find Nathan?" he asked her. "You can stay with Meagan. I'll go find him."

She didn't answer.

"Kelsey, what can I do to help you?"

She said nothing but went back into the room and clutched her daughter's hand. He followed her in, unable to leave well enough alone.

"You don't like hospitals," he stated, as he looked for any type of connection.

"I don't mind them." She shrugged, as she came back to the present. "Naturally, I don't want to see my family here." She turned toward Meagan. "I really must go find Nathan. I just came back to ask if you need anything, sweetheart."

The girl shook her head and rolled her eyes. "Nathan's probably stealing donuts downstairs.

Don't forget to take your purse." Then Meagan's eyes thinned. "You have money, Mom?"

"I have enough to buy a donut, Meagan. Watch your attitude." She kissed her daughter's forehead. "And welcome back. I have never been so thrilled to hear you nag."

Meagan smiled. "It's a gift."

He longed for someone to acknowledge the love and healing that had filled this room only moment's ago. No mistake—it was God—the love of the Father. "You're not going to talk about what just happened? What we just witnessed?"

"Pardon me?" She did not appear the wilting violet type, but poised and ready for battle.

"Your daughter. Five minutes ago you were in fear that she might not live, and now you act as though she never belonged in this room at all. You saw that light. I know you did. You felt it."

Kelsey's teeth clamped down. She spoke without moving her lips, like a bad ventriloquist act. "Meagan never did belong here. She has endured enough in this lifetime. If you'll excuse me." She tried to breeze past him, but he stopped her by clutching her arm. His actions surprised him more than it did her.

"Life isn't fair, Kelsey. Were you under the impression that it was fair? God sometimes allows—"

"Don't!" She put a hand up to his mouth. "Don't you dare say it! Trust me, I've heard enough preaching to last me a lifetime, and we've got no use for any of it. We're well aware that life isn't fair at our house." She trembled as she spoke.

"I'll admit, I don't know what happened to your family, but—"

She cut him off. "I know you mean well. I really do, but I've got all I can handle right now."

"So let me help you carry some of the burden. I'm offering."

"Do you know why Christians are ignored here in Santa Cruz, Alex? I mean, does it ever cross your mind why you're irrelevant here?"

He did. But somehow, he doubted Kelsey Mitchell harbored his answer.

She was mere inches from his face. Her green eyes pooled with tears, and it melted his heart. "I know the gift we received, Alex. I just wonder what it'll cost us."

Her words were a fist to the gut. She thrust her shoulder away, wrangling free of him, and he wanted to cling to her and tell her it would all be all right.

In his head, he tried to count the number of single mothers at Santa Cruz Evangelical. He knew there were some. They had a single parents' group, but that wasn't his department.

"We have a single parents' group," he said as some kind of victory, but as he said it, he realized single mothers weren't part of his domain, and he was the *family pastor*. A light bulb went off. In their own way, the church was saying singles weren't real families.

Kelsey's shoulders slumped. "I have nothing against you, and I appreciate all you've done here today, but—"

"Do you, Kelsey? Do you appreciate it?"

She slipped a lock of loose hair behind her ear, and he could literally feel her desire to get away from him, but God help him, he couldn't let it go.

"I do," she answered quietly. "But I don't want anything to do with your church. I hope you don't take that personally."

"I only meant—" Nothing came out of his mouth the way he meant it to. Everything he said only alienated her more. "I only meant that we have resources to help your family."

"I've made my choices and I'll live with them. The fantastic part is that you don't have to. You're free to forget you've ever known us and go on about your life."

"But I'm not." He leaned against the wall. "What happened to you? In my church, I mean. What happened?" He felt as though she held some kind of key. "If you're going to miss this miraculous moment, don't you think I have a right to know why?"

"If I don't notice this moment, it's my business. You can rest assured that my family is no longer your responsibility. We're not members of your church."

His teeth clenched. "I don't care if you're a member of my church or not." He ventured closer. "Why are you so angry with me? All I did was pray for your daughter. She spoke to me. I heard her when she was supposed to be dead, and God performed a miracle. Right in front of *your* eyes. Excuse me if I'm awed for the moment, but if you think I have all the answers, I can't remotely answer this one. So forget I'm a pastor for a minute. I only want to understand what happened. Don't you?"

She clasped her eyes shut. "No." She shook her head like a defiant toddler. "I don't dare ask any questions. If you were me, you wouldn't either."

Behind her anger, he saw tears beginning to form, and his stomach plunged. He could see her pain then, fresh and raw. "Kelsey." He cleared his throat. "Mrs. Mitchell, I just wanted you to appreciate the moment with me. I'm sorry if I brought up something hurtful from the past. I want you to see what God has done. Acknowledge it is all, tell me I just witnessed what I think I did."

"You needn't have me for confirmation. I'm only a woman, after all." She hiked her purse strap over her shoulder and looked away from him.

He raked his hand through his hair. He needed to find out what happened to Kelsey. He witnessed the remnants of her sweetness, the beauty of her naiveté, stripped bare by some ugly force. He needed answers. Sadly, he knew where to start. With his boss, Pastor Underwood.

"Give me a chance to fix this!"

A nurse came out of a room and shushed him.

Alex nodded and returned his gaze to Kelsey. "Whatever happened to you in that church, it was people. It wasn't God. God gave you back your daughter this morning."

He saw her release the breath she held so tightly that her body almost seemed to deflate. Tears pooled in her eyes again and she emitted a pained, choking sob. She steadied herself against the wall and met his gaze. Truly met his gaze, as if for the first time they were actually in the same place that morning. "If I let go, everything will fall apart again. I can't afford to let my guard down."

He didn't know what to do. If he possessed any relational skills, he would take her into his arms and just hold her. She needed someone to tell her it would be okay, but his own frame stiffened. He couldn't afford to let his guard down. Not with a wounded woman like Kelsey.

"I'm grateful beyond belief." She emitted another sob. She began to crumple, and he caught her before she hit the ground.

"I think you need to eat something."

One hand pressed to the wall, Kelsey righted herself. "I'll be okay, Alex."

"Let me go get you something and I'll find Nathan in the process. Go in with Meagan. It will make you feel better to see her. Kelsey, you don't have to ever see me again, but let someone help you. Please?"

"No, no, I should get him. It's me that needs to explain the truth. Well, as much of the truth as I can tell him without harming him." She tossed her head forward, burying her face in her hands. "What have I done? I'm so angry. I knew I'd blow it, I knew it." She unearthed her hands, dropping them to her side.

"Maybe you should give yourself a break, Kelsey. None of us is perfect."

"Alex," the way she said his name warmed his heart. Her voice was soft and full of purity in an honest way, and he longed to get to that part of her not hardened by the harshness of life. "The very thing I tried to keep from happening, happened. I married for protection." Her eyes, a clear, dark mossy green that seemed endless in their depth, searched his, as though she wondered if he could be trusted, but she clearly needed the release. "I married for protection because I knew I wasn't capable. And I was right, but I learned the hard way that I had no choice. I am capable."

"Yes, but—"Alex halted his words because even though he knew better, he wanted to offer advice, as if he had any. The irony of his arrogance. All he could offer was more pat answers. Answers she'd heard and discarded already. He longed for words to comfort her, to be the man to come to her rescue, but his mind was as blank as an empty canvas. Kelsey wasn't the type to pour out her soul, that much he could tell, and she stood before him. The way she stood there looking at him, believing in him… But he had nothing. The bases were loaded and he swung and missed.

"You think I should be more relieved," she finally said when he didn't reply. "The pressure is over for you, your prayer was answered and you go on your merry way, but my life doesn't work that way. One crisis dies, another arises. Wave after wave in supernatural proportions, so if I didn't seem wholly excited, maybe I'm only waiting for the other shoe to drop. Your God seems to take pleasure in watching my family suffer."

He shook his head. "No Kelsey, I may not know a lot, but I know God rejoices in nothing of the sort. I don't know what happened before…with Pastor Underwood or with your husband for that matter, but this is the closest I've ever experienced God. We felt His presence together and you can abandon me and forget about it all. But I won't."

"Alex, I know you believe with your whole heart that your church will be there to help me, but my rut is too deep and people are afraid of falling in. They avoid me, and I can't blame them. I'm a menace."

"I wouldn't avoid you."

"Well, you should avoid me. Or haven't you heard my toxic reputation from Pastor Underwood yet? I didn't think they kept us pariahs a secret very long. They have to protect you men, don't you know?"

He ignored her jab. "You can believe what you like, but I believe if God would go through all this trouble for you, this life-altering, energy-induced proof of Himself, that tells me a great deal about how special you are." He cleared his throat. "To Him. How special you are to Him." Her gaze floated to the ceiling. He felt the desperation of losing her again. "You think I'm naïve?"

"Don't knock it, Alex. I'd give my eyeteeth to be naïve again."

"Kelsey, you don't have a clue. I've dealt with more than you can imagine in life, so don't go judging me as some backwoods preacher a few cards short of a full house. Explain to me what happened in there then. If you have an explanation, I'm all ears."

"You used a gambling reference. Is that allowed?" She shot another glance to her naked arm, looking for a watch.

She infuriated him. It was like she was unconscious and he wanted to shout, *Stay with me now, Kelsey. Stay with me.*

"I need to find my son."

Alex clutched her hand and pulled her back to Meagan's room, where the little girl was examining the contents of a nearby drawer. She snapped it shut when she saw them.

"You felt it, Meagan?" Alex asked, seeing her eyes now propped open wide.

"I remember calling you." Meagan looked up at him with wide, joyful eyes. He gazed down again at the little girl who a few moments ago lay lifeless and pale. Her eyes were bright, but she looked to her mother and her expression fell. "God must listen to your prayers."

He felt completely alone in the room as if no one knew what he spoke of and he was the one who just woke up from some type of daze.

"You'll excuse me," Kelsey said curtly. "Meagan, try to eat something, I'll be back soon."

"Kelsey, please." He wanted her to tell him he wasn't crazy, that he hadn't imagined the entire scenario. Was he so overwhelmed with his lack of power that he'd actually created a miraculous event? Alex noticed for the first time that her hair was tangled and wet, and she smelled of vomit. In a strange way, the repulsive sight brought him comfort that he hadn't imagined the entire morning, whether they chose acknowledgement or not.

Kelsey embodied that girl-next-door image he'd dreamed about his entire life. She, like her daughter, had those green eyes that seemed to sparkle with life, even though she'd just experienced one of the worst days of her life. Or the best, depending upon your viewpoint. He watched her push her hair back as she bent over Meagan, and he watched the gentle curves on her neck. Shocked by the feeling of intimacy the sight brought him, he turned away abruptly.

"Meagan, Mommy will check with the doctor on my way out. I'll be right back. I promise, but I've got to find your brother." Kelsey pushed the nurse button, and then brought her magnetic eyes to Alex. She unnerved him by her direct eye contact. One day, he was going to find one of those sturdy girls who brought him dinner in casserole dishes, and he'd settle down and marry. One day he might be godly enough to realize he could overcome his false hopes in finding Mother Theresa in Heidi Klum's body. A woman who made him sweat by the shallow gaze of her green eyes was his carnal lust, nothing more.

"Mom, I'll be fine. But you should thank Alex. He healed me. I may have not felt it, but I know I asked him to, and then I felt the sickness go away."

"God healed you," he said.

The little girl shrugged her bony shoulders. "Semantics, really. He wasn't going to do it for my family."

"Semantics?" he questioned, more for her use of the sophisticated word than her meaning.

Kelsey suppressed a smile. "If you're expecting a Shirley Temple answer, you've come to the wrong family. I'm afraid Meagan was born with the mind of a forty year-old scientist." She stopped smiling the minute she met his eyes, and his hope of her warmth dissipated. He wondered what it took to make a woman like Kelsey giggle. Maybe she wasn't the giggling type, but he could foresee the future enough to almost hear her say, "You're a good friend, Alex." The kiss of death to men everywhere. While he knew he didn't stand a chance with a woman like Kelsey, it didn't stop him from wondering what kind of guy did. She didn't have good taste in men. He remembered that much.

Her ex-husband had been a strong-jawed, handsome sort with an athletic physique and cocky air, as if the world was all one rung beneath him and he could kick their grip off that rung anytime the mood struck him. He hadn't let himself go after his family came along, that was certain. His priorities included hours in the gym. He would swagger into the church office, dragging his wife by the wrist, no doubt to hear one of Underwood's infamous submission speeches. If Alex had heard even one of them before he was hired, he wouldn't have accepted the job. Not because he was anti-submission, but because Underwood never said a thing to the husbands about loving their wives, laying down their lives for them, so Alex failed to see how his counseling would help. As far as he knew, it took two people to be married. Of course, he had yet to commit to any relationship deeper than dog ownership, so he steered clear of the counseling argument.

Todd Mitchell was the kind of guy who took himself too seriously. Alex suddenly remembered a scene, in which Kelsey walked into the office behind Todd, her head bowed low. He remembered because it struck him as odd, with as much beauty as she possessed that she seemed like such a miserable wretch. That morning, his thought was that her husband should simply buy her a full-bodied burqa to make his point.

Of course any man who studied Shakespeare couldn't help but wonder if this particular wife was Kate the shrew in need of a little redirecting.

What kind of man who had access to a woman like Kelsey didn't hold her hand or open the door for her? A sudden awareness that haunted him swept the room. Why hadn't *he* asked that question two years ago? Why did he stand by idly and expect someone else to do it? Maybe this is why God had brought the family back into his life. God had a way of doing that. If you didn't learn a lesson once, he'd bring it around and around again for an encore presentation, until you got it through your thick head, you were the one who didn't act. Kelsey and Meagan bantered back and forth while he stood lost in his thoughts. He didn't want to miss his lesson. Not this time.

"A 40 year-old scientist?" Meagan looked appalled. "I've told you, I'm going to be a CEO, like Ivanka Trump on *The Apprentice*. They dress better and they have great hair."

"You're forgetting Ivanka had a head start with her father owning half of New York."

Meagan rose up from her reclining position, and her face turned red. "I won't need a head start," she said, as she pointed to her head. "I've got everything I need."

"Great hair?" Kelsey laughed.

"I wouldn't underestimate her," Alex said.

"Trust me, Alex. I could never do that."

"You two enjoy your time. I know this hospital like the back of my hand, and Meagan needs you. I'll find Nathan." He didn't wait for her to protest.

She watched him, and he could almost see her willing herself to trust him. "No, it's me he needs. I said something I need to explain." She crossed her arms, obviously hoping to intimidate him, but Alex stood firm, stretching out across the doorway.

"You're not going anywhere, Kelsey. I wouldn't underestimate me either."

"What do you think, Meagan? Is he trustworthy?"

Meagan nodded violently. "I wouldn't have called to him if he wasn't. If I trusted him when I was dead, I think we can trust him now that I'm alive."

Kelsey pursed her lips, as if to convey not to speak of such heresy.

"We'll be fine. We always manage," she said abruptly, eyeing the door. "If you don't mind, we can manage."

He felt his own jaw twitch at her dismissal. Whatever warmth or trust she'd shown him, it was gone now. "Sure."

"Alex, there you are." He turned around to see Dr. Mackinaw's on-duty nurse, a shapely young blonde who wore her uniform in the same cut an acting nurse on a daytime soap might wear. "I'm so glad you're still here," she said breathily. "Dan's asking for you. Crystal's taken the kids out of the room."

He felt a sick knot in his stomach.

"I called your cell," the nurse told him. "But you didn't answer."

Instinctively, he felt for his phone, which he'd never heard. "Thank you. I'm on my way." He didn't want to leave Kelsey's side. In some small way, he felt she needed him more than Dan. "Kelsey, if you need anything—" But the moment was gone and her stony expression returned.

"We'll be fine."

"But if you need anything at all,"—he handed her a card—"my cell number is on the back—"

"I'll be sure to call and let you know how Meagan's doing."

The nurse waited outside in the hallway for him with her arms crossed. "She's not going to call."

Alex wondered if he looked so naïve as to believe otherwise. He jogged down the hallway, dodging gurneys and wheelchairs and groups of staff to get back to Dan's familiar room. He found it undisturbed. The walls were plastered with homemade drawings and family photos, even familiar furniture from home. Dan's room resembled a retirement apartment he'd been there so long. The doctors wanted him to go to hospice, but somehow Dan sensed his time was more limited than the paperwork warranted, and he'd chosen to remain. That's what he'd told Alex.

Dan figured by the time they got him transferred to a home (he hadn't wanted to die in his family's home or burden his wife or sallow the memories of their home for his kids), he'd be dead. It had been two weeks to the day since hospice was suggested, and by tomorrow, it would be required.

To ignore the obvious, the family brought more mementos so he'd feel like he was at home, but the room had started to resemble a garage sale more than an imitation of his house.

Dan worked hard to make the home their own, so the family wouldn't have to be displaced when he was gone. The more Alex thought about Dan, the more remarkable the man seemed, the more unfair his early death felt. Human understanding may have been limited, but loss hurt just the same.

Alex pulled the Bible from his chest pocket and started his normal procedure, but Dan grabbed the Bible from his hand and placed it on the bed.

"You're awake." Alex startled.

"Take care of her, Alex. The church will tell you it's inappropriate, but I need to know you'll do it. None of those Daisy Do-Gooders making her feel she's unworthy, you got it?" His voice was hoarse and barely audible.

"I got it. Anything else?"

"Encourage her to remarry. She'll do me no favors by living alone the rest of her life. She's the best wife a guy could ever have, it's no wonder He wants to share her with more than me." Dan moved his eyes toward the ceiling. "I never deserved her."

Alex didn't want to promise a thing. He knew Crystal wasn't the type to accept help, and what did Alex know about her life? He barely managed the dog.

"Promise me!" Dan croaked.

Alex thought this amounted to blackmail, but Dan had been one of the few who fought for his pastorship when he was up for candidacy. It was his job to look after the widows and orphans, that's what the Bible said, so he exhausted his guilt quickly. "All right, Dan. You go in peace. You have my word."

"She won't want your help and she certainly won't look like she'll need it, but I want to make sure it's you, not the old biddies in the congregation looking after her."

"Don't plan my future for me!" Crystal appeared in the room, her plump face red and tear-stained, but her smile winning out. "With my luck, I'd marry that guy from *Sleeping with the Enemy*. I'd have to escape with four kids, and we'd be a *Lifetime* movie, *Not Without My Ducklings*." She grinned, and Alex noted when her eyes caught Dan's, he could nearly feel the force of their affection toward one another. He had never in his lifetime been around another couple that personified sacrificial love.

"Do you see Alex? What a drama queen I married. She's going to find another Brad Pitt and forget all about me. They'll have six more babies, travel the world and--"

"Poor Alex, do you see how deluded the meds make him? He thinks I'm Angelina Jolie."

"No," Dan said. "I think you make Angelina look like dog food."

The two of them laughed together and Alex wondered if it was the last time. They grasped hands tightly, their eyes saying the truth of their situation. The levity gone, the reality present.

Alex moved aside, and Crystal sat on the bed and molded her head against Dan's chest. "One true love in this life is enough for me, for anyone really. I don't have the energy for it again. You can pad my nest in heaven. Buy me a better mattress this time, okay? No pokey springs, all right?" She kissed his neck and brought his frail hand to her lips. "You're a stubborn one, you know? They keep telling me it's nearly over, that you're leaving me, and I keep getting to see your gorgeous, loving eyes." She sat up and searched Dan's eyes so intimately, Alex felt uncomfortable in his own skin. "I won't let the kids forget, how you worked like a dog through chemo to pay off their home, how you got them that ratty dog even though I fought you all the way. I won't let anyone forget you or your joy, it's my legacy. You're the love of my life, Dan."

He closed his eyes and smiled. His breathing was deep and strained. He exhaled deeply. And then, he was gone.

## Chapter 6

Kelsey walked out into the sunshine and dropped her neck back to feel the rays on her face. The slightest bit of foggy haze marred the morning sky, but not enough to keep Nathan from its pull. He was a magnet for sunshine and escaped to it every chance he got.

As she searched the parking lot, the phone calls she needed to make rushed through her mind. School, her parents…Todd. She couldn't bring herself to do it, so she called her best friend, Martha.

Martha was the antithesis of her name – which may have been in direct response to her mother naming her that, as she possessed a defiant streak. She always bore a disheveled, overuse-of-cotton, flowing sixties appearance. Martha herself was beautiful – a runner, who didn't possess an ounce of body fat, not in a place she didn't want it anyway. That, after three kids. Kelsey would have hated her if she wasn't so infinitely loveable and always there for her.

She had blonde, curly tresses of a mermaid – never brushed, of course – so they looked like she'd just emerged from the depths, creating an image of foreign innocence to the culture.

When Martha didn't answer, Kelsey severed the connection, feeling all alone in the world. She had no one else to call. It would have been easy to blame her lack of friends on Todd and his strange behavior, but ultimately, she believed she possessed some terrible character flaw and kept herself isolated by choice.

The shrill of her phone gave her a start. She exhaled deeply at the sight of Martha's name on Caller ID. "Martha?"

"Kelsey, where are you? I'm at the school. I called your cell, you didn't answer. I called you at work, you're not there. Everyone is worried sick. Where are the kids?"

She waited for her friend to finish. "I'm at the hospital."

Martha gasped. "Is everything all right? It's not the kids? Is it Todd? Is he back?"

She waited for Martha to pause. "Everyone is fine now." How did she explain only moments before she thought Meagan might die? That her only daughter may have actually been dead except for a miracle. Could she call it a miracle?

"I had to turn off the phone. Martha." She allowed herself to finally feel. "Oh Martha, I thought Meagan was gone. I've had the worst morning of my life. Nathan is missing somewhere here at the hospital, and I haven't called work. I can't even bring myself to care."

"Oh baby, you're overwhelmed. Kelsey, anyone would be overwhelmed. What happened?"

"They thought Meagan might have had bacterial meningitis, but then as soon as she got sick, she was better again. I can't explain it all right now."

"You don't need to explain it. I'm calling your work and I'll be right there. Santa Cruz General?"

"Yes. I tried to get her to Stanford, but—"

"Explain it to me later, Kels. I'm on my way." In the background, she heard Martha's car start, and she felt her heartbeat slow with help arriving soon.

"I hate when Nathan disappears!" She choked back a sob.

"He's not his father, Kelsey. Every time a teenager does something does not mean he's got a mental illness. Teenagers are moody!"

"He knows I can't deal with this right now. His sister needs me."

"He needs his mom, too. Teenagers don't have time to think about what their parents deal with – get real. Idiots!" Martha yelled at some driver on the road and followed it with a honk. "Okay, I'm just a few blocks away," she said calmly. "Any sign of Nathan yet?"

"No. Martha, he heard me say that his dad was living with a harem. That's why he ran out." She longed to tell someone the truth. The whole truth.

"This is not your fault, Kelsey. I always thought you shielded too much from them."

"It is my fault. Who else is here to blame it on?"

"Enough of that garbage. You're a wonderful mother. Did you say meningitis? That can be deadly."

"Mm hmm."

"But you're telling me she's fine now?"

"Mm hmm. Like nothing ever happened."

"Then what do they think she had?"

She didn't feel like replaying the whole weird miracle trip. She didn't know what to believe and sometimes felt like everyone was watching her for her own signs of mental incapacitation, so she brushed past the scenario.

"She started vomiting this morning, then got lethargic, and now she appears fine. They're not releasing her just yet. They want to keep her for observation."

"What can I do? Do you want me to call the school and give them more information?"

"Would you? And can you bring me some shampoo? I have barf in my hair."

"Yes, as a matter of fact, I have an organic bottle I bought for you right in the car. How's that for serendipity?"

"Fantastic. What would I do without you, Martha?"

"You'd be fine. You don't give yourself enough credit. I'm getting off to call your work now."

She exhaled. "Martha, do you remember that young preacher the church hired awhile back? Right before Todd left. Alex, I think his name was?" She knew his name, of course, but she didn't want to give too much away, so she let the information trickle. She needed to ease into the story.

"Alex Bechtel?"

"Yes." Kelsey didn't want to sound too intrigued either because every time she said a man's name, Martha was ready to shop for wedding gowns – Martha was convinced Kelsey could find love again, but the very idea sent a surge of panic through her.

Life taught her some hard lessons – but marriage taught her she wasn't cut out for partnership. And the church taught her she'd had her one shot and blown it.

"Sure I do. He visits Mrs. Willits. She's the neighbor I've been trying to introduce you to. You would love her, Kelsey. She tells it like it is, and she's lonely. I think—"

"Martha, focus with me here -- Alex. What do you know about him?"

"He used to be an accountant or something until the ministry called to him. I think he's a fairly normal guy. He's waiting for Underwood to retire, but until someone throws a wad of dirt on the casket, I don't see that happening. Why?"

"He's just been here at the hospital."

"Why do I think there's more to this story?" Martha asked.

"I remember him from Pastor's office back when we did *counseling*." She said the word with all the disdain she felt for it. "I found him in Meagan's room. Praying over her."

"He's not a pedophile or anything. Is that what you're asking me?"

"He had his hands over her, like he was some kind of magician levitating an assistant in sequins."

"Before or after she was pronounced better?"

Kelsey ignored the question. "I don't think I was all that pleasant to him, but I was thankful. I was too much in shock to say so. If you see him, you know…when you're at church…maybe you could pass that on."

"Kelsey…were you rude to him?"

She pondered the question. "Maybe a little. He was a strange man. With his hands over my daughter."

Martha sighed. "I heard Dan Tognotti is dying, Alex was probably there to pray for him. He's not the sort to float in and out of hospital rooms if that's what you mean."

"Who is dying?"

"Dan Tognotti. Crystal's husband. They have a bajillion kids. You might not remember them. Their kids aren't in school yet, and I think their kids were too young for you to know when you were at the church. I taught them in Sunday school, oh my gosh, they are the sweetest things. She homeschools them, bakes, everything that I'd aspired to be. Amazing woman. Her day makes me want to shoot myself, but that's another story." Martha honked again. "I'm pulling into the parking lot now."

"What's the matter with him?"

"Alex? Nothing that I know of. He keeps to himself, I suppose, but who wouldn't with all those desperate grandmothers trying to set him up. I kind of equate him with Saint Paul. Really focused and intense – gifted, but sort of missing that people gene, you know?"

"Not Alex, the man who is dying. What's wrong with him?"

"Oh, Dan? Cancer, I think. Never smoked a day in his life, ate well, exercised. The nicest man…naturally. God never seems to take the jerks, does He?"

She understood exactly what Martha meant, and it was true. It *felt* true anyway. "Oh, I see Nathan, I'll call you later."

"Do you want me to call your parents?"

"Is that a joke?"

"No, actually. They might want to know their granddaughter is in the hospital."

It never occurred to her to call her parents in times of crises. If anything, that was the time to avoid them, unless she wanted a lecture on how she'd created the current crisis. "Yes," she finally said. "Why don't you call them? You can get the lecture instead of me, and be sure and have the vaccine argument ready. She'll go after that, first thing. Avoid dramatics, won't you?"

"They thought your granddaughter had meningitis. She's fine now. Nothing dramatic in that. Oh, and your grandson was missing. Nice to talk with you. Something like that?"

"My mother hasn't seen them in two years. It will probably be like hearing the weather report – but of course, she controls that too. Nathan's not missing. I've got him in my sights. So you can keep that part to yourself."

Martha laughed. "I'll see you in a few minutes. I'm calling your boss first to see if the ice queen can defrost."

"Okay, bye Martha."

"*Ciao Bella!*"

Nathan's lanky body bent in the strangest ways. He was all angles and knobby joints with lengthy limbs in between. He perched himself against the cement wall near the emergency exit, oblivious to any concern he'd caused. Dr. Levin stood nearby, smoking and exhaling, turned away from Nathan's direction. The two of them seemed deep in conversation, and she felt self-conscious as she headed their way, but the peace she felt at the sight of Nathan enveloped her. He was a great kid, just naturally thought of others first, so it wasn't like him to take off.

"Dr. Levin, I see you finally got your smoke. Was it worth the wait?"

"Mom!" Nathan said. "Quit nagging." His words stung.

"She's right, Nathan. It's a terrible habit, but every time I kick it, I get fat. I wear my ugly inside now on my black lungs, better than a spare tire on a doctor. Everyone sees that."

"You shouldn't joke about that," she chastised. "Sorry. I'm nagging again."

"No," he said as he snuffed out his cigarette on the sidewalk. "I shouldn't. So Mrs. Mitchell, Nathan was telling me you all live in that old condominium building near the lighthouse. I was telling him how lucky he was to have such a view. I grew up overlooking the cow pasture, and for fun we might have a rousing game of chip throwing. If we were really feeling our oats, we'd go out at night and tip cows. Now that, son, that was living." He hacked a laugh.

Nathan's arms were crossed and he never looked up. "I told him we only have a view from the corner of the bathroom, if you're standing on the toilet."

"Well, you can always walk outside, Nathan. It's not many kids who get to live across from the Monterey Bay," Dr. Levin said. "Some people go their entire life without ever seeing the ocean, and you live across from one of the best spots on the Pacific. Not bad."

Nathan shrugged. "Whatever. Mom, can you drive me to school now? Mrs. Bates is going to have a fit." It wasn't like her son to not focus on the silver lining. Or to be rude.

Dr. Levin winked at Kelsey. "I should know better than to try and impress a teenager. I have three of my own. We're all idiots until they turn twenty-five."

She flushed at the doctor's attention. She'd almost begun to believe she was invisible. When anyone looked directly at her, she seemed to remember that she existed and immediately wanted to crawl into a hole and hide.

"You have three kids or teenagers?" she asked.

"Teenagers, and to make matters worse, they're all girls. Do you know they want a hundred and fifty dollar jeans? One pair! I told them the designer should come and sew it on their backside for that price, and they should embroider my name on the butt, not their own. But they pair them with 'vintage' shirts, which means *used* to you and me, and try to convince me it all evens out in the end." Dr. Levin smiled with his eyes but not his mouth.

He obviously delighted in his daughters, and Kelsey wondered what it was like to have a father like that. She'd grown up with a mirthless father, and though she'd known better, married the same type of man.

"You should quit smoking so you'll be around to see their weddings." She couldn't believe that had come from her mouth.

"You're right, Nathan," Dr. Levin said with another wink to her long-limbed son. "She is a nag." Then he looked straight at her. "But she's a beautiful nag and that's worth something. Some people have to hear it from a woman who looks like Ernest Borgnine."

"Who?" Nathan's features scrunched.

Her stomach plummeted at his gaze. Today, she felt like God had called her out into the light, and she didn't like it one bit. She marveled at the sound of her son's laughter. It had been too long since she heard it. She looked back at the doctor. "I'm a nag? Because I want your daughters to have someone to walk them down the aisle?"

"No, because you don't mind your own business. No woman does. It's part of their charm, I suppose."

"And no man thinks he lives with any faults of his own." She regretted her words the moment she said them. Dr. Levin had kept the conversation light, and her own anger reared its ugly head once again. While Todd had been around, maybe her lack of control made sense. But what excuse did she have now? For the time being she was free — maybe not emotionally, but certainly physically. How did she purge that part of her? She thought it only a matter of ridding herself of Todd, but he'd left a residue that she wore like a winter coat.

She looked down at her feet. To hear a man talk lovingly about his wife was always a knife to the throat — a reminder that only she wasn't lovable. "I'm sorry, Dr. Levin. I've forgotten my manners. You've been so kind to us this morning."

The doctor kicked the cigarette butt off the curb. "You and I make a fine pair, Mrs. Mitchell. I don't believe I had any manners to begin with. I'm going to check on your daughter, who my nurses tell me never had anything like meningitis. I must have been imagining it." He shook his head. "These nurses think we doctors aren't worth the paper our degrees are printed on. I suppose I was imagining her test results as well."

She paused, ready to tell him about the flash of light, but she clamped her mouth shut.

Dr. Levin shook his head. "I'm a doctor, I don't explain the miraculous. You, Mrs. Mitchell, must have done something right in this lifetime for that one." He walked away, and Nathan stared at her mercilessly.

"Did you have to nag?"

"No, I didn't. I'm sorry."

"His wife just left him, Mom." Her stomach tightened at the news. She felt like Todd himself, a person with no empathy or understanding for another's plight, because her mind was so filled with her own pain.

"I apologized. I'll go apologize again if—"

"Just leave it."

"Did you want me to take you to school now? Or Martha can take you. She's in the parking lot making some phone calls for me."

Nathan just shook his head. Whatever was on his mind, he wasn't going anywhere until he talked it out.

"Meagan's going to be here for observation," she told him. "I'll come back with a book for her and sit with her." When he didn't answer, she kept speaking. "You should see her Nathan. She looks incredible! I've never been so scared in my entire life."

"Dr. Levin told me about Meagan. *He* didn't forget his daughters because his wife threw him out. He picks them up and takes them out to dinner every week. On the weekends, they spend their afternoons playing tennis together."

Her heart pounded. So that was the reason for his mood. "No, most people wouldn't forget, but your father is not in the country either." She had noticed that Dr. Levin spoke higher about the woman who tossed him out than Todd had ever spoken of her in their fourteen years of marriage. It made her feel dumber than a bag of rocks. Why had she stayed so long?

"Is it true he's crazy? That's what the kids at school say. What if he is really like Noah and heard something from God, like build an ark, and we're all wrong about him?"

She didn't know how to answer that question. "It's complicated, Nathan."

"If there's something wrong with his brain, maybe he doesn't understand what he's done to us."

The words gave her chills. "I did all I could for him, Nathan. He believes God told him to leave."

Nathan straightened suddenly. "Maybe He did. Did you ever have any faith in him?"

She rubbed her temples. "Do we have to do this now?"

"Why did you marry him? He hates us. All of us."

"He wasn't like that when I married him, Nathan. He was very sweet, involved in campus ministries, he fed the poor. You wouldn't have recognized him back then. Life just happened, and he couldn't take it when it spiraled out of his control."

"Is that what's happening to Meagan? Is she going to be angry like Dad? She likes to control everything."

"No!" She grabbed her son's hand. "Meagan's illness is totally unrelated. Your father's angry, Nathan. Deeply angry, and it's changed who he is inside."

"What's he angry about?"

*There it was.* The question she could never answer. The secret she harbored for Todd and would be forced to keep forever.

"Mostly about the unfairness of life, I suppose."

Nathan glowered. "Then he should have stuck around to see how unfair it could be."

"He needed to get to a place he could manage better."

After children, Todd couldn't control his universe, and his sanity slowly started to unravel. He couldn't handle little people with their own minds. He couldn't stomach a wife who had a mind. With all the "defiance" around him, he moved deeper into a world he could control; where his charm and charisma got him exactly what he needed, compliance.

"He said he needed to get away from *you*, Mom. He said you were destroying him."

She nodded. "He did say that."

Nathan squeezed her hand. "It wasn't true."

"Thanks, sweetheart." It didn't matter if it was true or not. It *felt* true. "There's Martha. She'll take you to school." She pointed across the parking lot to Martha's black SUV.

Nathan made no move toward Martha's Mercedes. "I don't want him to come back, but I'm afraid if he doesn't, no one will help him. If he wasn't always like that. He can be like he was."

She drew in a deep breath. How did she explain? The early warning signs were all there, even when Todd was a pillar of the community. She'd only missed them because she was too anxious to get away from her mother. Out of the fire, and into the frying pan, as they say.

"Jesus went after the one lost sheep, Mom. I don't want to be like those people at church when Dad left."

"Nathan, you could never be like that."

"I worry about him in a foreign country. What does he know about those people, Mom? I think we should go get him. He doesn't have anyone and he needs us."

He didn't have anyone because he'd shoved everyone away.

"He has his mother, and not having us was his choice," she reminded him. But they both knew his mother was largely responsible for Todd's destructive ways. She excused all manner of abuse, and if it weren't for his religious preoccupation, who knows what Todd may have felt entitled to do?

"He only has us, Mom. Would you leave us if we needed you?"

"Of course I wouldn't, but Nathan—" She didn't like where this conversation was headed.

"Dr. Levin hasn't left his family just because the marriage hasn't worked out. Families are supposed to stick together. We can't leave him so far away, Mom. Even if we don't want him back, we have to try to get him help." Nathan always was her heart child, the child she knew would care for them in their old age. Though Meagan would no doubt organize all the details, Nathan would do the compassionate work.

She imagined the one sheep of the Bible hadn't fought like a jungle cat and ripped its rescuers to shreds. "If I learned anything being married to your father, Nathan, it's that you can't force someone to do something your way. Ultimately, they have control over their own actions. This is the way he wants it."

"Mom, we have to get him. If we don't, no one will."

She felt horrible to think how that thought comforted her. For once in her life, she had control over her destiny and she wasn't about to invite trouble back into their lives. If it made her a heartless, selfish soul, she could live with that. Looking into Nathan's dark, thoughtful eyes, she saw remnants of Todd, but none of his darker side, and she was determined to keep it that way.

"We'll talk about it when we get home," she finally said. "Martha's waiting."

## Chapter 7

"Pastor Underwood is waiting for you to start the staff meeting." Loretta, the pastor's secretary, met Alex at the door with the unfortunate news.

"I need some time first." He hung up his jacket on the mahogany coat tree. Everything in the church was mahogany. Mahogany pews, mahogany pulpit...from what he understood, there were mahogany floors under the ghastly wine-colored carpet. When he left the office, he shunned light like a naked mole rat. His body still buzzed from the extreme emotional ride he'd been on that morning.

Loretta shook her head. "He's in one of his moods and he's been waiting for you all day. Visitations aren't supposed to take that long, he said." She paused. "He's pacing. Maybe you could take care of your things later." She made this suggestion sweetly, but Alex only felt it as manipulation.

Loretta's sweet tone said it all. He had no choice in the matter. "I'll be right there. Let me get my notebook."

He called Loretta, *the extinguisher*, because she put out Pastor Underwood's fires like an experienced captain. Without her, the church would cease to exist. If Loretta said, "now", it meant Underwood was beyond her capabilities that day. Alex tired of the old man's moods determining everyone's behavior. As the younger pastor, Alex gave Underwood the benefit of the doubt and tried to imagine the fire and brimstone preaching set the Christian world aflame back in the day. When Underwood hired him, Alex was on top of the world, thinking he'd learn from the best. A man who could grow a church with unrelenting energy, though the senior pastor was well into his seventies. Alex thought, like Jesus at the temple, he would sit at Underwood's feet and drink in the knowledge.

"There's fresh coffee in the conference room, Alex." Loretta gave him a motherly smile. "You look as though you could use some."

"Thanks Loretta, I'll grab my cup while I'm in my office."

Most pastors took Mondays off. Pastor Underwood used them as a fifth quarter to tell the team what went wrong on Sunday. *We fumbled. We kicked when we should have passed.* He had an incredible way of lighting a fire under his congregation, but his staff seemed to be another story.

"You're late." Pastor Underwood didn't look up as he said the words.

"Dan died this morning," Alex said. "I was at his side."

Pastor Underwood moaned and nodded his head. "That's a shame. But this isn't a one-time occurrence. This meeting is held at 10:30 every Monday morning, and yet you always manage to be late. How is it possible that one member of our team can never seem to get in position?"

Alex looked around the room and noticed no one reacted to the man's words. They all kept their heads lowered, hoping to escape the wrath for that morning. In a way, Alex thought they might be glad for him on the staff. He provided the sacrificial lamb.

Ryan Talbott stopped thumbing through a folder of sheet music and tried to salvage Alex. "I thought we might up the tempo a bit on, 'The Old Rugged Cross' next week. I've noticed some of the younger members are dropping off during worship. They come afterwards."

"They come to hear the sermon. That's what they're supposed to come to church for, not entertainment. If we start playing to an audience, do you know what we'll become? A theater, and we are not in the business of providing entertainment for the masses. I'll make an announcement next week about punctuality. Loretta, write that down."

If Ryan were a dog, Alex thought, his head would hang low and his tail would be permanently bent downward to show submission to the leader of the pack. He'd lost any sense of fight that used to be in him, and Alex worried how long he could last in this environment before becoming identical.

Santa Cruz Evangelical Church was dying, and its slow and steady death appeared imminent if Pastor Underwood refused to give. It wasn't about entertainment; it was that the language changed. People said altar instead of Ebenezer, they responded to Truth combined with warmth, authenticity combined with love. The alternative they found hypocritical. The harder that the congregation tried to move forward, the more stalwart Mel Underwood became.

In less than two years, the church had gone from a thriving community to one behind dead grass that constantly preached on tithes. A congregation could only take so much. Alex could only take so much, and yet he felt the weight of the church on his shoulders. He longed for a revival. A rebirth. Because he loved the members and saw they wanted it, too.

"Loretta," Mel said. "Find out when Crystal wants the ceremony and make sure the church is cleaned before the event. They had many ministries outside the church. We'll have a lot of visitors that day. We want to make sure the church sparkles. A filthy church sets a bad precedent."

So they had heard. Alex's ears perked, but he judged other's responses to see if he'd heard correctly. Judy Blotson, the children's director, nodded her head so he knew he hadn't imagined it. "Excuse me, Pastor Underwood, but Crystal Tognotti has already made the arrangements. She'd like to hold the service at the soccer field where the kids played and Dan coached preschool soccer. Dan and I talked about it and he'd like all the kids he's coached over the years to come and have a game in his honor."

"What a great idea," Judy said. "That sounds just like Dan."

"That's not a funeral. That woman cannot expect me to speak at a soccer field! Loretta, call her and talk some sense into her. Give it a day to let her grieve."

Alex paused as he thought of the best way to handle Pastor Underwood. Straightforward generally didn't work, but he couldn't think of a way to meander through the backwards thinking today. "Dan wanted me to do the ceremony because we were so close, and I agreed on something short after the soccer game. A local ice cream store is going to donate cones with a portable freezer, and the local Pizza Hut is offering pizza. Dan wanted to purchase small trophies for all the children, and I told him the church would help with those expenses."

"I do the funerals." Underwood slapped his chest, not unlike the gorillas at the zoo.

Alex stretched out in his chair and said with a tired yawn to imply his lack of concern, "Dan didn't want to trouble you with this, Mel. He realizes it's out of the ordinary, but life ending at 39 is out of the ordinary. This day will remind the children that life will go on and that their father will be coaching them from the heavens."

Underwood wasn't fooled by Alex's tactics. "Loretta, get the widow on the phone so I can talk some sense into her. Honestly, where is the decorum in this generation? No respect for anything, just want to turn every event into a self-serve buffet with all-you-can-eat shrimp. It's about the Gospel!" He slapped the table.

Pastor Underwood used the word "Gospel" as a noun, a pronoun, an adjective, and most often, a verb. It never made any sense in most contexts, and with all Alex's seminary background, he still didn't fully understand the man's usage. Underwood used it as a weapon to shut down a conversation or veer it into a place where one got so lost in his word salad, they just shut up rather than try to figure out what he'd said. As if their IQ's weren't high enough to keep up with him. It was only after Alex had taken careful notes at a meeting, he finally realized Underwood made no sense. *Gaslighting*, Alex believed was the technical term. *Gospel gaslighting* he'd come to call it. Where everyone acted as though they knew what Underwood meant, and they all sat around nodding in agreement. Like the *New Yorker* cartoons, Underwood managed to make everyone think it was them. That's why nothing ever changed, why nothing ever got done. He eventually wore out everyone.

Today, Alex had enough. "What is about the Gospel?"

"The funeral. Life. Everything's about the Gospel. Don't you understand?"

"I have four years of seminary. I hope I understand the Gospel. I'm not quite sure of your usage in this particular context."

"Don't patronize me, Bechtel. People want to be entertained. They want to be enraptured. They want everything to be fun and games. Isn't it bad enough we don't call them 'funerals' anymore? Now they're 'celebrations of life'?"

"People cope with death differently. Dan was a believer, so he's in heaven with Jesus. That's the Gospel the family wants reflected. I think we should honor their wishes and the way they want to celebrate his life."

"There you go with those cockamamie words again. It's about the Gospel!"

"Exactly! It's about the Gospel and how Crystal and the kids can celebrate the fact that they'll see their husband and father again. It's going to be hard on them. Why make it any more difficult?"

"No!" Mel slammed the table again. "It's about the Gospel!

Everyone stared at Alex. This is how the conversation usually ended, but Alex couldn't bear to drop it. He'd lost a good friend, and he wasn't about to let Mel ride roughshod over him and perform a one-size-fits-all funeral where people remembered why they stopped going to church. "I don't know if you and I mean the same Gospel. What exactly are you talking about?"

Alex thought he heard a collective gasp. The room was silent as he looked around. Six people ignoring the fact that for years they'd all sat and listened to this over and over, not a one of them understanding his meaning. Loretta, the supportive secretary, who always wore a brown outline on her lips, had missed her mark that morning and her mouth morphed into a jagged 'O' like a confused 70's era clown. She sat perched to come to Alex's rescue and divert Mel.

Alex turned to Ryan Talbott, the worship leader, who obviously just hoped to make it out of the meeting without being noticed. He tapped his pencil on his pad. Darren Kites, the youth minister who didn't understand kids, looked at the prayer requests on the wall. Judy Blotson, the middle-aged children's director, who'd been at the church as long as anyone could remember, bit her lips to avoid laughter. It was all the encouragement Alex needed.

"I mean no disrespect, Mel. I'm trying to understand your meaning."

"My meaning is that this is my church, and you will not correct me when you have no idea what you're talking about. You will come to understand the Gospel means everything."

*Clearly,* Alex thought, in Underwood's world, the entire thesaurus could be replaced with the word.

Loretta spoke meekly. "I think, Sir. I mean, Alex knew the family so well. I think the church might do best to honor their wishes. They have four young children. They probably don't want his death to fill the neighborhood children with sadness. Or fear. If the Tognotti's dad could die, couldn't any of the kids' dads die? I'm sure he wanted to avoid that."

"Death is a fact of life. When did you get so soft, Loretta? Call the widow and let me speak to her. She won't be regretting this funeral on my watch."

Loretta rested her hands in a genteel manner, folded over her notebook. "I'm sorry, sir. I can't do that. I have to respect Dan and Crystal's wishes. They've been longtime members of our congregation. I have to believe they knew what they wanted."

"And I have to respect the Lord's wishes. Do you think He wants to be mocked out on a soccer field in a matter so important as the taking of a Christian life? My God will not be mocked."

"I don't feel He will be mocked," Loretta continued softly, brushing her gray bangs off her face. "I feel like He'll enjoy seeing the children's laughter and playtime. I can't call Crystal, Pastor. They've been through so much already. I think we should support them." She kept her hands clasped on her lap.

Underwood turned toward Alex, his eyes narrowed. "Have you ever done a funeral, Alex?"

"Well, no, but I've been to many that you've performed, Pastor. As you know, in my job, I've come to see a lot of death. I send off many, so it's something I have to learn. What better way than outside on a soccer field? If I screw up, Dan would forgive me, and the children won't be paying attention anyway. Why waste your time on this? With my doing the service, no one will question your good taste in the matter, Mel."

"If you go into it thinking it doesn't matter if you misspeak, you will do so. Performing a ceremony as important as this is a calling. It is not something you lightly step into as if there were no regard for the Lord's precepts. You're sending someone off into the next world, into the heaven they've waited for."

Alex assumed they were already there, well out of earshot of the pastor's sermon. He had to believe if someone had a choice to be at the Lord's feet or listening to an Underwood's sermon…

Still, he listened with his head drawn to his chest in deference. The argument wasn't worth having because he would perform the ceremony and he would do it exactly as his friend asked him to. If that happened to be preschoolers running around a soccer field, smudging him with chocolate ice cream, well so be it. It couldn't be more humiliating than the weekly staff meeting.

"Next on the agenda," Underwood shouted. "Is the matter of tithes. This church isn't tithing properly. I counted 147 people in the church yesterday and we collected only $730 and that's a high for the month. Loretta, put it on my calendar to run the tithing sermon again. Test me in this, God says. Test me in this. We can't afford our expenses if people aren't going to care for their church. It's their responsibility." He shook his head.

"The Lord healed a girl today," Alex blurted out to end the tithe conversation. "He used me to do it. I saw it happen. I felt it." He nodded for plausibility. He still had trouble believing it himself.

Santa Cruz Evangelical Church barely survived as it was, give that man any more leeway and it would be over. Underwood used to be a good preacher, a solid man of God, but lately he'd gotten so angry in the pulpit, people had started to avoid Sundays. The pews became emptier, the man became angrier. It was a vicious cycle.

The members owned the church outright, but developers were knocking at their door. The scent of a dying congregation was like blood to a shark. The dead landscaping out front, a small clue as to the gasping breaths inside the chapel. The Tognottis were one of the only young families in the congregation. Judy's job became pointless every week with dwindling numbers of children. She fidgeted every time the dropping tithe conversation came up, because she knew what that meant to her. Mel didn't seem to understand what the loss of a young congregation meant to them all, though.

One good concert at the Beach Boardwalk on the weekend, and the young families who had remained didn't bother to fight traffic or parking woes. If the Lord didn't act soon over Underwood, who'd become more and more independent in all his actions, the church would be no more, and all these people would be out of a job. He, for one, was tired of listening to the same depressing rant every Monday. It gnawed at him and he felt his face grow redder. His voice became boisterous, to the point it surprised even him.

"God used me to heal the Mitchell girl, who had possible meningitis. She's healed," he stated emphatically. "Can I get an Amen?"

He felt the slaps on the back, and that same rush that he felt in the hospital room came over him once again; the surge of energy that made him feel invincible, but it seemed like that was all the encouragement he'd receive that day.

Underwood stared at him as though he'd just announced he had grown another head. "You can save that for our answered prayers agenda. The Mitchell girl, you say? The daughter of the divorcee?"

"She was abandoned, wasn't she?" He blinked and tried to appear innocent with his comment, but admittedly, there was passion behind his statement.

"I don't think they're divorced," Judy intervened. "Just separated. But last I heard, he's in a foreign country on some mission."

"He's on a mission without his family?" Underwood scratched his head.

"He's not there with any church support or official ministry. I'm not sure I'd call that a mission."

"Look, it's clear we're going to get nothing done here today. Everyone is exceptionally chatty. If you all want to murmur about a woman who didn't follow her husband along on his mission, you go right ahead. I have a sermon to prepare."

*I hope it's about the Gospel*, Alex thought to himself with smug, and surely sinful satisfaction.

## Chapter 8

The surf exploded into white blooms and sprayed the bike path and street. The droplets invigorated Kelsey's senses. With all the loneliness she'd endured, the ocean kept her company. It reminded her that she was so small in God's scheme of things and to be grateful.

She stood at the edge of the cliff and stared into the vast blue that was Monterey Bay. Its color was deep like sapphires, with sparkling diamonds at the crest of each wave. The sun's reflection glimmered on the tips of the waves and created an idyllic picture straight from a postcard.

"And I get to live here," she said aloud to the blue sky. "Is that my consolation prize, God? In return for being unlovable?"

Kelsey pulled her hair back and stepped closer to the edge. Though only twenty feet or so below, the shallow, swirling surf covered a collection of enormous granite rocks at the ocean's edge that made the shallow surf seem tiny and innocuous by comparison. Kelsey felt the same way. Small and insignificant next to the world. Todd, by comparison, was his very own continent—his universe. How on earth could she rescue him? It was simple really. She wasn't meant to, but why had he sought to drag her down with him?

It was her own fault. Her view of love was skewed. Her high school years were filled with the tortured souls of gothic literature – Heathcliff on the Moors, the miserable Rochester shackling away his mad wife, the lonely wife in the shadow of the elegant first Mrs. DeWinter, Rebecca – these heroines made their mark. To her, romance was an illness, a temporary leaving of the senses that in novels ended happily ever after, but in reality none of the crazy went away with marriage. It only got worse. The happily ever after was the pot of gold at the end of the rainbow – always just out of reach.

A horn honk broke her thoughts. Kelsey turned. A brittle old woman crossed the street, and some off-season tourist nearly flattened her. Although bent at the waist, the woman carried no cane and ambled crookedly toward her, oblivious to traffic. The old woman never gave the car a second glance, and although her legs didn't look strong enough to hold her frail body, she moved quickly, like a fiddler crab sidling toward the water's edge.

"Young lady!" The old woman held up a bony finger and pointed at Kelsey.

She touched her chest. "Me?" The car brushed past, and so she shouted, "Are you talking to me?"

"Yes, you!" the old lady said. "I've seen many people go over those cliffs on days like today. I know it's beautiful, alluring and all that, but you must stay back. You mustn't take chances like that. Pretty girl like yourself."

"I—I…"

"Step back. Some of those people I'm referring to…"—she raised her eyes to the sky and crossed her chest—"are with their Maker now."

She stepped away from the edge. "The spray is invigorating."

"It makes this old woman's heart beat like a drum, and we can't have that at my age, now can we? You wouldn't want to be responsible for my having a heart attack, would you?"

Kelsey straightened and pulled back her shoulders. "No, absolutely not." She brushed off her backside. "I came out here to think, is all, just to enjoy the view. I live right there." She pointed to the scrappy building, painted to look pristine and worthy of the neighborhood. "I got fired this morning." She didn't mention that her daughter was in the hospital or the miracle healing, getting fired was reason enough to edge the cliffs, she figured.

The woman's face, etched deeply with lines, pursed her lips, deepening the crevices. "There will be other jobs. Not like in my day when you had to labor in the canning factories and you were happy for the work. I'll tell you, if I never see another apricot, it will be too soon for me. I'm praying it's the one fruit they do not have in heaven because I fear I may stand before the Almighty's throne and vomit from the smell. But heavens, God wouldn't do that to me, would He? He knows I loathe the apricot."

Kelsey laughed, despite her mood. "I'll take free apricots. I have two kids to feed, so I really have to find a new job." She couldn't explain why she elaborated, but she wanted the woman to know life was still hard, even without a war and sugar rations. "I'll have to find something quickly."

"Kids have too much these days, anyway. You'll be all right, young lady. You have to believe. We all did what we had to do back then. You moved in with your sister, or your cousin. Whole families, and there were none of these mansions back then, you were all crammed into a 900 square foot house. Eight of you, sometimes."

Kelsey nodded. "But I still don't think they should starve, do you? Video games notwithstanding?"

"They won't starve, don't put yourself on that plane and feel sorry for yourself. You look like a perfectly capable woman. No man about, huh?"

Kelsey's stance withered. "No."

"Even when times were really difficult, I never met a mother who'd let her kids go hungry. Go ahead and cry it out and then get back to the job hunt."

"I wasn't crying, I was—feeling the ocean's spray on my face." She shrugged. "It makes me feel alive."

"Everyone deserves a short pity party, but I'm requesting you find another place to have the soiree, you understand?" The frailness of her shook as she turned toward the street again. "You coming?" She glanced over her shoulder, her hands bent feebly to her hips. "Would you like to come have some tea with me? Since we're neighbors and all. I'll give you some sympathy and you'll be on your way to find a new job."

Her stomach dropped at the invitation. She couldn't have explained why, but at that moment, having a place to go felt heavenly. "Really?" Kelsey called after her. "I'd like that." She stretched out her hand. "Kelsey Mitchell."

"Alice Willits," said the matriarch, her arms bent at her side. "We don't need such formality, do we? Call me Alice. I'll call you Kelsey. I never met anyone named Kelsey. Where's that come from?"

Kelsey startled at her name. She rarely heard it used with only the kids at home. She dropped her hand. "I suppose we don't need formality. The name is my mother's maiden name."

"Odd." She paused and drew in a strained breath. "Is your mother odd?"

"Like you wouldn't believe." Kelsey laughed. "Mrs. Willits, I think you know my best friend. I've heard your name from her for years. Martha Kessler? She said you taught her in a Bible study years ago in a young-marrieds class. She wanted to introduce us because we were neighbors."

"Young, blonde Martha?" She sighed. "That girl reminds me of myself back in the day. Oh, she's prettier than I ever was, but she has so much energy, and she's always starting trouble. The good kind of trouble that makes people thinks about what they're doing."

"That's her!"

As they reached the sidewalk, Alice stopped and let her eyes scrutinize Kelsey. "So you're the infamous Kelsey Mitchell. I've heard a lot about you."

"You have?" Her smile flattened. "Church gossip?"

She nodded as she began walking. "Sure, you're the one with the crazy husband."

Kelsey halted, and Mrs. Willits looked at her.

"Oh, now don't be offended. Everyone knew everyone's business back when we had nothing to hide. It's not your fault you have a crazy husband. My sister did, too. Her man liked the drink. Put them all into an early grave, that bastard."

Kelsey followed along behind the woman, though she wanted to make polite excuses and get started on her job hunt straight away, but her loyalty to Martha wouldn't let her abandon Alice Willits just then.

"Is that what they say? That he's crazy?" she asked.

"They also say you drove him crazy, but I've lived too long to believe that business."

The two of them reached Alice's front porch, which donned a battered screen door and wood framing, weather-damaged to the point that Kelsey questioned the home's safety.

"You live here all by yourself?"

"Watch your step," Alice warned. "Lived here by myself for over twenty years now."

"How long have you lived here in total?" she asked, astonished by the number. The only thing in her life that had remained constant for twenty years was a mole on her lower back, and she had a good mind to get rid of that, if she had health insurance.

"Fifty-three years. Not much has been done since my husband died. Is that why you ask? I used to be quite handy with a power tool, but I shake too much these days. I guess all of us ladies were good with the tools, thanks to the war. But times have changed, the mind is willing, but the flesh is weak. Now I tap my arm muscle and it jiggles like Jell-O."

"I'm sorry. He died twenty years ago?"

"Eighteen years ago. The house got away from me, and now, I figure I'll be gone before it matters too heartily. I should have moved years ago. Too stubborn I suppose."

    Kelsey's lids popped open. "Gone? What a way to talk!"

    "It comes with age. It's a fact of life, why ignore it? I figure God's got a room up there for me in heaven and Stanley has probably already made sure there isn't an apricot in sight. He's had eighteen years to accomplish this mission I entrusted him with. We said we'd be together praising Jesus one of these days, and I had about all I can take of this world. Who would have thought you'd turn on the television and see people parading about in their underwear? It's almost a surprise when I see someone fully clothed. Even the newscasters wear their shirts to display the goods. God must have something left for me to do, because here I am."

    Kelsey couldn't tell if she was joking about the apricots in heaven, or if she meant it. She'd heard stranger things from Todd's mouth, so she didn't think to question Alice. They walked into the living room, and it looked like a sitcom set. The furniture was worn and ugly brown plaid, the carpet was that flat kind with the designs interwoven making some parts higher, and the walls all had their pictures hung too high.

    "Was Stanley a tall man?"

    "He was. How did you know that?"

    "Just a guess." Kelsey shrugged.

    "Don't you smile, dear? You'll get a better job. Come sit, I'll put the water on. Sit a spell in the kitchen and tell me what you hated about that job.

We never lose jobs we really want. You're probably not old enough to realize that yet."

"You have the same linoleum in here we have in the condominium."

"That condominium you live in was built by my husband, that's why. He got a great deal on this stuff, and you cannot pry it off the floor. If you ever want a new floor, you're going to have to cover right over it because Stanley, he didn't do anything if he didn't do it one hundred percent."

"Your husband built that place?"

"Sure, it was an apartment house back then. He built it with his brothers, then he managed it with tenants, and we lived there for a while before we had money for our own house, in the big unit on the ground floor. It was such a nice life," she said wistfully. "We'd go for our morning walk along the beach. Back then, they didn't have that nice bike path like they do today. Or even a fence. You took your chances." Alice looked out the window, lost for a moment.

She turned on the stove, which was an ancient white porcelain thing with four doors and red handles. Kelsey wondered how old it must be, but as she looked around the room, she saw that everything in the kitchen was original. From the ornate, scalloped cabinet moldings to the flecked Formica countertops. And everything looked brand new, as if Alice spent her life taking good care of her belongings.

"Well, that will be ready soon." Alice sat down and patted Kelsey's hand. "Are you feeling better?

My, you're such a pretty thing. So sad about your husband."

If she only knew.

She swallowed uncomfortably. "It's been a long day. My daughter was hospitalized this morning for meningitis."

"Meningitis?"

"But now she's fine, and they can't figure out what was wrong with her to begin with. She was watching TV and shouting out numbers for the 'Price is Right' when I left." She didn't mention that Meagan was a genius at the price of everything. Every time they wasted a bite of food, Todd would shout at them the lost pennies. *That bite cost me thirty-four cents. Now, you eat it.*

"It's a mother's worst nightmare," Alice continued. "My sister's daughter caught the scarlet fever, and then there was that awful polio. How old is your daughter?"

"Nine. I went to check in at work, and they told me not to bother coming back in. I suppose I haven't been a model employee, but my boss wanted a babysitter, not an assistant, so it's just as well. I'm weary of babysitting adults."

"We had it easier in my day. The other moms pitched in. It's not like that today. People are so alone. If you had a job, everyone knew you had to go, so the women who didn't, they took the kids. They were glad they weren't the ones who had to trot off. That's just the way it had to be, especially when there were no men around after the war. A lot of our men went to Japan to help rebuild."

"But you live alone now?"

"But I'm not alone, dear. I have friends come visit me, and the phone when I want to talk to the girls from high school. They don't get out much anymore. Then, I have Pastor Bechtel. He visits every week, but I see him checking up on me — usually every day." She smiled. "He's such a nice boy."

At the sound of Alex's name, Kelsey's stomach fluttered with butterflies. "Alex Bechtel?" she stammered.

Alice nodded. "He reminds me of my Stanley when he was young. Do you know him?"

"He was there this morning. At the hospital with my daughter. He prayed for her." Kelsey felt the same surge of energy she'd felt that morning, but she tried to appear normal, afraid she had lost her mind.

"He was supposed to be there for Dan this morning. He was with your daughter? Are you sure we're talking about the same man? Handsome thing, looks like William Holden."

Kelsey hated to tell Mrs. Willits that she had no idea what William Holden looked like. "I'm not sure. He was there to see someone who was dying. A young father, and he—"

"That's Alex all right. He was there for his friend, Dan. Well, I'll be. Small world. First Martha, and now Alex, it seems as if we were destined to meet, Kelsey Mitchell. Of course the Christian world in Santa Cruz is such a strange place, isn't it?"

*Too small for my liking,* Kelsey thought with a shiver. Something didn't feel right. First Alex, and now this, a neighbor who she'd never seen…hearing about Alex yet again. A miracle in the morning. It was all beginning to creep her out, and her skin crawled at the coincidences. The teakettle shrieked, and Kelsey jumped so she nearly fell out of her chair.

Alice patted her hand again before rising for the kettle. Her hand was soft, though her skin felt paper-thin and slightly cold to the touch. "Relax for a while. Being in hospitals is always stressful on one's soul. In fact, Alex was here this morning, trying to find a reason not to leave. I kicked him out the door. Sometimes you young people need that, a good kick in the pants. We had the war, but your generation doesn't have to fight for much."

"Yeah," Kelsey said absently. She'd fought for everything, and her mind was still back in the trenches of open warfare. Her battle was far from over. If she couldn't get Todd to admit the truth, she'd forever feel responsible for the damage he'd continue to inflict on others.

Alice placed a cup of tea in front of her.

"Thanks." Kelsey looked around. "You've taken such good care of this house. You can't tell from the outside. It feels so comfortable in here."

"You used to be able to tell from the outside. My husband had the prettiest garden out front. He told me once that he could bring me flowers, or he could plant them for me year-round, and that's just what he did. Stanley had the greenest thumb."

"He sounds like a wonderful man."

"Oh, he was. I was lucky to have met him. There's no question. Such a godly man."

The word *godly* caused Kelsey to flinch, and she placed her teacup down, missing the saucer and forcing hot tea all over the table. Alice was up in a single move and had a towel on the spill before Kelsey realized she'd caused the trouble.

Alice poured more into the cup and put her hand on her chin. "Is everything all right with your tea?"

"I'm just waiting for it to cool."

"It's Constant Comment. That was the first thing I served to Stanley when he came to my door over fifty years ago. That tea has been lucky for me."

"Maybe I should have had some when I invited Todd over the first time, does it ward off evil?" She snorted a laugh.

"You're divorced?"

"It's complicated."

"It isn't that complicated. You get married, you have good times and bad. That's what 'better or for worse' means, Kelsey." She nodded sweetly. "Is there a chance you two could work it out? That maybe he might get better?"

Kelsey blinked a few times as she pondered her answer. "No, I can say with complete certainty, it's impossible." She sipped her tea. *Not a snowball's chance in...*

Alice Willits drank from her teacup. "So what kind of job will you be looking for?"

"Administrative. I'm very organized and methodical, but only at work. At home, I'm a wreck.

Most of the executive positions that pay well simply require too many hours for me to leave my kids."

"Doesn't your husband have them some of the time?"

"My husband is in Laos."

"Laos?"

"I should really get back to the hospital." She stood suddenly and lifted her teacup and saucer to the sink. "I really appreciate the hospitality."

She raced through the small living room and felt Alice Willits on her heel. "Did I say something wrong?" Alice asked.

"I just noticed the time is all." Her gaze rested on the porch swing that she'd eyed so longingly since moving in next door. "I always loved your porch swing. Maybe we can have another chat someday."

"That swing is proof that life isn't always what you expect?"

"Pardon?" she said as she halted on the front path.

"That swing was a baby cradle. Stanley built it himself, and when year after year went by with no baby, he finally pulled it apart and made me that swing. 'Alice,' he said, 'there's no sense wasting this fine teak on a cradle. I don't think the Lord wants us to be parents.' So he took it apart, built that swing, and we used to sit on it, watching the kids in the neighborhood play."

Kelsey stared at the swing. How long would Todd have stayed around if she couldn't have provided the kids he'd wanted?

"We didn't have those fancy birth options in our day. You couldn't have a baby, well, you just couldn't have a baby, other than adopting, and we just never felt the Lord call us to that. We got used to our lives, just Stanley and I. He'd hand out candy to the neighborhood kids and they'd flock to us like seagulls."

She'd never be the kind of person who could look back longingly on her marriage or even her wedding day. She supposed women like her became angry, crazy old hens who had nothing good to say, and people avoided – like Kelsey's own mother.

"I think it's divine we met today," Alice said. "You have the saddest eyes I've ever seen, Kelsey. I know if feels bad, like it will never go away, but I've seen how God works. Just when you think you can't take anymore pain, something gives."

She had no such illusions. If God had a story written for her, it had to be a Greek Tragedy. She'd learned the hard way that's how Gothics really ended. She stared at the swing, and wondered what it was like to have a man who had the time to swing the afternoon away. "I didn't think that kind of love really existed. I thought people just pretended."

"Kelsey!" Alice's face straightened out. "That's the most dismal thing I've ever heard."

She felt exposed. "I've said too much."

"You haven't said anything."

"I don't go to church anymore. We went to Alex's church, well, your church I guess, before the separation. No offense Alice, because you are so sweet to sweep me in off the street today, but I don't have much use for religious people these days. They've done enough damage."

"That's what religious people do, Kelsey. You don't think I had a few of those in my lifetime? A few tarts who put on their biggest smile and their best dress for the pastor, but tried to steal your husband when you weren't looking? God's got no use for that kind of religion either, honey."

"I can't really see the difference."

"You can. You're not ready to see, is all. Someday…dear one. For now, you go ahead and question. God will be waiting."

*For the next act of my Greek tragedy,* she thought wryly.

"Thank you for the tea and for worrying about me across the street. I'm used to being by myself on the path. I go out there to think. I suppose I forget how odd I appear."

"Kelsey Mitchell, no one really knows what happened in your marriage but you. If you say it couldn't be salvaged, I believe you."

Kelsey froze. "It doesn't matter. I can't marry again. The Bible says that makes me an adulteress."

Alice shook her head. "You sure can recite the rules back to me easily. I want you to tell me about God's love for you, not his rules. You're attracted to the Pharisees of the world, you need to find the real disciples."

Kelsey nodded politely. She was legally separated, and the only way to get the divorce was to lie for Todd and there was no satisfaction in that.

"I may have met him once, your Todd. In Pastor Underwood's office. Is he tall?" she asked, as Kelsey looked at her back.

"Yes."

"Handsome?" Alice's pale gray eyes met hers. "Sort of looks like the mayor of San Francisco?"

Reluctantly, Kelsey agreed that he did. "Gavin Newsom."

"Kelsey, would you and the children like to come for dinner one night? I may not be able to do much, but I can cook, and I'd love to be around children again. You read the Song of Solomon and you come back with the children. We'll talk some more."

She questioned the invitation, but she didn't spurn it. Surprised, she heard herself agree, "We'd love to come." She scrawled her phone number on a scrap of paper and said her goodbye, but as she left the house, she turned to see Mrs. Willits gazing out the door at her. Her stomach stirred with warmth she hadn't known in a long time.

## Chapter 9

Saturday mornings in Santa Cruz buzzed with frenetic energy that seemed to force people into motion. For a clumsy, overly friendly mutt like Obadiah, a morning along the crowded bicycle path was like a video game to a twelve-year old boy: Addictive, overwhelming and sheer, unadulterated joy. The waves themselves felt this energy, and they crashed wildly, spraying the running path in rhythmic intervals. October sent home most of the tourists, and Alex felt like he had his town back to himself.

He jogged behind the furry, lumbering frame, jerking back Obadiah every time a biker or runner approached, for fear they'd all end up stacked like a log cabin. His dog's sole purpose seemed to be knocking people over with affection, explosively welcoming them to the day.

"Heel!" Alex shouted as Obadiah nearly took out a female bicyclist. The woman yelled something obscene as she passed, and Alex slowed his run to a halt, bent over with his palms clasped on his knees. "You're making this more work than it's worth," he said to the dog through labored breathing. He stretched out a leg over the wooden fence near the ocean and stretched. He kept his hand tightly tangled in the leash in case Obadiah got any ideas.

Unbidden, the dog gave Alex's cheek a giant lick and barked, as if to say, *Let's go. People to see, joggers to trip.*

They'd stopped right across from Mrs. Willits' house, and she shuffled onto the porch with a watering can in her hand then sprinkled an overgrown azalea. He could barely make out the front door behind the bush, and thought maybe her daily watering might be the problem. But he imagined, she couldn't lift the garden shears and she was too proud to let him do it.

Alex caught her attention. "Mrs. Willits," he yelled. He waved and waited for traffic to pass before crossing the street. Obadiah lumbered obediently behind him. Mrs. Willits scared the dog, who knew instinctively not to misbehave around the elderly woman.

"If that's the way you control that animal, you expect them to hand you a church? Who's walking who exactly?"

He laughed. "So you saw that, huh? We got kicked out of obedience school. Obadiah kept flattening a Yorkie."

"Well, it's no wonder. You two look like Abbot and Costello coming down the street. Did you notice the path clearing for you? It's like watching the parting of the Red Sea to see you coming."

He looked back towards the ocean. "I didn't notice a thing. I was just trying to stay upright." He kept Obadiah close so he wouldn't knock over the frail Mrs. Willits, but the dog sat down. "He loves Saturdays," Alex said, looking at the dog. "It's his one day to play, and now I have to lock him in the backyard for the day. Poor guy." He pat the giant head. "He has no idea what's in store for him."

"Where'd you find that mangy thing anyway?"

Alex covered Obadiah's ears. "Shh. He'll hear you. Someone dropped him off when he was just a pup. I couldn't bear to bring him to the pound, so I went and bought a metric ton of dog food, and we were partners for life."

"You should get him a friend. Maybe you should get yourself a friend while you're at it. You going to stay single all your life? In my day, we would have called you a confirmed bachelor by now. They don't live nearly as long, you know?"

"Hah! Another dog? Yeah, because I think there's a square inch of the yard not ripped apart. Besides, my landlord is all ready to kick me out as it is."

"I just wanted you to hire a gardener. I never said anything about kicking you out." Mrs. Willits laughed about being his landlord, stepped over to her porch swing and sat gingerly. "Quit avoiding the subject. My memory isn't that far gone. A girlfriend? A wife perhaps? We never talk about such things on a weekday. Doesn't seem right somehow. But it's Saturday, restore my hope in the youth of America."

His love life couldn't be less of a topic if he'd become a Roman Catholic priest instead of a minister. But Alice was primed for information, moving her lips about as if she were chewing a cud.

"I was thinking of asking this woman out, but I wasn't sure if I should bring her on a visitation first, or a funeral? I'm a barrel of laughs. This is assuming I could get to this woman's house before the old Lincoln decided to act up on me."

"You could walk," she deadpanned.

"Always an attractive trait. A guy without wheels."

"Why don't you meet her in the Sunday school class you teach? What young woman of God wouldn't want a man who is so passionate for the Lord? That way she wouldn't know you drove a jalopy."

"So, you're telling me you would have given Stanley the old heave-ho if he didn't have a decent car?"

"Stanley walked me home from school every day. I never did pay much mind to his shoes. A woman wants a good man who is passionate about his faith. What else is there?"

"I don't know, maybe a paycheck to cover groceries? My mom told me when I left accounting that women want security, and I'd be leaving that. She was right, naturally. My girlfriend at the time apparently thought so too. Dumped me like yesterday's trash."

Mrs. Willits laughed. "Oh now, don't you talk to me about poverty. This generation has never known poverty. It's not being without an iDop."

"iPod," he corrected her.

"Whatever it is. So God spared you a life with a greedy woman, that's a blessing, Alex. Greedy people always want more; it's like making life a giant race. Then, like Solomon, they have to figure out in the end that possessions didn't mean anything at all. That's a wasted life."

"It meant something to my ex-girlfriend. Let me guess, Alice, you're a prophet and you've seen my future wife."

"Good heavens, I'm old enough to be, but no. Well, maybe…no, she wouldn't be right."

"You *are* playing matchmaker."

"I just like to get under your skin, Alex. You take life too seriously for such a young buck. A bachelor." Alice pursed her lips. "It won't do for much longer, now will it?" She had a way that told you the argument was over, and she'd won. Regardless of the outcome, you felt so merry at the end of it, you were happy to call her the victor.

"I suppose not."

"I read in the paper, the funeral is this morning. So you should get that mutt home and go get dressed."

Alex nodded. "It's why I needed the run, to occupy my mind rather than focus on preparation or Dan's funeral." He'd been a fool to think he could pull it together for this. He thought of Dan's children staring at him while he tried to preach. His throat clamped shut just thinking about it.

"You shouldn't panic, Alex. Pastor Mel will do a nice job. He always does. He adds a certain resonance and an air of importance – as if he will escort the deceased to heaven himself."

"I'm doing the ceremony," Alex clarified.

"That's not what it said in the paper. It said services held by Santa Cruz Evangelical, Pastor Mel Underwood presiding, and then it gave the address at a local soccer field. Do you want me to get the paper? I thought the soccer field location was strange, but I figure Mel knows what he's doing. He's probably trying to honor the man's wishes, otherwise I can't imagine he'd do something like that."

Alex felt all his muscles tighten. "I have to run, Mrs. Willits." He grasped the leash and tugged on Obadiah's collar. He ran into his house, a crumbly old place that would need the love of a good harem to appear presentable. He showered and dressed, tossed the dog in the backyard with a giant bowl of kibble and drove to the local soccer field, muttering to himself all the facts of Dan's life.

Flocks of children in colored soccer jerseys dotted the field. The oversized bouncy balloons and inflatable slides gave a carnival atmosphere that would most likely attract all the tourists from the Boardwalk if they happened upon the scene. Alex stepped onto the field and his stomach turned. Children squealed at the base of the playhouses while their mothers wiped away their own tears to focus on encouragement. The children needed none. They didn't care why the bouncy house was there; they only wanted the line to go quicker.

The atmosphere before him was exactly what Dan requested, but the reality sent a sick wave through Alex. Drawn faces of his congregation appeared everywhere, and he felt their glares one by one as though they each slapped him. He wanted to crawl in a hole and disappear.

Mel came toward him with a somber expression, dressed in a dark suit, his small travel Bible in his hand. Alex looked down at his own shoes and thought he should have polished them before the occasion, even if they were covered in inch-high grass. It didn't look respectful.

"Have you seen the widow yet?" Mel asked.

Alex shook his head. "No. I just got here. It looks like a circus."

To Alex's surprise, the old pastor didn't take pleasure in his being right. Underwood actually wore a calm expression. "It's not a happy event when someone goes before their time. The unfairness of it always overshadows what young people want for their funerals."

Alex dropped his gaze.

"No matter how strong their faith, no matter what kind of life of the party that he or she was, no matter how easy that person tries to make it on those who are left. It's still hard." Mel looked at his closed hand. "You're simply not ready to let go." He let his hand bloom.

Alex nodded. "You're right." Everyone, at least two hundred people, stood around the field, staring at him as if hoping he had the magic pill to make this go down easier.

Crystal approached with her four kids in tow. He hadn't seen her since the hospital, even though he'd promised Dan to look after her. The women in the church had taken charge, and he melted into excuses for having to make the funeral arrangements. The ladies brought Crystal meals, helped with the kids, and spent the night so that she wouldn't be alone. Alex hardly thought there was a place for him. At least not in the present.

The widow wore a navy dress covered in flowers. It reminded Alex of his mother's sofa. The kids were dressed in their Sunday best, sporting tennis shoes with their childish suits and dresses. The finishing details told him Crystal wasn't herself yet. Normally, her kids were steamed and pressed. But today, when they'd bury their father, they took on the appearance of street urchins dressed for a handout.

"You all look wonderful," Alex said and kissed Crystal's cheek.

"Do we? We feel terrible. Don't we kids?" But she had lost their attention to the bouncy houses.

"Can we go play?" The oldest, Dan's namesake, asked. "I'll watch the babies. Please," he pleaded, his hands clasped over his mouth, as in prayer.

Crystal looked at them all. "They haven't had a moment's normal since…Lord, I can't even remember when." She exhaled raggedly. "Go ahead, Danny, but be sure and stay with the little ones. Frankie, you help with Charlotte and Jonathan." She stared at her watch, which was missing and only bore the tan lines to mark its place. "Come back in twenty minutes so we can start."

"He knows twenty minutes, right?" Alex asked.

"No, but he knows to come back and he'll guess." Crystal drew Pastor Underwood into a hug, and she closed her eyes and allowed the embrace to last. "Thank you for all the church has done, Pastor. I don't know what we would have done without Pastor Alex's visits and the ladies' fine meals." She pulled away and took Alex's hand. "He's truly been a godsend. Dan looked forward to his visits every single day. Sometimes they'd argue Scripture, sometimes which football team looked good this year. And for you both to organize all this for Dan…" She searched the field. "It's incredible. The ladies have brought food back to the house to feed the entire congregation and then some. It should be a good day. I only wish Dan could be here to see it." The last of her words faded, and her eyes drooped shut before she swooned. Pastor Mel clutched her in his arms.

"Alex, get her. She's collapsed!" Mel shouted.

The funeral happened without him. Mel took care of those assembled, and Alex earned a first-class ticket back to the hospital in a wailing ambulance.

## Chapter 10

Kelsey needed a job, and she needed to keep Todd in the dark about Meagan's illness. He'd only blame her and use the information against her in court. Her entire life was one big chess game, trying to outmaneuver an opponent whose only definition of winning was to destroy the enemy; namely, her. It made no logical sense, which is exactly why her life looked like the very definition of insanity.

When she entered the university's physics' laboratory to see Todd's former employer, it looked the same as it always did, with tubes, wires, and several oversized computers blinking and humming. A bevy of inhuman activity in sharp contrast to the beautiful redwood forest it overlooked.

The scientists were a ragtag group of doctors and post-doctoral fellows, who could offer a detailed description of particle string theory in physics, but couldn't match their socks. There were no women on staff, and she supposed if there were, the woman would be as Spock-like as the rest of them.

Dr. Massimo Campelli stood at a chalkboard, scribbling an unending series of numbers, letters and symbols while Kelsey stood by silently and waited. No doubt he'd forgotten their meeting. He would have forgotten his pants if his wife weren't at home ensuring he left dressed. He made odd grunting sounds while the chalk clacked against the board, then he dropped the chalk and turned around suddenly.

"I thought I sensed someone. Kelsey, how are you?" He kissed her cheek and his scratchy beard tickled her. He wasn't like most scientists she knew, but she thought it was his Italian upbringing.

"I'm doing well."

"And Todd?"

She shrugged. "He's in Laos. I don't know if he told you."

"He's not allowed to have contact," he reminded her. "I seem to remember something about him moving. Have a seat."

Kelsey found an empty metal stool and pulled it out with a screech. Dr. Campelli sat across the lab table from her and focused his attention with laser precision onto her. She felt as though she were under a microscope.

She sucked in a heaping helping of oxygen and rambled her words before she chickened out, "I know the last time you saw me that things hadn't gone well. You might find it strange that I'm here, but…"

"I'm Italian. I love to look at beautiful things and so a visit by you is always welcome."

She giggled outright as her nervousness pulled away. No matter how old Dr. Campelli got, and he had to be closing in on retirement age, his smooth talk stayed as European as if he were straight off the airplane. It wasn't very many scientists that possessed his charm.

"Don't throw me off. Wait until you hear what I have to say."

"You're not suing us, are you? Everyone is always suing the school, as if we have any money."

"I'm not suing you, no. Is there a reason I could?"

This time, he was the one who laughed.

Kelsey saw that her hands trembled, "Dr. Campelli, I wouldn't ask this, but I need help. I didn't know where else to go, and you're probably the last one who wants to help us, but –"

He perused her over his glasses and rubbed his scruffy beard. "If you're going to ask me if Todd can have his job back, I have to say no." He opened a drawer and dropped a giant folder stacked with papers in front of her. "That's your husband's file, Kelsey." On the front of the folder was written, *Do Not Rehire*. "We have a restraining order to ensure he's not allowed back on campus, much less the lab. I know it's a terrible waste of talent, but my hands on tied here."

"Estranged-husband," she corrected. "He's in Laos and no, I'm not here to ask for his job back."

"Well, that's a relief. I thought he might want to come back. Excellent physicist, but one never knows when that other side of him will reappear."

"No," she shook her head. "Not coming back." She would have given anything to reach out and scan that folder. "May I?" she reached for it.

Dr. Campelli swooped it up, "Confidential. I'm sorry, Kelsey."

"He did more than the one day of damage?"

"Let's just say we were trying to get rid of him for years. He finally gave us the opportunity."

"No one ever said anything. I thought he was doing fine, here. That it was just bad at home."

The doctor shook his head. "I'm afraid not. Your husband…I'm sorry, estranged-husband is a brilliant man. He seemed to know just how far he could take his behavior, which is why I had trouble believing he was mentally ill. He sure became sane when threatened."

"He's nothing if not a survivor, Dr. Campelli. He simply sucks the life out of those around him and he's reenergized."

He nodded understandingly. "So why are you here if it isn't to find him a job?"

"*I* need a job," she said without looking at him. "I got fired earlier this week after Meagan had to go to the hospital." She struggled to hold back her tears. More rejection.

"Meagan went to the hospital?"

"She's fine now. Just a little scare, but between the chicken pox, lice outbreaks at the school and dentist appointments, I'm not exactly a great nine-to-fiver. That's what made me think of here. This place is going twenty-four hours a day."

Dr. Campelli looked around the empty lab. Although it was Saturday, soon it would fill up with students and research doctorates. She felt a rush of anxiety.

"Please Dr. Campelli. If you can't hire me. Look me in the eye and tell me. Give me that much."

"What would you do, Kelsey?"

"Look at this place? You need someone to help you organize and I know the work well enough to do that. I know who studies quarks and who is dealing with string theory. I can help here. I know I can. The scientists won't know how to ask me, but I'll know how to help them. I'm very good at reading scientific minds and they'd be more effective with help like that. More published papers, more results."

He leaned back in his chair, "I wasn't expecting this."

"Dr. Campelli, it wouldn't be for long. I can find something else soon, but just for a couple weeks, to get things organized and find something that works in my schedule. The school year has just started and this place is already a disaster. We could help each other."

He scanned the lab, "Well, I wouldn't say it was a disaster."

"I can label everything. Don't tell me you all wouldn't benefit from me with a labeler. I'll buy my own. You wouldn't believe how much easier it makes for people to put things away in the right place with a labeler. I can guarantee, the lab wouldn't take months to clean up at the year's end!" She couldn't promise any such thing, but that didn't stop her from believing it. They weren't known as evil geniuses for nothing.

"You know most of the professors. Won't it be awkward for you to be here?"

"Naturally, it will." She thought of her appearance at church and how she felt being left was contagious and the wives — the wives of men who loved them — ignored her like the plague. She remembered herself. "It's more awkward to buy my groceries with food stamps or have to move the kids again. I bought a condominium, an apartment really. It's in bad shape, but it's the one piece of stability that we've had in years. Please," she pleaded, not caring how pathetic she sounded now. The more he thought about it, the more chance he had to come up with reasons why they didn't need her.

He drummed his fingers on the desk, "You're putting me in an awkward position. I can't simply hire you. There are forms to be filed and grants to be applied for—" he shook his head, but she could see him wearing down. His Italian heritage and her damsel in distress nature weakened him.

"I'll type them. I'll start for nothing until we can get the funding. I know I can get it, Massimo. Please."

He raked a hand through his hair, "Kelsey, I cannot say no to a beautiful woman. You do this to me on purpose. You could have gone to Finn."

"Finn's not in charge," she said appealing to his power nature. "I came to the man who had the ability to get this done."

He laughed, shaking his head. He bobbed his forefinger at her. "You're good, you know that? I should run the other direction. A beautiful, manipulative woman is not what we need around here."

"No one will notice either, except you. I'll stop off for a drawn double espresso for you every morning, and have it on your desk when you arrive. How can you resist that? Fresh espresso and typed papers. How can you resist that, Massimo? I know which journals to submit to, so that's taken care of."

He pressed his palms to the air, "I give, I give! Enough. Mrs. Campelli won't take kindly to the fact that I cannot resist a stunning woman."

"Trust me, I am smart enough to know my limits, Doctor. I would never mess with the Mrs. An Italian man is one thing, I know better than to mess with his Sophia Loren."

He laughed again, "I'll tell her you said so. You can start two weeks from Monday?"

She nodded.

"Eight a.m. Sharp. And I expect my espresso hand-drawn. None of that power machine garbage."

"I wouldn't think of it."

"We haven't discussed salary. Or hours."

"I'm writing for a grant. Don't worry, I'll make sure it's a good grant."

"Until then, we'll get you paid on temporary stipends."

She thought she might cry, "Thank you, Massimo. Thank you."

"I want your word that you won't be bringing Todd here. He's not welcome."

"No worries there. He's not welcome at home either."

"He ruined my lab, you know. Years of research gone."

Her family's life was the same: A pile of wreckage from a disaster that no one could ever pin on Todd. He'd create a tsunami's wake around him, and the only people who could prove it had been systematically stripped of their reputations. There was no justice, but there was freedom, and she had the only thing that mattered: her family.

As she hiked her handbag over her shoulder, Massimo had one last word to her. "I need to know if I provide you with security badges that you'll never let them out of your sight."

"I promise. Todd won't even know where I'm working."

Massimo looked slightly ill, as though he'd regretted his offer. "If you get word that Todd is back in the country, I want you to let me and campus security know first thing."

"Please trust me, Massimo. I won't let you down."

When she left the lab and drove down the hill through the dark canopy of old grove Redwoods, drawing in their rich, moist scent, she felt invigorated as if she could accomplish anything. Only four days and she had a job. And she had a good job. With someone who understood her plight, and her needs for the kids. Granted, no one would talk to her all day, but she'd grown used to that with Todd. Scientists were compartmentalized that way. She would be Uhura on the ship, relegated to the corner as a species no one quite understood. Which was fine with her.

She rushed home, anxious to see how Meagan fared under her brother's watchful eyes. She didn't leave them home alone very often, even though Nathan was at legal babysitting age. She had a hard time letting go, and after the scare of the week, she'd grown more wary by the day. But there was no choice. It was either find work or move again. The family needed what little stability they could grab and so she was forced to trust Nathan.

Arriving home, nothing seemed awry. The house, dare she think it, actually looked better than when she'd left. She walked down the hallway and found Nathan in his room, "Can I turn on my music now?"

She nodded and walked briskly to Meagan's room. Kelsey fluffed her daughter's pillows, and felt proud and a tiny bit sad that no one had missed her at all.

"Do you have everything you need, Meagan?" She felt her daughter's forehead, certain some other frightening symptom or malady would appear at any moment. Every cough or sniffle brought terror to her heart.

For now, the lab represented safety to her; the only other people on earth who knew who Dr. Todd Mitchell really was, and not his carefully crafted alter ego.

"Mom, I told you, I'm fine. God performed a miracle, why is that so hard for you to understand?"

She crossed her arms. "Really? You're going to ask me that question?"

"Doesn't matter if you believe it or not. Pastor Alex knows the truth."

"Pastor Alex? You're on a first-name basis now?"

"He's a Christian, Mom. A real one." She sighed. "Go take a bath or do something. Clean something while you're telling us what pigs we are; that always makes you feel better. I bet you'll find Nathan's underwear on the bathroom floor if you go in there."

"I've found a job."

"Really, Mom? Seriously?"

She nodded and heard Nathan bound down the hallway.

"You got a job?"

"At the university. I start a week from Monday." She felt light and full of life. It was such a foreign feeling that she didn't want to waste a second of it.

"Mom?" Meagan questioned slowly.

"Beauty is right here with me, and I want to appreciate every moment of it. I have my kids. I have a job. I have a home." She paused before thrusting a fist to the sky. "Wahoo! This is what it feels like to win! The best part is, no one has to lose for me to win. Isn't that lovely?"

"Does that mean I can get out of bed?"

"No."

Meagan's smooth brow crinkled. "Wait a minute. Did you say a job, at *the university*? Isn't that kind of…weird?"

Kelsey flittered about the room as though she had cartoon birds at her feet. It was as if the spell of gloom had been broken.

She'd endured four days with Meagan in the hospital, worried that she'd imagined the entire experience and that she might wake and find out it was all a nightmare, Meagan wasn't with them any longer. Every morning she woke, that terror was her first thought, then joy infiltrated like sunlight. It was like being given a gift every morning. It always had been, she'd just been too busy with a harried schedule to know it.

"Life is precious, Meagan."

"Okay. Is that a Meme on Facebook or something?"

"When you came home, it just freed me from fear. Strangest thing. A little humiliation was standing between me and a job, as if I had any self-respect left, so I marched into the most humiliating place I could think of; Dad's old lab."

She'd begun to feel again. She'd survived her marriage by numbing herself to reality – not only to pain, but also to joy and gratitude. And now, life suddenly felt like it was in high definition and she wanted to examine each pixel. In her children, Kelsey saw the babies that she'd fallen in love with, while acknowledging the years in between were a blur. Meagan's sparkling green eyes brimmed with life, and Kelsey cupped her face in her hands. "Have you been watching the Hallmark channel again?"

She focused on her daughter's eyes and locked in a grateful gaze. "I'm thankful. That's all. Thankful. You and Nathan are the best things that ever happened to me. Have I told you that lately?"

Meagan rolled her eyes. "Can I have a cell phone?"

"Not on your life."

"Just checking if you were still my mom. Can you let go of my cheeks now?"

She smiled smugly. "I start a week from Monday. If you're ready to go back to school, that is."

"What does it pay?" Meagan maneuvered her luxuriously long eyelashes into a thin slit. "What *kind* of job? Is it legal?"

Kelsey stood proud. "Meagan, for goodness' sake. I went to Harvard, darling, and when you can say that, you can't imply I'm some kind of intellectual deficient. Until then, mind your manners. It's none of your business what it pays."

Meagan wore her father's disapproving glare, and it could bore holes in one's soul. "We got worried you weren't going to find something." Meagan and Nathan glared at one another, and a familiar uneasy feeling roiled in her stomach.

"I called Dad," Nathan said. "He said the insurance was just a misunderstanding and he'd clear it up."

She grabbed her throat. "Nathan, you didn't."

"It's all right, Mom. He was the old dad when I talked to him. He was really worried about how you were handling everything. He knows you're not good in a crisis."

Todd Mitchell had made her whole married life a crisis so that he could swoop in and play the part of hero. "I hope you told him I had everything covered. You told him that Meagan was fine, and there was no need to worry?" No need to come back and check on her.

Nathan said nothing and then blurted what he was really thinking. "Mom, we can't help him if he's over there."

"I've told you, he doesn't want our help." She felt paralyzed by Nathan's calling Todd. If her son had any idea how dangerous his father really was, he'd let go of his fantasy to "fix" him.

"He's coming home," Meagan said.

Kelsey's heart was instantly in her throat. She'd never escape. Her kids were her weak spot and he knew it. He'd only had time to gather strength, to perfect his wiles and to take down the last crumbling wall that protected them. "No." she shook her head and refused to believe it but saw the truth written on Nathan's furrowed brow.

"I called Dad. Dr. Levin let me use the hospital phone and I called Laos. At first, I just wanted to tell him about the insurance and how we needed it, but he kept asking questions, and you know how he is…I kept answering him."

"Great." Her lids withered shut. "I'm sure they'll add that to our bill." It was as though her son invited the devil back into their midst, and she wanted to shake Nathan and scream, but she felt herself go numb in the circumstance.

"It won't be like before, Mom." Nathan convinced himself it was true, and how she wished it were. For now, she had to take precautions.

## Chapter 11

The doorbell rang and Kelsey froze. "He couldn't be here that quickly."

Nathan grimaced. "He left on Tuesday."

"Why didn't you tell me this before, Nathan?"

"Because I knew you'd make us leave before he got here. You don't want us to have a father!"

There was truth in that statement. She didn't want him to have a father like Todd, but kids loved what they knew: the familiar.

She didn't bother to address his accusation. "Did you give him our address? Could this be your father on the other side of the door?" She pointed down the hallway.

"He's our father! Just because you don't like him Mom, it doesn't give you the right to shut him out of our lives!"

The doorbell rang again. "Stay here with your sister." Nathan didn't listen and was behind her as she peered through the peephole. Todd stood on the other side of the door dressed in a crisp white shirt, and she gathered the collar of her sweatshirt in a tight knot. She raised herself up and looked through the peephole again, hoping for a different result. She could tell by his expression that he was lucid. His eyes were clear, his hair well groomed and cut. Lucidity was the enemy. When lucid, Todd could charm the skin off a snake.

Kelsey prepared for the worst. Whether lucid or not, Todd only had one way of thinking: his. Unfortunately for Kelsey, his truth changed like the tides.

"Is it him?" Nathan asked anxiously.

"I can't do this," she muttered. If there were any way out but the front door, she would have taken it.

"Mom, he came all the way across the world."

She felt Nathan's frantic energy. *It's starting again.* "I don't care!" she snapped at her son. Todd would inevitably keep his cool while she grasped desperately for reality.

"Kelsey," Todd said from the other side of the door. "I can hear you talking. Open this door." He pounded his fist against the door. "What is wrong with you?"

"Why are you here?" she said breathlessly as she wrapped her arms tightly around Nathan's chest.

"I'm not going away. I've come all the way from Laos to see my kids and if I have to knock this door down, I will. Now, open this door before I call the police."

Kelsey prepared for the worst. She hadn't time to gird herself against Todd's version of reality and she knew how easily she fell into the rabbit hole. She hadn't played his games in so long, she wanted to forfeit before they started again and she was begging for mercy.

"Mom, he's waiting!" Nathan said as he wrangled free. He reached for the doorknob, and with her son's small betrayal, her knees buckled.

The sight of Todd caused her body to hum with tightness. Her emotions slipped down a familiar slope of numbed existence, where he couldn't access the part of her that was still alive. He had such a strong essence, an overbearing, unwilling-to-share-space air about him that made her feel smaller in his presence.

"Dad!" Nathan opened his arms, and Todd slapped him on the shoulder. It was an awkward movement choreographed to avoid touch. Todd never could handle human contact. Early in their courtship, she'd taken that to mean he respected her. She rolled her eyes at the ill-conceived notion.

"Nathan, you've grown like a weed!" he said, with all the normality of a special holiday visit by Santa himself, not a father who'd removed himself from his children's lives for nearly two years. He wouldn't make eye contact with Kelsey, and she tried to force his gaze to hers, so he'd know she wasn't the same weakened woman he'd left behind. She knew eye contact was his kryptonite. The one deficit he carried no matter what state his mind he was in at the time.

"Kelsey," he said, as his eyes scanned her body without meeting her eyes. "You're not running anymore, I take it?"

"Somehow it slipped from my schedule."

"Self-control is everything in this life, Nathan. Don't forget it. You can't have what you want in life without self-control." He drew up his shirt and touched his taut, muscular belly. "Look at that six-pack. No one would ever guess my age." He let his eyes drift to her hips. "Taking pride in oneself is not something that ends simply because you get married. God gave us these vessels to care for."

"Dad, did you bring me anything?"

"Son, I'm here for Meagan. I didn't have time to shop."

"Yeah, I knew that," Nathan said, and Kelsey felt the boy's inflicted shame.

Todd threw a soft punch at his son's belly. "Feeling a little jiggly there, son. What sports are you playing?"

She knew the comment was meant for her alone. A barb meant to denote that he knew there were Pop Tarts in the cupboard and ice cream in the refrigerator.

"It must be nice to have time to keep a six-pack. Some of us work to feed our families. Not much time for balanced meals and preening like a lovesick peacock."

Todd ignored her. "Never use excuses, son. Excuses are just that. They are reasons that the weak cannot keep up with the rest of society." He cocked an eyebrow toward her.

She wanted to let him know there were benefits to gaining weight. Todd had never loved her like Ben & Jerry had.

"Nathan," Todd shook his hand in Nathan's hair. "Nathan tells me he's very interested in the things of the Lord. Kelsey, I thought we'd agreed when we married that we would raise our children in a godly household."

"I thought we agreed to be married too, but life doesn't always work out the way you planned."

His mouth flattened, "Here we go again. You're putting down my ministry yet again, and in front of my son."

"I'm sorry. Forget I said anything."

"I told Nathan," Todd went on, "That God will allow very few of those called into the Kingdom. People are out there living practically like atheists, calling themselves chosen. I told him, 'Son, none of those people will see the Kingdom. God wants to see action on our parts. That's how He separates the wheat from the chaff."

"Todd, do you mind?"

"What? Don't you want to see your children saved? Or do you want them burning in eternal separation from their Maker with their defiant mother?"

"Can we not have this conversation now?" How many ways could that man tell her she was going to hell? Didn't he ever tire of it?

Todd's eyes flashed and he went back to his former sermon. "Just so you don't let the kids gain weight. Every day is a choice, Kelsey. You are choosing to be too busy to prioritize food. You'll saddle them for life with those extra pounds. Did you know children who are obese are now showing signs of high cholesterol and Type II diabetes? It's criminal. Parents are killing their children. Seriously, parents should be prosecuted."

*Like when they abandon them and leave them without health insurance?* "You're going to give me parenting tips?" She took a deep breath and loosened her muscles. *Breathe*, she told herself. *Breathe; let it slide off your back.* "Well, as you can see, Nathan's weight is fine, and I think you'll find Meagan to your liking if you swirl her bouquet," she said in reference to his love of wine tasting, which became a sin of the worst measure a few years later when religion became his newest addiction.

"It's more important for Meagan. No one will date her if she has extra pounds in high school. They'll write horrible things about her on her Facebook page. I've seen this happen."

Her jaw dropped. "No one will date her? So an overweight person has never ever been on a date in high school? I think we should alert the media! That's big news."

"Can we go out to dinner tonight, Dad?" Nathan cut her off. "To celebrate your coming home? We could still go to our old pizza place, remember?"

"Pizza?" His lips curled in disgust. "Eating out is one of the primary causes of weight gain in children. Fast meals, foods drained of their nutritional values and laden with fat, it's an equation for disaster. They don't have these problems in the East. You'd love it there, Nathan. People have time for God. They have time for health. They aren't rushing everywhere trying to avoid God's Word."

"Have you put an end to crime, as well as fat?" She despised that side of her. The one that heard something barbed in his every comment. Granted, she knew he meant them, but it still did her no good to stoop to his level. People only saw her as cruel and paranoid. In fact, those had been Pastor Underwood's exact words.

"Ever the sarcastic one, Kelsey." Todd grinned. "Mock me, but order and schedules are the most important things for children. They need continuity. There have been so many studies about how consistency helps a child thrive."

"Like continuous health coverage. I couldn't agree more." Honestly, these conversations are what made her first think she'd lost her mind. Conversations were never reciprocal, never without a sermon on some perceived defect in her character. He spoke so rationally, so measured, and he said all the right things — actually acted as though he did them. After all, who could argue that children needed well-balanced meals and consistency?

His smug face went back and forth. "Kelsey, don't tell me that you didn't pay the health insurance bill," he exchanged a look with Nathan.

She'd forgotten how smooth he was, how easily responsibility slipped from his shoulders. In the past, in the name of submission, she'd let it go. Early on, she'd believed it all, thought she'd developed a memory problem and looked up early-onset Alzheimer's.

Until a simple diary of recorded facts changed everything.

"So Dad, it's soccer season," Nathan interrupted.

Kelsey couldn't drop it. "The separation agreement states you are the sole provider of medical insurance, and you will keep it current. Would you like to see a copy? I keep one handy for just such an occasion, like the other morning at the hospital."

Nathan grimaced at his mother. "Yeah, it's soccer season. You should come see me play Sunday. I'm a forward."

"Sunday? Kelsey, you let him play soccer on Sunday?"

"I assume you're here to see Meagan," she said, a faint darkness in her voice. "She's in her room, second door on the left." She followed him down the hallway. "If there's no insurance, you'll be responsible for half the debt at the hospital. All of it, if I choose to go to court. I'm afraid I had no choice but to sign paperwork agreeing to cover the financial costs."

He turned, his look menacing. Instinctively, she stepped back. "You can't wait to come after me, can you? It's like it's your favorite sport." Again, he focused on her hips. "Kelsey, when are going to do something about your anger issues. Isn't it enough you've gained the weight?" He clucked his tongue.

"Weight? I lost a good 175 pounds that I needed to lose," she said, adding in her head, when you left for Laos and took your baggage with you.

He dropped his head as if he pitied her. The movement riled her and she felt sick to her stomach that he could still get to her.

He gazed at her as though he felt sorry for her. "How is she?" he asked with all the oozing empathy of a soap star at someone's bedside.

"She's doing very well. Go see for yourself."

"I came as soon as I heard. I even cancelled services on Sunday."

"Services?" She knew better than to ask, but it was out.

"The women of Laos are very devout. They're not content to worship just once on Sunday. We meet in the morning, and then in the evening. It's like I was saying, people have time for God there. He is not some afterthought before Sunday Brunch."

"Are there any men in your church?" she asked.

"Leave it to you to take something good and beautiful and turn it into something filthy."

She took the attack with a grain of salt and noticed that he hadn't answered the question. Naturally, there were no men in his church.

"I'm glad you've finally found your calling," she said. "When will you be heading back?"

"Naturally, my first calling is to my earthly children," he said, as though he hadn't just up and ignored any parental rights when he'd taken off for another country. He looked to Nathan who had followed them into the hallway. "I had my entire congregation praying immediately. Those women are warriors. I intend to tell Meagan who is responsible for her healing."

"She won't believe you," Nathan said. "She claims it was Pastor Alex."

"Pastor — who? What is he talking about, Kelsey?"

"The family pastor from the last church you dragged us to." They'd never stayed at a church long, but Pastor Underwood seemed content to listen to Todd's corrections, so they'd managed to not get asked to leave within the first six months of attending. "Pastor Alex was on duty the day Meagan was brought into the hospital. She claims his prayer healed her."

Todd's jaw tightened, and she saw the muscle twitch. "I'll set her straight."

"Don't upset her, Todd. She's only been home for two days, and Pastor Alex was very good to her. He came to visit her every day that she was in the hospital."

"I've never heard of this guy. You let a perfect stranger near my daughter?"

"He's the protégé of your favorite, Pastor Underwood. The one who thought I might be possessed. Remember him?"

He grunted, but said nothing more on the subject. She stared at Todd, who didn't look a day older than when she'd met him in college. All the girls would swoon. *"You're so lucky to have caught Todd Mitchell,"* He'd said.

Yes, she'd thought later, like a terminal virus, she'd caught him. He'd been only charm and charisma then. She'd searched for signs of his critical nature early in their courtship, but Todd was so well masked, so heavily draped, he didn't allow anyone close enough to find his truth. As his fiancée, she'd been allowed to see what he'd wanted her to see. As his wife, she'd unearthed his flaws, and that was wholly unacceptable.

Todd rapped three times and then opened Meagan's door. Her eyes were wide at the sight of her long-lost father.

"Meagan!" Todd said, with his arms outstretched, but he made no move to hug his daughter, as he got closer. He sat at the end of her bed; his rigid stature rose above the bedpost. "How's my girl?"

Meagan, God bless her, had been born with the honesty gene, and nothing bothered Todd more than a truth different from his own, so Kelsey stood watch.

"I'm fine," she said as though they were casual acquaintances. "You?"

"I've been very worried about you. I booked the first flight I could to get home."

"What are you doing there in Laos? Do you have a job?" Meagan asked.

"Of course I have a job. I'm a pastor. It's more than a job. It's a calling. Sometimes, God's will overrides our expectations and delivers us into a life we'd never imagined. If I wasn't called, how could I justify leaving my family back here in the states?"

"Don't you have to go to school for that kind of thing? Pastor Alex went to divinity school after he already went to school to be an accountant. He said

God called him out of accounting, but he still had to go to school for it."

"There are lay pastors. Pastors like myself who bring real-world experience to a third-world country that—"

She couldn't listen to any more. She made her way down the long hallway and eyed all the things she loved. The cheap Ikea furniture she'd put together herself, the corner of board games she played with the kids – out for anyone to see – and the warm atmosphere that screamed *home*. It all looked different to her with Todd there. She saw the dust and the clutter – how there was cereal boxes right out on top of the refrigerator. And no one cared.

"Mom!" Nathan shouted and roused her from her thoughts.

"What is it, Nathan?" She ran back down the hallway.

"Mom! Mom! Meagan's turning blue!" Nathan shouted, and Kelsey sprang into action.

"Nathan, get on the phone and call 911!" She tore down the hall into her daughter's room.

## Chapter 12

Most pastors didn't make it three years in the profession, and at two and a half, Alex felt slated to become a statistic. Alex sat in the hospital's waiting room and waited for word on Crystal's sudden illness, which he assumed was only the stress from the day.

His mind drifted to the little girl Meagan, and why he couldn't get that family off his mind. Something in their shared moments in the hospital connected him, and he felt an inexplicable responsibility to them, that he wasn't done with them. His sixth sense never felt so strongly about anything before.

Pastor Underwood would have told him it was inappropriate, well, he knew it was inappropriate, but he was haunted by Kelsey's far-off gaze. The tale they told wouldn't release him from Christian responsibility, but he'd be loathe to explain it.

The feeling wasn't mutual. Although they'd spent the majority of last Monday morning together, he'd be surprised if Kelsey could have picked him out of a line-up. She looked, in a word; *traumatized*. He couldn't shake the feeling that his church, or the very least, Underwood, had something to do with it.

The doctor finally came out of Crystal's room, and Alex refocused on the reason he was there. "Dr. Mackinaw…"

Dr. Mackinaw, Dan's oncologist, saw Crystal as a matter of principle. He'd obviously grown very fond of the Tognotti family like Alex had.

The doctor grinned. "You're the family now?"

"I suppose I am. Everyone else is still at the park for the service. Is Crystal all right?"

"Crystal's fine. She's dehydrated is all. Probably in the chaos of the morning, she forgot to eat. I have her hooked up to an IV. She's getting fluids, and we've moved her upstairs to a room so she can rest. She flipped on the television and said it's been at least a year since she saw anything uninterrupted. She's watching college football." Dr. Mackinaw bent toward Alex. "I think she needs the break."

"Got any pull to get me a bed tonight?" Alex laughed. "She was supposed to be my responsibility today."

"Dan wouldn't have asked you for anything if he didn't trust you."

"You don't have to soothe my feathers, that's my job. Should I wait?" What was the proper protocol for taking care of your friend's widow? He imagined Underwood had a manual on it somewhere. The longer he had this job, the more convinced he'd picked the wrong vocation. He should have stayed an accountant. Simple math, simple procedures, and then the day's over and maybe you watch a ballgame.

"I think it's best to keep her overnight," Dr. Mackinaw said. "I'm not worried about her physically, but I'd like her to build back her strength. She has a lot in store for her and she needs the rest. I'll write her down as severe dehydration for insurance purposes."

"I'll find someone to watch the kids. Thanks Doc." The kids. They had to be mortified. To them, the hospital was a place parents didn't come home from. He felt overwhelmed by the magnitude of Dan's death and protecting the little ones. "I'd better get back to the park."

The doctor kept on speaking, lost in his own version of mourning, but the ER doors and the familiar face on the gurney diverted Alex's attention.

"Excuse me, Dr. Mackinaw," he said absently as he jogged toward the ambulance entrance and drew closer to the patient. "Meagan?" The little girl's eyes brightened. "Meagan, it's Alex."

Alex's gaze came to rest upon Kelsey's hollow eyes. She wore biker shorts and a UCSC sweatshirt and her hair was thrown up in a loose, jangled mess with a yellow pencil stuck through it. Her face was naked and pure, free of any hindrance to hide her beauty. He heard himself swallow.

"What's wrong with Meagan?" His voice squawked. Not the manly, protective image he'd hope to offer. Something deep within him wanted to make Kelsey feel safe in the world again, and the feeling put far too much pressure on him.

"Alex." Just the way she said his name, with a new softness, embarked on dangerous territory for him.

"Mom," Meagan whimpered. "There's nothing wrong with me. Can we go home now?"

He looked at the little girl, then back to her mother, opened his mouth, but stopped short when he noticed Todd Mitchell between the automatic doors. He hadn't seen Todd for two years and wouldn't have thought he'd recognize the man, but on sight, dark memories rushed to his mind and he knew he hadn't imagined his feelings of impending doom.

Alex shuddered at the uncomfortable rigidity in Todd's stance. His form was like a male mannequin, wooden and posed. Todd was tall, physically fit to the point of irritability on Alex's part, and so very cocky. It was as if Todd was created to look down his nose at those beneath him.

Kelsey's eyes met his. Time stopped for a moment, as her green eyes seemed to plead with him. *She wanted his help*. He didn't know how he knew, but her silent plea came through as though she spoke loud and clear the way Meagan had done previously.

Todd posed in the doorway and raised his hands and his voice, "Heal my Meagan, oh Lord!" Todd walked towards them as though it was the most natural thing in the world to burst out into prayer while making certain all eyes were on him.

The waiting room had frozen at his outburst. Children sidled up to their mothers, the security guard at the door rested his hand on his gun, and Alex tried to make sense of the scene. He looked at Kelsey for answers, but she was questioning a nurse.

Alex stepped closer to Kelsey and Meagan. *Let no man put asunder*, a small voice reminded him, but an untold, stronger force held his feet firm. *Protect the widows and children*. He was at war with himself.

Kelsey visibly stiffened and she evaded Todd as though they were complete strangers, not people who had created a life or a family together. An invisible barrier separated them, and Alex took comfort in the sight.

Kelsey's eyes darted about the emergency entrance and she drank in everyone's reaction to Todd, once she was done speaking to the triage nurse, she stood outside the admitting window. Todd waved her off, "I'll take care of this."

"Sir, as I was telling your wife, your insurance isn't good here."

Todd leaned on the counter and allowed his elbow to rest as he moved close to the nurse. His voice was low and smooth. Whatever the guy was saying, he believed it wholeheartedly and from the look on the nurse's face, she was inclined to agree. The woman smiled up at Todd, her eyes wide and hopeful. She nodded and Todd seemed to garner energy from her reactions, his movements became bigger and more animated. In contrast, he noticed that Kelsey's arms were twisted unnaturally across her chest and while she nibbled on her forefinger.

Alex thought the man had watched too much religious programming. Either that or the guy had dreams of starting his own television ministry. Regardless, there was nothing authentic about any of his behavior, but the nurse seemed to notice none of it. Seeing Todd's command over the room, Alex felt the weight of what Kelsey must have endured. Or maybe he'd only imagined it because he wanted it to be true. He took the opportunity to approach Kelsey.

She gave him the slightest smile while watching Todd work his magic on the admitting nurse. "Alex, it seems we frequent all the same happening spots."

Meagan looked pretty as a picture and she smiled up at him with her mother's sparkling eyes. "Hi Pastor Alex."

"Hello young lady, what are you doing here? You're not sick again?"

The little girl smiled broader, while she shook her head. "I knew you'd be here."

He cocked his brow, "And how did you know that? I'm not usually here on Saturdays."

"God told me you'd be here," she answered matter-of-factly. "That's why we came," she looked up at her mother.

Kelsey dropped her gaze and followed a nurse who grabbed Meagan's gurney into the long hallway. "We're admitting her," the nurse said as she wheeled Meagan along the hall behind the double doors.

Alex trailed along behind them, as if pulled again by some unseen force. He turned to see the doors shut and separate Todd from them.

Soon, they were in a room and he stayed as though he was a. Invited and b. Invisible. A nurse plied Meagan with machines that took her vitals. Meagan pulled the cords off of herself before the nurse could get any readings and she grabbed the nurse's wrist. "There's nothing wrong with me." She looked up at her mom. "I faked it."

"You what?" Kelsey said. "You about gave me a heart attack, what do you mean you faked it? Do you think they'll fake our bill?"

Kelsey's eyes, a paler shade of green, but with enough brown to render them magnetic, burned as she turned toward him. He felt all the venom she kept slated for those who hurt her family, and he felt the weight of responsibility. Nothing scared a man more than an angry woman, and with Kelsey's glare, he knew why.

He touched her arm gently. He had no words for her, but she softened at his touch. "Meagan, what are we doing here then? We can't afford this. Your father is out there working to get the insurance reinstated. It will be at least a month before I have insurance at my new job. What could you be thinking?"

"Mom," Meagan said. "Dad was doing that thing again where he acts like he's having a conversation, but really he's just giving a sermon. You don't act right when he does that, and I don't want to go back to that mom," she sounded petrified. "I just wanted Dad to go away and leave us alone, but he wouldn't listen to us. Nathan was falling under his spell, Mom. You know that look and I couldn't risk it. I told Nathan I couldn't breathe because he thinks Dad can change."

With one glance at Kelsey, the nurses filed out of the room. Alex sought to calm the little girl. "Anyone can change, Meagan."

She met his gaze with all the wisdom of an elderly woman. "If they want to they can change. If they don't pretend to be someone they're not."

He certainly didn't want to give her any Bible quotations for the moment. Truth be told, Kelsey might slap him if he'd been able to come up with one.

"Mom," Meagan clutched Kelsey's arm. "Listen to me." She looked intently into her mother's eyes, "I'm trying to tell you. There's nothing wrong with me and I'm sorry I did this, but I saw that look in your eye and I got scared."

Kelsey raised her lids, flashed a humiliated grin and placed her hand over Meagan's. "I'm the mom. It's not your place to take care of me. It's my job to take care of you, so if you were worried, you should have said something."

Meagan shook her head again. "No, you can't see it. You all think I'm imagining it, but I'm telling you, he's getting to you. To you and to Nathan, that's why I told Nathan to tell you I was turning blue. Once you're under his spell something happens and I can't talk to either of you. I don't want to be alone again. I don't know why I'm impervious to him, but I am. God just made me that way."

Kelsey's voice oozed comfort. "Meagan'—"

Meagan would have none of it. "Nathan was talking about us being a family again. Mom, he doesn't remember and something's already not right with Nathan. Even before Dad came back."

"What on earth do you mean something's wrong with Nathan?"

"Dad's here for something and it scares me. Whatever it is, it's not good and Dad's gonna go after Nathan, I can feel it."

Kelsey rubbed the back of her daughter's hair. "You've had a frightening week. It's natural to have anxiety over seeing your father. It's been a long time, and we haven't had a man in the house other than

Nathan. I'm sure his voice sounds scary after just me at home."

Meagan crossed her arms and spoke at Alex. "She's trying to calm me down, but she knows I'm telling the truth. If something happens to her…it will be my fault."

"Nothing is going to happen to your mother. You can't be faking illness. If you're frightened, you need to call the police." Alex told her, but he saw her reject every word.

The little girl was vehement. "He'd never do anything for anyone else to see. He'll get away with it. Don't you see? If he can't get to mom, he's going after Nathan because that's what matters to her. He knows I'm onto him."

Alex looked for the truth in Kelsey's eyes, but he couldn't separate fact from fiction. Still, Meagan seemed so certain and she'd known he'd be there. How could she have known that? He hadn't even known that? But he'd seen too many Christians embroiled in ugly divorce battles. Whose to say this wasn't just another one? Two sides of the same wretched coin? No one was fully innocent in a divorce battle and maybe Todd wanted his son now that the boy was entering puberty. It made sense.

The door burst open and Todd filled the doorway. Meagan clasped her eyes shut and lay back on the gurney. "Insurance problem is all settled. I explained to he nurse that you tended to overreact, Kelsey. It was all a misunderstanding. With me being in Laos and the insurance company being a conglomerate, I suppose it was bound to happen.

No harm, no foul." Todd scanned the room. "Where are the nurses?" He called at the open door, into the hall. "Nurse, my daughter needs help!"

When the nurse returned, Meagan allowed the finger pulse machine to be attached to her. Todd's honeyed words of prayer came again and both Kelsey and Meagan stiffened. Alex tried to make sense of it all. Todd may have been desirous of a TV evangelical's job, but he didn't seem dangerous in any way.

Alex felt useless, but as he saw Dr. Mackinaw through the thin slotted window, he roused and opened the door. "Doc? Can you come in here a second?"

"Now Meagan," Todd said calmly. "I had an entire church praying for you." Todd's brow darkened. "You won't get sick again, do you understand?"

"I know it. Alex healed me," Meagan said, as if daring her father to challenge her. "I felt it. Mom felt it. Right, Mom?"

Kelsey rubbed her forehead and another loose tendril fell from the pencil over her ear. She sidestepped Meagan's question and spoke to Dr. Mackinaw. "My son Nathan, he's thirteen, and he said she turned blue, and I didn't want to take any chance because she was hospitalized this week with possible meningitis, so I called 911, but she seems fine now."

"No, of course you wouldn't want to take chances," Dr. Mackinaw soothed. "This is our little miracle, is it? I heard about you, Missy."

Todd strode forward and stroked Meagan's hair clumsily. His voice took on the tone of someone reading his child a lullaby as he mumbled a prayer. Her heart began to beat rapidly on the computer screen.

Dr. Mackinaw paused with his stethoscope in hand. "Would you mind stepping outside?"

Alex made a move toward the door.

"Not you, Alex, this gentleman here," Dr. Mackinaw motioned toward Todd. "You seem to be exciting the patient."

"It's been sometime since I've seen my daughter," Todd said by way of explanation.

"If you'd just step outside, please." The doctor put the stethoscope to Meagan's chest. "Breathe deeply."

Todd stepped out of the room, and there was an audible sigh of relief from Kelsey.

"Has he hurt you?" Dr. Mackinaw asked the two green-eyed girls who'd stolen his heart. "Has he touched you?"

"No," they both said in unison.

"So, you want to tell me what this is all about?" Dr. Mackinaw pulled his glasses out of his pocket and stared at Alex. "Are you trying to keep me in a steady stream of patients? Because I do all right, you know."

"Doctor? Mom… would you mind giving Pastor and I a minute?" Meagan asked the question as though she were a fifty-year old woman, and Doc laughed.

"Absolutely. I have cancer to cure anyway." He slapped Alex's back. "That church of yours all hot, single moms?"

"I guarantee you, it's not," Alex answered. "Most of them are old enough to be my grandparent." Once the room cleared, he looked down at the small patient. "Well? How are you feeling now, Meagan?"

Before the little girl had a chance to answer, Kelsey slipped back in the room and again, his gaze was arrested by her presence before he caught himself.

"Mom!"

"I'm too old for this kind of excitement. Honestly. If there's anything left in your college fund, it may have to go to the hospital bill."

"Mom, I can't help it."

"Honey, I'm sorry. I didn't mean it that way. I was griping out loud. Shame on me. This excursion didn't do a thing but force the inevitable." Kelsey kissed Meagan's forehead.

Alex wanted to go to Kelsey's side. He wanted to share his insurance coverage with her. He wanted to protect her, but Kelsey's husband was on the other side of that door. The thought of it tightened his jaw.

He wasn't that different from Todd Mitchell. Not really. He wanted what he wanted; in this case, Todd's wife. Well, the wife Todd discarded like yesterday's trash before leaving the country. At least, that was the story he wanted to believe. Either way, it made little difference in his position. He was a pastor. She was a married woman and in his denomination, even if she were divorced, it wouldn't have mattered. She wasn't available to him.

His stepmother would have called this a Superman complex and told him that a woman like Kelsey would have no part in his fantasies. Then, his mom would have rambled off more psychobabble about how men were shallow, and told him she'd raised him better than that. Jesus intervened before he went too far down that track and his mind snapped to the present.

The way Kelsey stared at him now, with mistrust in her eyes, his mother's echoed reminders resonated, and he repeated a favorite Scripture in his head. Kelsey cocked her chin slightly as if she could read his thoughts.

Like Todd, he was little more than a peacock strutting about, fanning his feathers. In his defense, she was the kind of woman a man wanted to impress. Innocence indwelled her and in her eyes was warmth and kindness, worn down perhaps, but still present. In fact, Meagan appeared more worldly than her mother in many ways.

"You're embarrassed?"

She clasped her eyes shut and nodded.

"Why?"

Her gaze bore straight through him. "I picked him." She side-glanced her daughter. "I did this to them. They bear the brunt of my mistake…my sin," she corrected herself.

"Let it go, Kelsey. It means you're human, that's all. Welcome to the real world."

Her eyes flashed. He hadn't reached her. He watched her long, slender fingers as they reached for Meagan's gurney, and he grabbed her hand in his.

"Kelsey," his voice was a growl. "I mean it, let it go."

She closed her eyes momentarily, blinking a tear onto her cheek, and he felt her hand close around his, and she tightened her grasp. A current shot through him. Kelsey's watery eyes looked up at him, and she nodded. "Meagan's right. He'll make me crazy again and I won't know right from wrong or up from down. Alex--" She wanted to ask for help, that much was apparent, and it wasn't something she'd been used to doing. She obviously didn't know how he could help either, but she was like a drowning woman, grasping, reaching for anything to pull her up to the surface. He just happened to be there.

"He won't make you crazy." He stated this factually, and in his mind, it was. He wouldn't let that man near her. Meagan was right about one thing. He did have eyes to see.

Her smile was sheepish, a virtual pat on the head. "It's subtle, like an invisible, toxic vapor...what if—?" she let the question hang.

"Not this time." If there were two sides to this story, he wasn't capable of seeing it and that's what frightened him. Something about Todd rubbed him the wrong way, not the least of which was the fear he saw in Meagan and Kelsey's eyes.

"Nathan doesn't see it, Alex. He loves our dad and wants to help him. I want to help him too, but I can't watch us all live like that again. Mom wanted to die. Didn't you Mom?" Meagan's tears ran unabated down her plump cheek. "No one sees it, but I know you're here because I prayed for you to come. You're the one. You can see, Alex. God's called you."

"Meagan, --" He felt a burgeoning warmth in his chest, but it wasn't normal for him to be a discerner of spirits. However, when he'd looked at Todd, he'd known the whole story. Not in detail and drama, but in effect and outcome.

"We can't do this again. Mom can't lose it anymore or we'll have nothing, no mom or no dad. God sent us you, Alex." She grew restless and desperate.

"I'm not going to lose it, Meagan. I promise you. No more. I understand now."

This child was nine years' old, and she'd been sick with a very high fever in the past week. He searched for any reason to disbelieve her. Mostly because he wanted so desperately to believe her. This situation was what every pastor was warned about. It could ruin him and yet, he couldn't have stopped himself if he tried. He'd never felt so strongly about anything before and he couldn't justify himself. Not to Pastor Underwood, not to anyone who believed in the sanctity of marriage.

"I don't want Nathan to go to Laos, Mom!"

Kelsey sat on the side of Meagan's gurney. "Is that what you're worried about? I have both of your passports. I have to sign for anyone to take you out of the country."

"He wants to go. You know how tall he is. He could just say he was seventeen and go."

"Nathan doesn't want to go to Laos."

"He does," Meagan cried. "He's saved over $200 to go and that was before Dad came to get him. Now he'll believe that he can save Dad and he'll be lost to us."

"Where did Nathan get that kind of money?" Kelsey's voice stayed light.

"He's been selling his lunch tickets and then he eats the leftovers people leave on the table."

Kelsey's eyes immediately floated behind more tears. "He does what?"

"He's eating people's garbage. Jaslyne Kimbert's brother saw him and told me it was true. That's why he got beat up last year. They call him Trash Eater."

"Meagan, I give him money for lunch every day." She looked to Alex. "He doesn't eat homemade lunches anymore. He claims they're for little kids and he likes the pizza they have at the junior high school."

"His money is in the bathroom if you don't believe me. Behind the broken tile," Meagan said, by way of proof.

"He's not spending the money I give him for lunch?' Kelsey looked mortified and kept badgering Meagan obviously hoping that it was all a story. He thought things were starting to sound extravagant; maybe Meagan was one of those children who needed excessive amounts of attention. That would explain everything.

Meagan shook her head. "He writes people's papers for money too. Sometimes at lunch, the kids leave special things just so they can make fun of him. Last year, they left dog poop in a fast food bag. Jaslyne said that's why Nathan threw the first punch that time he got suspended."

Kelsey sat slowly in a nearby chair. "He got suspended," she said to him. "I had to take the day off of work. Meagan, kids say crazy things—"

"Check the broken tile, Mom. What if Nathan has whatever makes Dad act that way? What if that's why he's so desperate to help Dad?"

As though on cue, Todd stuck his head in the door and thrust his hand toward Alex, "I don't think we've been properly introduced. I'm Dr. Todd Mitchell."

"Alex Bechtel."

Todd pumped his hand hard. "It seem as if I owe you a huge amount of gratitude for caring for my family while I was away."

Alex was in over his head. Everything in his mind told him to run, but something bigger drove him and wouldn't set him free. This family needed help. Kelsey, Meagan and Nathan needed Jesus in skin, but what on earth did that look like? A godly man didn't get in the middle of a family.

# Chapter 13

Kelsey unlocked her front door when her blood ran cold and she froze at the sound of her name.

"Kelsey, is that you?"

Slowly and with dread, she turned to see her mother in the dark hallway. There was no mistaking the perfume, the shrieking voice and the clang of gold jewelry.

"Mom?"

"You don't tell your own mother you've moved?"

"How did you find us?"

"Your old neighbor, that friend of yours — the one with the wild hair and crazy outfits—"

"Martha."

"Martha, that's right." Her mother unclasped her purse and grabbed a handkerchief, most likely to defend herself against the bacteria of the aged moss-green carpet beneath them. "Have you and Todd fallen on hard times?"

She hadn't exactly explained to her mother that Todd lost his job…or that he'd left them. She just continued to send Christmas cards with pictures of the kids and no rambling explanation as to why she or Todd didn't appear in the smiling photos. It was easier that way.

"What are you doing here, Mother?"

"I came to see my granddaughter. I have to learn on Facebook that she's been in the hospital?"

"I didn't realize you were on Facebook," she said to avert the subject while she jiggled the keys to avoid the inevitable.

"Of course I'm on Facebook. And the Twitter."

The hallway seemed especially pungent that afternoon, and she was glad she couldn't see the looks on her mother's face. No doubt her father would get an earful when Mother got home, "If only Kelsey had listened to me…you wouldn't believe the state they're in—"

"I should warn you. This is a new place for us. It needs work."

Kelsey realized she held her breath and she exhaled too loudly as she awaited her mother's commentary. When her mother visited last, her family lived in luxury; a five-bedroom house with sweeping, ocean views, a gourmet kitchen and the mirage of one happy, functional family. Back then, Mother droned on so about how the kitchen should be closer to the dining room. Well, now they were pretty much one in the same, so that complaint shouldn't be on her list.

Kelsey hoped Nathan hadn't made a mess while she'd been across the street, though she couldn't imagine why she cared. Mother would find something to devour with her eyes, it might as well be the mess.

Nathan treated the world as his garbage can. She could tell what he'd eaten just by following the trail…cereal box…milk…strawberry carton…orange peels…empty chip bag. It wasn't that he was careless or even disrespectful, just in his own special world where he didn't notice things like…filth. And when he was onto the next thing, what was behind him hardly mattered. She supposed Todd was like that too, only he'd left the remnants of a family, so Kelsey made sure Nathan understood cleaning up his own messes because it was her fear that he might instinctively expect others to do so through merciless genetics. Her heart ached at the thought of him rummaging through other people's trash to find something to eat. There was no earthly reason for it, so it made her fear the worst. Now that everything was at its breaking point, who should appear but her long-lost mother who'd been far too busy with world travel and hosting political banquets to be concerned with anything as mundane as grandchildren.

"Mom, this is our house now, and I'd appreciate it if you kept your opinions to yourself."

Mother shrugged her bony shoulders and the sound of clanging bangles followed. "What would I ever say? I don't understand how you failed to send your own mother a change of address card, but I haven't said anything about that, now have I?"

"I did. Thank you." Kelsey had usually walked into her condominium with a sense of triumph. She'd overcome abandonment and bankruptcy, to buy her own place and create a home with the small amount of money she'd stashed away when she worried that Todd hadn't been paying the bills. No luxury ever had more value than freedom.

She suddenly saw the house through her mother's eyes. With its moldy, old lady-smelling carpet stained with heaven knows what, and sprinkled with sand from the nearby beach. Without further ado, she pushed open the door.

Meagan and Nathan were standing in the living room like two lost urchins gazing at them with wide, sad eyes, not like the independent latchkey kids she'd raised. "Look who's here," she said.

"Grandma?" Meagan asked.

"Of course it's your grandmother. Now come here and give me a hug." Mother stretched out her spindly arms, and the cold, clank of metal offered no further indication of warmth.

Meagan allowed herself to be swallowed up for the perfunctory hug and Nathan stepped forward with his languid, boneless stride, but lost motivation on his way and crossed his arms in the center of the room.

"So Grandma, how's Boston? Is it cold yet?" Meagan clearly wanted to dilute the musty, tired smell of the condo, but her mother's eyes were wide as she spoke absently back to Meagan.

"Oh yes, we've had our first snow already. Had to cancel my bridge night on Wednesday. Is this the right place, dear?" Mother looked around as though some thug would enter the doorway and attack her at any moment.

"Yes, Mother. Did you see how close we are to the beach? The kids love it. They see so much wildlife in the Bay, it's incredible. Just a few seconds outside and they'll see a porpoise or a sea otter. Obviously, I have a bit to fill you in on. It didn't seem right to say all of it in a letter and I guess time got away from me. I thought I'd wait, and now look, here you are," she said too enthusiastically.

"Well, how long have you lived here?" Mother said from her upturned nose.

"Are you tired? Maybe I could make you some tea."

Meagan nodded too joyfully, and Kelsey realized how often she'd acted maniacally like that to improve other people's moods. It was a skill she didn't want to pass on. She wanted her kids to understand that just because someone threw a tantrum, it wasn't your fault.

"Sit down, Grandmother. Mom has taught me to make a proper cup of English tea."

"I'll put on the kettle," Meagan said.

The apartment still felt humid from her morning shower. The vacuum cleaner stood in the corner, a testament to all she meant to accomplish, but the countertops were cleaned and there wasn't a shoe on the floor.

Her mother politely covered her nose, so as to be unnoticeable, but she'd taught Kelsey the move, so it was hardly inconspicuous. "Kelsey, did something happen to Todd's position at the college?" Mother approached the small, bar-shaped counter for two that separated the "official" kitchen from the rest of the room. "I heard the housing market in California was difficult, but, dear me, this is quite the transition from your last home."

"Well—" she stammered.

"When's the last time this carpet was cleaned? Well, no wonder Meagan was sick. Kelsey, carpet is bad for children. It induces allergies, hides bacteria…you need to get hardwood in here right away."

"Right after I get the granite countertops, that's my first priority."

"Are you joking?" Mother asked. "I never can tell with you."

"Mom, I'm joking. Todd's not working at the university anymore."

"He lost his job?"

"Well, yes."

Meagan grabbed Nathan and the two of then stole away to the front door. "We're going to the beach," she announced.

"Wait a minute! Nathan, don't you have something to say to your Grandmother?"

"Hi Grandma," Nathan said without meeting her gaze. The two of them shared a rocky relationship if they shared anything at all. Grandma Dee Quinzel couldn't help herself to offering helpful tips to Nathan on his manners, most of which could be attributed to his shyness. A sensitive child, Nathan felt his grandmother's condemning stares deeply, and Kelsey couldn't bring herself to force Mother on him, regardless of how the woman viewed her son's manners. They were in direct response to Mother's obvious dislike of the boy. As a three year-old, he'd steered clear of her mother from the time he crawled away from Dee's outstretched arms. That moment captured their entire relationship, and neither one of them looked back.

Her mother opened her arms. "Is that any way to greet your grandmother?" Nathan obediently went to her and froze long enough to get a hug. "Your grandfather wanted to be here, but he couldn't get away just now."

Their grandfather hadn't wanted to be *anywhere* since the lunar shuttle landed.

"Where's Todd?" Dee asked.

"He went to the grocery store." She thought she might leave it at that, but Mother's gaze pressed her. "He's actually just returned home from Laos."

Laos as an excuse worked for all school functions as well. It didn't matter if he was there for a short time on business, perfectly reasonable in the Silicon Valley area, or if he happened to be there starting up an all-female cult. She'd grown quite accustomed to the skill of omission. She'd find another opportunity to interject they'd been legally separated for two years.

"We'll be back in an hour," Nathan said.

"Don't go down to the surf, you two. Meagan, stay with your brother. And here, take my cell."

Nathan grabbed the phone. "Mom, you have a text. Martha says Grandma is on her way."

*Blasted texts*. She never could remember to check them. The kids ushered out the door.

"Wait a minute!" Mother shouted in a low, authoritative voice. The kids silently backed up. Mother glared at her. "You're going to let them go to the beach. By themselves?"

"It's right across the street. They go every day. You can go stand in the bathroom if you want to see them. The window over the toilet." Her mother hadn't laid eyes on them for over three years. Not since they'd gone back home for a Walton family Christmas that seemed to put the fun in dysfunction.

"Even worse that they go every day. Someone might recognize their patterns and be casing them," Mother said. She'd lost the ability to hear the truth or have a casual, lighthearted conversation. With Todd, every sentence had a deeper meaning; a critical implication that would rise up like a blade and cut her, and she'd learned to hear everything that way. Even if the other person meant nothing by a simple comment. Listening to her mother go on, it was no wonder she'd selected Todd. Criticism was her first language.

"Mom!" Nathan whined. "I've been stuck in this house all week! I need air! It's hot in here." He looked directly at his grandmother. "And stuffy."

"Just go," Kelsey told them.

She opened the door to Todd, his fists on his slim hips. The kids whisked past him, but he was so focused on Dee, he didn't notice. He held out his hand to Kelsey. "I need to borrow some cash. I'm glad you live on the ocean. I'd lost my bearings since I've been here."

"You don't have any money?"

"I didn't have time to exchange it."

*In other words, no, he had no money.* "I'll get my purse."

"Dee," he said.

"Todd."

"I ran into that pastor from Underwood's church at the grocery store."

She stopped rummaging through her handbag, "Alex?"

"He offered to pay for the food when I went over, but I said I'd just run back here. Decent of him, though. I told him that you and the kids really needed a home church. He offered to let me stay with him while I'm here."

"Alex? Alex offered to let you stay with him?"

Mother stepped forward. "Why would Todd need to stay somewhere?"

Todd looked at her, but she simply shook her head. Let Todd explain himself.

Much to her surprise, Todd spoke. "I live in Laos. Didn't Kelsey tell you?"

Dee glared at him and Kelsey noted that for the first time, her mother might have seen through Todd's charming exterior. "Am I to understand that you don't live here with your family? What about your job at the university?"

"I'm a minister now."

"Is that so?" Dee didn't look pleased.

Kelsey felt ill at the thought of the two of them arguing and her mother taking her side — it was such an unnatural feeling, it robbed her of security. Todd and Dee had always been allies, they were definitely two negative forces, and together, they created a positive. Her mother and Todd loved the concept of achieving human perfection — usually by taking aim at the flaws in others. She worried the world might fall off its axis if the two went up against each other.

"God called me to Laos," he answered dismissively.

Dee wasn't as easily put off with half-answers. "What exactly does that mean?"

"Kelsey will explain. Kelsey, the money?" He kept his hand outstretched, and she placed a twenty in his palm.

"That's all I have."

"This is ridiculous." Dee rifled through her purse and produced two more twenties. "Do you mean to tell me Kelsey has been here alone with the kids? Kelsey, why on earth didn't you call me?"

The answer to that question seemed obvious. She'd made a mistake and she didn't want the painful truth used against her.

"She's been here for two years by herself," Todd sang with a distant nyah-nyah tone.

Mother dropped her handbag on the sofa, and Kelsey braced for her mother's lashing when the most incredible thing happened. "You left my daughter here alone with two children and no support?"

Todd flinched. "I was prayerfully supporting them daily. That's far more important—"

Mother snatched the money from Todd's hand. "Get a job. That's what I have to say to you. Get out of this house." Dee stretched out her gaunt arm and pointed at the door.

"Dee." Todd offered his warmest smile. "As an unbeliever, spiritual matters—"

"Get out! Don't try any of that pious business with me," she said again, and this time, Todd moved toward the door empty-handed. Kelsey actually felt sorry for him.

"Mother, he needs money for groceries."

"Then, he can find the money for the groceries. What have you had to do to pay bills all this time?"

"Well, I had to get a job," she answered sheepishly.

"Exactly."

"I think I'll take the pastor up on his offer to stay there."

"I think that would be wise," Dee answered.

The last thing Kelsey wanted was Alex's church having any more information on her situation than necessary. "You can't get a motel? I think Alex was being polite. He's very fond of Meagan."

"He wouldn't have offered if he hadn't meant it. I came here commando without money. I told God, just take care of me, and He has."

"By sponging off other people?" Dee quipped. "That's how God takes care of you, by transferring your responsibilities onto innocent bystanders?"

"I'm leaving. I don't need this disrespect. Now I see where you got it, Kelsey!" He slammed the door and she realized only half the problem was gone.

"Before you say anything, Mother—"

"Kelsey." Mother took in the condition of the sofa's ratty upholstery, and then lowered herself to the edge of the cushion. "Why would you keep something like that from us?"

"Because it gets worse, and quite frankly, there's no way you could understand."

"He's going through a mid-life crisis. Men do that, Kelsey, but you have to play hardball. You can't let him come and go like he pleases. No man respects a doormat!"

"Mom, he's not coming back."

"You have to forgive him, Kelsey. He's a good man. Lost his way maybe, but he's a good husband and father."

"Mother, he's not."

"You always were so particular."

Kelsey couldn't believe her ears. "I'm really not, Mother. If anything, I've been too forgiving, too willing to make something work that simply doesn't work."

"Not if you don't put any effort into it. Kelsey, a woman needs to stay beautiful for her husband, she needs to make the home a haven. I can tell just by looking around here that this isn't a place any man would want to come home to."

"That's a good thing because no man does come home to it. It's all mine. Would you like some coffee instead, Mother?" She started fiddling with the coffee machine, an old white "Mr. Coffee" stained with other people's coffee. She'd sold her Cuisinart at a Garage Sale. She'd purchased the machine at the Goodwill, a small fact that would have paralyzed her mother. No more fresh-roasted beans or home grinding. She bought the grocery store brand, already ground. Stale and pale, she called it.

"What happened to the sofas from the house?"

"We sold them on Craigslist. Well, and we had a garage sale. Bought a month's worth of groceries until I found work."

"I still can't understand why you didn't ask for help. I'm mortified at my daughter suffering through this alone."

She poured water into the coffee machine, giving up the idea of herbal tea for some power-induced caffeine to calm her troubled soul.

"Todd said he saw some type of angel who told him to go to Laos. Before he left, he went on some kind of rampage at the lab, destroying years worth of data."

Kelsey wondered if the "angel" appeared to Todd before or after he got fired. One thing could be said for Todd's rewritten history, it was consistent. He never questioned it, not until he found the need to rewrite it again. How she longed to make sense of it all, but Todd was never the same person twice. "Kelsey, he's sick. He needs help." Her mother surprised her with her sudden desire to fix Todd's problems, but then again, Kelsey would be viewed as a failure with divorce on her résumé.

"I know, Mother, but he won't accept help. He doesn't think anything's wrong with him. It's the rest of the world."

"That sounds dramatic."

"Does it?" Hearing Todd con them for grocery money made her question her own sanity. It was so expected; it hadn't even struck her as strange until she'd seen her mother's look.

"He must think something is wrong if he's married, but his family lives across the world."

"He doesn't see the connection."

Her body heaved an exaggerated sigh. To think she'd ever fallen for Todd's smooth lines forced her to ask herself if she had an IQ in the single digits. It was systematic though, his dismantling of her thought process. Opinion by opinion, she slowly shed herself, like a snake sheds its useless skin, only hers didn't grow back. The innocent, trusting Kelsey was long gone and that's what bothered her most. Or maybe her mother was correct and Todd would right himself for the right woman.

"What about all those church folk you two hung around? No one showed him the error of his ways?"

"They don't know the truth, Mother. They only knew the truth that Todd allowed them to see, and in that scenario, I was a very bad wife and he was a tortured victim."

"And in your version?"

She choked on the truth, which was knotted, in her throat and for the first time, in danger of tumbling out.

"Kelsey, I asked you a question. What is your version of why Todd chooses another country and a following over his family?"

"I'll just say that Todd has struggles, Mother. He doesn't know how to deal with them, and so he suppresses them and keeps busy. With religion, with rituals, with prayer. With anything that keeps him from facing his demons."

Her mother played with the bangles on her wrist and clanked them nervously. "You're talking in circles Kelsey. What is it that is stopping you from helping your husband?"

Her throat caught. "You won't believe me anyway, so there's no use in my telling you…in my telling anyone. Todd has covered his bases very well. All that's left with me telling my version of truth is Todd sending out the men in white coats. He's already had me taken in for a three-day evaluation, Mother. I can't afford to lose custody of my kids, so I can't afford to tell the truth."

"An evaluation?" Mother shook her head. "Nobody ever claimed you're perfect, but your father and I didn't raise a…loon! Why would you make up such a crazy story? Must you destroy that poor man just because you're not together?"

"It's taken me two years to get my footing again, and I don't want to threaten the health I've worked for. It's like an oxygen mask. I can't save anyone else if I can't breathe. Do you understand?"

Mother shook her head. "I don't understand." She pointed. "Now, don't get me wrong, I don't believe in any man not working. You heard me tell Todd off. Had that been your father, I would've kicked him to the curb. But, don't you love your husband enough to fight for him?"

"Mom, Todd is not husband material and I never loved him. I loved the man he pretended to be. I didn't even meet the real Todd until I married him. I was so naive."

"What is that supposed to mean? No one truly knows anyone until they're married. It's all well and good until you shut the door and live with someone's habits."

She turned, leaned against the counter and faced her mother. "Todd can't admit it, but I'm telling you with all sincerity that my husband is…he's…simply not interested in being married. At least not to me. To any woman, regardless of what his actions state." It was the first time she'd said it aloud, but she relived the shame of that truth as though she'd just made the discovery. Her story was as raw and wounding as the day she'd first faced it, that her husband was incapable of loving her because she was not what he wanted. His vile hatred of women ran deep and she felt certain she knew its source, but still had yet to say it aloud. "He was convinced getting married would make his uncomfortable feelings for women go away, and when I didn't, he convinced himself that he married the wrong woman."

"That's crazy-talk." Though her mom looked visibly shaken. "He's the father of your two children. Of course, he loves you. Or at least, he did."

Her breath left her as she realized how ironclad Todd's story was. He might have desired men, but having no proof of her reality was the apparition that haunted her home. How ironic that she proved the alternate reality. That Todd was indeed a family man.

"Are you implying that Todd has feelings for men?"

She could cite the reasons for her mother; his dismissal of her on their honeymoon, their lack of a healthy intimate life, Todd's inability to notice anything but her flaws and use it as his reason for not desiring her…

"Well, if that's the case, you have to *make* him get the help he needs. If he chooses to live a married life, then he's not gay. He's choosing otherwise."

*It seemed like it shouldn't matter.* She understood from the outside how it must look, but having lived with the daily rejection of being unacceptable to the person who chose you to spend their life alongside was a dreadful cruelty. *You are not woman enough to make him change.* "Now, he's chosen to leave." She walked to the door and held it open. "You know, Mother. I think I need some time alone."

Her mother awkwardly jutted her arms around Kelsey and squeezed. She stood stiff in the embrace, unable to contemplate her mother's affection or let go of the doorknob. "Mom?"

"There, there, dear." Her mother patted the back of her head, rubbing Kelsey like one might pet a big dog. "It's going to be all right. You'll tell him you're sorry and he'll come back. Marriages have these difficulties. We'll get him the help he needs, darling. You just leave it to me. I've had friends in rehab."

Kelsey ignored her mother's words and tried some denial of her own. She crumpled into the expensive silk, knit sweater and let herself be the little girl who longed for such a hug. She held on firmly, but life felt so out-of-whack, so wrong, she couldn't even find comfort in what she'd longed for her entire existence. After all, it wasn't real. Love didn't want a person to live a lie. Love didn't push her back towards a man whose seething hatred of her emanated from his every pore.

What about her? Did anyone care about her? Why was she expected to be Todd's Jesus and die for the lies?

## Chapter 14

Alex plastered a smile on his face as he opened the door to Todd

Mitchell on his doorstep. "You're here?"

"It's safer for me this way. I hope you meant your invite. I don't mean to intrude, but as you can imagine, Kelsey is not happy I've returned.

You know what they say about a woman scorned and she seems determined to teach me a lesson."

Obadiah appeared at the door, bared his teeth and growled. Alex felt the same way, but since he'd offered, he had no choice but to let Todd inside the house. He couldn't go back on his word, no matter how much he might want to. "Let me put the dog out back."

Todd was still speaking when he came back into the room. "I'm hoping to arrange a meeting with Pastor Underwood before I head back to Laos.

I think it would be good for him to talk to Kelsey about her hardened heart. A marriage can't succeed when a heart is hardened."

"I thought you didn't want the marriage to succeed," he said.

The man grinned as if he held some great secret to the universe. "I want Kelsey to know the Lord. I want to know that my children aren't being raised to think of their father…of men in general, as the enemy. Right now, I can't guarantee that. Kelsey's not in the church. She's not living a godly life and she thinks I'm to blame for all of her problems. What kind of man would I be if that didn't concern me?"

Alex's jaw tightened hearing Kelsey spoken about in such disrespectful terms — and by the man who had sworn to love and cherish her. Alex wasn't a violent person, but the idea of parading Kelsey in front of Underwood for another helping of submission-gone-wrong-talk made him want to hit something. "So you're saying you do want the marriage to work out then?"

"I'm saying that we could have worked on it if Kelsey's heart wasn't hard. There is no forgiveness in her soul. A marriage can't succeed when a partner can't forgive."

"If you want to work on the marriage, I suggest you move back to the States to be with your family."

"I did everything in my power to bring Kelsey and the kids to Laos. She's so defiant, and all she wanted to do was accuse me of seeing other women. I think she has some definite issues with paranoia.

When my son called me from the hospital, I honestly had to stop and wonder if this was another one of Kelsey's ploys to lure me back into her web."

"I thought you were here for a divorce."

Todd offered up a broken expression. "Is that what she's told you? That I've come for a divorce?" Todd checked out the pictures on the mantel before he faced him with a direct, hard gaze.

"I came to make sure my kids were safe, even though I thought this might be another one of her episodes and not Meagan being sick at all. I'm worried about her with the kids. She's so desperate for attention, she's been known to make these things up."

"Make things up? Like her daughter having possible meningitis?"

"I know it sounds ridiculous, but I thought if I got away from her, and she only had the kids to worry about, that her health might get better. But now, I fear that her paranoia may have returned." Todd dropped his head. "So she told you I was back for a divorce, did she?"

Alex didn't say a word.

"I'm more convinced than ever that the kids need to be with me. I thought if I got away from her and she only had the kids to worry about, her health might return to her, but now I'm hearing more of this paranoia, I'm more convinced than ever that I should take the kids out of that house."

Everything suddenly made sense. Todd wanted his family as living proof that he was a good man, a protective dad and most importantly, not a failure.

He simply didn't have need of Kelsey any longer. Maybe she understood that divorcing him gave him the ammunition he'd need, and that's why she said she wouldn't finalize things. The entire scenario didn't make sense to his rational side. These were the kind of conversations you had with friends of decades. Not a virtual stranger who took you up on a polite offer of a place to stay. Something wasn't right.

"Won't you have a lot to overcome with the abandonment? To get custody I mean?"

Todd's steely blue eyes flashed. "There's a record of Kelsey's mental health, and I know that Pastor Underwood would attest to the fact that she hasn't been emotionally stable."

"I've never seen anything in Kelsey to imply that she's unstable."

Todd shook his head sorrowfully, "Not even the creation of meningitis, then a false claim of a miracle?"

"*That* I know for a fact. There was a miracle," he said sternly.

"You see my worry. Now she's using the children in her game. Alex, don't think I haven't been where you are. Kelsey is beautiful and a man wants to come to her rescue and be her knight in shining armor. You think I don't understand where you're coming from?"

The red heat of shame washed over him. "Why don't I show you where you'll be staying. I didn't see your luggage."

"I don't have any luggage. I came commando — just on faith. I figured what I needed God would provide. The important thing was that I get to my children and fight for their health as soon as possible before things got any worse."

If he were held accountable for every ungodly thought that entered his mind, Alex doubted he'd have the faith necessary to get him to heaven. Hadn't Todd just said that he didn't believe Meagan was really sick?

"You said Kelsey refuses to forgive. What is it she won't forgive? If you don't mind my asking."

"Heavens no. I have nothing to hide." Todd spread his arms across the back of the sofa, but stood as Alex passed to follow him to the guest room. "Kelsey expected me to be perfect, and whenever I made a mistake she'd hold it over my head forever. There was no making her happy, and one day, life just got overwhelming. Once I lost my job, through no fault of my own, budget cuts you know, she was unbearable. I was losing my relationship with the Lord by trying to lower myself to her worldly standards. It was as if she was my god, not the Father Almighty. I had to get out to save myself."

"Understood." He led the man to his extra bedroom, which was a wreck of theology books, an old oak desk and a hideaway bed. "This is your room. I'm sorry I didn't have a chance to clean it before you showed up."

"No worries. I'm grateful to have a place to stay."

"There's an new toothbrush under the sink in the bathroom if you need it."

"So, do you think you can arrange for Kelsey and I to have a meeting with Pastor Underwood? I'd like someone to hold her accountable for working out the details to the divorce."

"I thought you weren't here for the divorce."

"I'm here for my family, but if it comes to that, I may have no other church. I can't speak to her rationally. If Pastor Underwood can get through to Kelsey, naturally, I want to work things out, but I have to be prepared to do what I must. If you'd arrange the meeting I'd be most grateful."

"I'm going to start dinner," he said. "Do you want something or will you be joining your family tonight?"

"Not tonight. My mother-in-law is there. I figure I'll give them time and maybe she can break through to Kelsey. Maybe her mother can help her see that family is more important than being right all the time." Todd focused on the laptop on the desk. "Do you mind if I Skype back home and stay in touch with my congregation?"

"Not at all. There's no password on the laptop." He shut the door, and a sense of uneasiness drenched him like the unruly spray of the ocean. He had no proof against Todd, nothing but his gut to go on, and maybe that was skewed by his feelings for Kelsey — another man's wife. The irony wasn't lost on him, but he remembered that Mrs. Willits called Todd "Kelsey's crazy husband," and that meant something. Right now, it was the only evidence he had. That, and his gut, which reminded him that Todd's story, didn't add up.

The door opened again and Todd stood before him with the laptop. "I'm going to sit out on the front porch. The wireless reach out there?"

Alex nodded. "Be my guest."

Kelsey's husband walked out the front door with his laptop, and it crossed his mind that it might be the last time he saw either one of them. He was infinitely more worried about his computer.

Alex opened the back door and was met by Obadiah who slobbered all over the hammered leather leash in his mouth. "No boy, no walk." He looked at his watch. "It's only five o'clock and I'm ready for bed. I still have a Sunday school lesson to prepare."

After a few minutes of respite in prayer on the sofa, the doorbell rang, and he realized his momentary peace was over. Maybe Kelsey was right; maybe Todd's presence did make one crazy. It sure made him confused.

Jessie Miller stood at the door, a casserole dish in her hands. Jessie was a solid girl who dressed in loose, cotton skirts that puckered under her belly. She always wore a scarf that seemed to purposely clash with the skirt, as though she was telling the world she wouldn't be confined by society. She never wore any makeup and looked and walked like a boy with her arms hulked out to the side. Only her skirts gave away her gender.

"Hi," she said, nudging her head in the house and looking around.

"You busy? I just met your houseguest. He came through the gate. Very impressive. I didn't know you knew any missionaries from Laos."

"Hi." Alex stared at Todd, tempted to say he didn't know any missionaries in Laos. He had a policy about women alone in his house, so he left the door wide open when she entered.

Even though Todd was there to chaperone, he could hardly trust the man, though maybe if Alex took his mind off Kelsey, he wouldn't feel so guilt-ridden about inappropriate pastor behavior.

"The funeral party was nice today. I'm sorry about what happened. We videotaped all the people for Crystal, I'll burn you a CD if you want to see."

"Nah, but thanks. Pastor Underwood will tell me all about it."

"Pastor waited for some semblance of order, but it never happened.

He finally threw his hands up and went home. I sang because I thought it added a sense of seriousness to a ridiculous situation." She pressed her bulbous lips together, rolling her eyes back in her head.

It seemed she suddenly remembered Alex planned the funeral. "But it was nice. Really nice. Dan would have loved it."

"He would have laughed anyway, and Dan loved to laugh." The two of them were so uncomfortable together; one could almost feel the tightness between them. Jessie didn't flaunt her availability to Alex and he felt relief over her casual ways.

They walked to the kitchen, as he assumed that's where the casserole dish would end up. Todd came into the kitchen behind them, unloaded the casserole dish from Jessie's hands, and took the foil off the platter. "Mmm, what's this?"

"Salisbury steak," she answered. "It's warm. Go ahead and have some."

Todd found the silverware without asking, which Alex supposed wasn't too difficult considering the kitchen only had two drawers. He peeled back all of the foil and began eating straight from the casserole dish.

"Jessie, you say your name is?" he said through bites. Alex would have liked to have said this was disgusting, but Todd had such an elegant way about him, he managed to make his boorish behavior seem polite and even encouraging. "This," he pointed with the fork. "This is incredible, Jessie. Do you cook for a living?"

"No." She blushed. Jessie hadn't seemed capable of blushing. "I'm a vice principal for a high school."

"Wow, this, and you work too? Doesn't seem fair that all that beauty and talent are given to one woman."

"Are women allowed to work in your church?" Alex asked, feeling suddenly protective of Jessie.

"Of course they work, Alex. How else would they tithe? This isn't the Dark Ages."

Stupid Alex. How else would they support Todd?

"Have you thought about your eternal destination? If you're on the path to enlightenment?"

She laughed nervously. "You sound like my mother, and she prays to crystals."

"I hope not. I don't believe in the power of rocks. There's only one Rock, and that's Jesus."

"You're a missionary?" she asked with too much interest.

"I'm someone who is here to tell women how God loves them

unconditionally. That He is here to be a husband to them, a soulmate. You see, so many women waste their days looking for Mr. Right, when He is there waiting all along."

Alex took note of how Todd used all the right words to lure a woman into his web. In fact, if he weren't so disgusted, he might have taken notes. As rough around the edges as Jessie might be, Alex imagined she dreamt of her wedding day just like the next girl. He caught a slight grin on Jessie's face, and he could tell Todd had come on too strong.

"Excuse me, but who are you again?"

"Todd Mitchell," Alex said. "Kelsey Mitchell's ex."

"Now hold on there. We're not officially divorced." Todd lowered his gaze to Jessie. "My wife is an unbeliever."

"I'm so sorry."

"I never thought I'd be in this situation. It's true, Kelsey and I were married, but our marriage will be annulled and I'm presently living in Laos. I've planted a church there."

"Annulled?" Jessie's face wrinkled, "Are you Catholic or something?"

Alex had to look at his feet to avoid breaking up. So now, he was getting an annulment.

Todd smoothly brushed off her question with a smug smile and with it, the inclination that she was far too ignorant to understand his higher ways.

"Jessie," Alex interjected. "Thank you so much for the Salisbury Steak." He ventured a peek at the dish in Todd's hands. "I'll see you tomorrow at church." He walked her to the door, his hand on the small of her back. What choice did he have? He offered his room. He stepped onto the porch with Jessie and made his excuses. "I'm sorry if that was awkward."

"No, he's lovely."

"Oh hey, Alex." Todd stuck his head out the doorway. "If you're leaving for awhile, can I borrow a pair of boxers?"

Alex felt squeamish, but he nodded rather than have Todd mention wearing his underwear in front of Jessie again. God providing. Honestly, in his day, they called that begging. At this rate, he might as well supply Todd with a cup full of pencils and send him out to the boardwalk.

"I think I'll take a walk. Be back soon." Alex shuddered at the thought that he'd come back to Todd in his underwear and made a mental note to purchase new boxers.

Alex walked Jessie to her car, a beat-up Prius that had probably been one of the first off the line. He looked into her eyes, which were a flat brown with no sparkle or life to them at all. Jessie had always struck him as stingy in every sense of the word. When she gave, she acted like it was worth more than it was. Like the seller at a garage sale who can't part with anything. Jessie didn't give of herself lightly, and being from the Midwest, Alex saw this as an extreme character flaw and one he'd grown accustomed to on the west coast. He knew the steak was more than a standard gesture for her.

"I'm sorry I didn't get to try your food yet."

She tossed a hand. "No biggie. How long is the missionary staying with you, anyway?" she asked dreamily. The fact that the man traveled without underwear did not seem to bother Jessie in the least.

He shrugged. "I'm not sure exactly."

"Well, you might want to find out before you run out of boxers."

"I just came over because you looked bummed today at the funeral. I mean, I know your friend is dead and all, but still, you looked discouraged. I wanted to let you know that you did a great job leaving with Crystal. That was the right thing to do. My mom and I both said so."

"That's nice to hear, thank you."

"You're more of a behind-the-scenes guy anyway, so I guess the funeral happened the way it was supposed to."

"Oh?"

"I have to run," Jessie said. "Have fun with your friend. Good looking guy." Her car door lurched open, and she threw a knit purse onto the passenger seat. She grinned up at him, slammed the door and sped off. He stood and stared at the empty street before him. A behind-the-scenes guy? Was that what he was? How did he use his teaching gifts like that?

Todd stood on the porch again, his fork perched in the casserole dish. Alex's life made no sense. Todd Mitchell was back from the dead, with his squirrelly smile and slithering walk, his boisterous laugh and desperate need for approval from everyone within a five-mile radius.

Alex relived the way Meagan reacted to her father, and he knew the child had been given discernment for a good reason. The temptation to call Kelsey and check on her was drowning out the voice.

## Chapter 15

Fall arrived in full. A rogue wave exploded over the cliff and onto the bicycle path, landing in a white spray on the road just as Alex dodged the sheet of water. The wave's strength was like an industrial clicking sprinkler – the kind he and his brother would hold each other next to the stream until their shins became red with pain. Like a badge of honor, they wore their strawberry bruise home with pride, each claiming to their stepmother that theirs was worse.

"Well," she'd say. "I think you're both dim-witted for doing such a thing."

Their father would laugh. "Not dim-witted, honey. Just boys. Be glad they're not setting anything on fire. That's what my brother and I did."

He and Adam would look to one another and laugh. They figured setting plastic army men on fire in the field hardly counted, so why cop to it?

He missed his family, and as the holidays approached it always seemed lonelier in California. After two years in his position, nothing had changed in his life, and he wondered if he hadn't misunderstood God's prompting to leave the Midwest. Maybe that's why his morning jog was easier without Obadiah along, though he felt guilty when the dog moaned mightily. He needed time to think, and keeping Obi in check was like herding cats. After two nights with

Todd in the house, he needed time alone. He imagined Obadiah was just as anxious to escape, but God and he had some deep talking to do, and he wouldn't stand for Todd's interruptions. The man knew no boundaries.

As he finished up his run, he sat on the bench overlooking the ocean. Drops of water seeped into the back of his pants, and he laughed at the thought of looking as though he'd wet his trousers. An appropriate beginning to his Monday after a weekend without relaxation. He checked his watch and noted, it was only 7 a.m. and already he felt worn from the endless discussion back at the house. He was swiping his backside when he heard a voice.

"Alex?"

He tilted his gaze up, and Kelsey's brilliant eyes came into view. The way her presence touched him seemed supernatural, and he wondered if God's healing of Meagan had something to do with their connection. He blinked a few times to make certain he wasn't dreaming. Her dark hair whipped in the wind, and she matted it down with her hands, but her actions proved futile. She soon gave up the fight and let the wind blast the wayward strands.

"Kelsey…you're jogging?"

She shrugged her tiny shoulders. "I thought it might help me focus again. When Todd's around, I tend to get confused."

"I can imagine." He wanted to tell her that he couldn't hear himself think in Todd's presence. That he understood what she'd been talking about — that no one could really understand unless they'd spent inordinate amounts time with Todd — when he'd slowly let down the religious façade.

In public, Todd was the cat's meow, the charming salesman who could sell salt water to a thirsty fisherman.

"I don't want to interrupt," she said quietly. "I just wanted to say hi and thank you for hosting Todd. We wouldn't have had room for him." She grinned. "Not in my head or in the house."

He stood as she started to leave. "Are you done running?"

She nodded. "I'll find another bench to cool off. I'm certain you've had more than enough of my family."

"No!" he said with too much force. He whisked the water off the bench, using the edge of his T-shirt to get all the droplets. "Sit down, please. It's nice to see a friendly face, and I was thinking about you. A lot actually."

He didn't know if he should mention the girlfriend that Todd spoke to every morning. Somehow, he imagined that Kelsey knew of the other woman, but he was reminded that she didn't want a divorce and he needed to respect that. Even if he didn't agree with it or understand it. The Bible said not to divorce, and he couldn't deny her interpretation of Scripture, even if made no sense to him.

He didn't believe a man like Todd wanted what marriage required, only the benefits that it brought him. When he'd heard him on the phone, sweet-talking another woman, discussing when the divorce would be final — the divorce Todd claimed that he didn't want — it enraged him. The truth was not in Todd Mitchell, but he did a good job of keeping up his image.

"I must look a wreck," Kelsey said.

He squeezed the excess water from the bench out of the edge of his T-shirt. "We're a matched set." He wanted to ask her about the separation, the annulment – whatever Todd had asked her for on that particular day, but he feared he cared too much for him to be impartial.

He wanted her safe from Todd, but with the facts so dicey, he wasn't quite sure how to go about protecting Kelsey from something he didn't fully understand. He just knew he felt inclined to protect her.

"It's good to come out here and know you're not alone in the world."

She sat beside him with her long legs in oversized sweats. Her small frame swam in her clothing, and he wondered why she hid her delicate curves behind so much fabric.

She boasted a sun-kissed, olive skin tone even though it was late October.

His mouth betrayed their casual meeting because he simply couldn't figure her out. "Why won't you divorce Todd? He's been gone for what, two years? You could file and claim abandonment. You don't even need an excuse in California. It's a no-fault state."

She stared at him with a shy smile. "You wouldn't believe me if I told you."

"But I would. I've heard so many conflicting stories out of Todd's mouth, I'd have no choice but to believe you." Somebody had to be telling the truth, or something that resembled the truth.

"It doesn't matter really, does it? I don't want to shock a good preacher like yourself with my weird version of reality. Look at that sunrise—" she stared off into the distance.

He laughed at her words and she raised a brow.

"I only meant that I doubt you could shock me." A good preacher? He wanted another man's wife. That hardly made him pure in any sense of the word. It made him human — carnal— in the worst way. He hadn't earned her trust and if he were honest, he hadn't deserved it. Not when he, like Todd, had ulterior motives. Even if he hadn't voiced them. She stirred visions of a future within him, elements of commitment he hadn't entertained prior.

He shook it off. It was probably nothing more than the miracle in the hospital, the death of Dan. He was in recovery mode. That was all there was to it. Kelsey was unavailable and that made her the forbidden fruit.

She sputtered a few syllables and then finally spoke. "Did you believe in miracles before Meagan's healing?"

"Of course I did. Maybe I hadn't had it happen so literally, but I believed," he said.

"I did too. I believed God could overcome anything in a marriage, that it was sacred and that He could work anything out between two people."

"And?" He leaned forward.

"And God let me down. Then, His people let me down and told me it was all my fault. All I needed was someone to tell me that I wasn't crazy, that there was relief on the way. No one else had marriage problems like me, what was wrong with me? I needed to know I wasn't crazy. Why was that too much to ask?"

"You're not crazy." He finally understood what happened. She'd gone to Underwood for help and he'd thrown her under the bus. Just like Todd had. All she'd wanted was some compassion and she knew exactly what she received from Underwood. The same thing he did: a sermon about her fundamental flaws while Todd got a free pass.

"I think I understand. The church likes when things are straightforward. I think your situation may have been too difficult for Underwood to comprehend." He hoped his words offered compassion, some form of comfort, but they sounded hollow.

"You think?" she answered sarcastically.

"But I don't understand what's stopping you now. From divorcing him."

She stared off into the distance and shrugged.

"He's gone anyway."

Kelsey shook her head while she tied her hair into a knot to keep it from blowing. He waited patiently, but in fear she'd shut down again and he'd lose any sense of trust she'd developed.

"I'm afraid, I guess. The hell you know is better than the hell you don't. Todd says he wants the divorce, but he doesn't. It's like my whole life with him — one big chess game, and the fear that one move will be worse than the other. If he knows I want the divorce, or that I support it, he will deny he ever wanted it because then he won't be the victim. If I don't want the divorce, he'll hold it over my head like it's a prize I must jump for while he holds the cards. As long as my kids are minors, there's no winning."

"Do you want to win?"

"I want to survive." She shook her head. "I want my kids to survive. That's winning to me. It sounds so simple. I give him a divorce, and he's gone, but you don't know him. He won't give me a divorce. It will be my sole responsibility, and then, once I have all the papers drawn up, he won't sign it. He won't quit until he's got everything: the kids, the money, and the house so I have to wait until they're grown. It's that simple."

She sounded paranoid, and he knew that's exactly what Todd accused her of. There were two sides to every story, and he felt guilty for questioning her. But surely Todd didn't really want to see his family destroyed. Why would he come back and visit his sick daughter?

He reminded himself that Todd was carrying on with another woman. That would free Kelsey from her self-imposed jail, and he wondered if he shouldn't tell her, but decorum silenced him. He wouldn't be the one to hurt her further.

"I've said too much." Her expression seemed fearful. "I need to get back to the kids."

He grasped her wrist to keep her from leaving, and he immediately caught himself. "I'm sorry." He gazed into her eyes and pressed his palm to his heart. "Don't leave."

She hesitated in her words and he waited. He had unloosed something in her, and when he reached for her, she let his hand close around her wrist. Without warning, she wiggled free, turned and ran from him. His heart sank as he watched her go because he knew instinctively, he'd have to build the trust again — like a sand castle washed away with each fresh wave. He wished he understood what pulled him to her so easily, what made him want to protect her and free her from this responsibility she carried, but he feared it wasn't his to own and that he'd already overstepped his boundaries. Once across the street, she turned and faced him again. He looked down so as not to frighten her further and he felt her coming toward him again. She stood across from him, and he felt stray strands of her hair whip against his arm as the knot in her hair unraveled.

"Todd never had a long-term girlfriend before me. That made me feel special, but now I see that everyone else was smart enough to see through it. They saw the cracks there before they tethered themselves to the broken vessel. I didn't." Kelsey reached out, as though to touch him, then pulled back her hand.

"I don't have the energy to fight him any longer, Alex. I don't. I thought it was over when he left. He'd stay married to me and use me as his excuse as to why he was there in Laos. Why things didn't work out, and I'd be here with the kids. That's all I wanted." Her voice quavered.

He wanted to promise her safety, that he wouldn't allow Todd to touch her, but could he promise such a thing with the legal system? With Todd's rights as a father? He couldn't, so he stood there feeling as useless as the stone surfer up the street.

"I still don't think you understand grace."

She rolled her eyes. "Please Alex, can we just not talk about
    religion? There's this whole world that goes on outside of what you
    people do at church. Can't you ask me about the weather? Or how I drive to work? Something

mundane and not like everything is dependent upon my eternal choices."

"I'm not preaching at you, Kelsey. I'm empathizing with you. I don't think you've ever known grace, so how could you possibly understand that the gift is free?"

"Nothing is free. And quite frankly, God costs too much."

"The most important things are free. The weather, how you get to work, your kids…eternal life." He couldn't help himself.

They sat then, staring out at the ocean, both of them lost to their own thoughts for the moment.

"Pastor Underwood empowered him, and that made life unbearable at home. Whatever the guy's intentions, he did the work of the devil. At the very least, he shouldn't have made things worse and there was no acknowledgment, no apologies."

"I'm apologizing Kelsey. For everything my church unwittingly did, I'm apologizing. Had I known, I would have come to your rescue immediately."

Kelsey shrugged. "Pastor Underwood is human. He fell for Todd's sympathetic stories… just as I did. I can't exactly fault him for that. He saw him an hour a week, I had to put up with him full-time, and he fooled me for a very long time. Underwood wasn't the final straw."

"He wasn't?"

"I had a ladies' Bible Study. Back then, those women were my lifeline to the world. During prayer time, I finally got up the courage to share what it was really like at home. Not everything, just what he was unhappy about with how I raised the kids."

"And?"

"Pastor Underwood's wife, who I respected a great deal. She said, well, why would a husband act like that towards his wife? You must be doing something to provoke him.'"

Alex couldn't hold back, he reached for her hand and grasped it in his. It wasn't romantic in nature, it was a comfort, to let her know that he heard her cries. "That's when you left?"

She laughed again, that sweet melodic sound he'd grown to love in their short acquaintance. "No, I'm afraid I'm a much slower learner than that."

"So then what?"

"I learned to keep my mouth shut. I learned to keep the secrets like everyone wanted me to do. I learned to stop trusting. Then, I dropped my Bible, and it opened to this passage, about a man giving his son a snake instead of a fish."

"Which of you fathers, if your son asks for a fish, will give him a snake instead?"

"Right," she said. "That one. Reading that verse, I figured out that Todd would have given Nathan a snake and told him all the reasons why it was just as good or better than the fish. My world snapped into view right then. I realized that it wasn't me. A man who didn't want good things for his children, better things than he himself had, it was his problem. Suddenly, it didn't matter to me what anyone at your church thought."

"I take it back. You understand grace. You understand how to extend it, just not to give it to yourself."

She pursed her lips, and he decided it best to change the subject.

"Everything okay with Meagan?"

She nodded. "She's fine. I'm sorry, you probably came out for some air too, and here I am filling it with all this negative conversation."

"You don't have to apologize to me, you know." Their eyes caught, and an invisible energy passed between them, an understanding that went beyond the normal lines of communication. He worried she'd close herself off again, like a sea anemone that perceives a threat. He reached for her three fingers as they retreated, and he studied her elegant hand by the gentle curves

visible underneath his own. She shook. Or was it him? He'd never

felt this attraction for a woman before as if her hand belonged in

his, small and dainty…waiting to be cherished. Neither of them dared to look at each other. Until she finally spoke.

"I knew I'd go to hell for my choices," she said. "But I don't care. I won't let him to do my children what he's done to me." Her eyes pooled with tears, and he pressed a thumb gently to her cheek and wiped a droplet away.

"Nothing," he started. "Neither death nor life, neither angels nor demons, neither the present nor the future, nor any powers, neither height nor depth, nor anything else in all creation will be able to separate us from the love of God that is in Christ Jesus our Lord." He quoted the verse from memory, and he noted her shoulders softened a bit. It gave him courage. She hadn't given up hope yet. That small kernel of hope.

"I can't trust in the invisible anymore. I trusted in this love and this sacred vow I made in front of all these people. Maybe other people get married and it doesn't work out and they move on. I'm not like that. I meant that vow until death do us part. I meant that promise and my world crumbled around me while I tried to keep it."

"You forget, I've met your husband. His love costs something. God's not like that. Think about your kids. Would you give up anything for them?"

"My very life if I had to," she said without pause.

"That's just how God feels about you."

Her eyes changed colors, a more brilliant green illuminated behind a fresh wall of tears. "You're determined to get me back to church, aren't you?" She laughed with a hiccup.

"I'm determined to show you who God really is. Honestly, I think that's why I might be here. I can't think of another reason that God brought me out to California. I've been without a path."

"I want to enjoy life again. Remember what it feels like to laugh, really laugh from the belly and not worry that he may have heard and I'll hear how evil my laughter sounds. I don't want to live by a bunch of rules and regulations and be around more people who judge me. It's taken me years in counseling groups to find out what I really wanted, and for the first time in my life, I don't want to run. I don't imagine escaping to a private beach any longer, never to be heard from again, and now he's back, and I want to run all over again." She spoke quietly, but loud enough for him to hear when the waves crested and crashed beneath them.

"So what is it you want?"

"I want to taste normal again. I want to buy a nightgown and not think about if Todd will approve of the color, or make me take it back because it's showing too much skin."

"A nightgown?" he questioned. "I didn't realize men wanted a nightgown to not show too much skin." He turned crimson speaking his thoughts and wished immediately he could suck them back in, but her tinkling giggle came through again.

"That's exactly why I want a taste of normal. I want more days where I don't have to do the math on the outcomes of all such decisions. I didn't take full advantage of it while he was gone. I was actually starting to not question everything I did on a momentary basis and the regrets…they practically stopped. Suddenly, I found out if I spent too much money that month, the kids and I had to find a way to eat, – so I learned the next month not to spend that much money. Do you see what I mean?" His thoughts were hardly Christian. He was still fixated on the nightgown conversation. He wanted to tell her to chuck the whole idea of nightgowns altogether. His carnal man was so near to the surface when he was around her. He could quote verbatim all the reasons he shouldn't be here, but those thoughts dwelled beneath the surface of his desire to be nowhere else but as close to her as possible.

"So, tell me something normal," she said. "What do you do in your free time when you aren't preaching to distraught single women and healing children?"

"I walk on water," he quipped

"That's not even funny."

"No, it's not. Sorry. I set up appointments with Pastor Underwood and fallen church members as an example."

"No," she said with both palms raised. "I wouldn't show up."

"Not you, Kelsey. Todd. We're meeting tomorrow morning with Mel."

"Both of you?"

"Yeah, why?"

"He won't listen. He'll lawyer up if he knows I've even thought of divorcing him and I'll lose everything I've worked for in the last two years."

"He might listen. We'll pray."

"Honestly, I hope you do get through to Todd. I hope you find him underneath that mess, but I refuse to enter the lion's den again. This is why that pastor's wife shot him, you know?"

"I'm sorry?"

"Oh they'll forgive her for killing a man, but not for divorcing him. Todd knows that." She rose from the bench, her hard exterior resurrected, the sand castle he'd built so carefully washed away.

He stood up beside her. He felt guilty to realize he'd never thought of reconciliation, never crossed his mind. His motive was to destroy Todd's cult before he caused further damage. He'd heard in seminary that people who fall for cults weren't stupid. A charismatic leader knew just how to reel them in, how to target their weak spots.

"You were attracted to Todd's leadership skills?"

"I'm 34 years old, Alex and I'm just now learning to think for myself. It's sad, really, but I will not give up my freedom again."

"I never thought of reconciliation." He looked out over the bay and a dolphin leaped just as he turned. "Did you see that?"

"You never thought of it," she said, thrusting a hand to her hip. "Really?"

"Really. I never thought of it because if I'm honest Kelsey—" he let it drop, but his eyes said what his mouth didn't. He emptied any thoughts of her in his life. He too, had treated her like an object and as he stood looking into her eyes, he confessed it to the Lord. His tongue was in knots and he stumbled to find a new subject. "Did you go to school?"

"Harvard. I didn't finish so don't be impressed, and I think my father may have paid someone off to get me in there."

"You sell yourself way too short. Do you always do that?"

"I don't need to. People around me do it for me." She laughed, but he didn't find any humor in her words. As the resident 'nice guy', he didn't understand why girls like Kelsey ended up married to men like Todd. It was all too common, and it made guys like him want to throw in the towel.

"Then you should surround yourself with better people. Honestly Kelsey, since we're steering clear of the God subject, if I had a shot with a woman like you, I'd tell her every day how lucky I was and to not even to think of nightgowns." Todd's an idiot and a moocher, he wanted to add, but he'd let Todd mooch for as long as he stayed. It was worth it, to keep him away from Kelsey and protect her in the only way he could, other than prayer.

"You say that. All men say that before they get to sleep with a woman, but then real life starts. The babies cry at night, the diapers cost more money than solid gold, the newspaper doesn't come in the morning, the kids barf on your shoes, and oh yeah, my California mission project is due tomorrow. You won't have time to tell your wife she has vomit in her hair, much less that you love her. Life just goes too fast for those niceties."

"No, it doesn't." Her eyes, the most beautiful shade of green he'd ever seen, appeared as small inlets, and he forced his hand down, rather than wipe her tears away again. Touching her moved him in a way he couldn't play with. "Kelsey, it doesn't. I saw my grandfather pick up my grandmother's frail, cancer-ridden body and take her to the bath until she left this earth. That's how you treat people you love.

No, it isn't always pretty, but that kind of love is truly beautiful."

The pools in her eyes increased and she turned away from him. He never wanted to see the woman he loved with this kind of sadness in her eyes. "I can't even imagine that." She shook her head. "Not in my wildest dreams."

"May you dream bigger then. My grandfather told me to find someone I could love through anything, and then to just do it. He was way before Nike's time."

She stared at him while she pulled her hair off her face and locked it up in a clip. "That's an incredible gift, Alex. You'll make some girl a very nice husband if you do just that." The way she said the words, in a motherly tone, bothered him. She thought of him as

nothing more than an innocuous friend. No threat whatsoever to her, and while that should have filled him with security, he agonized over the truth of his situation. She'd handed him the friend card.

Kelsey Mitchell was still a complete mystery to him. Maybe that's what he found so attractive. She seemed to harbor a secret identity within her, an unknown world, which made the Hardy Boy in him want to look deeper for clues and unravel her vague gazes and half-hearted responses. Maybe he was fascinated because she was off-limits and he didn't have to worry about any commitments in life. Isn't that what his stepmother always told him? That he couldn't commit to anything? Not a job, not a woman. Always made with the sad pronouncement that she'd never get grandchildren.

"Kelsey!" Todd appeared behind them. Instinctively, in a sudden flurry of protectiveness, Alex inched closer to her. "Kelsey!" Todd said again. "I've been thinking about dinner tonight."

"It's not even seven thirty in the morning."

"Hey Alex," he said coolly. It bothered Alex that Todd didn't have the slightest edge of jealous in his voice. Alex might as well have been a woman. He puffed out his chest in response.

"Todd." Kelsey seemed surprised by his presence and she sighed heavily. "The kids wanted a pizza. I was going to call it in on my way home." She mumbled the rest, "Not that I give a—"She wore her masked smile.

He peered at his watch. "I will be by the time you get dinner on the table. I wanted the crepes while I was here, remember?" Todd's voice took on a nicer tone, as though a child asking for more ice cream.

"We never discussed it," Kelsey said.

"We did." Todd turned toward Alex. "Kelsey makes these
 fabulous chicken/asparagus crepes I've been craving. I told her I've come all the way across the world for the dish."

"Asparagus isn't in season," Kelsey and Alex said in unison, before laughing at their sing-song answer.

"Is something funny?" Todd obviously thought they were laughing at him and his jaw locked. The ocean roared to life with a huge wave, and slapped water behind Todd. He jumped to drier parts.

Not since sixth grade and Joey Fisher carving a "J" in the back of his hair, had Alex felt the urge to fight, but he calmed down to find the right words.

"Being a farming community, we Santa Cruz residents like to eat in-season crops to support the local economy," Alex explained.

"Asparagus is an especially difficult crop for the soil."

"And it's been a particularly hard week for our family, Alex. I think the Lord will understand if we choose to partake of asparagus, whether it's originated here or a foreign country. Every good and perfect gift comes from Him."

"Everything is permissible, but not everything is beneficial," Alex shot back.

Kelsey yelled over the latest wave, "I'm just going to get a pizza tonight.

My mother offered it to the kids and it's been so long since they had it. I thought I'd take advantage of the offer. Alex, you're welcome to join us."

"They can have pizza when I leave, Kelsey. I've asked you for one thing since I've been here. You don't mind, do you?" Todd's tone had grown sharper, and as his friendly mask slipped, Kelsey stepped back and her voice became quieter.

"Actually, Todd. There's so much going on, I'd really rather not—"

"My church performs a miracle, you'd think I could get a chicken dinner out of it, wouldn't you?" Todd addressed Alex, and his words mocked Kelsey. Somehow, Alex knew that Todd wanted him to take credit for the miracle, but the truth was, he didn't care who got the credit, other than God. Meagan Mitchell was alive and craving pizza. That was all that mattered to him.

Alex knew his battle was not with Todd himself, but his struggle was with the dark world of spiritual forces in the heavenly realms. Which, in theory, made him feel better about wanting to beat the crap out of Todd.

It was apparent why Kelsey appeared the crazy one, the depressed one to Pastor Underwood. It was a hallmark of oppression. Todd Mitchell said everything in a persuasive monotone voice that epitomized logic.

Like Spock, he was void of emotion save anger and a seeming underlying hatred towards women. Todd sat in the middle of the wooden bench and stretched out his arms across the back of it like a demon with wings. "This cold spray stings a rainforest creature like myself. I haven't felt this kind of weather since I left California."

"Being from Michigan, I can't feel too sorry for you," he said.

"Did you want me to go with you to the grocery store, Kelsey?" Todd asked, as though it were a kindhearted offer, and not the subtle manipulation to get what he wanted. Kelsey rolled her eyes and walked away. Todd stared up at the sky, smiling to himself as though he'd conquered a great battle. Alex felt his battle was only beginning.

## Chapter 16

Another Monday morning. The days melted together like seaweed in a kelp bed. As though Alex's life consisted of pointless meetings, the dying and now, Todd Mitchell. With his unwelcome guest in the house for a week, even home had become a source of contention. Obadiah stayed curled up in the darkest corner of the laundry room, somehow sensing that Todd's nature shifted like the sand.

He'd made a point to avoid Kelsey after their uncomfortable connection on the beach. Pastor Underwood kept canceling Todd's meeting, not giving any thought to Alex's awkward living position. In short, the week had been the longest of his life. He'd never gotten a straight answer to the question did Todd want a divorce, and he couldn't stand that Kelsey might live in limbo while her husband went back to the women he'd left on the hook in Laos.

Life felt out of control and it was time he stood firm. Todd had commandeered the living room with a makeshift altar. "I'm going to work."

Todd slapped a Bible shut and looked up at him. "I'm heading home in the morning."

"To Laos?"

"Of course."

"Without a divorce?" He hoped he'd finally get a straight answer out of Todd.

Todd only smiled. "I've decided that would hurt my ministry. A man of God has to think in the long-term – in the eternal."

His jaw clenched. He wondered how the woman waiting back in Laos would feel about that eternal perspective. "Have you thought about Kelsey's eternity?"

"It is what it is. I'm a minister with a wife who's an unbeliever."

"Kelsey is not an unbeliever!" Not that Todd hadn't tried his level-best to turn her against Christianity.

"You seem to know an awful lot about my wife. Is there a reason you're so concerned with my wife leaving me?"

"I'm going to work," Alex said by way of crying uncle. "Tonight's dinner is at Mrs. Willits' house. I left the address on the kitchen table. Her house is basically next to Kelsey's condominium — you can walk there."

"I'm warning you as a brother. She'll ruin your ministry as she's ruined mine."

He stopped at the door. "If there were something between Kelsey and me—"

"You couldn't marry her anyway, because your church doesn't allow for it. I married her not knowing she wasn't a believer. You'd have no such excuse."

"It's crazy to even have this conversation. I barely know Kelsey. I'm concerned about her family because of what we've been through together.

Because Meagan and Nathan didn't have a father here when he was needed. They were abandoned."

"Abandoned?" Todd picked up on the accusation. "How dare you, when you sit behind a desk and do nothing more than Mel Underwood's bidding. How dare you judge me, an oracle of the Lord. By the same stick, you will also be judged." He pointed his finger.

"Bring it on," Alex said before going out the back way with Obadiah and slamming the door. Obadiah stretched and dropped to the ground and turned over to have his belly rubbed. "The stress is getting to you too, huh boy?"

He looked in the window and saw Todd stick his head back into his Bible. How anyone could spend more time in the Word and yet pull nothing more out of it than his own righteousness shocked Alex.

Todd Mitchell never slept. He literally stayed up all night, preaching to himself in the guest room. With Santa Cruz in the throes of Halloween, Alex prayed like never before. With a fervor. The entire town felt like a black cloud hung from the sky, stirring up the city. At night, he imagined the cackling covens nearby practicing their witchcraft while they slipped into society as if God had no place in the world any longer. He marveled darkly at how close the world had come to believing it. He walked back into the house and Todd looked up at him from the sofa.

"Be there tonight," Alex commanded. "The address is on the table. Six O'clock."

Todd's face took on a rusted stoicism — he was a man who bucked authority. Any authority, no matter how kindly given, no matter how much to his benefit. In truth, he hoped Todd didn't show. Then, he could have Kelsey all to himself. He gave Obadiah a last pat, shut the door behind him and passed the Lincoln for a chilled walk in the morning fog.

Alex still had no idea why he was involved in any of this, not the miracle, not the ludicrous houseguest, the funeral he'd botched. Life felt so random and disjointed. He couldn't even see the finish line any longer, much less know if he were still on the right path.

Women were a mystery to him. Even old Mrs. Willits got her groceries delivered and knew everything that went on at Santa Cruz Evangelical, though she never left the house and didn't drive any longer.

"Are you all right, Mrs. Willits?" he asked as he stepped on her property. He found her in her porch swing, looking wan and tired. "The dinner party is not going to be too much for you, is it?"

"Oh Alex." She patted the seat beside her. "Come sit by me, what's a little dinner party? I used to feed half the town when the church had its revival."

"I'm not sure this qualifies as a little dinner party," he said ominously.

"Because of the drama, you mean? You kids think you invented drama. Honestly, there's nothing new under the sun."

"Drama?" he questioned as innocently as possible.

Her face brightened and her wrinkles creased. "I'll never give up your secret, Alex."

"My secret?"

"How's Crystal doing? And the kids?"

She was toying with him. Like a lion with its kill, only far more devious. "Crystal's as fine as can be. I'm watching the kids for her next week so she can take care of some business, but then I think I'm going to plan a trip home to Michigan. Get out of here for awhile."

"If you think that will help."

"Crystal wants the kids to be around a younger man. I guess Grandpa gets worn from all the chaos." He tried one more time. "You're not going to tell me what you think my secret is."

"We both know it. Let's not pretend. There's a certain glow a pregnant woman has and one that a captured man dons. I've seen enough of it in my lifetime. You can deny it all you like."

His heart pounded. "Somehow, I think you've got an edge on me, Mrs. Willits. I'm not sure what it is. You're not a prophetess, are you? I've already got Meagan in my life for that."

"Heavens no, and if you think I'm as old as the Prophetess Anna in the Bible, we have another issue."

He chuckled. "Absolutely not. If I know anything about women, I know better than to discuss their weight or their age."

"Or their natural hair color," Mrs. Willits added. She placed the watering can on the grass and patted her swing. "Come sit by me. I won't bite."

He sat, and took in the view. The ocean calmed his senses, though he had no reason to feel relaxed. When he looked out at the vast blue, he somehow realized his place in the world, merely a grain of sand, so how dire could any situation truly be? "I wish your husband was still here to enjoy His creation. What a life you two must have had."

"I thought he'd live longer too. With all this salt water, we used to joke we were preserved well until the next life. We'd arrive pickled. But he was a hard worker and he rarely sat here with me. There was always something to be done. Not until he was older and he felt the damp in his hips. God forced him to sit more. Oh but listen to me, I'm sounding like one of those old women again." Mrs. Willits stared emptily into the horizon. She paused for a good, long time. "She's beautiful, Alex. You shouldn't beat yourself up. A man can't always help who he falls for."

"Who is?"

"You know who I'm talking about."

He nodded. "Jessie Miller."

She pursed her lips and all the lines radiated from her mouth like the sun. "I'm not so much a codger as to believe that." She waited again.

"Mrs. Willits, you're not climbing those stairs?"

"Well, the front door isn't coming down to meet me."

"I shouldn't be a pastor. My life is going to be half-way gone before I figure out what to do with it."

"You've figured it out. It's just getting harder because life isn't matching up with the way you've always seen it. It's not so black and white, is it?"

He dropped his head in his hands. "Nothing feels simple anymore. Todd's going to leave and nothing will have changed." He rubbed his temple. "But everything has changed."

She patted his leg. Though it seemed she ignored his topic, Mrs. Willits generally took a circuitous route to what she wanted to say. She measured each word. "Alex, if I had a grandson, I'd want him to be just like you. I think you can be anything you want to be. Not too many of us around who still remember the young Graham Underwood, but oh how he could set a room on fire! You've got that passion in you. I suppose it depends where you'll use it."

"Is that a warning?"

"Not so much a warning as a reminder. We only have so much energy to give to this world and it's up to us to decide where to expend it."

"Where do you think I should be expending it?"

Mrs. Willits shook her head. "They're not my choices to make. I've made my bed, and it turned out to be right comfortable for me. There's no one right choice, barring salvation, of course." Whenever he needed a good dose of realism, he knocked on her door. People weren't like that anymore. They were afraid of showing their truths, afraid of being vulnerable, whereas Mrs. Willits reminded him if you lived a good life, you didn't have much to hide.

"I think you're probably more useful now, than as a young woman. Look how many people don't have time for prayer, and you're a warrior over here in your swing. You're probably accomplishing more than ninety percent of us do in a day without ever leaving this swing."

For the first time, he noticed Mrs. Willits didn't appear to pay attention to what he was saying. Usually, she clung to every word as if it were spun gold. When Mrs. Willits listened, it was as if the world stopped for you, but maybe that was his problem. He thought too much about himself lately. How he came off to others, how he did, how he could improve. Me. Me. Me. And then, an echo, Kelsey, Kelsey, Kelsey.

Mrs. Willits stared off into the distance. "This swing is falling apart. I'm just hoping it doesn't give out before I do. I feel so close to the Lord when I pray here."

"I could refinish the swing for you and grease the chains." He looked closely at the fine workmanship that had gone into the swing. They didn't make things like this anymore. "You know, my mom had one vacuum cleaner for my entire existence. This swing was made like that. Built to last. It only needs maintenance."

"Ah, maintenance. An old person's worst nightmare. I'd rather have my own joints oiled than waste a can on this old swing. Waste not, want not."

It puzzled him how anyone he'd known who survived the Depression had such a difficult time spending money on themselves. Mrs. Willits had no problem suggesting he hire a gardener for his rental, but her own front yard, overgrown with wild bushes, she watered anyway, rather than face the real issue that she was too fragile to wield clippers, too frugal to hire a gardener, and too proud to accept help.

"Since you won't say her name, I will. Kelsey Mitchell."

Her name alone sent his body surging with electricity, but reality quickly thrust him back to ground level. Mrs. Willits gazed out over the ocean. She wore a mask of serenity and he couldn't tell what she was thinking. He wanted to shake it out of her was the truth, but he bit his tongue and waited with the patience of Job until he measured his reply. "Todd leaves tomorrow."

"Yes, our dinner party will be our last opportunity to get through to him." Now she looked at him with a pointed gaze.

"You don't believe it will happen."

He took solace in her statement and immediately felt guilty. "I don't know, Mrs. Willits. If you're a pastor, shouldn't your first concern be for people's eternal salvation?"

"It should probably, but then our humanity gets in the way, doesn't it? Always stopped me cold when some sweet thing flirted with my husband in front of me."

"You're trying to make me feel better."

"She seems so sad for such a young person. She needs healing, Alex."

"You mean, Meagan?" he asked hopefully. Though he knew exactly whom she meant.

"No, I mean Kelsey. You know I mean Kelsey."

"We have the opportunity to make things right for her tonight. Help Pastor Underwood see where he went wrong."

Alice rubbed her withered hands together. "Is that what you're hoping for?"

"Divorce happens every day. Why should Kelsey have taken the blame for the breakdown of that marriage? I've lived with him, Alice. He's deranged, and the only reason she won't leave him for good is out of fear. Why can't Pastor Underwood see that?"

"Why does it matter, Alex? You see it."

He looked down.

"Alex, she's a beautiful woman, there's nothing wrong with you noticing that."

There was. And he knew it because he'd done more than notice. In his mind, he'd planned a future. "What can I do? That ex-husband of hers is a Svengali of sorts. He never sleeps. I slept with a baseball bat under my bed, doesn't that tell you something?"

"Well, we needn't get into character assassination, Alex."

He felt chastised, but it didn't change his opinion. He didn't have a spiritual leg to stand on, other than being the Good Samaritan and protecting the weakest, and if that were his only motive, he would have slept peacefully at night.

"I was thinking perhaps you have the gift of healing, Alex. I know everyone is talking about young Meagan, but I remember Mr. Stalworth being released of his cancer and ol' Emmeline Lambert overcoming shingles. All after you prayed for them. Maybe you should pray for Todd Mitchell's healing. Maybe he's not right in the mind and that's why he was brought into your life."

"There's my good friend Dan Tognotti who I prayed for fervently, and he's dead."

"God determines who gets healed, Alex, you know that, but I got to thinking, what if God were to restore Meagan's family? To bring them back to wholeness. I think you should join me in prayer for her father to be healed and come back to his family. As long as he is still alive, there's hope for reconciliation. Can you imagine the victory?" She clapped her hands together.

Alex jolted and tried to recover. "Of course. Of course I should be praying for him." *Should* being the operative word. Maybe Todd couldn't help himself, but Alex had a hard time finding any compassion for him. Nathan needed a father. Meagan needed a male role model! It convicted Alex to realize he didn't think about Kelsey needing a husband, and his own feelings were convoluted into the mess.

"I don't think I'm the person for this job, Mrs. Willits. Is that where your mind is today?"

"You'll pray for Dan's widow, Crystal," Mrs. Willits said. "She's single. Is this because Kelsey is single – and beautiful? Crystal, after all, is able to remarry in the church — her being a widow and all."

He got the distinct feeling Mrs. Willits was testing him. "Crystal is my friend's wife. I'd do anything for Dan."

"It's easy to pray for Crystal, is it?"

"Of course it is!"

He didn't like where the conversation was going, and he focused out on the horizon rather than meet her gray-eyed gaze. Mrs. Willits seemed to look through you, rather than at you.

"Do you want me to say it, Alice? Yes, I think Todd Mitchell is a hateful man who bears no responsibility for the downfall of his family and I can't bring myself to pray for or to even want his healing because I see how Kelsey's eyes are so haunted and drained of life when he's around. I felt it myself when he was in my home."

"So was Hitler, and we prayed for him during the War. It's what Christians are called to do. Pray for their enemies."

His whole body seemed to rise up in rebellion. The very thought of Kelsey's ex made him shudder. "Then you're a better person than me. Until I see some sign of repentance in Todd Mitchell, I can't bring myself to wish him on his family."

"I agree with you—"

"You what?"

"I've seen Todd's type before. I only pray for him because I'd love to see the weight lifted off that poor girl's shoulders, but I'm no more hopeful than you. When a man is that addicted to religion without an ounce of empathy or compassion, nothing good ever comes of it."

"I have to get to the office. I don't have to go to the hospital this morning, and for once, I'll be on time to the staff meeting."

"She'll be your downfall if you're not careful," Mrs. Willits said, as he rose.

"Maybe she will. I'll see you tonight. I'm bringing dessert and the Underwoods will bring the salad. If he can't get through to Todd, I don't know if anyone can."

"I've already put the turkey in the oven," she said. "It's going to roast extra slow. The way my husband used to like it." Then, Mrs. Willits focused her guilt-inducing gaze on him. "Alex, just be careful with Kelsey. She's been through a rough time, but she can rescue herself."

He couldn't possibly be that transparent, he hadn't even voiced the thought to himself. He hadn't allowed it, but he stared back at her. "I haven't done anything, if that's what you're implying." He examined her passive face. "I've got to get to the office. Kelsey Mitchell is none of my business. Your point is well taken."

Mrs. Willits lowered her eyes to the ground and began singing a hymn. Apparently, that was the only farewell he was getting. He hiked the rest of the way to the church, trying to convince himself no one else saw in him what the old woman had. Such feelings were not there. God had used him to heal Meagan. Period.

## Chapter 17

Kelsey arrived back at her apartment to find her vacuum cleaner put away with the cord wrapped tightly and the floor free of Nathan's remnants. The kitchen counter was void of clutter, and the rooms, a series of small, lightless squares, now smelled like the clove cinnamon candles of her childhood. Underneath the heavy scent, she could still smell the musty, dungeon-like odor that came with the apartment and lingered. Before she left, her home showed haphazard and imperfect, just the way she liked it.

That had been the problem with her childhood house. Nothing was out of place and everything took on the glinty sheen of untouchables as if they lived in a china shop. If Mother could have put Kelsey behind a glass door...

She frowned at the sterile picture of her apartment as though she'd wanted to live like her mother, but was incapable. Of course, Kelsey never employed a staff to do her bidding.

"Mom!" she called into the apartment. "I'm home!"

Her mother must not have heard very well anymore. Kelsey found her wandering through the apartment, annoyed that she had nothing more to accomplish. It surprised her to notice how tiny her mother really was, a little minx of a person, really. She'd always thought of her mother as giant in every sense, her confident direction being given for every aspect of life.

"I've been trying to get a handle on this clutter. How can you live like this?"

"I don't have time to look for stuff, Mother. It's easier if it's out in the open."

"The kids are at school?"

"Both of them. Meagan's friends came running out to the car to get her. It was lovely to see."

"This is how the homeless live so that they can see everything they own."

"Actually, when we were homeless, we kept it all in a plastic bin in the rear section of the mini-van. I didn't have trouble finding things that way either, though it was much more cramped."

"You're mocking me."

"I'm not. When Todd left, I learned that he hadn't made a house payment in nearly a year."

"Well, how was that your fault?"

"Apparently, the bank didn't care whose fault it was."

"You're trying to press me. You always did find a way to get under my skin. It's as though you were born to be the thorn in my side, to make sure whenever there was happiness in my life, you were there to numb it like a Novocain. There to remind me how I used to be beautiful and the apple of your daddy's eye."

"Such a warm thought, Mom. Thanks." She wasn't surprised that her mother hadn't worried about her daughter or grandchildren being homeless.

As usual, Dee Quinzel managed to make a painful truth all about her.

"We have more in common than you realize, Mother." Kelsey tossed herself on the old sofa. "I used to think I was the apple of Todd's eye. I believe, for a brief moment in time, we were both the object of their obsessions. Then, when they possessed us body and soul, they quickly moved on to their first loves. Daddy to his money and winning, and Todd to his quest to be like God."

"You speak like a disgruntled poet, Kelsey. Such fantasy goes on in that mind of yours. Always dreaming without regard for the practical, like how you managed to miss that your husband wasn't making the house payments. Prince Charming isn't coming to rescue you. Love isn't meant to be a consuming passion for a lifetime, so you need to get Todd back on track and make this work. You have two kids to raise."

She reached for her mother, and like a black spider, Dee scampered away to her corner. Retreating as though human touch would weaken her further. "I am raising them. Alone."

"As what? Some retail clerk?"

She opened her mouth but stopped short of telling her mother she'd be working at the university. That information would only be used against her at a later date. "I'm an administrative assistant."

"Who doesn't notice when house payments are due?"

"The person who doesn't know what's in the checking or savings account, Mother—or even if we've got money and where it is."

"You should've made it your business to know." Mother dismissed her with a wave. "I'm going to be gone soon, you do realize? I won't be here to protect you if that's what you were planning." Her mother reached for her crocodile handbag.

*Probably real and extremely fitting,* Kelsey mused.

"I'd be more worried about myself if I had turned out relatively normal."

"I'm going out this morning to find you a new floor. You need hardwood in this house for the kids. If Meagan did have meningitis, it was probably from some air born bacteria from this carpet."

It was hard to feel any gratitude, but she forced it. "Really Mother, you're going to buy us a new floor?" The fact was, the only way Dee Quinzel could show love was with her pocketbook, and Kelsey needed love. In any form she could get it. "Thank you, Mother." She managed to peck her mother's cheek before the older woman could spirit away.

"I simply didn't expect my daughter to be a single mother, raising two kids on her own in some cramped, little apartment. This is not the kind of thing that happens to people like us. You must understand how difficult this is for me." She made a smacking noise with her tongue. "How ever will I ever tell your father?"

"You'll find a way." Kelsey was so over guilt – guilt implied Todd's leaving was all her fault, and while she may not have been perfect, she'd agreed to do what was necessary to keep the marriage together. Todd didn't want the marriage, not even the pretend version they'd managed for years. He only wanted the ring, the safety shield that kept him free of real commitment.

Mother's black eyes darkened. One only noticed her pupils, which grew more severe as her hair lightened. In Boston society, Dee would be considered quite a beauty, but from the time she could remember, Kelsey feared those eyes. As a child, she felt enamored of mothers who brought a sense of warm into a room, who filled their homes with an aura of comfort and the scent of fresh cookies.

In contrast, Kelsey never felt peace in her own home. She learned to stand up straight, clean up after herself and hold her breath subconsciously. As a teenager, food lit fireworks at the table, and calories became her archenemy. One less pound, she used to think, and I could disappear altogether…

"If you get this house looking more presentable, Todd may stay."

"Is that what this is about? Mother, Todd is not coming back. He's addicted, do you understand me? He's addicted to the idea that he has a special mission for God and I cannot help him complete his mission. He's delusional, Mother."

"Marriage is not something we Quinzels look to as disposable. I only have your version."

Blasé? Hadn't she cried herself to sleep for over a year? Called out to God? Fret about where their next meal would come from? Pride settled in her chest, though. She wouldn't have called her parents unless life on the street became their only option. She'd been taught not to be needy. The needy were useless to the Quinzels, victims of their own stupidity, and Kelsey had learned well.

When she'd found the lost, offshore account that hadn't matured, she took it all and poured it into the apartment. A small sense of satisfaction she still found hard to digest. Todd never forgot money, and she waited in vain for him to come after her, but by then he'd racked up some stiff penalties himself in regards to child support. She supposed he decided to call it even.

"Todd is a lovely man, Kelsey. You can't throw him away when his mind isn't working right. Your father hasn't been perfect, but did I throw him away when his stock dipped?"

"Somehow, leaving me bankrupt, taking up residence with other women and deserting his children—I don't know, it feels somehow, different, than a husband's stock losing value. Maybe it's me, but—"

"You're making fun of me!" she shrilled in that screeching tone she took when she might lose the point. "A divorced daughter." Dee shook her head. "I'll have a divorced daughter. None of my friends' daughters are divorced."

It really was all about Dee Quinzel. "Would it be easier if you told your friends I met an unfortunate end? Tell them a rogue wave took me out to sea and I haven't been seen since."

Her mother actually paused. "No, that wouldn't work. I won't lie for you."

Nothing had been demanded of her mother. The woman had lived her entire life as though on stage with an audience waiting for the *America's Funniest Home Video* moment. Fortunately for Kelsey, she'd taken the clumsy plunge into the water; the baseball to the groin; the face plant to the ground – and she'd survived them all and, she'd delighted in the humor of the situation. She'd moved on. As a human, she'd left the larval stage behind.

The front door swung open with a crash. Meagan appeared crumpled at the knee, gasping for breath. She heaved, and lifted her forefinger.

"Meagan! What on earth are you doing here?" Kelsey ran to her side, and rubbed her back gently. "What's the matter, sweetheart? Take a deep breath and try to calm down. I knew I shouldn't have sent you to school."

Meagan's innocent eyes loomed enormous with fear and despite Kelsey's current lack of faith, she prayed silently and waited for her daughter to breathe rhythmically.

"Mom! Nathan! Gone!" Meagan groped for air, bobbing up for it like an aquarium guppy at feeding time.

"Honey, calm down." Kelsey patted her back. "How did you get here?"

Her mother chimed in, "Kelsey, I thought you took Meagan to school. Young lady, what did I tell you yesterday about walking around town by yourself?"

Meagan continued, "I ran! Mom, Nathan left with Dad!"

"Nathan's at school, sweetheart. I dropped him off at the junior high right after I dropped you off at school. Remember? You need some rest." She tried to guide Meagan to her bedroom.

Meagan shook her head. "Stop!"

"Did you want to have breakfast with me? I could make your favorite." She refused to hear what Meagan was telling her. It simply couldn't be true.

Meagan's face flushed red. Her cheeks bulged, clammy and moist. "Mom, stop and listen to me. Nathan's gone! He left me a note in my binder. And the iPod to give back to his friend." She gulped for air again, holding up the iPod, which Kelsey grappled with. *There was a friend.* He hadn't eaten garbage to earn an iPod. Nathan Mitchell had a good enough friend to lend him an iPod."

"I didn't open it until I was in class!" Meagan shoved a crumpled envelope toward Kelsey. She rifled through the envelope to pull at a hand-written note in Nathan's careful, small script.

*Meagan,*

*Tell Mom not to worry. I've gone back to Laos with Dad.*

*I feel like I'm the only one left he'll listen to. I'll call Mom as soon as*

*I can. Pray for me. Pray for Dad to have ears to hear. It's our*

*only hope.*

*Nathan.*

*P.S. Dad is happy I'm coming and I'll take care of him.*

Kelsey clutched the letter to her heart and ran into her bedroom, tripping over a shoe of Nathan's. She picked it up and took it with her, clutching it under her arm before it dropped with a thud when she bent at the filing cabinet. She yanked out the drawer and rifled through the folders, scattering them onto the carpet as she pawed clumsily to get what she was looking for. She stopped at the kids' birth certificates, social security cards and passports and pulled the folder out, panting as she did so. All of Nathan's papers were gone. Something inside her died. "Nathan, why?"

He'd passed on that crazy Superman gene of his. Why hadn't she seen it? Why hadn't she known Nathan was headed for trouble when he was thumbing through his Bible every night as though he was cramming for a test? She'd chalked it up to puberty, but how ignorant was that? Teenagers don't rifle through the Bible to avoid puberty. She ran back out to the living room.

"Get in the car, now!" Kelsey grabbed her purse and her keys and ran down the steps. She could hear Meagan behind her. When she reached her minivan at the curb, the tires had been punctured. The van sank into the street, crippled and useless. Todd sabotaged the car. They must have just left. Think Kelsey, think! She rubbed her forehead. "Call the airport in San Francisco. Tell them there's a child whose father doesn't have custody and that the documents are forged! Then, call 9-11."

"Honestly Kelsey, she's nine. Do you expect her to know what that means?" Her mother grabbed her cell phone and started punching buttons. Kelsey sunk to the ground, paralyzed with fear. She needed to give chase, to use her adrenaline, but her mind felt as though it might explode.

She sat on the curb, paralyzed by fear and livid that she'd slipped back. She'd fallen for the lies again. She'd let her walls come down and he'd gotten the best of her. The truth was not in him. So why, oh why, did she continue to believe him? She'd known he'd only come to save face. What on earth could he want with Nathan?

"Get up, Kelsey!"

"Can it, Mother! I just need a minute."

"You don't have a minute!" Her mother's far-reaching forefinger pointed to the car.

She banged her forehead with the flat of her palm. "Think! Think!" Her mind swelled. With all the excess security, there was no way Todd could sweep Nathan out of the country, but her gut told her that was a lie, like everything else where Todd dwelled. In her mind, Todd had already swept Nathan onto the plane and out of her grasp. She tried to take it to the worst possible outcome like she'd been taught in counseling so she might overcome her fear and react. *The plane going down over the Pacific. Todd is hiding Nathan from her until he is grown. He's teaching Nathan to hate her, to hate all women. He's raising Nathan as heir to Todd's religious preoccupation and lack of all human emotion.*

As quickly as it hiccupped, her brain started up again as though she'd turned an ignition. She roared to action leaving her old self behind.

"Mother, I need the keys to your rental car."

"I took the car back. I hadn't realized how close everything was, and you have the minivan, so I didn't think—"

"Never mind. You pick now to save money?" She yanked her mother's cell phone out from her grasp and pressed the buttons, muttering another prayer in her head, *I know I said if I had that one thing, it would be all I asked, but I'm here again. I need my Nathan! Even if Todd is a favorite, leave me with something, won't You?*

Their time with Todd had passed as like a vapor and now she understood why. Todd never was an integral part of the family unit. He dwelt on the peripheral, always edging in toward them, but never infiltrating. This was his way of forcing himself into their lives, making himself known and exerting his position of leadership. He'd steal whatever he could not have.

"This is Martha, leave me a message and I'll get back to you ASAP!"

"Martha! It's Kelsey, please, please, please pick up!" There was no answer, but Martha didn't like to be disturbed when deep in conversation. It wasn't likely she'd forgotten her cell, she'd be more likely to leave a child behind. So Kelsey pressed redial again and again until Martha picked up.

"What?" Martha yelled in her ear. "I don't recognize this number! This better not be a sales call."

"Martha, don't hang up. It's me, Kelsey. I need help!"

"Whose phone is this?"

"My mother's. Martha, listen, I need a ride to San Francisco this very minute. Todd's taken Nathan, and they both think they're going to save each other. It's a long, convoluted tale, but Nathan's no match for Todd, Martha. He's such an innocent. Hurry!"

"I'm on my way. Wait out front! I'm calling the church to get them to pray."

She didn't have the strength to argue. "Just hurry!"

Her mother ripped the cell phone from her vice grip. She pressed a few buttons. "Get me the San Francisco International Airport."

Kelsey took Meagan's cheeks in her hands. "Meagan, you're so flushed. You need to rest. What was I thinking sending you to school?"

"You didn't know Dad would do this. I should have known. I checked the loose tile yesterday and the money was gone. Nathan was talking to Dad on the beach the other day."

"This isn't your fault, Meagan."

"If Nathan gets to Laos, we'll never see him again. Dad doesn't know how to share."

"It's not going to happen. Go upstairs and lock the door behind you. You need to rest. Grandma will be up when Martha gets here."

"I will own that airport if you don't get me the head of security right *now*. Do you understand me? This is Dolores Quinzel of Boston, Massachusetts, and I have an emergency." For once, her mother's bull-in-a-china-shop personality came in handy, and Kelsey took solace in the deep crease that made its way between her mother's eyebrows. Botox be hung, Dee Quinzel did have a heart.

Kelsey paced the sidewalk, back and forth, muttering to herself like a lunatic. "Nathan, what are you thinking? He doesn't want our help. He doesn't want to be fixed."

Meagan grabbed her around the waist and rested her cheek on her chest. Kelsey held on firmly. "Nathan wants to rescue us, Mom. He wants to be our hero because he's the man of the family."

"I said that, didn't I?" She covered her mouth. "I never should have said that. It was never Nathan's job to take care of us."

Meagan clung to her tightly.

"You two are already my heroes." Kelsey stroked her daughter's hair. "It's my job to protect you both. I am very bright, Meagan. I'm not stupid like your father thinks." She whispered the next part, "And maybe Grandma thinks, but it's not the truth. I've made mistakes, but that doesn't make me a failure. You only fail when you don't get back up."

Meagan nodded.

"I don't need either one of you to take care of me. I love you for wanting to, but it's not necessary."

Meagan nodded fearfully and instantly, her wide eyes calmed Kelsey.

"Even if I do have a hard time waking up, I get up. Though I don't want to dry my hair, I dry it. I put makeup on, and I feed you breakfast. You have never been late for school, Meagan. Not once in your life. I have never sent you out hungry or with holes in your pants. So while I may not iron, I don't need saving. Not by anyone. Not by Dad, my parents, or you."

Meagan's round, bottom lip quivered. "I don't want Nathan to go!" she wailed, finally sounding like the child she was, the age she was supposed to be.

"Nathan's not going anywhere. You remember that Bible story about how the shepherd will leave the ninety-nine sheep and go after the one?"

"You'll go after him," Meagan stated.

"We'll go after him if necessary and we won't come back without him. We're a family."

She embraced her daughter and Meagan clutched her tightly, like the little monkey she used to be, before she got old and versed in the ways of the dark world.

When Todd announced his departure, his first departure, he'd looked at Kelsey with pure hatred in his eyes. "I've been called Kelsey. The Bible says the time is short. For those of us who are married, to live as though we are not." The words haunted her. "What do you expect me to do when I stand before God? Would you have me say, 'Sorry God, I listened to my wife instead of you – like Adam listened to Eve when she told him to eat from the tree of knowledge?' She brought sin into the world. That is why God wants man in control.'"

She paced the sidewalk with Meagan at her side. The ocean, fittingly, erupted across the street, exploding with energetic intensity and collapsed onto itself with a thunderous strike. In contrast, their neatly manicured apartment with its shorn lawn and managed shrubbery held all its drama within, all its passion neatly shut away behind the everyday, ordinary image.

A horn honked frantically, and she swung around and saw Martha's black SUV come into view. She let go of Meagan's hand and watched as the little hand searched for Grandma's, only to be spurned as the old, tentacle-like fingers dug in her purse for a house key.

"We're a family, Meagan!" Kelsey called to her daughter. "Pray and we'll be fine." She wondered if that actually came from her.

"You can do it, Mom!"

## Chapter 18

Alex imagined himself in a different life, but he couldn't form a complete picture in his head. The vision lacked focus and left him believing it was only another round with discontent. The coastal town looked tired, its endless construction projects came and went, like the block buildings of his childhood. Up and down, up and down, eternally in transition, no sufficient ending ever found. As soon as the gleaming, slick asphalt covered one road, the next looked worse and the jackhammers returned. As members of Santa Cruz Evangelical died off, their homes and the lives within them transformed too.

The church building, an old brick Methodist structure lilted to one side as though trying to escape the mighty Pacific and its soppy, destructive weather. The wooden stairs at the front needed a good paint job and in all honesty to be rebuilt so they didn't end up with a lawsuit on their hands.

"Alex, what are you doing out here?"

"Oh Loretta, I was just—"

"Avoiding the staff meeting?"

He glanced at his watch, "It hasn't started yet, has it?"

"I just don't want you to be late. You've already got pastor coming out for dinner tonight, and you know how he doesn't like to go out in the evening."

"It's important, or I wouldn't have asked." He looked back up at the peaked roof, "What is it, Loretta? What's missing here?"

She turned around and stared up at the church, crossing her arms and securitizing the building. "It looks fine to me. Why are you acting so strange lately?"

"Am I?" he questioned.

"You forgot to check on Crystal this morning, and she called here checking because she had to get one of the kids to preschool."

"I forgot!" he slapped his forehead. He should have known the morning was too quiet.

"You'd better come up with a better excuse before the meeting." She looked out to the street, "Where's your car?"

"At home," he said absently, still focused on the bricks. "It's all pride, isn't it?"

"I beg your pardon?"

"I used to want to hand out hope to the hopeless like free popcorn. I wanted to teach His

Word and have people zealous, like they were drunk on the Spirit as in the Book of Acts."

She gazed wide-eyed at him, her mouth with its carelessly placed lipstick rounded into an "o".

"I wasn't one of those Christians whose passions wore off, like my mother said it would. I was happy to annoy people with my Jesus-speak. Perfectly willing to tell them their eternal soul rests upon the matter of the Gospel, while they look at me blank-eyed and searching for the nearest exit, but I didn't sound any different from the likes of Todd Mitchell. Except he does his version with more finesse and a willing audience. He tells the lie better than I tell the Truth."

"Is this a midlife crisis?" She frowned. "All men go through this, Alex. If you want to buy a new car, just go and do it. You don't have to feel guilty for wanting something that everyone else has. Maybe that will make all this introspection go away."

"I don't want a car," he laughed, to avoid confessing what he did want. He wanted a woman. His mind was filled with her thoughts of her crowded his subconscious, so that he couldn't concentrate on anything else. How could he be so commonplace? Even when he coveted that which he could not have, he was banal.

"It's not a car I want," he finally said.

"Good heavens, you're not gay, are you?"

"Loretta!" He didn't know who was shocked more, Loretta for suggesting it, or him for what the accusation might mean. "Of course, I'm not gay. Why on earth would you think such a thing?"

She shrugged. "You're single. You live alone. You're well groomed. It's not a giant leap when you live here, you know."

"It is if you see my rental. I have absolutely no taste."

"That's right. Mrs. Willits said that was true."

"How would she – never mind."

"I'm going in to put the coffee on. Whatever it is you want, either decide for it or against it. Don't stay in that place of decision forever. It's the worst thing you can do."

He missed Dan. *Dan,* he'd say. *I've fallen for a woman who doesn't know I exist. I can't marry her and keep my job, and she wouldn't marry a preacher besides. She hasn't fully rid herself of the last one.*

"Loretta," he called after her.

She swung around, a skinny A-shape pirouetting on the steps, "Honestly Alex, you don't have to solve the world's problems this morning, do you? Just get into the meeting on time."

He held no respect here. No place of honor or esteem. That much was obvious. God must have sent the miracle to humble him, to remind him that apart from God, He could do nothing. God sent the miracles, God chose who would be healed. He felt weak with humility.

Life wasn't fair. He knew it. Rain fell on the just and the unjust, but lately, it was a downpour. He was an optimist by nature, and if he'd known he would see and feel a miracle in progress, he would have said that was it. He'd be on fire for life. Yet, here he was a week later, pining for a nearly-single mother who wanted nothing to do with him, stuck in a dead-end job where he'd never get to preach and living with a guest who stole underwear. Did it get any lower?

Santa Cruz Evangelical had sunk into a depression of sorts. The Supernatural of God, the miraculous gift of grace, they hid behind a veil of rules and regulations. Standards that had become the Gospel to Mel. The darkness enveloped him, allowing only small darts of light to seep through, and it wasn't enough. He craved and though he knew God was within reach, he didn't feel he had the power to reach Him. Evil surrounded him.

Why did children have to suffer?
Why didn't men want to care for their families?
Why did Christians suffer betrayal?
Why did Christians behave so hatefully to one another?

He knew the stock answers. And he believed them, but his faith was like St. Peter in the water. He'd taken his eyes off Jesus, and he was sinking deeper and deeper. He clung to the figurative ledge and needed to pull himself up.

He just needed a little time. Maybe a good morning of prayer. More prayer. His dark-stained, box of an office, and its books, representing years of study blurred in his eyes. His desk, cluttered with papers and open theology teachings, ebbed away as priorities. Christians would argue Scripture for an eternity. Until Jesus returned and what good did it do anyone? Alex groaned, wearied by it all and the emotion took him by surprise how lax he'd become.

What did it matter? Did God plant him here to argue about the right way to believe? When he disagreed with the wrong person, his career was thwarted or worse. The fervor he once felt for the Lord's work was lost in a sea of church politics and red tape.

Mel Underwood looked for a battle. Anywhere, he could make a jerk out of Alex, Mel stood tall, booming out his knowledge, cutting the young pastor to the quick. He had been taught to respect his elders, and early on he'd seen the tendency in Mel and swore he wouldn't be swayed by the legalistic tendencies. Give experience its due and all that, but if he listened again to a blowhard argue some circular conversation just to hear himself talk, his head might explode.

His only friend in Santa Cruz was well over eighty years' old and he wasn't sure she wasn't becoming dotty wanting him to take on healing prayers for Todd Mitchell. He couldn't help but wonder how much of Todd's mental illness was his own pride and inability to hear input from another person. "But I'm putting my fleece out, God. I'll keep praying, but if it's time for me to go, lead me on."

His cell phone chirped, "Alex Bechtel speaking."

"Alex, it's Martha…from church. I'm Kelsey's friend."

"Right."

"I'm calling about the dinner tonight. I've already called Mrs. Willits. Kelsey needs to cancel."

"She can't!" Without Kelsey there, he wasn't sure he could stomach another meal with Todd.

He'd probably have to make sure Alice put the good silver away. He cleared his throat and started calmly, "Martha, this is our last chance to approach Todd about his…his work. I wanted us to pray for," he swallowed hard. "Healing."

"Alex, you need to get the prayer chain started now. I can't get a hold of Loretta. She's not at her desk. Todd's gone. We think he may have taken Nathan with him."

"What does he want with Nathan?" Alex tried to wrap his mind around it. Todd acted as though his children were still across the world, not a few blocks away. He'd made no attempt to go and see them, nor did he give any indication he wanted them with him until he'd come back and seen how Kelsey raised them well enough to be deemed fit.

"Kelsey said she stopped trying to figure out his motives a long time ago. If you understand the crazy man's motives, you're probably crazy too."

"Todd's ticket." He searched his memory. "I saw it, Martha. He said he'd have to print out a new boarding pass, that was his old one. He was supposed to leave originally at 2 p.m. How could he have made any changes? He doesn't have a credit card. Nail me on the boardwalk, I am as dumb as a plank."

"We're heading to SFO right now."

"No! He's leaving from San Jose because his International flight is going out of LAX." He exhaled. "Is Kelsey with you?"

"She's right here."

"Let me talk to her."

He could hear them wrestling over the phone, Kelsey saying plainly, no, no until she came onto the line, "Hello."

Alex's breathing quickened, "He's at San Jose, flying into LAX on Southwest. I should have figured it out, Kelsey. I'm so sorry."

"He has no money, Alex. Did you give him money?"

"No, I didn't—" he stopped and plucked his wallet out of his back pocket. The cash was gone. The credit cards were missing, and he could guess where his car was headed. "I'll get him, Kelsey. If I have to go to Laos myself, I will get Nathan and bring him to you."

"Forget it, Alex. I'm not blaming you." She sounded weary, as though she'd given up. "Forget it all right? It's not your problem."

"But—"

A long tone answered him. He rubbed the back of his neck, feeling immobilized and yet overflowing with adrenaline. He tried to think of a way he could help, and wanted to dash to the car, but without a car, he was as crippled as he felt. He looked at the dark ceiling, "It's because I looked down on the Lincoln, isn't it?" He dialed the first name on the prayer team and then, he kneeled near the window and called out to God. "Not Kelsey, Lord. Not again. She can't take anymore. Relent! Let me bear this burden."

The light burned his eyes when he opened them, and reality flooded in, erasing his momentary sense of calm. Mel stood in the doorway, with the shadows it was like Alfred Hitchcock walking into view to make his presence known. His belly hung over his pants, wrapped in his striped dress shirt, and slung in front of him like an earthy mother carrying her newborn. "Loretta promised me you'd be on time for the staff meeting. Imagine my surprise when you don't show up. Again."

"Something came up."

"Something always comes up." Mel waddled his side-to-side walk and shut the door behind him quietly. "Alex, you understand, I can't have you ignoring the rules. It makes the staff question me and it rings of disrespect. If I let you have other priorities, all the pastors will have other priorities. There's always something to be done, Alex. If you don't learn to protect yourself, build yourself some boundaries, you will bounce around like one of them kids in the bouncy house at the funeral."

"I understand," Alex put up his hands. "I know this comes at a really bad time, Mel. I promise to be here at all the meetings from now on. I promise to make it my priority and explain to the staff that I'm going to get better at time management. I'm not going to go this way and that just because someone has a need. I'm disrespecting you all. I understand and I apologize profusely. I'll bring donuts next week and apologize to the entire staff."

"Well," Mel had nothing more to say, but he'd no doubt told the staff Alex was going to get a good talking-to, so he couldn't go back yet either.

He had enough presence of mind to be sheepish in asking, "If I might borrow your car, Mel.

This one last thing is so important. I feel that someone's soul depends on this errand."

Mel's face bloated like a red, birthday balloon. "You can't be serious."

"Oh and can you let the staff know they need to pray for Kelsey Mitchell. I already started the prayer chain. We think Todd may be trying to take their son to Laos. I think he has my credit card." Alex opened a drawer as though it might suddenly appear.

"So call the bank and put a stop to the card, but you don't need to run out of here like a chicken with your head cut off. That's exactly what we've been talking about. You hear something and you think you're the only one to fix it, and you dash out of here before you have prayed about it, asked for wisdom from others, or understood that you have a job here."

He settled into his chair, "Fine, I'll call the bank."

"Kelsey's soul can't be saved by you."

"I was talking about Todd's."

"His can't either, and no, I don't think you were talking about Todd's."

The unspoken accusation hung there in their midst, until Alex found his tongue, "What are you trying to say, Mel? If there's something you're accusing me of, please say so outright."

"You're a proud man, Alex. Full of pride and all the zeal that accompanies your youth, but I do think you've got a good heart and that can always be trained. But you're an island. You think you can accomplish it all by yourself and we're the little people lifting you up. One miracle and you're suddenly believing you have the ability to heal the world."

Alex shook his head, "I haven't told anyone about that miracle. Only the staff that morning, and I know full well that I had nothing to do with it."

"I'm not sure it ever happened. You can't stand to be in my shadow, I understand that Alex, but you're not ready to take over this church."

Like his brother's surprise backhand to the jaw, the truth jarred him unexpectedly. "I've got it. By George, I get it!" God was showing him all along what Kelsey had endured. That niggling, layer-by-layer loss of belief in the truth set before him. Another person who had no concept of who you were on the inside telling you exactly who you were, with no bearing on the facts. "Excuse me, Mel. I have to get to the airport."

Mel blocked the doorway with his generous frame. "I don't think you want to do that, Alex. You don't want the church to be the source of common gossip. We've already worked out this Kelsey Mitchell scenario once in our history, I don't think we're ready for a command performance. I know that Todd seems odd and misguided in his actions, but Kelsey," Mel shook his head. "That woman is like a spoiled child who throws a tantrum whenever circumstances don't go her way. If you'd seen her in my office." Mel shook his head back and forth causing his jowls to waddle like a turkey's. "All those times, crying her eyes out, and sobbing as though she'd lost her mind. How could a man work all day and come home to those kind of dramatics? No marriage is one person's fault, Alex. Is that what she's led you to believe? I've seen her in action and trust me, she can make Scarlett O' Hara appear the beacon of tranquility."

"Correction Mel, we, as a church, never worked anything out. We threw Kelsey overboard and sacrificed her, letting her fend for herself against a man who is void of love, except for that which he sees in the mirror each morning."

Mel chuckled at him, in his condescending way as if Alex was a child and he had to simplify things for him. "Alex, she made a promise to that man. One never knows what really goes on in a marriage and I'll grant her, Todd is most likely crazier than a loon, but that doesn't erase the commitment she made before God. It doesn't mean she's not crazy as well."

"So what's the church's position on this? When a husband abandons his family and relinquishes all responsibility toward them, we act as though she deserved it?"

"Of course not. Kelsey Mitchell kept coming to the church. She acted as though everything was fine, but when I asked her what she might do to bring her husband back to the family, she snapped. She told me something I can't repeat and we never heard from her again. If that's the extent of her faith, I say good riddance to her. A little yeast in the dough Alex, that's all it takes to destroy an entire congregation."

"If you're using yeast to mean sin, then the entire congregation is made up of yeast, so how does that work exactly?"

"The church can't go around giving people the idea they can abandon their commitments without setting off a firestorm of divorce every time someone's unhappy. You don't feel the weight of it because you're too young to know the fallout." Mel pointed toward the window, "Those other churches can lie to people, and tickle their ears with what they want to hear, but I won't do it. Do you understand? Nor will I let anyone on my staff make a mockery of the marriage covenant by telling a woman she chose badly, so she can move on. That's not what the Bible says!"

Alex felt his head nodding on its own volition. "Fine. But answer me one question, Mel. Would you let your daughter stay married to such a man?"

"How dare you?"

He wouldn't answer. Alex knew as much, "I'm going to the airport."

"We have a staff meeting."

It was a thinly veiled threat. Alex knew if he walked out the door, he could kiss his job goodbye. It wasn't Kelsey he left for. Deep down, he'd been flailing in his job for more than a year, and too paralyzed to move on that niggling voice. *The economy*, he'd say to himself. *The congregation needed him*, he'd reason. So he stayed, running around in circles and accomplishing nothing except when he broke the rules. Didn't that tell him anything?

Mel crossed his arms, and lifted his great, wire brush eyebrows as he removed himself from the doorway. "Do you think any man is above temptation? Least of all, a young, unmarried one?" His expression recoiled and Alex felt a fire in his chest for being accused and convicted without so much as a hearing, but the writing was on the wall regardless. It was time.

"You've never liked me, Pastor Underwood. I don't know why you hired me in the first place. Do I remind you of someone?"

"It's a shame it's come to this, but I'm glad to know your position on important matters before any more damage was done. "

Alex knew when to shut up, and he did just that, hoping Mel would be done and leave him for dead, but he went on, empowered by his own higher nature, "You're going to have to learn things the hard way, and you may as well start now. I'm doing you a favor by cutting you loose. Whether you realize it or not because no man without humility will make it as a preacher. Temptation will be your downfall. Don't think I didn't hear about Jessie Miller being at your place the other night. Alone."

As for humility, Alex had yet to see any in Mel Underwood. He supposed Mel meant everyone else needed to be humble. Sometimes he felt Christians were just plain paranoid, as if they dangled temptation from the rafters hoping you'd reach for it, "Aha! Caught you! I knew what you were made of!" As if Christians had no will of their own, but were mere puppets on Satan's string. He didn't take temptation lightly, in fact. He simply knew that for him, it didn't lie with the likes of Jessie Miller.

If Alex wanted a woman, he could have a woman. It was so easy today; it pained him. Women seemed to offer themselves freely, as though they had no value and, like common prostitutes, they used their body for power. He wanted more. He didn't think himself immune, Kelsey Mitchell was proof enough of that.

"I have to go." He spied Loretta in the hallway and her lips were pursed. She was a mother hen to him, and she wanted him to make the right choices, shamed him into it. But when push came to shove, she handed over her keys and $20 bill.

## Chapter 19

Kelsey rubbed a picture of Nathan from her wallet. "Nathan has such a good heart."

"He does," Martha assured her. "He got it from you. I remember a time not so long ago that you thought you could save Todd yourself."

"I never really knew what he was thinking. How could I save him when he couldn't even tell himself the truth? I spent years obsessing about it and it wasn't until he left that I finally got why he hated me so."

Martha looked at her briefly. "It never dawned on you that it was his issue? I always knew it was his issue."

"But did you know what it was? Could you have rested until you figured it out? I mean, why did he marry me? Why did he stay married to me? Why wouldn't he divorce me before leaving for Laos? The questions tormented me."

Martha said nothing.

"Did you ever think that Todd didn't…you know…like women?" She hoped she put the question delicately enough. There was no easy way to ask it.

"From the moment I met him."

"Really?"

"He was never comfortable in his own skin and it made others uncomfortable."

"That's why I lost all my friends, I suppose."

Martha laughed at her. "Not all of them. I think you're finally coming back to us, Kelsey. When I first met you, you would giggle constantly. I haven't heard that infectious laugh in ages."

"You make me sound like a disease. Todd didn't like my laugh. He said it sounded evil."

"I think you're coming back up to the surface. You know you can handle anything life dishes out now. You believe in yourself, but more importantly, I think you know Who is in charge, and that you don't have to carry the weight of the world anymore."

"I thought maybe it was just that extra cup of coffee."

"Oh you."

An ominous voice came out of the dashboard, "Turn right in one-quarter mile."

"Oh that stupid navigation." Martha said, slapping her dashboard. "I can never figure out how to turn it off. The kids mess with it, and put in directions to the arcades, the mall, places I am not taking them, so I am tormented all day by the voices." Martha appeared harried and flustered, pushing buttons frantically. "Figure out how to turn that woman off, before I reach in there and put an end to her for good!"

Martha hated her car, which was everything she wasn't, flashy, expensive and obvious. In Santa Cruz, Martha blended in as easily as tie-dye, but her husband, an investment banker in love with all things image-inducing, didn't make it easy for her. Kelsey and Martha bonded years before, like most work widows, over their inability to fit in with the standard society wives. In the world of Santa Cruz money, it seemed Kelsey was nothing but jewelry, to be taken out for special occasions.

The only difference between Edward and Todd, was that Edward loved Martha and treated her with kid gloves. Perhaps, it wasn't the love Martha craved, but she relished his attention, regardless. Edward bought her material things like expensive cars and bottled perfume, Martha would say, 'thank you Edward, but I'd rather have you come home for dinner.'

The navigation voice reminded Kelsey of her mother: "I hope my mother doesn't say anything to Meagan to upset her while we're gone."

"Dee raised you and you're still alive. She'll be fine for a couple of hours."

"She barely raised me, and probably only because of the nanny. I would have been quite feral if not for that."

"You had a nanny?" Martha found this hilarious, but in reverence of the situation, she bit back her laughter. "You're serious?"

"You can laugh," Kelsey told her. "Go ahead."

"I just pictured your upbringing more like Annie's in the orphanage than Annie with Daddy Warbucks. Did she dry your hair for you in the morning? Is that why you hate to do it?"

Kelsey sat up straighter, "The nannies all blur together, so I don't remember. No one could work for my mother, so none of them lasted very long. I finally started calling them all Nanny, so I didn't have to remember their vile names as they passed through college and out my life."

"Should I turn on some violin music now?"

"What does Todd want with Nathan, Martha? The boy is so sensitive. He's nothing like his father and why wouldn't he take Meagan too?"

"I think you know the answer to that question."

She did. No doubt Todd was afraid Nathan's sensitive nature meant that he too, would battle the demons Todd battled privately — wanting so badly to be normal — to be holy in his mind — and unable to overcome.

"Todd's like the California Condor." Kelsey said.

Martha lifted her eyebrow, "The Condor?"

"You know, when the scientists tried to breed them because they were going extinct?"

"Vaguely."

"The scientists celebrated like it was 1999 when let those birds out into the wild. They had overcome nature with science. They had proven that they had the power over nature."

"Is this going somewhere? Besides Todd not being all that attractive to me, I fail to see the connection with the Condor." Martha took the windy road with racecar skill.

"They let them loose and within days, the birds were attracted to the pretty, pretty, green broken glass. They ate the broken glass — essentially, pretty garbage and died."

"Do you have a point to this story?"

"Remember how the environmentalists battled for the Condor and their right to live in this new world that didn't seem to have a place for them anymore."

"No, I don't."

She pursed her lips, "The scientists blamed people for the Condor, saying that it was us who littered, and otherwise the Condors would have been fine. They wouldn't have found broken glass, they wouldn't have eaten it and the condor population would have flourished."

"This is like Todd?"

"And you know, when young men stop drinking beer in the wilderness, maybe then the California Condor might live – but no! They spend countless dollars and they try again, and then, the dumb birds die of lead poisoning, because they ate the carcass of some animal shot by hunters. Again, it's the people's fault, we shouldn't be hunting."

"Kelsey? You're going to have to close this one up for me because if you talk like this when we get to the airport, it's you they're going to take off in the white coat."

"Exactly!" She pointed at Martha. "That's exactly my point. My point is that no one wants to say the truth because the truth is painful. The bird is too stupid to live. He's today's Dodo bird, which by the way, is extinct. It's always someone else that is responsible. The humans, as though we have no right to infringe upon the world of a vulgar vulture, which eats dead things and is too stupid to live. We're supposed to feel guilty and wallow in our shame! We've relegated ourselves to the bottom of the food chain, instead of the top. And we want the whole world to change, rather than just admit the painful truth. That the bird is too stupid to live."

Martha rubbed Kelsey's knee, "Are you all right? You need something to eat?"

"Don't you see? Todd isn't functioning at work and he blames me. He's stressed at home and he blames the kids. He leaves because he can't handle the responsibility and it's entirely my fault. No one wants to say the awful truth, that Todd was ill-equipped to handle the stresses of life because he can't admit the truth." Kelsey shook her head. "He never wanted what he was supposed to want. He didn't want the good Christian family because he doesn't want a woman, but rather than admit that, like the condor scientists, he blames us — his environment."

"Kelsey, I never will understand how your mind works," Martha smoothed her knee. "But I can't imagine what you went through with a man who didn't want you. I just don't understand why you never said anything to the myriad of counselors he paraded you in front of."

"I could never prove it. It would have just led to more blame." They were at the summit of the mountain and she felt breathless at the travel still to go. "We're at least thirty minutes from the airport."

"It's only ten-thirty, we've got time and the airline is warned."

She struck up her shallow conversation again rather than think about Nathan and the distance between them.

"It's simple, really. Science is based on observing, the study of how things work. You watch things, see them in their natural habitat, and you learn."

"I'm afraid to ask," Martha said.

"A scientist is supposed to observe, not interfere. They're not supposed to come up with the outcome before the study has taken place."

"Why do I get the feeling you're not talking about an ugly bird with the wingspan of a Volkswagen?"

"If anybody at the lab had observed Todd, they would have seen the truth. The same is true for the men at church. But they all made their assessments without observing the truth. All these people blamed me, and by submitting unconditionally, I actually made Todd worse. I enabled him to believe in the delusions about himself until the problem got bigger and bigger and he couldn't contain it within the household anymore."

"What good does it to blame yourself now?"

"I'm still married to him, aren't I? Out of fear that he'll make things worse if he takes notice of what I'm up to, so I stay under the surface, hoping to go undetected. It's what I taught my kids, to stay out of sight."

"Kelsey, c'mon."

"I told my kids to believe in their father. I told them to avoid their truth and believe what I told them to do. Nathan's doing exactly what I told him, and I told him wrong."

"Nathan is the sweetest boy I know, he's not a thing like Todd. He's got a sixth sense. He'll be at the airport when we get there."

"You're right, naturally."

"There is no way with the kind of security they have today, someone is going to let him on a plane to Laos without proper identification."

"Todd may not lie, but he'll find a way. He only has to get him on the plane to LAX here. You mark my words. Trouble slips from his shoulders like a summer shawl."

"Don't think like that."

Kelsey turned somber. "What if he hadn't left us, Martha? What if he'd stayed? I think about that all the time, because I hadn't the mind to leave him by then. I was so confused if he'd told me my name was Bertha, I would have answered to it. If he'd told me I was African-American, I would have looked into the mirror and wondered how to do my hair."

They were on the mountain now, thrust into the canopied tunnel of Redwood forest that lined Highway 17 over to the San Francisco Bay Area. It was a fast-paced road, one the passenger always seemed to brake for the driver in their nervousness.

"He left. I thanked God he left," Martha said. "When everyone at the church said what a tragedy it was, I kept quiet, but silently, I praised God for it. The truth was getting fuzzier and fuzzier for you. It was like you were in a cult, disappearing before my very eyes and getting smaller and smaller while I called out your name."

"He won't ever admit his truth. He'll marry again as soon as our break-up is legal and he can't be judged by the people here."

"Does that bother you?"

"It bothers me that I worked so hard for something that wasn't possible." As they drove over the snaking Highway 17 with its dangerous curves and lightning speeds through the darkened, fog-heavy forest, she felt the shame of her marriage and its lies all over again.

"It's over. Can you leave it behind?"

"It's not over! My son is out there somewhere and I don't know where and he's with a man who is certifiable, yet no one believes it."

"Your daughter is with someone who is certifiable too, Kelsey. Did you forget that?"

"My mother would never hurt Meagan."

"Your mother is toxic, Kelsey. Another truth you fail to see. You'd rather live her lie so you can be the good daughter. You can forgive both of them, and still protect your children, but you have to embrace the hard truths. These people don't treat you with love. Pastor Alex? He barely knows your family and he treats them with love."

She felt flush at the sound of Alex's name and the kindness he'd bestowed on her family. "I can't even fathom what it's like to be treated that way. Alex will make someone a wonderful husband some day."

Martha turned and grinned, "I was thinking exactly the same thing." There was the rush of giant Sequoias whooshing by her window, a flash of the concrete median, and a crippled vehicle parked at a dead stop around the blind curve. She heard the thunderous crash and saw the flash of light and then, the overwhelming silence.

## Chapter 20

Highway 17 was one blind curve after another, but that didn't stop drivers who knew the road from driving it like they were at Indy. Alex slapped the steering wheel of the old Lincoln, "Come on, come on, come on…" Every time traffic slowed, he worried the old Lincoln would cut out and he wouldn't get it started again.

In the slick of the morning fog, the road was either clogged from too many yuppies getting over the hill to Silicon Valley, where they couldn't afford to live, or yet another speedster smashed into the guardrail after hugging the curve too tightly. Either way, he had no patience for the crawling traffic with Todd ahead of him.

Why didn't he predict this? Of course, Todd was going to leave without warning. It was in his nature to run when someone got close enough to get a good look inside. He tried to have mercy for the man, believe that Todd was filled with self-loathing and acted accordingly, but he didn't care. He only wanted Nathan safe and the fact that he wanted that more than the boy's father did told him everything he needed to know about Todd's fitness as a father. A real man didn't justify stealing a child from his mother and he felt certain Todd harbored some reason his actions were necessary. It hadn't taken long to notice that Todd had a reason for everything to go his way without exception.

His cell phone trilled, and he pressed the button on his Bluetooth, "Alex here."

"Alex?" Kelsey's shaky voice reached out to him — the very same way her daughter's gripped him in the hospital. He was drawn to into the sound and felt all the emotion it encapsulated. "Alex, it's Kelsey. Where are you?"

"Just below the crest of the hill. Traffic seems to be breaking up. I think I'll be free and clear here soon." As though he jinxed himself, traffic halted and once again, came to a standstill. "Never mind."

"We've had an accident. We're not hurt," she said immediately. "But the car is totaled. Can you pull over and I'll find a ride up to you? I've called the airport, but it's Todd and you know how he puts things."

Sadly, he knew what she meant: That with a few carefully crafted words, Todd would be on the airplane with his son. "Are you sure you're not hurt? Sometimes these things aren't obvious right away. I think you should stay and get checked out."

"I'm fine," she said with an annoyed tinge to her voice. "I wouldn't care if I wasn't fine, I need my son."

He stared at the traffic ahead. "Traffic's a mess and I don't know how far ahead of you I am, what if I miss them?"

"I've reported Nathan missing, so legally, he can't be put on the plane, but Todd can sell anything."

"Kelsey," the taillights flashed in front of him. "I don't want to risk coming back for you. We're probably only a few minutes behind Todd." He paused before he asked the world of her. "I need you to trust me."

"Alex, please! I can't do that."

"Don't ask this of me, Kelsey. I'll have no choice but to come back for you. I feel it in my bones, we can't risk it. You have to trust me."

He heard a small sob, "He'll get away with it. He gets away with everything and my son will come back to me ruined. I sound like a bitter ex-wife to the rest of the world, but as God as my witness, he will destroy that boy if given the chance."

"Not this time," he answered firmly. "If I have to go to Laos and get him, I will, but you're not alone anymore. I believe that he is without conscience."

A small cry came across the line. He felt his gaze drawn again to an accident ahead when he saw her eyes. Those wide, expressive and alluring eyes that he'd know anywhere. *It wasn't possible.* He was in front of them. By a good fifteen minutes at least. He swerved to miss the car in front of him and waited until the thin road widened to pull over onto the gravel shoulder. He scrambled out of his car, but before he could look up, he had to thank God for yet another miracle. There was no other way.

"Kelsey!" he screamed over the cars, which were mostly at a standstill.

It was as though time stopped when her eyes came to his. Her whole face lit up and he was Superman himself, "Alex? How?" She drew her phone down to her side.

"Come with me!" he motioned.

She looked at Martha, who was speaking to the CHP, and her lips moved. Martha nodded and waved at Nathan, "Take her!" she screamed over the snaking traffic.

Kelsey bolted across the line of slow-moving cars, like a real-life game of Frogger and came to his side. She stood momentarily still until she plunged forward and ran into his arms, grasping him like a long-lost friend. "Oh Alex, it's a miracle! The CHP wouldn't let Martha go, and I don't think her car is going anywhere. But no one's hurt. And she hated that car, so praise God. The cop said I could make a statement later if necessary. He said Todd hasn't done anything illegal yet so he can't help me."

Yet. He hated to think of that word in terms of what Todd might be capable of. He knew instinctively that Nathan was in danger, but he needed to know why. He needed the whole truth. He unlatched her arms, in disbelief that he was doing so. "We need to catch that plane, get in the car."

She did and she crossed her long legs before she connected her seat belt. "He won't quit until he wins."

"Wins what?" Alex asked as he eased back onto the road.

"To Todd, life is one big competition. It's not enough to be rid of me, he has to destroy me to feel victory. He knows the only thing that matters to me is the kids."

"How is that possible? That a father would want to strip a child from a mother's life?"

Kelsey's expression darkened and he felt the weight of her wrath before she spoke. "This is why I quit going to church. No one believes in evil anymore. Everyone is just misunderstood. No one could really be a sociopath and really trying to do harm. That's mythology."

"I never said—"

"You didn't have to. You're like the rest of them, you think I'm crazy."

"I don't. I'm only saying maybe Todd really is concerned with the spiritual well-being of Nathan and thinks this is best." Judging by her lowered brows, he may as well have said, "Get into that pretty white coat with the straps."

"Right. There are two sides to every story."

"I wasn't—"

"He's a—I believe he may be a homosexual," she whispered. "Not a practicing one, but—"

He must have misunderstood her, "Who's gay?"

"Todd. Todd Mitchell resents women because he doesn't want them and feels they are God's punishment to him. That is the secret that I keep for him because he cannot bear to admit the truth and he cannot bear to be alone, so he will destroy another woman. He will tell her that she's not thin enough, beautiful enough, desirable enough and then reject her with excuse after excuse. All while he hangs with his former male roommate, tells this Simon character all of his heart's desires, while he snipes at his wife that she's paranoid."

"He could just be—"

"Not interested in that part of life. Nice try, but Todd's Internet history will tell you the truth. As it told me all those years' ago." He instantly thought of the church laptop and his being fired. Would they find something on that computer when he turned it in that render Alex unemployable?

"Why didn't you tell Pastor Underwood this when you were in the counseling sessions?" His blood was beginning to boil. "How could Underwood help you if you weren't telling the whole truth?"

"I wasn't allowed to tell the truth without consequences and besides, who would have believed me? You don't believe me now. I'm just a bitter ex-wife out to steal her kids from her poor, estranged husband."

"I never said that."

"You didn't have to. Here's the thing about your opinion, Pastor Underwood's opinion and even Todd's opinion. I no longer care."

He turned toward her. "Did you ever?" It came out in a more attacking way than he'd planned.

"Yes. Absolutely. I cared because I trusted that Pastor Underwood was the mouthpiece of God, but I'd confused the voice of God with Todd's voice until I read the Scripture about someone bearing fruit. Todd bears no fruit to make him a Christian. No love, joy, peace, patience, kindness, gentleness or faithfulness. He only bears the image of it from the outside."

Alex contemplated the statement.

"But no one wants to judge. If the guy says he's a Christian, by golly, he's a Christian."

"You don't think Todd is a believer at all then?"

"I have no idea," Kelsey stared straight ahead at the road. "That's between him and God. I only know, from my perspective — which I grant you, could be off, he never showed me or my kids an ounce of mercy or compassion. So to me, his faith is dead, a clanging gong, but God sees the heart, I don't."

Alex pondered if her claim was true. Did his church give a free pass to someone acting hatefully because of mere words? "Would you convict a man based on his wife's word?"

She gave a half-smile. "That's the wrong question. Would you convict a man based on the testimony of many character witnesses? What about the testimony of a few who witnessed him commit his crime?"

He didn't know how to answer her. Sure, he understood that Todd wasn't right in his thinking, but had he truly hurt Kelsey and her kids? Other than abandoning them? "Maybe the best thing Todd could have done is leave. Did you ever think he was thinking of you when he did so?"

She turned and glared at him. So harshly, he turned back to the road. "You're forgetting Alex, I don't care any longer what you or Pastor Underwood think. It took me a long time to get to this place, but I know what the Bible says and I know the truth my kids and I endured. You and Pastor Underwood are welcome to think Todd is a gleaming saint for all I care, it doesn't change my truth. Nor will it ever do so. If I'm wrong, God will deal with me, but you can't have it both ways. Either the husband is the head of the household and bears some responsibility toward the downfall of his family, but the church can't call the man the head of the household and solely blame the wife when a marriage is broken apart."

"The church doesn't do that!" He felt suddenly very defensive.

"No?" she raised her brows. "You're right. Maybe some churches don't. Todd doesn't attend those churches."

The accusation rubbed him like the backside of a shark. Was he a part of that kind of church?

"So why would Todd take Nathan? If he's free to live the life you say he wants and you're still covering for him, why would he want Nathan?"

"He thinks Nathan is weak. He's worried that Nathan will struggle with the same thing. If I had to guess, I'd say Nathan would be encouraged to play football and grunt to prove his manhood to his father." She crossed her arms and turned toward the window.

Alex felt sick to his stomach. Because if he was honest, Kelsey's story didn't resonate. Had his emotions got the best of him? Todd possessed a manic energy, but that didn't make him what she accused. And what difference did it make if he chose to live a straight man's existence?

* * *

As his algebra teacher might have said, Nathan Mitchell grossly miscalculated his father. They weren't even at the airport when he'd discovered his error. The worst of it was that his little sister was right. That hurt most of all, that he'd pay the price for blowing off Meagan.

As the car sped down the freeway, he calculated his chances of bailing from the vehicle. They weren't good. His father drove like a bat out of darkness, scarcely noticing anyone in his path, around him or in front of him. Just zipped in and out of lanes like a real game of "Crazy Taxi" — but he didn't dare mention his fear or he'd get another talk on fear being a lack of faith.

"Dad, do you think you could slow down? I'm getting car sick."

His father swerved into the next lane. "Sure, we're almost there. I want to get us on that airplane before your mother discovers you're gone. She's the reason you come by that fear of yours honestly. She's a very anxious woman, that can't help but have tainted your thinking."

"Anxious?" He didn't think of his mother as anxious. Except maybe when his father was around.

"Nervous, you know what I mean?"

"I guess." He didn't want to talk about his mother. "I'm hungry."

"We'll get something to eat as soon as we're through security at the gate. It's time we bulked you up. You look as though you've survived a concentration camp. Did your mother ever cook you a meal or did she save them all for herself?"

He stared down at his wrists, "I'm skinny, Dad."

"You're neglected," he said. "Before you play your sports like soccer, you've got to load yourself with carbs. It's not enough to have a snack. I should have left instructions. Athletes have different needs for their body to run at optimum capacity."

"I'm not really an athlete."

"Not if you tell yourself that? Anyone can be an athlete with the right motivation."

His father looked like a juicehead. Plumped up with muscles on top of muscles. None of his friend's fathers looked like that. Most of them carried a beer belly, but the main difference was that his friend's fathers smiled. He never saw his own dad smile. He grinned sometimes at the end of one of his talks, but he never smiled.

"When will I see Mom again?" The question formed a giant lump in his throat and his eyes stung at the promise of tears. *He wanted to go home.*

"You'll see your mother on breaks from school. I wouldn't worry about her, Nathan. She's going to be a lot better off not having to worry about bringing up a healthy young man. That's my job. I should have never left you there to begin with."

He nodded. He did a lot of nodding with his father, unsure of the right answer. "What's Laos like?"

"Nathan, that's enough questions. You'll find out soon enough.

Dad's car's a disaster. "Where'd you get this piece of junk?" He lifted his foot free of the trash on the floor, mostly old fast-food wrappers.

"I've been meaning to talk to you about your tone. You may get away with that with your mother, but I expect more out of you and so will my followers."

"Your followers? You mean Jesus's followers?"

"You know what I mean and that's just the attitude I'm talking about."

"Whose car is this?"

"It's a friend's. He's going to pick it up at the airport when we're off."

"Does your friend bathe? Smells nasty in here, like the grease trap outside the taco joint downtown."

"Be grateful in everything, Son. We have a ride, don't we?"

Piles of old mail cluttered the dashboard. "What's your friend's name?" He only asked because he'd never seen his dad with a friend. No one other than that weirdo roommate he had in college. Mother didn't like that guy, so he rarely came around and that made Nathan happy. The guy gave him the creeps.

"Thomas," His father answered.

All of he mail was addressed to a James Williams, but he made no mention of that fact. "Doesn't your friend Thomas have a mother? Mom is always nagging me to pick up after myself." He hated to admit maybe his mother was right.

The airport was in sight and as they took the side road, a giant jet streamed in for a landing directly over the car. Reality struck him like a stone. There was no going back now. But he wouldn't cry. That was for babies, and his mom would understand. Dad needed him.

His father parked the junker on the top floor of the garage, "This is where I told my friend I'd leave the car."

He didn't answer, but instead followed him with his backpack, waited while he checked in for the two of them. No one asked for his student ID or anything and it seemed that he was really on his way to Laos with a short stop in L.A. Maybe it would be harder once they got on the International flight. He found himself hoping that would be the case.

His father stuffed the tickets into his shirt pocket. "We're off. Are you excited?"

"Yeah," he lied as he turned toward the automatic doors. His mother didn't even know he was gone yet. Would she think he'd abandoned and betrayed her too? No. This was the way it was supposed to be. Babies cried for their mothers. Men sacrificed for them.

"You're here!" A buff guy with his pink shirt opened down half his chest approached them. Nathan cowered and felt the desire to run. The guy side-hugged his dad, then held out a fist-pump motion toward him. He took a pass.

It was him. He shuddered at the sight of the man his mom called, "the creeper."

"What's he doing here?" he asked his father.

"Nathan, what did I tell you?"

He wasn't backing down. "Seriously, what's he doing here?"

"Simon, will you excuse us a minute?" His dad yanked him into a nearby bathroom. A guy at the urinal stared at them when his father gripped his ear and pulled him toward him. "Listen to me," his mouth twisted and in his eyes, Nathan saw murder. "You ever talk to one of my friends like that, and I'll have you for lunch, you understand me?"

"Mom said—"

"I don't care what your mother said, do you understand me? God created man to rule over women, not to be subjugated to them. You've been taught wrong and now I have to undo all that fault programming."

"Whose fault is that?"

His father's palm collided with his cheek with brute force. He heard the crack before he felt it, but then the sting reverberated down his body, but the physical pain was nothing to the discovery of who is father truly was: a fake and a fraud.

"You said you were taking me to Laos to start a new life! How is it a new life if you're bringing that dirtbag with us?"

His father's hand balled up into a fist. He forced his words through his tightly-clenched teeth, "You will go out there and apologize to my oldest friend and you will do as you're told. This is not a democracy."

"I won't!"

His father drew his fist back when Nathan felt himself yanked from its trajectory. He turned to see the guy who'd been standing over at the urinal. "You want to beat up on somebody, big man? You touch that kid again and I'll call the police."

His father took a swing at the stranger, and Nathan took it as his chance to run.

## Chapter 21

Kelsey understood she was on the verge of having Alex decide she was completely mad, but she hardly cared. What was one more? She took his laptop and followed his instructions to see where Todd Mitchell had surfed the Internet; an activity that once rocked her entire world when she discovered she had no idea who she was married to.

"He knew you'd check," she said slapping the laptop shut.

"What do you mean?"

"He researched undetectable poisons."

Alex's eyes grew large. "What does that mean?"

"It's a warning to me. Nothing more. He erased anything important to him out of the cache."

"How can you know that?"

She didn't want to admit how she knew it. She only knew it made her sick to discover what Todd really did with his time on the Internet. "He took what mattered to me. The poison is nothing more than a warning that if I come after what's mine, he'll take the only thing he can ultimately control: my life."

Alex raked a hand through his full, curly hair. It was clear he thought her a lunatic. Maybe she was. After years of living in a giant chess game that no one else was playing but Todd, who knew the truth anymore. She only knew the way his mind worked, and there was no motive for what Todd did, other than winning. Winning the imaginary game he played in his head. Where Kelsey was the cause of every disaster that went wrong in his life and revenge was his only recourse.

"You're saying he's a sociopath. Someone without conscience?"

"Why is that so hard to believe? Do you think they're mythological creatures? That they only come in the form of an ugly serial killer?"

"It's just — it's far-fetched."

She shrugged. "It's your prerogative to believe me or not. It makes no difference to me. I was done trying to prove it to others a long time ago. I've had to keep the secret from my children, which is the only part I struggle with — what should they know? What is too much? Now I fear with Nathan gone, I didn't tell him enough."

He kept stealing glances at her, as if he could read a crazy scale on her. It disheartened her that he was so wary of the truth. She wanted Alex to be different.

None of it mattered. In less than 15 minutes, she'd have her son back; she'd watch Todd depart for some country she couldn't place on a map; and she'd learn more about who she really was – who she wanted to become – and before she let anyone define her again. She would run the information through her own, newly reliable data storage bank and test the new definition. She'd try it on for size and if she didn't like it, she'd toss it away with the rest of the heap where words like *fat, lazy, ignorant,* and *selfish* lived, banished from her life forever.

Alex looked at his watch. "We're nearly there. Do you know which terminal American is at?"

She shook her head.

"Kelsey, I shouldn't have let this happen. I'll go to Laos if I have to, but why didn't you tell me there was a chance he'd run?"

"I thought with the dinner planned tonight, there wasn't a chance he'd leave. It was everything he loved. Parading me in front of the church as the corrupt, immoral woman who ruined his life. It was expanding his fan base, feeding his ego." She sighed. "He can still surprise me."

The endless construction that defined Bay Area airports hadn't changed. After circumventing the pylons and makeshift concrete barriers, Alex pulled into the parking garage of the newer terminal at San Jose International and parked haphazardly. Together, they dashed across the street to the terminal where she arrived breathless at the American Airlines counter.

"I'm looking for my son. He's thirteen—"

"I'm going upstairs to check the security line," Alex said before he took off.

""My son," she swallowed. "He's thirteen and he's with his non-custodial father. I don't have a ticket, but I need to get my son. They're heading to LAX." She brought out a scrap of paper that Alex gave her. "They're on flight 1079. It leaves at 2:25." It was only 11:30 a.m.

The woman, a short, squat, middle-aged woman with the proverbial mom haircut stared at her blankly. "I don't have any records here about a possible—," she stopped herself short of saying kidnapping.

"Please. Check if they've checked in," she opened her purse and took out her wallet and her identification. "This is me, Kelsey Mitchell. My son is Nathan Mitchell. He's tall, nearly six feet and very thin. He has sandy brown hair, and a sweet face with big, brown eyes and beautiful olive skin."

The woman beat a few keys, "Yes, here they are. They're all checked in and probably at the gate."

"The police were supposed to stop them. Is there any chance security stopped them?"

The woman pounded her keyboard some more. "I don't have any notes here. I doubt they would have been stopped for any reason, unless they —"

"Can I buy a ticket? Is that what I need to get through the gate? I need a ticket. To anywhere," she pulled out her Visa card.

"I can't offer you an assistance pass since your son may already be through the gate. I can offer you a police escort and they can take you to the gate."

"That's fine." She tapped her fingers as she waited impatiently for the woman to call the police in a non-emergency tone. She scanned the terminal for Alex, but he was long gone, and once again, she felt completely alone — as if she'd let her only son down by not telling him the whole truth about his father.

"They wouldn't be allowed to check in unless they took an earlier flight." Another attendant came to check out what was going on and looked at the records the older lady pulled up.

"Can they do that?" she asked. "Take an earlier flight?"

"If the flight had room. Do you have a picture?"

Another man came beside the first attendant. "Tall guy? Looks like Remington Steel? I mean that guy who played Bond in the 80's. Skinny kid about twelve or so?" The man asked with a Pilipino accent.

"That's them," Kelsey cried. "How long ago did they pass through? Did they have time to catch an earlier flight? Who do I have to see about getting past security?"

The security guard called another guard to the front podium and took her aside. Her heart pounded and she felt her head shaking of its own volition. "No hurry, Ma'am. There was an altercation in the restroom. He's with the police now. Follow that hallway toward baggage claim and you'll find an information desk. Ask there."

"Was my son involved? Is he there as well?"

The man shrugged. "I don't know, Ma'am."

As she rushed down the hallway, Alex came toward her and laced his fingers through hers. "Come with me," he mumbled under his breath. "I have Nathan."

He squeezed her hand, gently but firmly so that she felt the protection he offered. He marched her past baggage claim and she looked back only briefly. At the baggage carousel, a family, obviously just home from Disneyland judging by their paraphernalia, waited for their bags. The children giggled, each of them wearing a Mickey Mouse hat. The father, a pudgy, bald man in a *Pirates of the Caribbean* shirt, pretended to fight his daughter for a sip of her soda, and the sound of their laughter wounded her. The normalcy of it all. Did they have any idea what kind of blessing was in their hands?

Alex leaned into her. "Nathan's at my car. He says his father is looking for him. Let's go."

The words sent a chill through her spine. Would they ever be safe from Todd's games? Outside on the sidewalk, she caught a glimpse of the man who held more power over Todd than even his own mother and her gaze turned cold. "It's Simon." She unlaced her fingers from Alex and pushed him forward, "Take my son home. Don't come back for me, no matter what. I'm going to finish this once and for all."

Alex shook his head, "I'm not leaving you here!"

"Go, Alex, please!" She pressed both hands against his chest. "If he sees you, he'll know I have Nathan. Please," she looked directly into his eyes and noticed him once again as a man. She pulled him toward her and hid behind his masculine frame. "That's the man Todd would do anything for."

Alex started to turn and she grasped his chin and forced his gaze back to her.

"I've let this game go on too long. It's time I took control of my life. I'll never be a victim again."

Alex stood in front of her as he'd obviously talked his way out of any trouble already. He blocked out her view of Simon. The rage she felt well up in her at the sight of the man who'd always been a third party in her marriage felt like a gathering storm. The feelings had picked up weight and power over the years and once unleashed, she wasn't sure she could maintain control. She breathed in deeply and prepared herself with a silent prayer.

"Would you have really gone to Laos for Nathan?" she asked Alex before she made a move towards Simon.

"I don't say things I don't mean. Not intentionally, anyway." The charcoal pupils of his eyes were so deep; it was as though she could look straight into his soul. Her reaction surprised her again. She'd thought that womanly part inside of her was dead forever. Heaven knew it should have been and the collective strength of his gaze scared her. She buried her head in his chest rather than stay under his power. His arms came around her in a fatherly motion, with awkward pats to her back.

The swarm of violence died within her and with clarity she understood that Simon was not to blame for what Todd brought into their marriage.

She reached for Alex's hand and strode across the street back to her son — back to the life that mattered. Once at Alex's car, she caught sight of her son and ran to him. She enveloped the boy in her arms. "Nathan," she cried. "I thought I'd never see you again."

"Mom!"

"Don't *Mom* me. Did you think I wouldn't come after you?"

Her son looked shell-shocked, worn-out and if she wasn't mistaken, grateful.

"You're the child's mother?" A police officer in full, black uniform with a gun at his waist approached her. "We've had a report of abuse."

"I am. Kelsey Mitchell," she rifled through her purse to get her wallet and identification. "His father doesn't have permission to take him and was here to scurry him off to Laos."

"The report is on you, Ma'am."

Todd stepped next to the policeman, his eyes weapons of warning and mockery all at once. His expression, so cold and distant….aloof and above it all. *Inhuman. She could be anybody to him. Being the mother of his children meant absolutely nothing.*

"Can you state me your son's father's name? We'll need you to come down to the station and give a statement."

"Todd Henry Mitchell," she glared at him.

"Birthdate?" the officer asked.

"August 12, 1963."

"You wouldn't happen to know his social security number?"

She rambled it off without a second thought. "Can I talk with my son?"

"Not just yet."

Todd's face grew darker and his scowl more pointed. *Pure hatred.* She recognized the emotion she'd told herself he couldn't possibly feel for her. She'd created a life with Todd Mitchell and through his eyes; it was as though none of that existed. Like God himself, Todd thought of himself as outside of time.

The officer said. "We'll be taking the boy into custody."

"Custody? What has he done?"

"Protective custody," the officer said. "It's going to be up to Child Protective Services to decide the best interest for the boy."

Kelsey's heart sank. Todd had done it again. He'd taken the focus off of himself and created another web of lies so convoluted and tangled, it appeared a glistening truth. She felt Alex behind her. He'd placed his hands on her shoulders in a protective manner and she watched Todd, to see if another man's touch might irritate her husband, Todd stared right through her with his hard, incriminating gaze. Magically, he'd been able to do that, simply to look at her and make her heart race with shame and guilt. She'd want to wring herself out like a wet towel and destroy the terrible sin nature that filled her up.

His gaping gaze, like a slow burn, drilled into her. He used everything he had, but she felt nothing. No shame or guilt for being who she was, she felt only pity for Todd. He'd become an empty shell of a man and if it were possible, she wondered if his soul might have drained from his beautiful exterior altogether.

"I'll get my son back," she said with certainty as she sat in the back of the police vehicle. Her defiance spoke volumes to Todd and for the first time, she saw and smelled his fear. He wasn't impenetrable after all.

Nathan slipped into the police car beside his mother and allowed her to put an arm around her.

"Son, you need to come out of the vehicle. CPS will be picking you up."

Nathan crossed his arms. "I'm not going anywhere."

"Nathan, Honey, don't make things worse. We'll be home tonight together. I have nothing to fear."

Todd winked at her from behind the policeman. It was then that she saw Simon step behind her estranged husband and wondered what on earth she'd ever done to deserve Todd Mitchell's wrath.

"Nathan," she said quietly as though she might never see her son again. "Your dad is a very smart man, but he confuses the truth sometimes, and it makes it hard for you to grow up being told one thing, when you're seeing another. We're just going to make the best of what we have, is all. All right?"

He pulled away, and tried to shake off his childishness. "You don't have to talk to me like I'm four, Mom. I wish I'd listened, that's all." A part of Nathan's childlike wonder had been stripped from him, and Kelsey felt her inner turmoil starting to burn. Like a moth to the flame she kept trying to win Todd's attention.

*Here I am. Look at me, honey! Do you like this dinner? How about this dress? Is my hair okay?* And like the moth she'd get burned, disintegrated like a flaky piece of tissue paper. She'd give anything to ensure Nathan wasted no more time playing near the fire. She looked at Alex and thought about him, the peaceful Alex, sitting on the bench over the rugged cliffs and the pelting waves. He had his whole life in front of him. While Kelsey felt God's grace upon her, she couldn't say she'd ever entertain the thought of another in her life and an envy burned deep within her for couples all around her. How they trusted one another and had each other's back…she couldn't even imagine putting her trust in someone again and she mourned that part of her.

"Nathan, it's not you, Baby. I screwed this up. I didn't understand normal mommies and daddies and I married what I knew." She pined for what her kids had lost. "There will be so much in your future you can feel guilty for, you hand this one over to me, all right?"

Nathan laughed, "He doesn't look at me like a father looks at a son, more like he hates me. He never taught me to throw a ball or took me to the game. I miss that. I wish I didn't, but I do."

"There'd be something wrong with you if you didn't recognize that." She moved his hair aside and kissed his forehead. "I'll be home before you know it and so will you. Just tell the truth."

"He just stares at me, you know? Like one of those creepy clowns at the boardwalk, he barely blinks, like I'm some kind of specimen in his Petrie dish."

Kelsey searched for the right words. She lifted up his chin, "Nathan, I know. I know what it's like to want to believe in him. You're hopeful he'll be that kind of father who sacrifices for his children and brings home a pie just for the fun of it. I know because I hoped for fourteen years he'd be that kind of husband, but that isn't who he is, Honey. He loves you in the way he's able to love you."

She was proud of Nathan. If she'd been as smart as him, this situation would never have come to pass, but then again, neither would her children. And for all his faults, Todd left her with the best part of himself, even if he was too proud to realize it.

## Chapter 22

The police officer, a portly Hispanic who strained the buttons on his black, button-up uniform leaned into the backseat of the police car and spoke quietly to Kelsey. Contempt covered her like a flimsy veil as Nathan viewed his mother in the back of a police car. When would it all end?

"Your ex-husband is coming along to the station to make his statement. We have a bank robbery in process, so we're short on manpower." Todd slipped into the officer's car beside her. The irony that she should be forced to sit beside her accuser was not lost on her. "His character witness will also be joining you. Any problem with them coming along in the same vehicle?"

Simon smirked at her and emotions flooded her as history rolled tape before her. Simon in college organizing canned food drives "for men only"; Simon who hosted the Harvest Festival for "bros"; Simon who told her in a letter before her wedding to "do the right thing" and abandon Todd at the altar because "she wasn't worthy of him." Todd never stood up to Simon, or the Svengali ways that hypnotized him and dislodged common sense. She'd believed once they were married, Simon's power over Todd would diminish, and that she would outlast the fiendish friend and have Todd forever. How wrong she was.

"No problem," she smiled at the policeman. She'd played nice long enough, tried to be the good, Christian woman and support her husband. What trouble was it to hide her true feelings for another hour? She rammed herself against the passenger door rather than let a part of her touch her ex, but it hardly mattered. She could feel his dark energy emanating and pulsing beside her. She prayed for an invisible coat of protection, as she knew he'd use the time to wear her down and question her story.

"I didn't abandon my kids, Kelsey. I was called by God to a ministry that you wanted no part of — what was I supposed to do? Deny my love for God to prove my love to you?"

She didn't answer him. It was a rhetorical question meant to unnerve her.

"I sent Meagan a birthday card that year, and I bought Nathan a graduation gift for sixth grade. You can't act like I simply abandoned my children."

"Your mother sent those things, Todd. The kids recognized her handwriting. Naturally, they love their grandmother, but they wanted to know you thought of them. They didn't even hear from you for six months after you left."

"Communication was spotty. I was focused on the ministry and I knew they understood my love for them was based on the love I have for God. That had to come first."

She said nothing. Why even speak when Todd only wanted to convince her of her own insanity? She felt unstable enough as it was; she needed no help from him.

"I told you not to marry her," Simon said. "I knew you didn't have the kind of depth a serious man of God needed in a wife."

"My mother sent those things because it was cheaper to do it from the states." Todd snorted.

"Abandonment, Kelsey? Really? That's your story?" he scoffed. "You never understood my love for the Lord. You were always jealous of Him, always trying to niggle your way into a place that wasn't ever yours to begin with. Nathan understands. He'll tell the police what it's like to be sold out for God."

"This isn't about me." Her voice grew louder. "This is about your two kids needing your love. More love than you show say — your college roommate." Again! She'd fallen prey to his prodding again and shame washed over her like a rogue wave.

"You won't keep me from my kids. Do you think there's a court of law in the world that won't see the truth? That won't see how you're trying to keep the kids from their own father because I had to follow my faith? If they lived with me, they'd have godly women taking care of their every need. They'd see their father in the role that I was meant to play. You can't think keeping them here as latchkey kids can possibly compare."

She should have known if she'd wanted Todd in her children's life, all she'd had to do was threaten to take them away and suddenly, Nathan and Meagan would become his deepest priority.

"Kelsey," the way he said her name chilled her. It was the gentle tone, the one that made her feel like she ignited his passions, and left behind his dry scientific persona only for her. The voice that captured her in its elegant web. His eyes bore through her, and Simon's glare faded into the background.

Todd looked at her. Really looked at her and she saw the humanity in his eyes again, something she hadn't seen in years. Like a torrent, the memories flooded her mind. Her life played before her and for the first time in a long while, she saw the good times: the man who worked tirelessly with the homeless on campus, the brilliant physicist who captivated his student audience with the wonders of the universe, the joyful father who lifted his giggling children in flight. She grieved that loss and wondered when religion had replaced his faith?

"You have to know how hard this is for me," Todd said. A tear sparkled in the corner of his eye. "You can't see what this has cost me, can you?" He dropped his gaze. "I lost my family, Kelsey. My family."

"You could have been faithful without leaving." She wasn't without hope after all, she was anxious for him to come back to reality — away from the powers of his mother…of Simon…of his false prophet business. A Scripture floated into her mind, and for once, she wielded it like a sword, as Todd always did. "Let us not love with words or tongue, but in action and in truth. This then is how we know that we belong to the truth."

His expression darkened, the blank stare of hatred returned and a cold chill prickled down her spine as she backed into the car's door further. If the policeman hadn't been standing outside the car, she had little doubt he would have struck her.

"You always had such an anxious temperament," he said the words like he was casting a spell, but she no longer felt his power. Fear snapped her back to reality.

"Is that so?"

His voice lowered. "The problem with you, Kelsey, is that you don't have the first idea of the truth. The truth is that no man could ever please you. There are countless women who would love to have a godly man like me. Women who would honor me and treat me with the respect I deserve as their husband. Your problem is that you continue to think you're not the issue. Without that humility, there is no hope for a life with you."

No hope.

With those words, a great weight lifted. She possessed hope and it wasn't in Todd. It wasn't in the church; it wasn't in Martha or Mrs. Willits or even Alex Bechtel. Her hope was in Jesus and she wouldn't play the role Todd created for her ever again. She wouldn't allow false hope give way to reality. Not ever again. She'd struggled her whole life venturing to be loved by people who were incapable of the emotion. Finally, she trusted herself because God had her back.

In the distance, Nathan was escorted away by a woman she imagined from Child Protective Services. Her heart swelled at the sight of Alex behind her son and her breathing calmed. She saw in Alex the kind of faith that colored his entire world. If she garnered one last wish, she wanted to be the kind of woman who was worthy of a man like Alex.

His rakish good looks were different than Todd's. Todd had that striking appearance, like that of a movie star that silenced women when he walked into a room. Todd commanded attention. He couldn't be missed, which probably accounted for why she'd felt so special when he'd pursued her. She'd felt special on his arm because everyone else wanted to be there, only to discover the chain he'd silently latched to her while he continually reminded her how fortunate she was.

Alex, on the other hand, Alex's beauty came in the form of his warmth. The way the thin, smile lines radiated from his eyes, as though he'd spent many blissful days under the sunshine; the way she felt safe in his strong arms, brief as it may have been, as if the weight of the world didn't rest upon her shoulders. His face was more rounded, but ended with the perfectly rounded, sharp chin. His cheek flinched when he didn't like what was being said, and under his morning stubble, the gold in his hair seemed like an angel's halo.

*This*, she thought, *this is what a partner is supposed to do in life. Help you through. Be there for good times and bad.* She'd spent her life being told to go after the best, own that which everyone else wanted. Now she understood, loving a man in secret, for what all the rest couldn't see was love. She got no more of Todd than anyone else did. How she prayed that Alex would find the woman worthy of him. As she watched him with Nathan, it was clear he tried to calm the boy and her heart quaked. If Alex treated strangers this way, what did he have in store for the woman he loved?

"I want that Alex Bechtel to mind his own business."

"He might have been able to do that if you hadn't bedded down in his apartment for the week."

"I told you, I came on faith. I'd do the same for a man of God who visited my congregation."

"I'm sure you would."

Todd seemed agitated, excited to prod at her while she sat beside him and Simon, the man she felt invaded their marriage from the start. As the waited for the officer to finish his paperwork outside the vehicle, Todd couldn't help himself, "That pastor is only doing his job. Don't get any ideas that he cares about this family."

She didn't answer him. He only meant to get her hysterical, so he could prove his claim that she was an unfit mother. She searched Todd's soulless eyes and then allowed her vision to swim toward Simon, a man who wore his aversion to her like a badge of honor. Her gaze floated back to her husband and an unnatural tenacity bubbled to the surface. "Why live a lie, Todd? What do you authentically want? Do you even know?"

"I don't know what you're talking about."

She looked to Simon and back to Todd. "I won't tell your mother, but I ask that you have the courage to tell yourself the truth. If no one else. I don't really care what your truth is, only that you let me go."

"Let you go," he laughed at her in a way that cut to her soul. "I don't want you. Is that what you think? I'm engaged to be married in Laos. I just want my son to have a proper mother who loves the Lord."

She ignored his profession of his upcoming marriage, which seemed infinitely easy in a country where marriage could still be a purely financial decision. Todd should have selected that option from the very start, so that nothing emotional was expected from him.

"Why would you marry again? Todd, neither you or Simon want you to be married, so why ruin someone else's dreams of happily ever after?" She felt her pulse hammer against her throat as she finally said her thoughts out loud. She'd never come that close to accusing him of what she'd suspected for years.

"How dare you accuse me of —"

"Enough!" Simon twisted, backed out of the vehicle and strained to regain balance. His tortured gaze, thunderous with hate aimed at Todd and before she could react, a deafening noise pummeled her ears, followed by her own blood-curdling scream. Simon's eyes were like lasers; red, angry and focused and another bang peeled and echoed off the concrete structure. She looked down and saw Simon's hands gripped a gun, but as quickly as she saw the weapon it disappeared from her view along with Simon.

Then, she saw the blood. Its red, metallic-scented trickle pulsated from Todd's abdomen and she reached to block its exit, "Todd!"

Time rushed past her. Someone gripped her shoulders from behind and yanked her out of the police car so that she fell hard on the asphalt below. She cried out and tried to get to the blood oozing from Todd and stop it. Alien sights mingled with the normal, the dark floor of the police car and Todd's cold stare. Her eyes focused on the metal object pointed in her direction, but it took a moment for her brain to work out that it was the gun from Simon's tight-fisted grip. She struggled against the hands that grasped her and strained to break free, but they bore down on her with an incredible force and eventually, she gave in to their will and felt herself dragged away from the scene. Another shot peeled through the concrete bunker of the garage.

She felt herself dragged against the rough cement until a large concrete post stood between her and the scene. "Kelsey, stay down!"

She swung around and realized the brawny arms around her weren't that of the police officer, but Alex. "Where's Nathan?"

"Shh," he whispered. "Shh, he's gone with Child Protective Services. He's safe, Kelsey." Alex held her tightly from behind and her body settled into his chest.

The wail of sirens filled the air. "Is it over, Alex?"

"It's over, Kelsey." Alex wrapped his arms firmly round her. "It's over. I won't let anything happen to you."

She turned her cheek to Alex's chest and allowed herself to be comforted. It would never be over, but for that moment, she rested in a loving man's warm embrace. If she never felt it again, for that brief flash in time, she felt loved and safe.

# Chapter 23

Alex brought Nathan home to his grandmother with permission from CPS, as the social worker thought he'd endured enough trauma for the day. It took every ounce of strength he possessed to keep his emotions in check and remain calm for Nathan's sake. His father had been shot, his father's college roommate killed by police.

As he dropped Nathan off with Kelsey's mother, he felt as if he committed the ultimate betrayal as though he himself committed child abuse. Nathan's grandmother offered no comforting words. She nearly ripped the door off its hinges as she screeched, "First you worry your mother to death and now this?"

The older woman in full makeup said nothing to Alex, not even a thank you for bringing the boy home. She simply slammed the door in his face and left him standing numbly in the hallway. Alex knocked on the door.

"What is it?"

"Don't you want to know what's happened?"

Dee slammed the door again and he wasted no more time in getting home.

Alex took comfort in Obadiah's welcoming lunge as he came through his front door. "How ya doing boy? Good day?"

Everyday was a good day for Obadiah. How he envied that. He felt useless at home and wished he could go to Kelsey's side, but he had no right. The thought plagued him, how little he meant in her life, how much more he wanted to matter to her.

He didn't want to be alone, but he wasn't fit for company, so he took Obadiah on a long run and prayed with each exhale, as though his life depended upon it. All he could manage was the word, "Jesus" as he thought about Kelsey in some dank police office. He probably envisioned a bad television version of her circumstances, but it hardly mattered. He couldn't protect her and he wanted nothing more. She needed a rescuer and whether by divine right or not, he believed the job fell to him.

When he returned to his home, he dialed Martha to check on her, but also for moral support.

"Alex? Are you all right?" Martha asked when she answered.

"I'm fine. What about you? No problems from the accident?"

"Just my Mercedes, that's all. I hated that thing anyway."

"Before you hate it too badly, consider that it saved your life."

"Touché." She cleared her throat. "Kelsey's still not answering her phone."

"She's in police custody. I think they might believe Simon was "the third party" in the marriage, but it's not the way they're imagining. It's not Kelsey who was seeing him."

"Ah. I honestly can't believe he didn't shoot Kelsey. He always hated her. You could see it in his eyes. It's only our prayers that spared her. I believe that."

"If she calls you, Martha, will you call me? I don't care what time it is."

"Sure Alex. It's nice of you to care so deeply. You're a good man."

He wasn't such a good man. He loved another man's wife. When he thought of Todd not even trying to protect Kelsey from Simon, he could have finished the job Simon started. That scared him, how depraved he could be, how bent on revenge Todd's actions made him feel.

"Remember, anytime. And can you call and check on Meagan for me? Kelsey's mother is a piece of work."

"I will. Rest, Alex. It's been a long day for all of us."

He hung up and fell back on the sofa. He fell into a fitful sleep with Obadiah curled up at his feet, which slung off the couch. He kept waking with a start. The thought of Kelsey being shot haunted him and the reverberating sound in the parking lot echoed in his ears as though he were still there. He was grateful that Todd's disturbed friend hadn't been able to touch Kelsey with his evil intentions, but he wanted to see her — to know she was safe.

Strange dreams invaded his sleep for the rest of the night.

*Alex walked along his darkened neighborhood to the hollow sound of silence. An eerie stick-figured man in a black suit with a black fedora sat atop a roof, playing a violin. His face glowed bluish-white, as if lit by black light and his lips parted to reveal sharp, animal-like teeth of the same color. The tune he played screeched and reached irritatingly high notes, until Alex covered his ears. He walked by, as though the scene were rational, when suddenly he turned, looked up and said, "Wait a minute! I know who you are!"*

*The creature smiled and tipped his hat, before disappearing with a guttural scream. Alex tried to get the words out of his mouth, "I rebuke you in the name of Je—" Over and over again, he tried to get the words out, but Christ's name caught in his throat and the scene was dark once again. He wielded no power against the creature and struggled to breathe as an invisible hand choked the air from him.*

Alex awoke in a sweat, clicked on the lamp and opened his Bible, reading Scriptures out loud stressing the Names of God. The Word would weaken any evil around him and although awake, he still felt shrouded in a clinging darkness. His phone rang, and he started at the sound, tried to make sense of where it came from and then noted Obadiah staring at the phone. He grabbed his running pants off the floor, fumbled in the pocket, and finally got the phone to his ear. "Hello?"

"Alex?"

He tried to place the voice, but couldn't. He squinted his eyes and looked at the clock. It was only 12 a.m., but he felt as though the entire night had passed him by. A late night call after his nightmare was the last thing he needed. "Yes, this is Alex Bechtel. Who is this?"

"Alex? It's Sally Underwood. Pastor Mel's wife."

"Sally?" he sat up and leaned against the sofa's back. "Is everything all right?"

"Mel's had some sort of incident, we're at the hospital."

"Is everything all right?" he repeated.

"I'm not sure. Mel says he's feeling much better, but he's pale as a ghost, and he's having difficulty breathing."

"Let me talk to him," he heard Mel growl. "Sally, I said give me that phone!"

Mel's booming voice became more distant and Sally went on, "He said earlier his arm was having shooting pains, so naturally I'm thinking about his heart, but I don't want to worry you. It's bad enough I woke you." Sharp noises came through the phone, "Mel, be quiet, I'm trying to listen."

Alex smiled. If only the rest of them could handle Mel as well as Sally did, there would be no problems at Santa Cruz Evangelical. "No, you didn't wake me," he lied. "I'll be down in a few minutes if you think it will make him feel better." Alex doubted his presence would do anything to calm Mel, but for a plate of Mrs. Underwood's chocolate chip cookies, her form of payment, he'd visit Darth Vader himself.

"Tell him to get down here Sally!" Mel's voice boomed.

"Yes, do come Alex. He wants to see you. He's persistent."

He muzzled his apprehension, "I'll be right over, Mrs. Underwood. Can I bring you anything? Something to eat or read?"

"You're such a gentleman, Alex. We're fine here. Just bring yourself. Mel wants to go over some of the things that need to be done at the church tomorrow, and I think it would calm him to know you'd taken care of everything."

He hung up, not mentioning the fact that he'd been fired and wondering what Mel had to say to him. Maybe Sally didn't know he'd been let go yet. He prayed the entire route to the hospital, for Mel, for Kelsey, Nathan and Meagan, and for his rampant impatience at being out of the loop.

When he arrived at the hospital, it wore that eerie, sallow glow of night. Alex didn't understand why a hospital felt so creepy after dark, but he'd avoided them at all costs in the evening. The Bible said to visit the sick, but it didn't say to visit them late, he reasoned. The familiar halls were like ice down his back, chilling. He woke up straight away in their midst, and all dreams of sleep melded into the familiar background. A night nurse gave him a second glance, but he must have looked innocuous enough, because she went on her way without questioning his presence. During the day, all the nurses were as familiar with him as any doctor on staff. Did he still qualify as clergy?

Sally, Mel's wife, was sound asleep in the guest's chair when he entered the room. She was everything you'd expect from a longtime pastor's wife. Calm, at least publicly, self-sacrificing and she still wore the veil of younger beauty. He stepped quietly so as not to wake her, and found Mel watching him, assessing his thoughts as if Alex spoke them aloud.

"Mel," he said, startled at the old man's wide-eyed scrutiny. His coloring wasn't good. He appeared pale, and he didn't look dreadful, as Sally had implicated by phone. He seemed, in a sense, knocked down a peg or two. Alex was surprised he had so much compassion for him lying there, but he did. It reminded him so much of when his own father lay broken in a hospital bed. That scene was never far from his mind, and he wished that he could erase it forever, but God seemed determined to bring him through it daily with Alex's duties at the church.

"Alex, my boy." Mel said. "Sit down. I suppose you're wondering why I wanted you to come so late. You're probably thinking I might have waited until morning, but when you get to be my age, and you endure these little scares, sometimes you wonder if the morning will come."

"I'm sorry about --" they said this in unison and laughed at their faux pas.

"No, really--" they both started again.

"Let's forget it," Mel offered. "I get too caught up in management sometimes. That's why I asked you here. I'm hard on you," Mel said. "It's because you, more than any of the others, remind me of myself. You might think I was always like this, harsh and worried about the tithes. But I didn't used to be like that. I started out like you. Eager, wanting to change the world one person at a time, wanting to be at God's disposal. It got lost in the day-to-day. That's bound to happen, I think, but I don't consciously remember it happening."

"I can see where that would be the case," Alex said.

"My point is, I don't want it to happen to you, son. I want you to get out there and live the life I probably should have. I don't want you to turn into a bitter, pencil-pushing administrator. It's not your calling."

"Are you saying you know what my calling is?" Alex scratched his head, just to make sure this wasn't all a part of his creepy nightmare.

"I believe you were sent to our church to show me some lessons. I think God wanted me to find the passion of my youthful zeal again, not be so worried about the tithes and such. I didn't like being faced with it. You forced me to look at myself and as hard as it is to admit, I'm grateful for it. A man never likes to ask for directions, you know."

"I sure do."

"I wanted to tell you that I'm sorry."

Humility. The very soul emotion he didn't think Mel capable of, and he worried this conversation was all in his mind. Served him right for judging his fellow man of God.

"I had an old friend contact me today. He's got the perfect position for you, and I got so caught up in the day to day, I forgot all about it until I had a dream tonight, and I didn't want to go until morning without telling you. I fired you for your own good."

Again, Alex scratched the back of his neck. "I'm sorry too, Mel. About the way I treated you with disrespect. It was never my intention, even if it was my way."

"There's a parachurch organization that ties together the Monterey area churches. Their goal is to bring churches together to meet the physical needs of those less fortunate in the area. They generally work with the elderly and the crop pickers, taking care of their families, organizing medical care, helping churches start up ministries that care for our community."

Alex thought he might cry, "This is the job?"

"They need someone with the gift of prayer and mercy. I thought about you first thing, and I felt like I got to start over." Mel shook his head, his jowls quivering. "Then I had that dream again, and I knew I had to give you the information before something happened." He handed him a scrap of paper with the name of the organization and its leader.

"Mel you'll be fine. You wanted me to pray for you, is that why you asked me here?"

"Dream is the wrong word. It was more of a nightmare, really, Alex. You know me, I'm a practical man." He looked over at his wife, as if to ensure Sally was really asleep. "I've never had something like this. It was disturbing. Made me wonder if my life was at stake and perhaps I had some unconfessed sin or such. It was a ghoul I saw, and he had a hold on me."

"Are you all right, Mel?"

"I'm not sure, Alex. If my time is up, I want to be sure that I've done all God has asked of me."

"Your time is up? Your time isn't up, Mel. You're strong as an ox. You've had a scare, that's all."

"I never had a nightmare so real. I need to be certain. I was walking in a neighborhood, and it was late at night. Not like anything I'd really do, but the scene didn't strike me that way. I felt like I was out for an evening stroll, even though I could feel it was midnight or later. That's not true, I had one once before and that's why I was concerned. It was the night my daughter died."

"Your daughter?"

"That's why I reacted so strongly when you asked me if I'd let my daughter stay married to a man like Todd. It wasn't fair to you because you didn't know what you were saying, but God knew what you were saying. That convicted me."

"Mel, I never knew, I'm sorry or I would have never—"

"She died in a car accident," Mel continued. "I saw that same ghoul in a nightmare that night. Never before or since. So naturally, I had the fear that it was my time to go, and I wanted to be ready."

Alex nodded.

"Jessie Miller's car was T-boned on Highway 1 and Sarah was gone instantly."

Sally nodded, having suddenly awoke. "It changed us, Alex. We weren't the same people. I don't think we clung to Jesus like we'd always thought, it took the wind out of us. We kept on breathing, but we didn't live anymore. We should have left here if we weren't prepared to fight for our church. Somehow, we didn't see any of this then. We only knew that when people came to us in pain, we harbored a little less compassion. After all, no one had endured what we had: the loss of a child."

Alex sat stone-faced, unsure of what to say, so he simply nodded, hoping to give them the right amount of compassion.

"We should have left and started over."

"I wouldn't let him go," Sally explained. "I couldn't leave Sarah's grave. Oh, I knew it was only her bones in that plot of land, that her soul was dancing and singing with Jesus, but I couldn't leave her. Without anyone to put flowers there and let people know she was dearly loved. It was like saying that we'd forgotten her, and moved on with our lives."

"Now I see that Sarah would have liked us to move on with our lives. She'd be sad to see what we've become. What the church has become," Mel said shamefully.

"When that little girl survived such a miracle, of course we thought of our Sarah. She was sixteen at the time. So while we're ecstatic for Meagan Mitchell, it brings up our loss. I didn't understand it. Meagan's parents had done everything wrong, they didn't deserve that miracle. That's when it hit me. That I didn't deserve it either. That's what grace is," Mel said.

"I can't believe I never heard about this," Alex scratched his head.

"It's been twelve years now, but it's like yesterday to us. Sarah and Jessie were good friends in school, until she told us Jessie had taken to casting spells. We put an end to the relationship, right then and there."

Alex took an emotional punch to the gut. "She's a principal now. Well-respected and liked."

"But we never forgave her," Sally said. "Not really. In our hearts, while we may not have ever said it aloud, we always wondered why it wasn't her. She was the one playing with the demonic side of life. Sarah was a good girl."

"The rain falls on the just and the unjust."

"It does, but it's still so hard when it's your child, your unfairness," Sally said through tears. "Sarah told us that Jessie said there was a spirit of death over Santa Cruz. I've felt it. First with Sarah and then, many times after that."

"That's why you don't visit the sick," Alex surmised, looking at Mel.

The old man nodded.

Alex had been at Santa Cruz Evangelical for two years and he understood now that he was a complete outsider. Only Mrs. Willits had allowed him into her circle, and even there, she kept Mel and Sally's secret. No one discussed spiritual warfare, the pain of the past and nor did they feel God's victory when miracles did happen. Everyone at SCE kept their secrets, while the darkness grew in power and influence. The wrong action with the right intention was still wrong.

"So I'm apologizing to you and come Sunday, I'm going to apologize to my congregation. In the meantime, you're going to do that job," he pointed to the piece of paper. "I've never met a more perfect job description for a man." Mel actually laughed. "But first, I want you to preach this Sunday. I'm not going to be up to it, but I can make my apologies if God's willing."

"You're letting me preach?" Alex shook his head, but his heart leapt. To preach. After two years of endurance. He wanted it so badly, he could see the crowd in his mind. "One sermon."

"To send you off and raise more money for the organization. "

Joy filled his heart. Mel had a daughter. No wonder Kelsey's miracle had been so hard for the senior pastor to digest, his own daughter hadn't been spared. Alex had to be fired before he finally got to preach to the congregation. God indeed worked in strange ways.

## Chapter 24

Alex gathered up the morning paper from his beachside bench, tucked it in his laptop case, and walked Obadiah to Mrs. Willits' house. She sat on her swing as usual, though the air was brisk with an early winter so she wore two of her ratty cardigans: one, a bright, royal blue and the other a deep, blood red. Next to her green, fern-printed dress, one would easily take her for a dotty, old woman. He laughed at the notion.

"Anything today?"

"It's not easy to get a pastor's job when you've been fired, but believe it or not, Mel has found me something." He straightened up. "And you'll never guess…I'm preaching on Sunday."

Alice Willits grinned broadly, looking out over the ocean. "Well, I'll be. I thought it would be months before you found something."

"You never let me wallow, do you Alice?"

She held in her mirth, "There's no point in it. I told you, that's what your mother is for."

He smirked at her, "My mother told me I should have stayed an accountant."

"Well, maybe you should have. You wouldn't have to check the pulse of little old ladies in that case."

"So what's got you in an ornery mood his morning?" He wrapped Obadiah's leash around the lamppost.

Her grey eyes kept their gaze on the horizon. "I think it may be time for me to move into one of them retirement homes," she scoffed. "What would Stanley say to that?" Her head shook as though she failed on some level.

Alex strode to the homemade porch swing that held so many memories for Alice. "He'd say be sure and tell them how you want your tea served if that's what you want." He noted that the clapboard house was getting worse with the small amount of rain they'd had already that year, and he saw that the puddle that pooled in the middle of the red painted porch grew deeper. Worse yet, he saw that the happiness that emanated from her soul seemed withered and troubled. Once again, he saw his own failure in the house's condition. "Here's the tape of last week's sermon," he pulled it from his shirt pocket.

Alice lifted it from him and laid it beside her on the bench. "I'm anxious to hear your tape next week," she grinned and for a moment, she obviously forgot about her idea.

"Alice, what do you need to stay here? I know I can get whatever you need. Help with the laundry? Painting? I just can't see you can't go to a retirement home. It's just not you and I feel like it's your way of saying you're done with the world."

"Oh, I'm done with this world all right. Stanley is up there and he's prepared a place for me, I'm certain of it. I'll bet he explained to Jesus just how I'd like things."

"I'll bet he did." He loved to hear the elderly woman talk with such love and confidence in her long-gone husband. He hoped one day that a woman he loved would be able to say such things about him, and not be grateful he was buried and in the grave. "I noticed your garden is cleaned up. It's not you, is it?" He let his eyes scan the cut grass, and the snipped foliage that surrounded the small house.

She patted his hand as he sat down. She forced a smile.

"You don't know how to ask for help, do you Mrs. Willits? Now that it's your turn, you can't do it. There's nothing wrong with needing people. It's how we were created."

"Spoken by a man whose only companion is eating my juniper bushes."

"Obadiah, sit!"

"I'm not afraid to ask. Martha brings me my groceries and takes the check to the church, now that – well you know – and Kelsey's son mows the lawn now. Did you know that? He's got quite a green thumb that boy, and he's so polite. I nearly had a heart attack when I heard he disappeared with that father of his."

"I didn't know that, but Nathan's a great kid, so it doesn't surprise me. How long has he been doing it?"

"Since I met his mother that day on the beach. I thought she was going to jump. Did she ever tell you that?"

He grinned. "No, but I bet she found that funny."

Mrs. Willits gave a knowing smile. "One day Nathan is going to grow into those legs and oh, my, Kelsey will have a barrel of trouble then. The girls will be ringing her phone off the hook. And Martha brings me dinner most nights now. Her chef makes extra."

"I wondered how you managed the world from this bungalow."

Alice pursed her lips. "I'm just so sorry that Kelsey and her family couldn't make it to dinner last night. It doesn't seem right what that poor girl must endure all because of marrying the wrong man."

"Kelsey," he said her name just to hear the sound of it on his tongue. He found his voice again,

"So, back to you. What else do you need to stay here if everyone is taking care of these things?"

"I need to do something for others, Alex. I need to be useful and I can barely wash my own dishes after tea. I just feel tired all of a sudden and I fear it's because I just feel useless."

"No," Alex snapped. "You are not going to give up and be ready to die on me, Alice. You're sad, I get that, but winter's settling in, and the world always looks different when spring comes. I know what you need."

"What is that, young man?"

"You need a Christmas party. A big, joyful, loud potluck with everyone who loves you here and gathered around in our family. We'll make a big turkey with stuffing and gravy—"

"Alex, I had to give last night's turkey to Martha. She had a car accident yesterday – oh yes, I guess you know that."

"Not you making Thanksgiving dinner, *us*. Your crazy, patchwork family. We'll cook the feast and if none of us can do it, we'll buy it at Safeway. The point is, you need something to look forward to. We all do."

She laughed at that. The animation in her eyes returned. "I could teach them to make my candied yams. No one can rival me in the yam department. I did not spend my early years with apricots and not learn a thing or two about sweetening the pie."

"Do you think you can handle all the commotion?"

Her brows darkened and he knew that Alice Willits was back.

"I'm going to get started on it right away."

"I guess you should. Nothing better to do, us retired folks gotta keep busy." Alice's eyes brightened, "Well Nathan, what are you doing up so early?"

Alex turned to see Kelsey's son on the walkway standing alongside his little sister. "Our grandmother had to go out this morning. We thought we'd come garden. If that's all right."

Meagan ran up to him and wrapped her arms around his waist, "Hi Pastor Bechtel."

"Hi yourself," he said as he returned her hug. "Where's your mother this morning?"

"She's with Dad at the hospital," Meagan said.

"He's in stable condition."

At the news that Kelsey was with Todd his heart started to pound. It wasn't safe. "I've got to get Obadiah home and work on my sermon this week. Nice to see you all." He unloosed the leash and bolted back to his house, where he quickly shed his running clothes and whipped on a suit as though he were making the rounds for visitations like any other day.

He didn't know what he expected to find at the hospital, he only knew he had to get there. It was the same calling he felt that day when he heard Meagan call out his name by some unseen force. He was compelled to get to Kelsey's side.

\* \* \*

Kelsey didn't go to the hospital out of love, or the memory of love for the father of her precious children. She went simply because she worried that if she didn't, she might be capable of becoming like him; a soulless creature who cared less for his own children than he did himself.

With Simon's shooting officially an open case, a policeman stood sentry outside Todd's hospital room. "Kelsey Mitchell, here to see Todd Mitchell," she told the officer.

"Open your bag."

She did as she was told. He ran a metal wand up and down her person and it remained quiet, so she gained entry.

"Fifteen minutes."

She nodded. It wouldn't take longer than that. Todd's disturbing glare met her with the intimidation it intended. Once, she might have wilted under his formidable gaze, but she'd been too browbeaten for that now. Like a seafaring block of glass pummeled and softened by the tumultuous waves in the ocean, she'd become relieved of her rough edges and more exquisite for the trip.

"You killed him," Todd accused. The words smacked her with their weight. Even after being shot, Todd felt no responsibility for the damage in his wake. Nothing would ever be Todd's fault, but she wouldn't be there for him to blame any longer.

"If the death of your best friend…and whatever else he may have been, doesn't faze you, what would, Todd?"

"Doesn't faze me? You'll see how it fazes me when you stand up in court accused of his murder."

"He wasn't ed, Todd. He was shot for pointing a loaded gun at a police officer."

"None of this would have happened if you'd stayed home where you belonged. Nathan is my son and I have a right to him!"

"A right to him? He's not a piece of property. He's a child. Do you even know what kind of music he listens to? What his favorite video game is?"

"You've raised him in the world. He wouldn't have had access to any of that devil worship had he been with me in Laos." Todd's mouth practically foamed, and she kept back from his bed, nearer to the police officer than Todd.

"If you're feeling well enough to blame, I'll take my leave," she said. "I only came to let you know that the final divorce paperwork will be ready. If you won't sign it, I'll be filing abandonment charges so that your signature isn't necessary. It will make things more complicated, but easier when it comes to the division of assets."

He sat motionless, rigid and controlled like a sentry on night duty, while his magnetic blue eyes flashed. There was no other symbol of his seething rage and hatred of her, but instinctively, she understood its underlying threat. How every part of his body hummed with unspent anger.

"You're free," she told him. "Isn't that what you wanted when no one else was looking? You can tell everyone in Laos that I'm to blame. I'd be happy to admit as much on paper. Would that make things easier?"

"I forbid you to file for divorce. Do you understand me?"

She knew it had to be his idea. "You've left me no choice. I can't be responsible for any liability on the part of your ministry in Laos. It's strictly a legal move."

"You come in here acting as though you have power over me. Naturally, you do. I'm grieving. You've only just killed my best friend with your insane paranoia. He thought he was going to lose me to your craziness. You will not destroy my ministry by filing anything. Do you understand me?"

"What about your fiancé? How will she feel about this?"

"You have tried my patience long enough, Kelsey. I warn you that you will rue the day you messed with me." Todd said.

"Is that a threat?" She knew he wouldn't answer, just like she knew Todd wouldn't answer about his supposed woman back home. It didn't matter to him. Fiancés…women…were expendable; collateral damage in Todd's mission. "I know why you don't want a divorce: Simon's going with you to Laos. Is that it?"

"God does not take kindly to a woman who tries to rule her husband and you will learn there are consequences. It may seem for now that you've won, but God will not be mocked. Your punishment is imminent."

In Todd's lack of conscience and responsibility toward Simon's death, she realized how truly void of humanity her husband was. All that time, she'd thought she misunderstood him, that he hadn't been able to speak of his love, and he showed it in strange ways. It was so much easier to believe than Todd might truly embody evil. Admittedly, she'd searched for that small piece of goodness, that rich part of him that did for others when no one else was looking, but after fourteen years of marriage, she had yet to come up with one example. Why would she ever settle for such crumbs? If Todd were void of a soul, she felt void of a brain for believing in him.

"File that paperwork with the courts and you won't see Nathan or Meagan again. Do you understand me?"

"You would keep your own children from their mother? You'd really do that for some kind of invisible win?"

"You won't leave me. I won't allow it."

"She must leave you," Alex entered the doorway in a dark navy suit and bright yellow tie. He looked fresh off the cover of GQ and her gaze lingered slightly too long. He moved further into the room, and came beside her so that their arms touched. She felt the electrical pulse through her body. No one ever touched her; it felt foreign and no doubt she read far too much into the motion. "I've just come from the morgue and the autopsy may show some foreign substances in Simon's system."

Todd smirked. "Suddenly, everyone in America is CSI, is that it Preacher Alex?"

"I thought when you researched poison, you were looking to go after Kelsey, though she denied that you'd do anything more than scare her." Alex moved closer to the bed. "I know better. I know who you are, Todd Mitchell."

"I never researched any such thing, and if it's on your computer, it must have been you."

"Except the web browsing is timed, and I have an ironclad alibi. It was the one staff meeting that I actually attended." Alex rubbed his chin, which boasted a day's growth. "Unless Obadiah was searching the Net while I was gone, I think you're going to have some explaining to do."

"Todd has a lot of explaining to do," Her mother entered the room, decked out in her Winter White slacks and matching Cashmere twinset.

"Mom?"

"You were nearly divorced once already Kelsey, why did you stop the process?" She waved a manila envelope in front of her.

"I ran out of money and I needed more time to pursue abandonment. Life got busy with the kids, and it ceased to matter with him gone." It hadn't been like she was turning down options by the dozen.

Her mother walked toward the bed and tossed the envelope next to him. "She won't ever run out of money again, do you get that?" Mother bent low and nearly pressed her nose to Todd's. "Her father and I will see to that." Mother twisted in a way that reminded Kelsey of a great soap opera move with drama and flair. "It seems our preacher has been very busy trying to move all his assets — and your assets Kelsey to support this church of his." Mother lowered herself to Todd's face again. "You messed with the wrong account this time, Todd. That money Kelsey inherited was in her name only. Her father made certain of that because he never did trust you."

Kelsey didn't want to feel giddy over Todd's demise because it made her less of a person to want revenge on another living soul, but to be free of his wrath, for him to be caught in his own vicious web, she couldn't help feel a small, smug satisfaction.

"Time's up," the officer said and the three of them filed out of the room into the familiar hallway.

Alex smiled and she noted how every part of him seemed to evoke his emotion of happiness. It wasn't an empty gesture that hid a deeper motive. He simply radiated joy. "So," he said. "We meet again. Of all the hallways in all the hospitals around the world, she walks into mine."

She walked into his arms and wrapped him in the tightest, most heartfelt embrace. "Thank you for believing in me," she whispered.

"Thank your daughter. She prayed for my discernment. She's your heroine."

Everything about being in Alex's arms felt right…but it wasn't. Alex faced a world without baggage where he was free to explore everything God had to offer a man of his kindness and stature. She pulled away and didn't look into his eyes for fear she wouldn't be able to say what was necessary.

"Good bye Alex. God bless you." She followed her mother's angelic frame down the hallway and walked into her new life.

## Chapter 25

Alex kept his unspoken promise and left Kelsey and her family alone. He'd heard about her: snippets from Martha and Mrs. Willits, but anything more than that and he'd feel the misery of her absence, so he stayed in the shallow end of the information pool.

"Her new job is going well," Martha would say. "They've made her a permanent position. You should talk to her, Alex."

He'd nod.

"Nathan worked off that money he needed and do you know that child bought me a clock?" Alice was so animated when she'd discuss Nathan. "Come and see it, Alex. It's absolutely beautiful with gold baubles that spin and every hour on the hour, it plays, 'My Favorite Things." When Alex saw the clock, it was a gold-plated replica with some of its plating worn off, but the fact that it was invaluable to Alice made him tear up. She understood how special Kelsey's family was and that warmed him inside.

Although he'd seen Kelsey a few times as she sat alone on the beachside bench across from her condominium, he could never bring himself to speak with her. The timing just didn't feel right. Everything in her romantic history had been about manipulation and guilt. How would he have been any better if he'd taken her most vulnerable moment, the time when she could finally embrace freedom, to hit on her?

Halloween gave way to Thanksgiving and ushered in the Christmas season. He braced himself for the holiday celebration at Mrs. Willits when he finally trusted himself enough to see Kelsey without making a fool of himself.

\* \* \*

Kelsey thought Mrs. Willits' house looked like something out of "Cottage Life" magazine. Over the last few months an endless stream of Christmas elves from Alex's former church visited and worked daily. The house received a fresh coat of white paint. Stamped concrete that looked like flagstone was poured on the walkway and the porch. Martha donated new, double-paned windows along with new wooden door with glass cutouts. When the house was completed, Christmas lights were strung along every manicured hedge and at the roofline.

As Kelsey approached the house, she heard streams of George Winston's December album wafting over the low murmur of the crowd gathered within the house. "Meagan, see if you can fit those green beans in the oven to keep them warm. If not, just put them as close to the stove as possible and keep it covered with the foil."

"I'll try, but that stove of Mimi's is ancient. I'll bet it only has the turkey inside."

Kelsey loved how her children finally had a grandmother figure in their lives that baked cookies, showed them how to garden and even darned their socks if necessary. The kids had taken to calling Mrs. Willits' Mimi and they seemed more at home at Mimi's than in their own.

"You're probably right." Before she knocked on the door, she heard their names called out in festivity. Her hand trembled as she reached for the door. She hadn't seen Alex since before Halloween and she realized he'd probably be at the party with a date. It was only natural and perfectly right, but that didn't mean it wouldn't hurt. She knew Alex deserved better than her, and she wanted that for him, but none of that changed her feelings.

It was her first celebration since Todd kidnapped Nathan. While she paused, Martha came to greet her, "I'm so glad you're here! Let me take that. Go and say hello to my husband. He's sulking that we're around so many people on Christmas Eve and not at home with a ham sandwich."

Kelsey laughed. "Got it."

Crystal Tognotti, the young widow from her new Bible study that Mrs. Willits taught, tried to wrestle her kids into behaving, "Outside. Go into the backyard if you're going to play with those." The kids all donned black olives on their fingertips and like a train, huffed and puffed in a line, right out the back door.

Mrs. Willits sat in the midst of it all in her favorite chair, queen of all she surveyed. The older woman's joy was as big as the crowd. "Well Kelsey dear, I'm so glad you're here. Now that you're working so much, I never get to see much of you. Except at Bible study and that's not nearly enough," Alice clutched her hand. Then she looked at Nathan, "Get over here young man and give me a proper greeting."

Nathan came dutifully and bent to hug her. Meagan followed and Kelsey's insides felt as if they might implode from the sheer pleasure of having created a new family.

Alice stood up and wobbled a bit before steadying herself. "Now everyone, I want you to take a look at that beautiful clock there on the television set. This is Nathan and he bought that with his own money for me. What do you all think of that?" A round of applause erupted in the crowded room.

Love felt better than anything in the entire world, and Kelsey still chastised herself occasionally for not listening to her gut when she was told she was loved, but treated with hate. Protecting herself from real connection wasn't loving at all. She'd learned that it was far better to risk being made a fool of, than to feel the void that came with a battered wall around her.

Her boss, Dr. Campisi and his wife had been invited to the gathering, because they too, had nowhere else to go, and that made them family. He walked toward her with a big, wrapped box. "Buon Natale, Bella."

"Merry Christmas, Massimo," she took the gift and nearly dropped it from its sheer weight. "What is this?"

"Open it," Massimo said. "It's for you. Well, it's sort of for you. It's going to save you a trip in the morning."

She unwrapped the gift to find a professional, Italian lever espresso machine in all its shiny, chrome glory. "It's beautiful! Are you sure it won't get ruined with coffee stains? It seems too pretty to use."

"I'll teach you how to work it. It's not one of those ridiculous automatic things. This one lets you pull a shot as long as you'd like." He pooled his fingers together at his lips and kissed them, exploding them into a flower of sorts, in his Italian way. "Bellissimo!"

"Thank you," she kissed him on the cheek.

"You see? Now, she doesn't have to go and pick up my espresso," he said to his wife.

"I can make it for you on the job, is that right?" She laughed at his idea of generosity, "I'll cherish it, thank you." The fact was, he'd been more than generous with her by providing her a way to feed her family and put a roof over their heads. Nothing else would ever be necessary from Dr. Campisi.

"No more gifts until I say so," Mrs. Willits harped. "We're going to do them together. Put those under the tree," she told Nathan.

The house was a zoo. Alex's giant dog rumbled in the background chasing a mess of children, who had come in from the backyard. "Get that beast out of here!" Alice yelled. "Alex!"

At the sight of the dog, and the sound of Alex's name, Kelsey's stomach lurched. Her arms felt weak and without a word, Massimo lifted the espresso machine from her arms.

"Angela!" Crystal yelled, exasperated. The tallest of the kids,

a tow-headed blonde raced toward them, followed by a smaller boy who stopped abruptly by butting his head into Alex's nether regions. Kelsey met his eyes, and it was if time stopped. A smile automatically crossed her face and everything within her felt alight and bliss-filled.

"Uncle Alex, come on!" Angela tried to pull him by the hand. "Let's play!"

"Angela," he said without looking down. "Take Obadiah and go in the backyard. We'll call you when dinner's ready. You don't want to make Mrs. Willits angry, and I'll let you in on a little secret, she's not Obadiah's biggest fan."

The little girl dutifully rounded up her siblings, and headed again to the back door. Uncle Alex, the words finally registered. He was seeing Crystal. Naturally, he'd make a great father and she was widowed. He was free to date her. To marry *her*. The little girl pierced the room like a bullet, followed by three smaller caliber ammunition.

Kelsey saw them all, four little wonders, now fatherless in their world. Their emptiness, the inexplicable sorrow touched her. Like Nathan and Meagan, they too would grow up without a father and not because their mother made a stupid choice. Maybe they wouldn't grow up without a father. Maybe Uncle Alex already had that covered.

He walked towards her, and her body felt boneless, weak and feeble. A tear pooled in her eye as she calculated how long it had been since she'd seen him, since he'd saved her from Simon's gun, since he'd beaten Todd at his own game. She felt her tears coming for what her children would miss because of her choice. Crystal was powerless to help her children. It was God's will that they be without a father, but Kelsey had simply been ignorant and therefore, not powerless, she'd simply given away her life's power of attorney.

"Kelsey," he said smoothly. "You look beautiful. Red's the perfect color for you." She watched his friendly grin melt into a focused gaze. She didn't look away, though she knew she should have. His stare was extraordinarily intimate and she let her mind wander to a dangerous place where she wasn't alone in the world.

"Mrs. Willits, someone dropped the whipping cream in the kitchen!"

Kelsey, thankful for the diversion, immediately rushed to find a towel. She knew right where they were and she sopped up the liquid before she thought further about Alex's presence. Would it always be this uncomfortable for her? Would she have to watch him marry the beautiful, young widow? She could handle it. She could handle anything. God had shown her that much.

"Kelsey," she heard his smooth, low voice behind her. "Look at me." She held open her hands, still wet from one of the cream-soaked towels.

"Come over to the sink." He turned on the water, and she watched as he felt the stream of water waiting for it to warm. When it did, he pulled her hands into the stream and lathered up her hands with soap, lacing his fingers around hers as he did so. When their hands were both covered in bubbles, he stood closer and placed the softest kiss on her jaw, as though they were completely alone. She turned to see his face. It was a pull she couldn't refuse.

"Don't do this to me, Alex." She whispered. "I can't take it. I'm not as strong as you are."

"Meet me in the front yard," he whispered as the doorbell rang. Like a figment of her imagination, he was gone.

She rinsed her hands quickly, fumbled with a clean towel and wound her way through the throngs of people in Alice's small home. Crystal, the curvaceous blonde, and mother of the four children stopped her, "Kelsey, wow, you look great! Have you lost weight?"

"A little," she said. "I'm running again." Mostly, she was just doing what made her feel good about herself. She wasn't trying to live up to anyone's expectation any longer and the result was she was at her thinnest since high school.

"I have to get motivated. How do you do it?"

Kelsey looked toward the four small kids out the back door, "Well, you have a little more on your plate than I do." Kelsey remembered Crystal from a Bible Study they'd been in years before. That time had all but evaporated from her memory. All of it a great blank when she did nothing more than go from function to function, bringing food when necessary, a plant for a housewarming party, a healthy snack of cut fruit for a play day; All of it a blur, as though someone else lived that life altogether.

"Kelsey," the young mother said. "I'm so glad to hear you're back at church. Did you hear Alex preach? He's done it a few times now, when he isn't doing his other job. Isn't he great? He's just such a natural."

"I—I'm so sorry about your loss, Crystal."

She smiled serenely. "We're managing. We had a lot of time to say goodbye, and I think that helps. There's not a lot of time to sit around and feel sorry for myself."

"I'm glad. I'm surprised you remember me," Kelsey said, with her eyes on the door.

"We were in small group together for years, Kelsey." She gave her that confused look that always caused her to feel as though she was missing a few lights upstairs. "It was a stressful time for you," she added in an understanding voice.

"Your kids are beautiful."

"Can you believe it? All that time I used to whine we couldn't have them. Wasn't that my prayer request every week?" She laughed. "And boy, I turned out to be Fertile Myrtle, didn't I?"

She didn't know how to respond. None of it came back to her, none of this life sounded familiar. What was wrong with her that she'd lost so much of her memories?

"I've left something at home, I'm going to just run and get it," Kelsey said to make her escape.

"Sure, I'll see you soon."

Kelsey dashed out the door and saw Alex across the street on the bench in front of the sea. His broad shoulders and muscular arms took up the entire back of the bench, and she forgot to look both ways before running to him. A car honked, but stopped just the same, allowing her to run across to the beach.

Alex stood up, and took her hand, leading her to the bench. She shyly sat. "I remember the first time we sat here."

"You do?"

"We'd experienced a miracle together. We rescued your son. We put your ex away for what should be a good three years."

"If they can extradite him from Laos, and that's a big *if*."

"My point is, stop acting as though you barely know me."

"You kissed me," she said breathlessly. "In the kitchen…"

"I know. I'm so sorry, Kelsey. I had no right. I just hadn't seen you and I got carried away."

"Oh sure, I understand," she managed to stammer.

She watched his face change. Gone was the man who desired her, and in his place was a lifeless drone afraid of his emotions and any feelings he couldn't control. *Just like Todd.* Was she the one who shut men down? Had she caused Todd's reactions?

His hand brushed her cheek with the backs of his fingers, "I'm not Todd," he said as if he read her mind.

She closed her eyes, lost in the touch. "Alex, don't."

He pushed the hair off her shoulders. "I'll go away if that's what you want."

"Alex." She said breathlessly. "Don't start something you can't finish."

"Who said I couldn't finish it?"

She shook her head, "I know what you do for a living, and I'm a sorry excuse for a pastor's wife. Or for anyone's wife as far as that goes. You don't know me, what I've been through. You deserve a woman who is like you, fresh and naive of the evils in the world. Not someone like me who sees danger around every corner."

"Is that what you think? That I'm ignorant of the evils in the world? Kelsey, in my work, I've rescued babies from Witchcraft sacrifices. I'm not as naive as you might think."

"But see, even this. I talk to you and you give me an answer. I'm not used to that. I'm used to being shut down and —I just don't act right. I'm ruined, Alex. There's a reason the Bible says that the divorced woman is not to remarry. I'm that reason."

Alex shook his head. "I've tried to give you space, Kelsey. I've tried to forget you, but I'm not going to settle for some pale version of who I really want. That would be a far greater sin in my mind."

"Alex," she let her head fall to the warm crook in his neck and his arms sheltered her from the crisp wind off the ocean. "I can't let you do that. You've got your whole life in front of you. You don't even know me."

"It's deeper than that and you know it. I'll court you properly," he whispered in her ear. "I'll wait until Mel Underwood himself will perform the ceremony."

That made her laugh, "I don't think either one of us has that kind of time. His words were like honey to the tongue, but she couldn't help but remember that Todd's had been too, and she was a weak woman for words of love, something she lacked her entire life. What if it was only a tickling to her ear, a lie to get what he wanted? She looked into his eyes, which were as deep as the ocean in front of her. "I can't let you, Alex. I can't let you pay for someone else's mistakes. I'm full of fears and doubts, holes another person isn't expected to fill. No one but Jesus."

"He's already in your heart, so can you make some room for me?"

She shook her head. "What we feel right now will go away."

"That's true," he said. "Real love never feels like the thrill of first love, I've been told that a million times. Heck, I've even counseled dating couples on the matter. Real love is better than this. It's solid and stands on a firm foundation. Will you start building with me?"

She stayed quiet rather than let her lips betray her. She didn't want to say what she should say, she wanted to throw herself on his mercy and let life come at her.

"We'll start small. One date," he said.

She shook her head, but clasped her eyes shut rather than weaken.

"You're going to make yourself pay for your mistake forever. Jesus has forgiven you, but you're still doing your penance."

"It's not about me." She opened her eyes. "It's about you. You have the entire world in front of you. It's your oyster. You don't need to be held back by a worn-out bride and her two kids — one of them a teenager of all things."

"It's never perfect, just so you know. If it is, you might be worried someone's hiding bodies in the basement." Crystal stood behind them. They quickly separated.

"Crystal," Alex said.

The young mother smiled at them. "It's time for dinner."

"We're coming," she said as she stood.

Crystal pressed her back down to the bench. "Kelsey, life's too short to obsess on your mistakes. One just never knows…If God decided to take Alex tomorrow, could you live with that?"

Kelsey's tears came now, unabated. She shook her head.

"That's what I thought. I'll put dinner off for a few more minutes." Crystal turned on her heel in the grainy dirt, and ran back to the house where the party raged in full swing.

Alex pulled her close again, and they fought off the cold of the swirling evening wind while the sky around them changed from amber to orange to a deep red. The waves turned to a deep violet with their white caps rushing toward them.

"I'll mess up Kelsey. I promise you I will, but I can't think of any other woman I want to fight for, spend my life protecting and cherish. If there's anything I've learned about myself, it's that I'm stubborn to a fault. It was easier to be an accountant, but that wasn't where God wanted me. It might be easier for me to marry another woman…"

Nothing would be harder than to let him go now and yet still she struggled. As time stood still and her brain wrestled with her heart, she wanted to pull away. To do the right thing, but his pull was so strong. His eyes so warm and gracious that she felt as if she'd known him all of her life. She thought she'd only test things, just to know what it was like to be embraced by a man again. That's all it meant, it was just to know what someone's touch felt like again. To be desired had such an intoxicating effect on her, she felt powerless in Alex's grasp. She snuggled herself closer into his chest. Something jabbed at her, and she pulled out a notecard from his jacket pocket.

"It's my Scripture for tomorrow's sermon," he said.

"That's a buzz kill," she giggled.

"Is it?" He showed her the notecard and read it. "Perfect love casts out fear." He cocked his brows as he gazed down upon her in the soft evening light.

"Your choice, Kelsey. What's it going to be fear or love?" He didn't give her a chance to answer. He pressed his lips to hers hard and kissed her with abandon. Her body went weak against his and she braced herself for another round of his intense, impassioned kisses. Not the light, dull, perfunctory kisses she knew, but sharp, powerful and thrill-inducing kisses that made her feel what a woman should feel. It was as if the clouds parted and she suddenly understood all that had been stolen from her — the intimacy that never took place in marriage with a man who didn't want her. She was done for, putty in his strong hands, under his piercing gaze.

"This is what I've been missing?" she asked.

He pressed his lips to hers. First softly, then more insistent. "This is what you've been missing." She felt his hands on the back of her neck as he pressed her towards him. He kissed her with an intensity she'd never known. A self-assuredness and a desire that felt like abandonment of any front. She knew it was dangerous to play with such feelings, but she felt powerless to stop them, they came like enormous waves, undeterred by reality. There was a giant vacancy in her heart longing to be filled; only she hadn't known it.

"I'm a selfish soul," she said when he pulled back.

"Welcome to Earth," he kissed her again lightly. "Sinner meets sinner." Another gentle kiss. "They fall in love." He took her up tightly in his arms. "It's an age-old tale."

We should get back to the party," she said, clutching his jacket and drawing it tighter around her shoulders. She shivered, but it was not from the cold.

"Uh huh," he agreed, snuggling her closer. "We should." They watched the horizon in silence as the sun descended into the sea.

"For once," she said. "I'm not thinking about what someone else is doing across the ocean. I don't want someone else's life."

"There's nowhere I'd rather be, but I'd go to the darkest places on earth with you at my side."

"I've spent so much of my life swimming to the surface, gasping for air--" she said, through the smile she couldn't erase, though the harsh winds chapped her lips and made them stick to her teeth. She licked her lips, "I am not just swimming to the surface anymore. I am walking on water."

"Me too, Kelsey. Me too."

**The End.**
http://www.KristinBillerbeck.com


Enjoy this excerpt from Kristin's recent release with Thomas Nelson Publishers, The Scent of Rain.

**The Scent of Rain
by Kristin Billerbeck
Copyright 2012**

Could it be that the life Daphne's always wanted is right under her nose?

Daphne Sweeten left Paris – and a job she loved – to marry the man of her dreams in the U.S. But when he stands her up on their wedding day, she's left reeling and senseless. Literally. She's been trained as a perfume creator and now her sense of smell has disappeared along with her fiancé!

She has to figure out why her nose isn't working, fix it, and get back to Paris. Meanwhile, she'll rely on her chemistry skills and just hope her new boss at Gibraltar Produces, Jess, doesn't notice her failing senses. They'll be working together on household fragrances, not posh perfumes. How hard can it be?

As Daphne and Jesse work on a signature scent for their new line, she feels God at work as never before. And the promise of what's possible is as fresh as the scent of rain.

## Chapter 1

Daphne Sweeten's knees buckled beneath her, but Sophie, her maid of honor, kept her from reaching the concrete floor. She straightened and stared into her best friend's eyes, which were softened in pity. She searched for their meaning.

"He's not coming?" Daphne mouthed the words, but Sophie understood and as she searched the vast gothic church in front of her, the crowd stared back at her and she noted the absence of the groom's family. "He knew," she murmured.

Sophie nodded and pulled the bouquet from Daphne's clenched hands. "Let's go." Sophie tugged at her elbow, but Daphne couldn't take her eyes off the long aisle that she wouldn't be walking down. The one where she'd leave loneliness behind her. "Daphne, come on."

She should be embarrassed, humiliated and she knew it. The faces, familiar and foreign aimed in her direction and her in their scope. But something kept her there. Her feet firmly planted as she registered the peppery scent of freesias and the slightly-musty smell of the rental runway carpet. She turned to Sophie, ringed by the rest of her bridesmaids.

"Where's my father?"

Across the vast distance of white carpet in the gothic church, Preacher Riley stood alone on the altar. He cleared his throat to make some kind of Anne while pitying glances stared back at her from the rows of wooden pews. She held her breath. So much as a tiny sob and she would echo like a Swiss mountain yodeler in the cavernous cathedral, though by the look on everyone's faces, they knew everything. What was the point of saving face now? She may as well experience it all or she might miss something and then, how would she ever fix it?

Daphne followed Sophie out of the great double doors. She turned one last time to face the altar, in its far-off place, under its three grand stained-glass windows, littered with white rose petals, and dotted with violets. The petals felt like the remnants of her heart. Mark wouldn't be back and the altar was like the end of a rainbow; a destination she'd never reach.

"Daphne, let's go," Sophie whispered as she tugged at her arm. Resistance was futile.

"That was my wedding day."

"You're scaring me. Get in the car."

"Did you see his side? No one was there. He knew he wasn't coming! Why did he bother to rehearse last night?"

"I don't know, Daphne."

She allowed herself to be led outside the church, which stood atop Nob Hill in San Francisco. The steps between her and the limo seemed endless and as if her legs would never carry her the distance. It was an idyllic day in San Francisco, which was probably a bad omen. No fog. Only a light breeze and pure, California sunshine marked the day, almost mocking her in its perfection.

"Why did you stand there forever?"

She looked down at her gown and shrugged. "I'm wearing Monique Lhuillier. Face it, if you're going to go down in a blaze of glory, this is how you want to be dressed."

Sophie laughed. "That's the first sign I've seen of the real you all day!"

"I had a feeling he wouldn't show," Daphne answered. "I thought all brides probably had that little inkling of fear, but now I wondered if I noticed something. He must have given me some sign that I didn't want to face."

Mia, her friend from high school, lifted the back of her skirt. "It's always been frightening the detail you notice. I'm sure you did. Sometimes, you're like being friends with the Mayan calendar."

"Did you notice anything?" she asked Mia.

Mia shook her head.

"Keri?" she looked at her coworker and bridesmaid, who also shook her head.

Daphne and her four bridesmaids huddled in a circle on the steps of the church. "We look so good," she tried to make light of the situation.

"You don't have to be brave for us," Marguerite said. "You go ahead and cry if you want to."

Her blood ran cold as awareness settled in her veins. "I missed it. I missed something."

"Did you?" Sophie asked with raised eyebrows. "What did I wear the first day of kindergarten?"

"A purple dress with heinous flowers on the skirt," Daphne rattled.

"Be assured. Your obsessive nature is still well in tact. Sometimes, it's just easier to not see certain things." Sophie skipped down the long set of stairs toward the limousine and Daphne followed.

"What are you trying to say, Sophie?"

Sophie's flawless skin looked nearly plastic in the bright sunlight of the afternoon. Her strawberry-blonde hair wrapped in an elegant updo and the simple strand of pearls around her neck was the perfect complement to the dark sapphire bridesmaid gown they'd selected. One thing was certain; she hadn't missed a detail in coordinating her wedding.

"I'm saying," Sophie twisted so quickly, Daphne nearly crashed into her. "Maybe there weren't any signs. Maybe things were too perfect."

"Too perfect?" Daphne blinked manically. "Is that possible?"

"What was wrong with Mark? I mean, give me his imperfections. Just a shortlist."

Daphne turned to make certain they were alone on the staircase. "Lots of things."

"Name one."

"He couldn't get a job in Paris, for one. I had to give up mine to get married."

Sophie continued down a few more steps and Daphne shouted after her.

"Just because you spend all day with psychological problems does not mean Mark had one."

"Then where is he?"

She hated when Sophie got like that, so certain in her assessment of another person. Sophie barely knew Mark. "I'm sure he has a perfectly good excuse. Maybe he didn't want to get married at all. Maybe I pushed him into it."

"So it's your fault again. Like the excuse he had for not being employable in Paris. It's all very convenient and yet, you still stand here and defend him. He left you out like yesterday's trash and you're standing here making excuses for him."

"You never did like him," Daphne accused, shocked that her best friend would choose then to bring up Mark's faults. Did she need any reminders? She was standing alone in a Trumpet gown, tailored to perfection. The detailed Chantilly lace on the bodice with its hand-stitched flowers embellishments were reminder enough. Every detail was perfect save one. The absence of Mark Goodsmith, her groom. "Maybe that's why he ran! Maybe you were afraid of my not being alone. Maybe together, we scared Mark off."

As they spoke, random tourists applauded from the sidewalk below the famous San Francisco landmark. Daphne waved, rather than point out an obvious lack of a groom. They probably thought she and Sophie had just been married anyway.

"Call Arnaudt and ask for your job back," Sophie said.

Buy *The Scent of Rain* here:

## About the Author:

Kristin Billerbeck is a bestselling, Christy Award Finalist and two-time Carol Award Winning Author of over 40 Inspirational Novels and Novellas. She has appeared on the *Today Show* and was featured in *The New York Times* and *USA Today*. Best known for her comic take on Christian romance, this novel takes her work to a new level. Kristin lives in Silicon Valley with her family.

Printed in Germany
by Amazon Distribution
GmbH, Leipzig